MIDNIGHT CITY

MIDNIGHT CITY

A CONQUERED EARTH NOVEL

J. BARTON MITCHELL

THOMAS DUNNE BOOKS
ST. MARTIN'S GRIFFIN
NEW YORK

THOMAS DUNNE BOOKS.
An imprint of St. Martin's Press.

MIDNIGHT CITY. Copyright © 2012 by J. Barton Mitchell. All rights reserved. Printed in the United States of America. For information, address St. Martin's Press, 175 Fifth Avenue, New York, N.Y. 10010.

www.thomasdunnebooks.com
www.stmartins.com

ISBN 978-1-250-00907-4 (hardcover)
ISBN 978-1-250-01343-9 (e-book)

First Edition: November 2012

10 9 8 7 6 5 4 3 2 1

For Stephanie Gisondi-Little: manager, confidante, collaborator, and friend. This is your first book, too.

To love means loving the unlovable. To forgive means pardoning the unpardonable. Faith means believing the unbelievable. Hope means hoping when everything seems hopeless.

—G. K. CHESTERTON

PART ONE

CONQUERED EARTH

1. VULTURES

RIGHT ABOUT THEN, it became official: Holt Hawkins was having a bad day.

"Hey, you're right," one of the kids shouted, reaching for him underneath the crumpled old truck. "There *is* someone under here!"

The kids yanked him out from under the ruined vehicle and slammed him hard against its rusted door.

They were younger than Holt, but not by much. Seventeen or eighteen he guessed, looking at the black veinlike growths crawling through their eyes, the telltale sign of the Tone. It had a firm hold on them now; it meant their time was running out.

Holt sized them up quickly. They were shorter and thinner, weaker, less quick probably, but those things mattered a lot less when you had guns or knives, and these kids had both. Holt had left his with Max, near the tree line, not wanting to risk the weight on the precarious bridge. A decision he was quickly coming to regret.

The six kids holding him had small tattoos on their right wrists. The one with his forearm pinning Holt to the door sported a Scorpion. Two more, knives at the ready, had a Coiled Snake and a Heart respectively.

The wrist tattoos were bad news. It meant these kids were in the Menagerie, and the situation had just gotten a whole lot worse. Then again, Holt thought . . . maybe they wouldn't recognize him. He glanced at the single, fingerless glove he always wore on his right hand.

"Hey, this guy's a Heedless, look at his eyes!" one of them pointed out bitterly. They were right—Holt was Heedless. One of the rare few on the planet the Tone didn't affect. His eyes were perfectly clear; there were no signs of the crawling black tendrils. It was the only reason Holt had made it to twenty years of age. "Isn't Tiberius looking for a Heedless out here somewhere? Tall guy like this one?"

Holt grimaced. So much for not being recognized.

He peered upward, looking for any sign of the ship. There were no clouds, the sun was high, and in the blue sky it would blend in perfectly. He had no way of knowing if it was even still there. Which was unfortunate, because it was probably his only shot at getting out of this.

"One way to be sure," another said, younger still, fifteen maybe, with two tattoos: a Yellow Skull on his right wrist and an eight-pointed star on his left. The star had only two of its points filled in; the rest were just outlines. It was a sign of promotion—it meant he was an Adjutant, a lower-level commander in the Menagerie. As he rose in rank, more star points would be filled in.

"The glove," the yellow skull said. "Pull it down."

Holt's heart sank. He struggled when they went for the glove, but a couple more punches brought him in line. It was a leather one, and he wore it for only one reason, to hide what was under it: a black tattoo just like these kids' . . . only his was half-finished.

It was hard to make out what it would have been, but there were hints of a birdlike shape, wings, claws. Whatever it was, it was enough for the Menagerie thugs who had him by the throat.

"Yes, indeed!" said the yellow skull. "This is Holt Hawkins—Tiberius is paying big money for his head, no wonder he's hiding under there."

The funny thing was, Holt hadn't been hiding from *them* at all. He'd been huddled underneath the truck because of what had been circling in the sky. He glanced upward once more, trying to find it. . . .

"That what you were doing, Holt Hawkins? Hiding from us?" the yellow skull asked with a sneer.

"If you want the truth, I was taking a nap," Holt replied, holding the yellow skull's eyes as solidly as he could. He had to stall them, had to keep them talking. "Nice under there, you should try it."

Holt groaned as one of their fists made less-than-gentle contact with his stomach. The Menagerie still lacked a sense of humor it seemed. *Where is that ship?*

"You're a funny guy, Holt Hawkins," the yellow skull said, stepping even closer. "Didn't know that about you. Say something else funny. Go on."

Holt didn't bother. Instead, he glanced at the environment out the corner of his eye.

They were all standing on a massive, decaying steel bridge that spanned what used to be called the Missouri River. It stretched as far as Holt could see in both directions, and was filled with hundreds of old cars, where they had either been abandoned by their owners or blown to bits by Assembly gunships during the invasion.

Holt's fists clenched in frustration. Even if he ran, there weren't many places to go, other than taking a swan dive off the edge. The way Holt's luck had been going today, that probably wasn't the best idea.

The bridge's supports and cables were barely holding on, many of them had snapped already, and a huge crack in the asphalt near the middle showed where the bridge was pulling itself apart in slow motion. Of course, the bridge's state of disrepair was the reason he'd bothered to check it out in the first place. Places like this, precarious ones that were risky, they were where you still found valuable things for trade. It had been eight years since the invasion, and most everything not locked down had already been taken, unless it was difficult to get to. Clearly, these Menagerie thugs had been thinking the same thing.

"Get something to tie him up with," the yellow skull ordered.

The snake groaned at the implications. "We have to drag this loser all the way back to the Samneric?" he asked.

"The bounty says Tiberius wants him alive," the yellow skull said. "How else are we gonna collect it?"

"What do we tie him up with?" the heart asked.

"Rope. Wire. Your shoelaces—do I have to do all the thinking? Go find something," he said with impatience.

Two of the boys left to go find restraints. When they got back and tied Holt up, it would all be over, plan or no plan. As ironic as it was, he needed that ship. He just hoped he could draw its attention.

"Kind of funny, I guess," the yellow skull said, his eyes back on Holt. "Bounty hunter with a price on his head. Could've just turned yourself in, collected your own reward. You ever think of that?" The yellow skull laughed. The others laughed with him.

Then a strange sound filtered up from under the truck. The laughter died; the boys all looked down at it. It hadn't been there before, the sound. Holt knew why. What he'd left under there was starting to burn hotter.

"What's that?" one of the boys asked, kneeling down to look underneath. His eyes widened at what he found.

"Well?" the yellow skull asked. The boy grabbed hold of something and pulled it out. A long cylinder that sparkled bright red. Even in the daylight, the kids had to shield their eyes.

A road flare. Sparkling and burning hot.

If this was going to work, it would happen any second. Holt looked up into the sky. . . .

. . . and saw a flash of light, far above, as the ship twisted and caught the midafternoon sun. His heart made a hopeful leap in his chest.

"What did you do?" the yellow skull demanded, looking back at Holt, his voice nervous and unsure for the first time.

Holt smiled. "E.T. phone home," he said.

Something slammed into one of the boys, knocking him to the ground and pinning him at the same time.

Holt had just enough time to see the clawlike contraption, the cable stretching up into the sky . . . before it yanked the poor kid violently off the bridge. His scream quickly faded to nothing as he disappeared far above.

The others flinched, panicked, looked around the bridge in confusion. It was only the leader, the yellow skull, who knew what was happening. "Vulture!" he shouted, fear in his voice.

Another boy screamed as the claw ripped him upward out of sight. The rest bolted.

Holt rammed his head into the face of the lone boy still holding him, sent him reeling backwards. He was loose; the yellow skull was too shocked to react. Holt's kick found his knee, crumpled him to the bridge. The other Menagerie were already running, no longer interested in Holt, concerned only with escaping the horror circling above.

Holt didn't waste the opportunity. He ran with them, toward the edge of the bridge several hundred yards away. Unfortunately, abandoned, rusting cars blocked his path like an obstacle course.

Another boy went down, pinned by the claw of the Vulture scout ship above . . . and then screamed as it yanked him powerfully up and away.

Holt had seen the Menagerie approaching, knew the Vulture was circling above. The Assembly scout ships' optics were infamously powerful, so he'd lit the signal flare before the pirates grabbed him, hoping to attract the thing's attention. A gamble, but it had paid off.

Of course, there was no guarantee it wouldn't grab him next, but he liked those odds a lot better than the ones he would have gotten with the Menagerie.

As he ran, Holt leapt over the hoods and trunks of cars, sliding over them agilely, hitting the ground at a sprint. Ahead, the two Menagerie who had gone for rope were running back. They weren't totally aware of their predicament yet. They were still focused on Holt. He saw them raise their guns, and he ducked quickly behind a ruined station wagon.

Gunfire erupted from ahead of him. He flinched as slugs sparked on the hood of the car.

From the other direction, the remaining boys were closing on him, drawing their own weapons.

A scream echoed from in front of him. Another grapling claw yanked one of the two blocking his path into the sky. Immediately after, one of the boys behind him was ripped upward as well.

No Vulture could fire and retract its claw that fast. Holt ripped his gaze back up to the sky. He saw one flash above him. And then another, separate flash several meters to the north.

There were *two* of them.

"Super," Holt groaned. His plan had just backfired.

The kid in front of the car, just now figuring out his problems, stared up into the sky with terror.

Holt drove straight into him, sending him crashing to the crumbling concrete of the bridge.

He could hear the shouts of the other Menagerie pirates behind him, chasing after him. Gunfire sparked all around him as he ran, but Holt ignored it.

Only two pirates were left: the heart and the yellow skull leader. They rushed after him, leaping over the cars almost as agilely as Holt, guns drawn.

More gunfire shredded the bridge near his feet, barely missing him.

Holt lost his footing, stumbled forward, crashed into the open rear door of an old van, hit the ground hard. The wind burst from his lungs;

he struggled to get up. The kids were almost on him—he could hear their shouts, growing louder, their footsteps.

He got to his feet and ran. He had to keep moving, to get to the tree line on the other side of the bridge. It was his only shot.

The heart grabbed him from behind. Holt lashed out with a foot, managed to connect and sent him spinning away.

Another grapling claw blew the kid to the ground, pinned him . . . then yanked him with ferocity up into the air.

Holt stumbled to his feet, ran for the edge of the bridge. Above him, sunlight flashed off the metallic fuselages of both Vultures.

He dodged and shimmied past the remaining cars on the bridge, and came out the other side onto solid ground. Holt instantly turned right, down a grassy slope toward a thick line of trees just a few dozen yards ahead.

It was going to be close.

Holt reached and burst through the tree line with a sigh of relief. With the tree canopy above, he was safe, at least from—

Holt groaned as the yellow skull hit him from behind, tackled him to the ground. He tried to roll over, but the boy grabbed his hair, shoved his face into the dirt.

"You cost me my whole crew!" the boy shouted. "You know what that means?" Holt *did* know. It meant the Menagerie would hang the kid on sight, but right then he was too preoccupied to answer. The pirate pounded Holt's face into the dirt over and over, and he struggled to get loose, but the boy's grip was too strong.

Something growled behind them. The yellow skull gasped as a big blue gray shape rammed into him.

Holt rolled onto his back, saw the yellow skull wrestling with a large cattle dog, its mouth clamped down firmly onto the boy's arm, its eyes intense slits. It growled angrily as it tried to chew the kid's appendage off. The boy yelled in pain and shock.

Max. One of the few things Holt ever counted on.

Holt leapt for the yellow skull. Max was tough, but he wasn't a pit bull. The kid would get him off eventually; it wasn't a fight the dog could win.

Holt punched the yellow skull hard. Max let the pirate loose, barking furiously.

The two kids grappled, but it wasn't a school yard fight—it was life or death, and they knew it.

They rolled through the dirt, and the yellow skull maneuvered on top of Holt again. His hands circled Holt's throat, started to squeeze.

But Holt had seen it coming, got his feet underneath the boy when they rolled over. He kicked outward with everything he had . . . and the pirate went flying.

The yellow skull hit the ground and rolled right out of the tree line and back into the open field beyond.

Max barked after him, but Holt grabbed the dog and held him in place, staring at the open air beyond the trees with trepidation.

The yellow skull looked up in a daze. Then his eyes widened as he realized he was no longer concealed by the trees. The two looked at each other. Holt almost felt sorry for him.

Almost.

The grapling claw flashed down from the sky, pinned the pirate to the ground. Then he yelled as it ripped him upward out of sight, back into the deadly blue sky.

It was over. Holt let Max go. The dog brushed against him affectionately, licked his face. Holt smiled, tried to push Max off him, but it wasn't the easiest task. His fur was a mixture of gray and blue with spots of black, and under it rippled muscles made strong by years of carrying packs full of salvage . . . and chasing the occasional rabbit. Max was considered only a medium-sized dog, but Holt had seen him readily take on creatures and kids three times his size without any hesitation.

"Thanks, pal," Holt said, scratching the dog's ears. "Another one I owe you."

Holt found his pack and weapons where he'd left them, loaded up, made ready to move. He whistled three short notes. At the signal, Max bounded off into the trees ahead of him to scout.

Before he left, Holt looked to where the last Menagerie kid had been. Other than the scarred ground where the Vulture claw had punctured it, there was no indication anyone had ever been there at all. Here one moment. Gone the next.

Just like everyone else . . .

Holt set off through the trees, following Max's trail.

2. SCARS

HOLT CROUCHED in front of what was left of the cargo train, absently twisting the thick, black fiber bracelet he always wore on his left wrist. The train had careened off its tracks years ago, and tore a swath of destruction through the ground on either side. Most of the cars were rusting pieces of jagged metal now, overgrown with grass and weeds, stretching for more than half a mile. Some of them were still in one piece, and, even more shocking, one or two were still on the track itself.

Next to it lay the wrecks of military vehicles—jeeps, Hummers, an APC or two—all in a similar state of disrepair, most so broken down, they were unrecognizable. And lying next to the vehicles were dozens and dozens of skeletons, some still wearing the tatters of what looked like army uniforms.

As Holt took it all in, he put the pieces together in his head.

An army train. Probably running equipment to Fort Dearborn. And *they* had hit it. Within the first hour or two, he guessed, before the Tone went active.

There was something else, though. Something you rarely saw, then or now: a hulking, charred piece of machinery in a clearing on the far side of the tracks, crumpled where it had fallen and burned years ago. Looking at it from this distance, even in its destroyed state, it was very clear that it had never been anything of this Earth.

It was an Assembly combat walker. One of the big ones from the looks of it, a Spider.

Whoever was on the train that night, they managed to take one of those things with them. Judging by the skeletons tossed around the area, Holt doubted it was much of a consolation to them now. But it was something, nonetheless. . . .

Holt hated places like this. They were scars. Scars on the planet's surface, and the world was littered with them now. He hated them for the memories they brought back, the old images they forced him to see again.

Images of her.

If he didn't have to be here, he wouldn't. But he did.

Max lay next to him on his back, blissfully chewing on a big bone that probably came from one of the unfortunates scattered about the battleground. As happy as the dog was, something about it just wasn't right.

"Max, come on." Holt tried to pull the leg bone loose from the dog's jaws, but Max scampered off before Holt could grab it.

Holt shook his head, looked back to the tracks on the ground.

They were everywhere, tracks from dozens of people, dating back years. Finding the specific ones he was looking for wasn't impossible— there were ways to separate old tracks from new—it just took time. And a good eye. For instance, he could eliminate about half of them right away, based on their size. Most of them were too big. The one he was after had small feet and wasn't wearing boots.

It took him a moment, but he found the shoe prints he was looking for. After almost a week tracking them, he recognized them instantly. They moved off to the north, sidestepping the site altogether. They hadn't even bothered searching the area for useful salvage. Holt didn't blame the person: there likely wasn't anything here worth risking tetanus for. Whatever used to be here of value was long gone now.

From the far distance came an unsettling sound. A deep, concussive booming that echoed through the trees around him. Seconds later, two more booms, echoing and fading in the same way.

Holt looked up. He knew what the sounds were. Explosions. Large ones. Probably two or three miles away, to the northeast.

More sounds filtered through the trees, different from the first, more like staccato thunder.

Plasma cannon, the big ones. The Assembly was nearby and they were riled up. But over what? Whatever it was, it was probably better not to get caught outside the tree line.

Holt stood up to leave, and as he did, he noticed the train cars again.

Two of the ones that were somehow still standing were only a few yards away. He frowned as he studied them—there was probably nothing worthwhile there . . . but you never knew. Even if there were no supplies, the metal itself could be valuable if it wasn't rusted through.

Survival factored into every decision Holt made. It was what he lived by, and it meant many things. One of them was to figure out what was of value. If you had things of value, you could survive.

By Holt's logic, survival said that he had to at least investigate the train cars.

He moved for the closest one, its door yawning open. Max stepped into line next to him, the trophy bone still in his mouth.

Holt peered inside the first train car. It was just as empty as he expected, nothing but rotting wood and rusting metal. He moved to the next one. Its big door was only open a crack, preventing him from seeing inside.

Holt grabbed the edge of the door and pulled. It didn't budge. He cursed under his breath, pulled again, harder this time. It slid a little, but not much. He yanked it hard over and over, trying to force it. Slowly, it began sliding open.

From inside came a noise. It sounded like the shifting of someone moving. Below Holt, Max dropped the bone as his hackles raised. A low growl rumbled from his throat.

Holt stepped back from the train door, drawing the rifle from his back in a smooth, practiced gesture. The gun used to be a SIG716, the same kind his father used, but Holt had modified and updated it extensively. The wooden grip and stock were worn smooth with regular use.

He readied himself, quieted Max with a look . . . then spun around the side of the door, aiming into the gap he'd managed to open.

Holt instantly jumped as he saw a solitary figure standing in the doorway. It made him flinch so bad, he almost pulled the trigger.

The figure didn't react or move in any way, just stood stoically in place.

"Geez," Holt said, keeping the rifle trained on the shadow in the door. His heart felt like a drum in his chest. "Almost got yourself killed, you know that?" The figure made no response. Holt studied him closer. "Hey, anybody home? You hurt?" Still nothing.

The sunlight behind Holt revealed that the figure was a boy, about Holt's age. He was alive and real, not something hung from the ceiling as a decoy. But something was way wrong with the kid. He seemed to be sleepwalking or in a daze.

Holt could guess what it was, he looked about the right age. Holt drew a flashlight from his belt, flipped it on, aimed it up at the kid. When the light hit his eyes, the boy didn't react.

But Holt did. As he expected, the boy's eyes were a solid black. The snaking tendrils of color he had seen in the Menagerie pirates earlier had filled in this boy's eyes completely.

It was the Tone. The boy had finally lost his battle with it and Succumbed. He was now under Assembly control. Someone had probably sealed him up inside the train car, either out of a sense of kindness or a desire to deny the Assembly one more human adult for their growing collection.

When a survivor finally Succumbed, he began a long, slow, zombie-like walk to the nearest Presidium, the massive Assembly base ships that had come roaring out of the sky eight years ago, impaling themselves into the hearts of the world's great cities like daggers.

What happened (or was happening) to the majority of the human population inside the Presidiums, no one knew. . . .

And it was something Holt likely never would know. But even though he was immune to the Tone's call, he definitely had experienced its effects.

He stared up at the Succumbed boy with bitterness. A tingling of sadness began to surface from the usual place, the place where he had buried it long ago.

Holt felt it rising, wanted no part of it, pushed it back down again. Angrily, he stepped away from train car's door. After a moment, the boy inside hopped down of his own volition. His black gaze stared blindly forward, not even noticing Holt or his dog.

Max whined at the boy, unsure whether he was a threat or a harmless drone. To be honest, Holt wasn't sure either, when you came right down to it. He petted the dog comfortingly, held him back.

The two watched as the boy slowly turned and began walking to the northeast, compelled by some unknown force toward what remained of Chicago . . . and the dark Presidium ship that waited there.

Holt watched him until he became a small silhouette on the horizon.

The sight haunted him. He remembered that walk, knew if he closed his eyes he would see her walking that same way all over again.

So Holt kept his eyes open. He grimaced, forced himself to look away. "Come on, pal."

Max barked, grabbed his bone again, and followed him back to the tracks. He found the ones he was looking for again, heading north, back into the trees.

Holt and Max quickly set off into the forest, following the trail.

From the distance came more booming, more staccato drumbeats. They sounded closer now.

3. BOUNTY HUNTER

HOLT LAY AT THE EDGE OF THE TREE LINE, staring through a pair of small binoculars. Night had fallen, thick and dark over the forest, and the woods were filled with the impatient buzzings of locusts. Max sat next to him, chewing on a piece of cherry-flavored taffy from Holt's pack. Max had a wicked sweet tooth, and when Holt needed to keep him quiet, he gave him a snack to focus on.

Through the binoculars, Holt spied what was once a farmhouse beyond the trees. For the most part, it was still in one piece, though some of its windows were broken out and there was graffiti on its doors.

Holt watched each window on the bottom floor light up with flickering orange light as something moved through the house. A lantern, Holt guessed, held by the very person he'd been tracking.

He smiled. The bounty on this one would solve a lot of problems for him, but he'd have to be cautious, have to do this strategically. The person in there was supposed to be very clever.

Holt and Max moved for the farmhouse, closing the distance quick and quiet, keeping low. He could see the lantern light from an upstairs window now, which meant the bottom floor should be clear. Unless his target had set up traps or alarms, of course. It was a distinct possibility.

Holt opened the door and slipped in.

The farmhouse was dark, probably hadn't had electricity since the invasion. It had also been ransacked by looters many times over. What was left of the furniture was smashed on the floor, the cabinets and shelves all turned over and emptied.

Holt and Max moved through it all slowly, careful about tripping or breaking something, all the while scanning for traps. So far, Holt hadn't seen any.

They moved toward the stairs at the other end of the room. As they did, Holt noticed the walls. There were still a few pictures hanging on them. Family portraits, a picture of a man on a tractor, two boys and a dog, a girl dressed in a high school graduation gown. They were glimpses of a world that no longer existed, and in all of them was something that gave Holt pause.

Images of adults. Parents. Friends of friends. Smiling, standing tall over their children, strong and capable.

Holt couldn't help but stop and stare. It was almost a decade since he had seen anyone older than twenty-one or twenty-two. To him, the figures within those pictures seemed . . . alien. And even though they made him uncomfortable, he couldn't look away.

The ceiling above him groaned as somebody moved upstairs. It was enough to break the spell. Max stared up at the ceiling, sniffing the air curiously and growling low.

Holt silenced him with a gesture, moved away from the pictures, and started up the stairs, taking them nice and easy in case they were squeaky. As he moved, he drew his shotgun from his back, a faded, camouflaged Ithaca 37 he'd found at an old army base and restored back to health. He used it almost as much as the Sig. They were two of his best friends.

At the end of the stairs stretched a dark hallway, wallpaper peeling from it and littering the floor. The hall moved between several different bedroom doors, but only one of them had light spilling out of the doorway onto the floor and wall. The same flickering orange light he'd seen outside.

Holt and Max crept toward the door quietly, and reached it in about six slow steps. Holt pushed himself gently against the edge of the doorframe, listening and waiting. No sounds, no indication of who or what might be waiting.

It was now or never, he figured. Holt took a deep breath, gripped the shotgun, and spun around the side, raising the weapon as he did. He aimed down the barrel and moved quickly into what used to be a bathroom.

The lantern sat on a shelf, bathing everything in wavering hues of orange and yellow. In the center of the room was a large porcelain clawed bathtub, full of water and soap suds that covered a lone figure resting contentedly inside. The person didn't so much as flinch.

"Get out of the tub," Holt ordered firmly, keeping the shotgun aimed at the figure. "No quick movements, I know who you are."

Inside the tub was a girl, a little younger than Holt, eighteen or so. A cucumber slice covered each eye, and her hair was tied behind her head as she lay relaxed against the opposite end.

"I said out," Holt demanded louder when she still failed to move. Max growled low beside him, as if he were eager to leap in after the girl. He probably was, Holt guessed. The dog loved it when people resisted.

With a frown, the girl slowly plucked one of the cucumbers off an eye and leveled an annoyed look at Holt. "Do you have any idea how long it took to make this bath?" she asked in agitation. "Here's a clue: I had to use a teakettle for the hot water, so, yeah, it took me a long time."

"I'm not sure it would be possible for me to care less," Holt said, growing impatient. "The only thing I care about is the price on your head." He kept the gun raised. She seemed remarkably calm for her predicament, which in his experience was a bad sign.

The girl removed the second cucumber and stared at him evenly. Unlike his eyes, hers were laced with the black veins of the Tone, and the ratio of white to black had shifted dramatically to the darker side. They were pretty eyes nonetheless, Holt noted, flashing green in the candlelight. Up close, they probably sparkled. . . .

Holt quickly shook his head to clear out that thought. He had a job to do; he needed to stay focused.

"Another bounty hunter," she said, making no move to exit the water. "I've already left three of your friends in my dust—what makes you think you'll be any different?"

"Because I'm better than them," Holt said. "And I doubt they were my friends. Get out of the water, or I'll have my actual friend here *pull* you out." Max barked in anticipation.

"He looks like he could use a bath, too," she said. "No reason to be grumpy. Mind turning around while I find my clothes?"

Now, that was a new one. "You're . . . naked?"

The girl smiled. "That's typically how a bath works."

Holt hesitated, a bevy of images flashing through his mind as he looked at the bubbles lying like a blanket on top of her. But he forced those away, too, and concentrated on the issue at hand. She had a point, he had to admit. What was the harm? She was too far away to reach him even if she tried. Besides, Max had no qualms about looking away—it was all the same to the dog.

"Fine," he said gruffly, turning around but keeping the shotgun close. "But make it quick."

"Totally quick," the girl pleasantly assured him.

Behind him, she stood up in the water, keeping her eyes on Holt as she did so. Max growled as she stepped out, but she paid the dog no notice. Several necklaces hung from her neck, one of them a thin gold chain with a pendant made of a very odd combination of objects. Two dimes, a glass vial full of dark gray powder, and a red marble, all tied together with copper wire. The moment she was free of the tub, her hands shot to the pendant and ripped it off. She threw it hard at the floor where Holt stood.

Splinters of light exploded in a sphere all around Holt and Max as the vial shattered. Streaks of light streamed upward and brilliantly burst apart in the air.

Something ripped Holt and Max off the floor like they weighed nothing.

It yanked them straight upward, left them floating in midair, weightless, feet off the floor, spinning around helplessly. In shock, Holt tried to reach a wall or the ceiling or anything to give him traction, but they were all too far away. He was stuck, hovering uselessly in space over the crumbling bathroom floor.

Max spun around as well. The difference was, he seemed to be having a great time. The dog barked excitedly as he rotated and twisted, enjoying the weightlessness.

The girl laughed, watching them. "Well, at least one of you's enjoying it." She moved to her clothes, slowly gathered them up, and put them on.

The girl was thin and lithe, with short red hair that ebbed and flowed somewhere around her neck line. Her eyes, just as Holt guessed, were green, and they shone like emeralds behind the black of the Tone. She had the easy body language of someone capable, like most survivors these days. The ones who couldn't save themselves had long ago been weeded out, but there was more to her than just that. A polished savviness and lighthearted glint in her eyes that was earned only from numerous close calls and brushes with death.

Holt caught only glimpses of her as he spun, brief flashes of golden wet skin in the lantern light. Any other time, it might have been a nice sight.

"Let me down!" he demanded, managing to twist around enough to aim the shotgun at her. She just laughed, watching him with amusement. Holt felt a rush of anger, both at his predicament and at being bested by a girl. "I don't want to, but if you make me shoot, I will!"

He had underestimated her, he knew. Big-time. And he wondered how many others had made the same mistake.

The girl clicked her tongue disapprovingly. "Shooting a gun inside a gravity void's the opposite of a smart idea," she replied, calmly tying her shoes. "And Midnight City wants me *alive*. There's no reward for you if you shoot. And that means you won't."

The girl grabbed an overstuffed backpack from the floor and opened the bathroom window, letting the cold night air float in. She put one foot through . . . then paused, looking back at him.

"My name's Mira, by the way. Mira Toombs," she said, smiling as she stepped all the way through the window. "Did you think I wouldn't make you work for it?"

Holt could only watch as she dropped from the windowsill. He heard her hit the ground below and scamper quickly away, leaving him stranded in midair.

He cursed as he floated. A Strange Lands artifact. It must have been. The wanted poster had clearly said she was a Freebooter after all, an expert. He should have seen it coming. But he hadn't. And now he was trapped while all that reward money ran away from him.

But he wasn't going to lose it this easily.

Holt studied the room, noticed objects at the other end weren't floating as he and Max were. Whatever she had done to the gravity, she had done it only in close proximity to the two of them. It meant the "gravity void," or whatever she called it, didn't extend that far out. If he could just reach its edge . . .

But he couldn't grab a wall or the ceiling, couldn't grab anything to pull himself through the air. There was one thing, however, he *could* reach.

Max yelped as Holt grabbed him. "Hold on, pal." Holt flung Max forward. The dog flew over the floor with relish, then passed through the edge of the void and back into normal gravity.

He fell to the floor with a thump, and Holt quickly grabbed a spool of rope from his belt and tossed an end of it to Max. Half of it fell to the floor in front of the dog as it passed through the edge of the zero-gravity. The rest still hovered weightless above.

"Pull!" Holt shouted. Max grabbed the rope and started pulling, growling with enthusiasm.

Holt held on, being towed through the air. When he reached the edge of the void and passed through, he suddenly realized something. "Wait!" he shouted at Max, but it was too late. Gravity caught him and he dropped directly into the bathtub.

Water sprayed everywhere, blowing suds and bubbles all over the room. Holt, wet and angry, burst from the tub and immediately leapt through the window.

He landed on the ground outside, looking for signs of the girl. He was in time to see her disappear into the trees a hundred yards ahead. Max landed on the ground next to him, and Holt clicked his tongue twice. The dog darted after her, barking furiously, a missile over the ground. Holt ran after him, watched Max disappear into the tree line.

Holt rushed into the forest, dodging the hulking shadows of huge pine trees in the dark. Only the moonlight filtering in from above gave him light. Ahead, he could hear Max's barking, and he followed it as fast as he could.

When he burst through a mass of shrubs, he skidded to a stop right before careening off the edge of a steep cliff.

Only open air lay between him and a riverbank hundreds of feet below, and he stared down at it with alarm. Max was to his left, barking furiously. The girl was there, too, keeping the dog at bay with a tree branch.

Holt and the girl locked eyes. She smiled as she saw how drenched he was. "Guess you took a bath, too."

Then she simply turned . . . and leapt straight off the edge of the cliff.

Holt gasped; Max barked in frustration. They both looked out over the drop-off, expecting to see her splattered on the rocks below. Instead, they saw something completely different. Mira floated gracefully through the air, light as a feather, like she was being carried by an invisible parachute.

Another artifact, Holt thought with disdain.

Maxed whined pitifully, barked once, desperate to pursue, but without a way to do so. Holt watched the figure of Mira Toombs land on the riverbank and run toward the north. He stared after her, counting each footfall until she disappeared, becoming one more shadow among thousands in the dark.

He had to admit, she was good. No wonder her bounty was so high. But she was worth it, regardless. That reward was salvation, his ticket to the east, away from all his problems, and he didn't mind putting in a little overtime to get it.

4. FREEBOOTER

MIRA TOOMBS STARED NERVOUSLY at the huge, imposing structure across the lake.

In the World Before, it was called Clinton Station, a nuclear power plant built on the banks of Lake Clinton in Illinois, known for its bright blue domes and cooling towers. Now it was a crumbling, overgrown ruin. The towers still retained a little of their former color, but one of them had collapsed and the other was leaning badly. Holes where the facility had cratered in on itself were visible in all the surface buildings that still stood.

But it wasn't the place's disrepair that made Mira uneasy, or even the very real possibility of radiation. It was the fact that behind her, the sun was setting, a giant sphere that buried itself in the horizon and colored the water of the lake orange.

Normally it would be pretty, but right now it simply meant that night was falling. And that what lived inside the old power plant would very soon be awake.

Mira tried not to think about it. She had no choice, after all. She had to go inside, had to find what she had come all this way for. It wasn't just her own life she was trying to set right, she reminded herself.

From nowhere, a blast of sound filled Mira's mind.

It was like static, like the sound from a mistuned radio projected at full volume. The shock caused her knees to buckle, and she barely caught herself from falling when it hit.

It lasted only a moment . . . then receded back where it came from, to the edge of her awareness. It was still there, as always, the hissing pulse of static she could hear in the back of her mind. The ever-present effect of the Tone, the Assembly's little gift to mankind.

She heard it constantly now, and it was growing louder, but like most survivors, she had learned to tune it out. She still hadn't heard the voices, though, and she was grateful for that. The whispers that those who were older claimed they could hear underneath it. And it hadn't really tested her yet, hadn't fought her for control, but Mira knew it was all coming, the whole inevitable, grisly affair. As she got older, it would take more and more hold of her, and she would have to work harder to keep it at bay. Until, finally, she didn't have the strength anymore . . .

But that was a problem for another time. Right now, she had business to attend to.

She headed toward the power plant, scaling cliffs and pushing through overgrowth as she circled the lake's shoreline. The sun was almost all the way down by the time she finally reached the old gates and stepped through.

The open space in the middle of the plant was overgrown with weeds now. The fallen tower lay in a broken heap across the ground where it had crashed years ago. Part of it had come down on one of the administration buildings, crushing it to dust.

Unlike most abandoned places these days, Clinton Station had no graffiti, no signs of looting or pillaging, no indication that anyone at all had set foot inside in years.

Mira wasn't surprised. Some stories were scary enough to keep anyone out of a place, and given the original purpose of the power plant, those stories were undoubtedly hiding and waiting in the dark tunnels beneath her feet.

She moved for the nearest building, her footfalls echoing far too loudly for her comfort.

She stood at the door there a long time, trying to convince herself to simply open it. It wasn't easy. She could feel the fear trembling through her, fear of what might be beyond. But she hadn't come all this way, risked everything she had risked, to freeze up here.

Mira steeled herself and reached for the handle. The door opened with a groan of rusty hinges . . .

. . . and nothing whatsoever happened. No sounds of spindly legs rushed forward; no shadows writhed and twisted and lunged at her. Everything beyond the door seemed empty and devoid of life.

Mira stepped inside cautiously nonetheless.

It had been a control room of some kind, Mira guessed. The banks of knobs and dials were still in one piece, but covered in so much dust, they were impossible to make out. She brushed some of it away, revealing a host of gauges and switches whose original purposes were long forgotten.

She surveyed the room quickly, found what she was looking for. A big, thick, faded red door in the far wall. She moved to it and wiped the dust away from a sign fastened on its surface.

Clinton Station: main access route. Entry beyond this point limited to authorized personnel only.

"Jackpot," Mira said to herself, smiling.

But what if it wasn't here? She had traded a lot of artifacts (useful, valuable artifacts) for the information that led her here. Everyone she traded with had seemed trustworthy, but the world had evolved a certain degree of dishonesty. Everyone was a good liar when they had to be. You just never knew anymore.

It would be here, she told herself. It *had* to be.

Through a window in the control room, Mira saw the last traces of color fading from the sky, being consumed by the dark. She didn't have much time now.

She pulled her pack loose, set it down on the floor. On the front of it, something had been embroidered into the fabric in bright red thread. A letter from the Greek alphabet, the δ symbol, a marking used the world over now to identify "active" artifacts from the Strange Lands. Her pack was overloaded with them—batteries, watches, vials full of glittering powders, springs, pencils, a bag of paper clips, magnets, lightbulbs, nails, and, of course, dozens of different coins, each wrapped in separate pieces of plastic.

Whenever she looked at the artifacts, they all seemed to writhe and push away from one another, as if some subtle, invisible force was slipping in and out between them. Mira had never decided if it was a real phenomenon or just her imagination.

She shifted through them and found what she was looking for. A large antique lantern that looked like it was ready to fall apart . . . but Mira knew it never would. At least not outside the Strange Lands. Artifacts were virtually indestructible once taken out. Mira remembered the Librarian's theory that it was because their molecular structures "froze" once they were extracted. It was a good enough explanation for her.

Mira added oil to the lantern pan, then stuck a wick into a small hole in the bottom and fed it up through the top. But she didn't light it. Not yet. Not until it was time.

Mira slipped her pack on, grabbed the lantern, pulled a flashlight from her belt . . . and stared at the big red door waiting in front of her. Her heart beat heavy and thick in her chest. Outside, the sun had set. It was now or never.

Mira opened the door and stepped through. When it shut behind her, pitch black fell over her.

5. UNDERNEATH

MIRA NEVER KNEW A PLACE could be so dark. Shadows hung like thick curtains all around her. She quickly flipped on the flashlight, sending a beam of light shooting forward. It did very little to drive away the shadows that pushed against the illumination.

She was at the top of a concrete stairwell that descended downward into the dark. Her light didn't reach very far down, and where it ended, the stairs were swallowed by the thick blackness. Nervously, she started down, each footstep echoing loudly in the tight, concrete confines. Much too loudly.

As she descended the stairs, the shadows crushed in on her. But nothing moved within them. Not yet, anyway. The light in her hand wavered as her hands shook, and each step downward seemed to require more effort on her part to accomplish.

But Mira took every step. After moving for an eternity, she finally reached the bottom, where the tight confines of the stairwell gave way to a much larger tunnel.

Her light still didn't reach very far, but she could see the chalky concrete tunnel was lined with dark, dust-covered doors leading to different areas of the power plant's underworkings.

She tried to remember the map the kid in Faust had shown her, even though he wasn't willing to trade for it. The storage room should be near the end of—

A shuffling from behind her, like something slithering along the floor.

Mira spun quickly around, raised the light. She saw something dark scamper back into the shadows at the other end of the tunnel.

Or had she? Maybe her fear had imagined it for her.

She held the light where she had last seen . . . whatever it was, but nothing moved there now. Her heart beat heavy in her chest again; her breathing was quick and ragged.

More scampering, something moving for her from the other direction.

She spun once more, shone her light . . . and saw shadows slither away along the floor. Strange, unsettling clicking sounds—as if from dozens of teeth grinding against each other—echoed from the dark . . . then faded away.

Okay, that she most certainly had *not* imagined, and she forced herself to study every open door in front of or behind her.

And in the places where her light could not fully penetrate . . . the shadows moved. Dark masses of slow movement that writhed just out of reach of the light, waiting and watching.

More scampering, more shapes. This time on the ceiling behind her. Her light pushed it back. More from a door to her left, the hungry clicking sounds came again, louder.

Mira knew the flashlight was about to become useless. They knew she was here now, they would be on her any second . . .

She struck a match from a pocket and lit the wick jutting out of the lantern.

Brilliant light pulsed outward in a powerful flash unlike anything a normal lantern could create. A bright, radiant sphere formed around Mira, wavering and flaring intently, filling the tunnel with its luminescence, burning bright.

Mira held it up like a shield.

In its intense light, the skittering shadows all around her were horribly revealed. Hundreds of them, stuck to the floors and walls, dripping off the ceiling, pulsing inside the doorways. Hulking, cancerous masses of goo, thick and black, like oil, constantly morphing and blending into new shapes.

Jaws of black teeth jutted out from their bodies, formed for the express purpose of collectively shrieking in pain. Mira held her ears, almost dropped the lantern as the sickening screeching that flooded the tight tunnel. The creatures withdrew from the powerful light, disappeared into darker rooms and hallways of the old station.

It was just as she had expected. A Fallout Swarm.

When the Assembly arrived on Earth, their ships were covered in billions of microorganisms carried from the vast reaches of space. Their reaction to exposure with Earth's environment and atmosphere was to grow. Quickly. Within a year, they had become the huge, abhorant organisms they were now.

Globulous masses of putrid blackness that constantly changed shape and could form and dissolve eyes, maws, and other appendages as needed.

They were predatory to the extreme. Instead of the Assembly, the Fallout Swarms may well have overrun the Earth, if not for the fact that they found bright sources of light intolerably painful. Plus, they were attracted to sources of radiation; they seemed to live off it. Places like Clinton Station were natural homes for them, with its leftover radiation and its inherent darkness.

This Fallout Swarm had temporarily been pushed back by Mira's artifact. It was a major artifact, from deeper into the Strange Lands, and she had traded for it in Midnight City long before she had been forced to flee, thinking she might one day need it for just such an adventure. It was one of the few things she could think of that might help her survive entering a Fallout Swarm lair.

So far, it was working. In the bright light, Mira could see from one end of the tunnel to the next. And there was no sign of the swarm.

Except for the clicking. The sounds of gnashing teeth, from hundreds of sources, all ticking and grinding and echoing everywhere.

The swarm may not have been visible . . . but it was nearby. Looking for its chance to get to her and rip her apart.

She rushed down the hall, looking for the door she wanted. She knew the lantern wouldn't burn forever, She had to hurry. As she moved, the bright light pushed into and through each door she passed, followed by shrieks from inside as the Fallout Swarm twisted and crawled back into the dark. All around her, at the edge of the lantern light, the shadows writhed and fluctuated, following hungrily after her.

She found the door she was looking for and stepped quickly through it.

The room on the other side was immense, stretching high above her, most likely all the way to the surface. In the light, she could see crates of all kinds and shapes, stacked high off the floor, all sitting untouched and covered in dust.

It had been the power plant's main storage area, as big as a warehouse, and it was what she was looking for.

A lift mechanism sat in the center of the room, directly underneath a large mechanical door in the "ceiling" above. Mira assumed it was used for bringing material to and from the surface.

The Fallout Swarm had made this room its main lair, it seemed. It was revoltingly, impossibly, densely covered with the black, oozing creatures, all swarming and contorting throughout the room, dripping from the walls, the ceiling, the floor.

When Mira's pulsing lantern light entered, they emitted a collective shriek of pain and anger, swarmed up and away in a shuddering wave of blackness that receded into the shadows.

The clicking sounds were overpowering now, echoing everywhere. If the lantern were to fail . . . she wouldn't last long.

Mira's heart raced as she moved toward a series of stacked metallic crates. They were sturdy and solid, seemed to have weathered the years well. It was a good sign. She wiped the dust off one, revealing a circular symbol divided into six yellow and black triangles pointing at a black circle in the center.

In the World Before, it had meant radiation.

Mira's relief and elation were enough to make her forget about the clicking sounds filling her ears, the swarming mass of blackness trying to get to her outside her light. It was what she had risked everything for. And she had found it.

One of the crates sat by itself, and she undid the locks on its front, yanked it open. Inside, completely dust-free, was a layer of black foam protectively holding half a dozen water-filled glass cylinders. The cylinders were full of slivers of a dull, brownish compound.

Mira smiled at the sight. She reached for one of the canisters and pulled it free of its foam. At the same time she took something else from her pack. A strange conglomeration of different, mundane items: dimes and quarters, a green marble, coiled copper wire, two triple-A batteries, and other things, all wrapped in gold chain and blue thread. It wasn't big, Mira could hold the entire packet in her fist, and it was attached to a large watch band.

It was an artifact combination called a Dampener that she'd made before entering the dam. It would absorb all the radiation and heat the plutonium naturally gave off, making it safe to carry.

She quickly wrapped the band around the cylinder and tightened it. When the object touched the glass, there was a spark of light . . . and then a hum, like something electrical powering up. Mira felt the hair on her arms stand up at the charge.

When it was done, she held the cylinder up and studied it in the light from the lantern like a priceless treasure . . .

. . . just as the crates above her suddenly began to topple over.

In their fervor to reach her, some of the Fallout Swarm had climbed on top of the crates, shrieking and clicking, piling more and more of themselves on top of the stack . . . until it was too much.

The crates tumbled downward to the floor in a cascade, and Mira leapt away. She barely avoided them as they crashed down all around her, slamming into the floor and bursting apart.

Mira hit the ground hard and rolled away.

As she did, the lantern came loose, sliding away. It couldn't break, but the flame on the wick snuffed out regardless.

The vital, protective light it offered died, and everything plunged to black.

The glass cylinder skittered out of her grasp, rolling into the shadows.

Mira stared around her as ghostly shrieks shouted out and filled the huge room with frightening power. But the shrieks weren't ones of anger or pain this time. They were shrieks of glee.

Mira couldn't see them, but she knew they were coming, heard their slithering bodies dragging themselves across the floor toward her.

"Well, crap . . . ," she said, and yanked her flashlight loose once again. The light it emitted was puny compared to the lantern: it barely lit anything around her. Two of the creatures lunged for her from the dark, and she shone it right at them. They withdrew a little ways. But there were more. Many more.

In the decayed beam from her flashlight, she saw the Fallout Swarm streaming down toward her from every direction, unafraid now, hungry, angry, obsessed. Teeth and jaws and writhing mouths formed and jutted out from their bodies, ready to tear her to shreds. The clicking and gnashing of teeth echoed everywhere.

Mira knew she was done for. Whatever she did, she was just stalling the inevitable. She didn't feel fear now, just bitterness and frustration at having come so far and so close. Mira hated to fail more than anything, and she had failed gloriously here. She thought of goals unmet, promises she couldn't keep, and her anger began to rise.

She had been so close.

Nearby, she saw the outline of the glass cylinder, just out of reach. There had to be a way out. There *had* to be. . . .

Mira pushed herself into a corner, keeping the creatures at bay with the flashlight beam, shining it in every direction as the things screeched and leapt for her, only to withdraw at the last moment.

And, as bad as things were, she noticed something worse. The flashlight, her pathetic source of protection, was beginning to fade. Its batteries were running out. When they did, she would be all alone as the darkness consumed her.

6. SWARM

MIRA HUDDLED IN THE CORNER of the giant dark room, trying in vain to push her back farther into the wall. But there was nowhere else to go.

The Fallout Swarm screeched and clicked and scratched everywhere, shadows of dripping, putrid ooze full of claws and teeth darted in at her, only to be repelled by her flashlight.

But that wasn't going to last much longer.

It would be over soon, and given how many of the things there were, it would be over fairly quickly. It was the one consolation she had. Strangely, there was only steeled determination now. Determination to stay alive as long as she could. It was the only semblance of a victory she had left.

And then the roof of the underground warehouse, far above, miraculously filled with bright light.

A huge door in the ceiling groaned mechanically as it opened, and the structure's freight elevator began to lower downward toward the floor. Bright lights under it shone into the chamber with intensity.

It wasn't as bright as Mira's lantern . . . but it was bright enough.

The swarm shrieked in fury as one, a terrifying, inhuman cry that echoed back and forth between the room's walls.

They scattered away, some forming wings to bat themselves into the air, or tentacles to scale the walls, retreating to the far corners of the room, away from the light. They swarmed there, gnashing their teeth, eager for the kill they had lost.

Mira ripped her gaze up to the elevator, stunned. She could see a lone figure riding it down. A figure she recognized, revealed in the machine's light. And the sight of him made her frown. It was the stupid bounty hunter from the farmhouse. The one who'd interrupted her bath. He must have tracked her all the way here.

He saw Mira huddled in her corner, her flashlight fading. His eyes locked on to hers . . . and he smiled. Smugly, Mira thought. As if at the irony of her needing to be rescued by *him*.

Well, she didn't, she thought, glaring back. She would show him. He'd be sorry he followed her all this way.

The swarm's frustrated screams filled her ears, reminding her she had more pressing issues.

She looked back at the precious glass cylinder from earlier, spotted it again, several yards away, next to a stack of rotting wooden crates.

She smiled. Maybe it was going to be a good day after all.

One of the lights on the still-descending elevator exploded in a bright shower of sparks.

Mira looked up . . . and saw black shadows leaping from the walls and the floor, flying through the air and slamming into the lights, breaking them apart in showers of glass.

It was the swarm. While they couldn't get through the light of Mira's major artifact earlier, this light, though bright, they could force themselves to leap into.

More sparks as another light exploded. With every hit, the room was again plunging into darkness. In a few moments, Mira would be right back in the same situation she'd just gotten out of.

So much for the bounty hunter rescue.

Mira scrambled for the glass cylinder on the floor, just as the last light on the elevator exploded. Everything went dark, and the swarm screeched, hungrily closing in.

The bounty hunter wouldn't last long. If she could just make it to the lift, maybe with her flashlight, she—

Sparkling red light burst to life in the huge room. Not as bright as the elevator lights, but enough to push back the swarm. Mira looked and saw the bounty hunter holding two old signal flares, one burning in each hand. He waved them at the creatures as they lunged at him, sending them wailing back into the shadows.

So he was more capable than she thought. How nice for him.

The boy leapt off as the elevator touched down. As he did, he dropped one of the flares on the platform to keep it clear of the swarm.

The other he carried with him, waving it at the horrible oozing creatures. She watched as he drew a shotgun from his back and ran toward her.

She didn't have much time; he'd reach her soon. She turned and ran the opposite direction, toward the glass cylinder on the floor. Mira could see it just a few yards—

One of the creatures landed in front of her—two screeching jaws formed and pushed out of its body. She raised the flashlight . . . and then saw it was dark, the batteries had died.

She was defenseless.

Behind her, the sound of a shotgun filled the cavernous rooms like shots of thunder. The boy blasted the swarm as it attacked him, pumping the shotgun and reloading as he moved.

Mira had her own problems. She leapt out of the way as the thing in front of her pounced forward, barely avoiding its double jaws.

From a pocket, she pulled out a handful of quarters, each wrapped in light plastic marked with the δ.

The creature spun around, hissing and clicking as she pulled the plastic off each coin, and then gripped the first one between her thumb and index finger.

The thing scampered madly for her, shrieking and scratching across the floor.

With practiced ease, Mira snapped her fingers . . . and the quarter shot out like a bullet. When it hit the monstrosity, it exploded in bright sparks. The thing howled in pain, reeled backwards, stunned. Ooze from its body sprayed everywhere.

Mira placed the other quarters between her fingers, snapped them forward. They exploded into the thing like bullets, one after the other, sending it contorting and flailing backwards . . . then finally crashing to the ground, lifeless.

But there were plenty more to take its place, and Mira had no other Strange Lands coins within easy reach.

She twisted and ran, heading for the cylinder as the swarm writhed in a mass above her head, shrieking and darting toward her.

One of them knocked her to the ground, pinned her with its oily, leathery wings, and wailed into her face with three separate mouths.

Mira tried to get loose, but it held her tight. Its mouths parted, revealing dripping fangs, black tongues descending—

And then a shotgun blew the thing off her. It hit the ground, slid a dozen feet, and didn't move.

Red sparkling light filled the air around Mira. She looked up in a daze . . . and saw the boy staring down at her, holding the flare above him, keeping the creatures at bay.

"Hey, you look familiar," he said as he reached for her. "Are you following me?"

"Cute," she said with disdain as he yanked her to her feet.

The swarm circled all around them. On the walls, in the air, looking for their opportunity, a mass of screeching blackness in the red shadows.

He handed her the sparking flare. She took it. She had little choice: it was their only hope for escape. "We move for the lift, don't stop until we're there, I'm almost out of shells."

The cylinder sat a dozen feet away. Her eyes locked on to it. This was her only chance; without the lantern, she would never be able to find another one.

"Wait, stop!" she begged, resisting his efforts to pull her away.

One of the creatures lunged through their light.

The bounty hunter raised the shotgun, blasted it back, pumped the gun. "Keep the flare up!" he shouted at her. "If I have to drag you, I will, but I promise you won't like it."

She kept fighting him as the swarm pulsed and writhed around them. "Please, I'll come with you, I won't struggle," she pleaded. "If you just help me get *that*." Mira pointed it out to him, a few feet away, lying there by itself. "Please, you don't know how important it is."

The boy stared at it a moment . . . then rolled his eyes, started pulling her away again. "You don't need it where you're going, sweetheart." He pulled her harder, and this time she was unable to resist. He was too strong. He started dragging her away.

"No, please!" Mira cried, staring at the glass cylinder in agony as she was pulled away from it. "It's incredibly valuable, it's priceless almost."

And at those words, the boy pulled up short. He stared down at her. "Priceless?" he asked, a hint of a new tone in his voice. She almost smiled when she heard it. It was child's play now.

"Yes! You could trade it for *anything*!" Mira exclaimed. It wasn't a lie—you definitely could. She had known people who would kill for that thing, for the opportunity it presented.

The boy looked at the cylinder, seemed to calculate its distance versus the risk involved. The swarm was all around them, and Mira had to spin to keep the flare up to drive them away. "Please, I won't fight you if you get it. It'll be worth it. *More* than worth it."

When he looked back at her, she saw something remarkable. His eyes were crystal clear, no telltale tracings of black at all. He was Heedless, she realized in surprise (and envy). The Tone had no effect on him. "If it turns out to be a glass of water," he said with a hint of warning, "you're going to have a very unpleasant trip back home."

Before Mira could answer, he lunged forward into the shadows, leaving her holding the flare for protection.

But she didn't really need it. The sight of someone outside the protective cocoon of reddish light was enough to stir the creatures into a frenzy.

They darted downward at the bounty hunter, jaws and clawed appendages materializing from their bodies.

The boy blasted one that landed in front of him, sidestepped its corpse, and leapt for the cylinder.

He grabbed it as two more of the things flew toward him. The boy rolled away . . . and the things crashed into a stack of rotted crates. What was left of the heavy boxes came tumbling down in a mass of debris and splinters, burying the creatures.

The boy didn't stop to look—he ran back for Mira, firing his shotgun as he went. When it clicked empty, he sheathed it on his back and drew a handgun from his belt all in one smooth movement, fired at two more creatures, dropped them dead to the floor.

Mira watched in amazement. He was more than good . . . he was amazing.

He reached her, stuffed the cylinder in her pack, and shoved her forward. "Anything else I can get for you?" he asked sarcastically. "Forget your toothbrush somewhere? Maybe your favorite socks?"

Mira scowled at him as they rushed for the lift.

The elevator was clear of the swarm. The red flare was still flashing there, keeping them away.

They reached the lift, shut the gate behind them, and hit the button to start it rumbling upward. The creatures swarmed all around them, slamming into the lift, shaking it as they tried to get at them, shrieking and scratching in fury. But there were two flares now—the light was too much. There was nothing they could do.

As the creatures receded, Mira breathed a sigh of relief. She had done it. She had what she came for, she had survived—barely.

Then she gasped as the boy shoved her hard to the floor of the elevator and pinned her arms behind her back. She felt rope circle around each hand, and flinched as it tied them together tight. "Ouch!" she said angrily, glaring at the bounty hunter. "That hurts!"

His hair was thick and wavy and unkempt but somehow managed to look intentional in its style. He was tall and well built—streamlined was probably the best word, muscles and quickness earned from years of running and fighting—but there was more to him than that. Behind his brown eyes were confidence and cunning in a proportion Mira didn't often see, a calculated awareness of everything around him. He had . . . something about him—that was for sure. And it only annoyed her more.

He kneeled down to her, smiling as the swarm futilely pushed and shoved against the lift. "My name's Holt, by the way. Holt Hawkins," he said, mockingly introducing himself the same way she had when they first met. It made her blood boil. "And you were right. You definitely made me work for it."

7. COMING STORM

STARS PEEKED THROUGH THE TREE canopy high above the forest floor. Only the flickering light from the fire illuminated the campsite, but Holt was about to douse it. He built it as he always did, dug into a hole at the base of a tree, with limbs covering it. Doing it like that allowed the fire to still provide heat while drowning out most of its light and filtering the smoke. All to avoid detection. Not just from other kids, but from Assembly patrols as well.

As if on cue, the rumbling of distant explosions floated through the air, this time from the east. Strange, rhythmic percussive booms that hung in the air. The Assembly was still stirred up, it seemed.

"Excuse me," a testy voice said from behind him. Holt turned and studied Mira, tied to a tree at the top of a small rise. He had secured the girl with rope, tying her around the waist and binding her hands on either side of the trunk. She wasn't happy about it, but he didn't particularly care. She had already escaped once, and he wasn't taking any chances this time.

"Can you please make it stop staring at me like *that*?" Mira asked, nodding to Max, who lay in front of her, his tongue lolling out of his mouth, watching her like a prized bone.

"Sorry, but no," Holt said, dousing the fire with a pile of leaves he'd assembled earlier to block the smoke from rising in a plume when it went out. "Max is just doing his job. He knows you're his meal ticket."

"Oh, is that right?"

"You know how much your bounty is?" Holt asked. With the fire gone, the camp was thrust into the dark; only the filtered starlight above provided illumination.

"All I know is it's definitely less than I'm worth," Mira replied. She was just a dark shadow now against the tree.

"It's a tidy sum, the biggest I've ever seen." Holt moved to his cot, straightened his bag out. "Gonna solve a lot of problems for me and Max."

"Only if you can get me back to Midnight City," Mira said with a smile in her voice. "A lot can happen on a long journey like that."

"I'm not too worried, now that you've lost your little bag of tricks." Mira's pack, adorned with the δ, and all the artifacts it contained rested underneath Holt's cot for safekeeping. "Your wanted poster says you're a Freebooter. Carrying that many artifacts, looks like it's true. I thought Freebooters got along well in Midnight City. How'd you piss them off so bad?"

"Getting a price on your head doesn't take much these days," she said bitterly. "But it sounds like you know all about that, though. If you need my bounty to solve your problems, you must be on the run," she replied. "Who owns *your* death mark? Rebel group? The Menagerie? Some Midnight City faction?"

Holt frowned as he crawled into his sleeping bag, suddenly aware of the glove on his right hand. He didn't like her figuring out his predicament. It was best this Mira Toombs knew as little about him as possible, that she saw him only as her captor. But it was his own fault. He'd made the remark about needing her reward money, and the girl was smart, she knew what conclusion to draw. He'd be more careful.

Survival dictated it.

The sounds of explosions rumbled through the night air again, like strange, reverberating thunder announcing the coming of a storm. It filled the space between the shadowy trees, rattled leaves in their branches. It sounded farther away now, though, which was a good thing.

"What are they up to?" Mira asked quietly, almost to herself. "Something's had them jumpy for two days."

"Three, actually," Holt corrected her. "Some idiotic resistance group, probably. We're not that far from Chicago, it's probably the Blacksheep."

"The Blacksheep Brigade has their hands full, they never leave the ruins," Mira said. "And they're not idiots, they're good at what they do."

"Which is what, exactly? Getting killed? You're right, they're great at that." Holt made no effort to hide the contempt in his voice.

"They're resisting," Mira said firmly, "making a stand, you don't respect that?"

Holt laughed. "Challenging the Assembly isn't respectable, it's suicidal. No one can beat them."

"There's always a way," Mira said. "Always."

Holt shook his head at the conviction in her voice. "Eight years since the invasion, if someone was going to pull it off, they'd have done it by now." Holt rolled onto his back, stared up at the stars that he could see through the tree cover. "They crushed every military on the planet, subdued most of the population, all without lifting a finger. The only ones left to make your 'stand' are kids, most of them younger than us, and hardly any of them know anything about fighting. Not to mention we all seem more interested in killing each other than uniting and really facing them. The Tone takes more of us every day, and pretty soon, there's not gonna be anyone left."

"That's easy for a Heedless to say," Mira replied. "Someone who isn't living with a ticking clock in their head, counting down the moments before they lose their mind."

The words stung Holt, and his calm detachment melted away. He turned to the girl, could see her more clearly now in the dark. She was staring right at him.

"You don't know what it's like," she went on, "to have the static inside your head, to have it growing and clouding everything. You don't know the fear of hearing the voices . . . and listening to them slowly start to make sense. If you did you might be a little more motivated to find a solution rather than just hiding out here in the forest like a coward."

Holt glared at her, felt the anger (and the old pain) form and course through him. "I know more about the Tone than you can imagine," he said venomously. "I know more about it than anyone has a right to, trust me. This conversation's done. We'll get to Midnight City in three days, which means we're going to move fast and hard. I suggest you get some sleep, unless you want to be dragged all the way there. I won't have a problem doing it if I have to."

Mira didn't respond. He held her gaze until she finally looked away.

Satisfied, Holt rolled over. His hands trembled. He knew it would be a while before he could sleep. He wouldn't let her see how much of an effect she'd had on him, though. He had to appear strong, in control.

He hated this anger, because it was always tied to the memories. They were harder to push away when he was angry.

To his right, Max whined slightly. He watched Holt with his big round eyes, tilting his head sideways as he did. Holt reached out and petted the dog, scratched his ears. Max was a good judge of Holt's mood, and there was something about that that Holt liked. At least someone understood him.

When he withdrew his hand, the dog looked back to Mira, watching her like a hawk. Holt closed his eyes, trying to concentrate on the sound of the wind in the leaves and the chirping of crickets. If he could calm down, maybe he wouldn't dream about her tonight. . . .

8. DREAMS

A YOUNG HOLT, no more than twelve years old, exploded through the front door and out onto the lawn of the house they'd given his parents at Fort Connor. A quick glimpse of the living room clock as he ran past told him it was close to one in the morning.

Outside, the alert sirens were even more jarring. They were blaring all over the base, and he could see lights flickering on in windows up and down the street.

His sister, Emily, a tall brown-haired girl who was almost seventeen, stood with their father and mother at the edge of the house's small lawn. His dad was already wearing his fatigues.

Holt saw more people filling the streets, struggling into their uniforms and clothes. Civilian wives and children, too, all coming to look, all confused.

When Holt reached Emily, she took his hand, put her finger to her lips, signaled him to be quiet.

His mother spoke with her soft voice, but it was shaky with a kind of nervousness Holt had never heard before. He didn't like it.

A sound like rolling thunder reached them from far away. They looked toward the sound, past the buildings of Fort Connor to the skies above Denver. The sparkling lights of the buildings could be seen from the base. Masses of storm clouds had formed above the city . . . and they glowed in strange light. A dull reddish orange, almost like they were burning inside. Holt stared at them in wonder.

Everyone in the streets around Holt froze at the sight, listening to the long thunderlike rumblings wash over them. It wasn't like any thunder Holt had ever heard.

His mother moved closer to his father, and he put his arm around her. Holt felt his sister's grip on his hand tighten.

The glowing in the clouds grew, becoming brighter, the shades of red blooming vibrantly. The thunder rolling in from the city grew louder, too. Something was building; something was happening.

The clouds over Denver parted violently as a massive black shape exploded out of them.

Holt, Emily, and everyone else in the street gasped as it slammed straight into the heart of the city. An enormous fireball erupted where it hit, bellowing up into the night sky.

Seconds later . . . the sound of the impact hit them, a giant boom that shook the ground. People screamed; some fell to the street as if blown over. Emily moaned, her knees buckled. Holt held on to her tightly.

In the distance, the lights of Denver flickered once, twice . . . then went dark. Seconds later, so did the base, the lights up and down the street flashing out.

More sounds reached them, loud enough to carry over the distance. Pops and bangs, like firecrackers on the Fourth of July. But Holt knew they weren't firecrackers.

The city itself could no longer be seen. Only bright flashes near where the ground must be . . . and yellow pinpoints of light that flared from the sky to the Earth like how his dad once described tracer fire from the war.

It seemed pretty clear. Denver was under attack. But . . . by what?

The realization broke the spell. The people all around Holt ran in a stampede either back into their houses or toward the barracks to gear up. Holt knew his father would go with them.

Holt's mother had the same thought. She shook her head, gripped his shirt tight to keep him in place . . . to keep him with them. His father pulled her close, whispered into her ear. Holt couldn't hear what he said, but his mother relaxed a little in his grip, shut her eyes.

Holt and his sister watched their father kneel down to them. Holt noticed how calm he seemed in spite of all that was happening, in spite of the panic in the street. It made him feel better, made him believe things would be okay. His father always made him feel that way.

He said he needed them to help their mother, to pack the car and get ready in case they had to leave. He asked if they thought they could do that.

Holt and Emily both nodded, held each other tighter. Their dad smiled.

He looked at Holt, studied him in a new way, like he was seeing different parts of him he'd never recognized before . . . or at least never needed to until now. After a moment, his father nodded, pulled something from a pocket, and handed it to Holt.

It was going to be for his birthday next week, Holt's father said. But he'd decided he was ready for it now.

Holt stared at the object, a glittering, new red Swiss Army knife, full of different tools and blades. Holt smiled. His dad ruffled the boy's hair affectionately. When he got back, his dad said, he'd show him how to use it. Then he hugged them tightly, Holt and Emily at the same time.

His father stood up. His mother's eyes glistened. The sounds of explosions from the city were growing louder. Holt's father pulled her close, kissed her . . . then he was gone, running down the street with the rest of the soldiers.

Holt gripped the knife in his hand as he stared after his father. He watched until he faded into the distance, until he lost sight of him on the darkened street.

It was the last time Holt ever saw him.

9. BEST-LAID SCHEMES

EXPLOSIONS RIPPED THE AIR above the camp and yanked Holt from his dream.

"What was that?" Mira asked in alarm, still tied, but awake and alert.

There it was again, the high-pitched rapid-fire booms of heavy plasma cannons. Holt recognized them instantly.

So did Mira. "Raptors . . . ," she said. "We need to get out of here."

She probably wasn't wrong. Holt leapt from his sleeping bag, scanned what little of the sky he could see through the treetops. It was still night: the half moon had risen high above them, raining silver light downward on everything.

He heard it again. Above and to the west, coming fast. More cannon fire. With a grimace, he reached behind him and yanked the SIG from his back. Max was next to him, whining slightly, sniffing the air suspiciously. Holt reached out to pet the dog . . .

. . . and a blue and white Raptor gunship screamed by overhead, visible for half a second through the canopy. Two of its engines were burning, trailing smoke behind its signature crescent-shaped wings. Max barked angrily up at it, but Holt just stared in awe. He had never seen a wounded Raptor, not even during the invasion when the military had mounted its brief, lackluster defense. What could have done that?

A second later, he had his answer.

Two more Raptors roared by above, plasma cannons flashing, firing after the first gunship. They were gone in a second, but there was something different about them, and Holt knew what it was immediately.

Every Assembly aircraft or walker he'd ever seen had one thing in common: They were all painted blue and white. The patterns differed sometimes, but the colors never did.

But the two Raptors that just whipped by had not been blue and white at all.

They were a solid *red*.

Holt listened to the sound of the cannons as they became fainter, and then heard the rolling boom of another crash several miles away. The damaged Raptor must have finally gone down.

He clutched the rifle tightly, breathing heavy, thinking.

"Did you see them? They were red!" Mira yelled down at him from the tree on the incline. Holt frowned. She almost sounded excited. "*Red!* What's going on?"

"Good question," he answered. "Heard rumors of different-colored Assembly down south, but I never put much stock in it. And I definitely never heard about Assembly firing on *each other*."

The sounds didn't return. All was silent in the woods and in the night air. Maybe that was the last of—

A flaming, spherical Assembly ship exploded through the trees right above them.

Holt rolled, scrambled, and leapt clear before the thing hit, pulling Max with him. When it hit, it hit hard, plowing through the middle of the forest, tossing aside trees and foliage and leaving a gully sixty or seventy feet long. The impact sprayed debris and flame in a vicious sphere. Mira screamed from her tree, unable to move as debris flashed through the air all around her.

When it was over, Holt stayed motionless a long time, staring at the smoking crash site and the large round ship, its metal surface painted blue and white, as he was used to.

But while the color was familiar, nothing else was. He'd never seen a ship like this, a huge metallic ball. Flames burned lightly around it, starting to consume the nearby trees, but the vessel itself was no longer burning. It was, however, cracked completely open. Smoke poured out of its shell, blocking his view of the inside.

"You still alive, Hawkins?" Mira shouted through the thick clouds of dust and smoke. He couldn't see her through it, but he could hear her coughing.

"Yeah!" he shouted back. "Sure you're relieved."

The crashed sphere nearby groaned as something inside shifted. Holt's gaze snapped to it. Max growled low at the sound, the hair on his back standing straight up.

Something there was moving. Something inside was still *alive*.

Holt stood still, thoughts racing in his head. He'd never seen one of the Assembly. As far as he knew, no one had. They had always stayed locked up tight inside their armored walkers and ships.

Holt forced himself to be calm, to think. The red Assembly craft might be headed back. Or worse, they could have walkers moving in on his position. At the very least, the blue and whites had reinforcements headed this way. The prudent thing seemed to be to leave. What good was investigating an Assembly ship if he got carried away by a Vulture?

Then again, Assembly technology, regardless of what state it was in, was invaluable in trade. Two or three plasma weapons alone could feed you for a whole year. Who knew what lay inside the wrecked ship? And if he didn't loot the thing, someone else surely would.

Holt calmed himself and listened. A few sounds, but nothing threatening. Just the wind in the trees, the crackle of flames. No Raptor engines, no cannon fire, no metallic stomping of Spider walker legs. Still, he waited, listening, making sure.

The spherical craft listed again. There were more sounds of movement from inside.

That decided it for him. Holt sprang to his feet, moved for the craft, keeping low. He shoved the SIG back into its slot, yanked loose his shotgun. Better for the close quarters inside. Max moved beside him, his eyes focused on the shadows inside the craft.

"What are you doing?" Mira yelled down at him. "Please tell me you're not actually thinking about going *in* there?"

Holt ignored her as he moved for the ship.

"Hey! What am I supposed to do when you get killed?" she demanded. "I'll never get these ropes off."

Still, he ignored her. A few more steps and he was at the ship's hull, cracked open like an egg. Wires and tubing spilled out of it like guts. Sparks popped and fizzed everywhere. There was a weird whirring sound that was winding down, going lower and lower in pitch. Something mechanical dying, most likely.

Holt raised the shotgun cautiously, peering around the edge of the hull. The smoke was thick inside, pouring out in great plumes. He couldn't see anything, had no idea what was in there. To find out, he'd have to move in.

"*Hey*!" Mira yelled in anger behind him.

Holt tuned her out, took a deep breath, then he and Max pushed quickly through the smoke, into the strange ship's interior.

MIRA WATCHED IN ANNOYANCE as Holt and the dog disappeared inside the strange craft. Idiots. Going inside a crashed Assembly ship had to be the heavyweight champion of bad ideas. It was a miracle they'd survived this long.

Mira looked around at the campsite. Most of it had been thrown into disarray when the ship crashed, but she saw Holt's cot a few feet away. Her pack was no longer under it. Instead, it had been knocked closer by the impact, and she could see the red δ just out of reach of her feet.

Or was it?

If she could reach it while the dynamic duo was busy being eaten inside the ship, she might be able to make this whole thing play to her advantage.

Mira reached out with her feet, the only part of her the bounty hunter hadn't tied to the tree. His mistake, she thought.

Her shoe stopped just a few inches from the bag, almost there. But it wasn't enough.

Mira grimaced. She pulled against her bonds . . . and could feel the ropes give around her waist, only to feel them tighten against her arms, pulling them harder against the tree.

If she strained hard, she might be able to loosen the ropes around her legs enough to reach the bag . . . at the expense of what little circulation she had left in her arms.

It would be well worth it.

She pulled against the ropes with all the strength she had. And then groaned in pain as they tightened hard against her arms, the sharp bark of the tree digging into her skin.

But her legs were looser now. Mira reached for the pack again . . .

. . . and this time she looped one of the straps around her ankle and quickly pulled it to her. She had to hurry—who knew when the bounty hunter and his smelly dog would reappear.

With her leg, she tossed the pack backwards. It landed on the right side of the tree, just barely in reach of her hand. While Holt had tied her upper arms against the tree, he'd left her forearms free. She worked one of them out of the tight ropes, just enough to bend it.

When she did, she reached for the pack and flipped through it with her right hand. The first thing she looked for was the cylinder. After a moment, she felt its cool, glass shape inside among all the other objects and artifacts, and breathed a sigh of relief. Good, he'd brought it with them. All wasn't lost.

She rifled quickly through the other contents with her hand as it explored the pack's interior.

After a moment, she found what she was looking for, recognized the cold, metallic, angular shape. She grabbed it, pulled it out—an aging, rusted Zippo lighter—and smiled at the sight.

With her hand, she closed the pack, then grabbed one of its straps. With what little leverage she had while tied to the tree, Mira threw the whole thing forward through the air. It landed even farther than where she had originally grabbed it from, closer to Holt's cot.

She looked at the Zippo in her hand, closed her fist around it. She couldn't wait to see the look on his face. He'd be sorry he ever saw her wanted poster.

THE SMOKE WAS THICK and everything was dark. Holt could barely see the end of the shotgun. Max shadowed him as he moved, a gray blue blur below him. He was just a dog, probably no match for whatever was waiting in the smoke . . . but it made Holt feel better having him there.

The ship's interior, like its hull, was round. Hulking husks along the walls marked what probably had been control panels. Now they were singed beyond recognition. A few of them still clung to life, spraying the odd spark here and there.

Holt pushed farther in, sighting down the barrel, finger on the trigger.

The smoke was so thick, it was almost impossible to see. He coughed, dropped low, hoping the air was clearer closer to the floor. It was. He could see a little better, too, more of the ship's insides.

More fried circuitry, more splits in the ship's hull, some sort of fallen equipment rack, its contents in pieces all over the floor. But there was no sign of survivors, of whatever had made the noises he heard. He was running out of time. The Assembly would be here in minutes, maybe seconds. He should get out now, he told himself, it wasn't worth—

Movement, a shuffling from just ahead. He heard coughing.

Coughing? Did the Assembly cough? Did they even have lungs?

Steeling himself, Holt crawled ahead, shotgun ready, pushing through the curtains of—

Something long and thin and metallic materialized from the smoke, wrapped around his leg, and started to pull.

"Son of a—!" Holt jumped in fright, scrambled back. Whatever it was withdrew, fading into the smoke and dark.

He fired his shotgun after it.

Sparks sprayed from the opposite wall. There was an electronic-sounding screech, like something crying out through a broken speaker.

And . . . whispers. Hissings. Something almost like language, but not. Holt couldn't be sure if he was hearing it . . . or if it was in his head.

Shadows moved all around him, coming to life in the smoke. Max barked frantically, alarmed and ready to fight. Maybe this hadn't been such a good idea after all. . . .

Holt pushed himself back against the closest wall, raising the shotgun, trying to keep low enough to see anything advancing on him.

The shadows continued to pulse and move. The whispering grew louder in his head, harsher, more frightening. Was this what the Tone sounded like? Is this what the Succumbed heard in their heads?

Holt flinched as the horrible screech came again. Louder this time, grating, ripping his ears. Something sprung for him. Something big. The whispers again, louder, angry . . .

The Ithaca exploded to life. It was a combat shotgun—it could fire shells one after the other if he needed it to, and right now, he did.

The shotgun fired again and again, blasting the huge shadow backwards. It wailed its strange electronic cry . . . and then went silent, fading into the dark.

For a moment, there was no movement. No sound. Max whined next to him.

And then a shuddering. That was the only way Holt could describe it. As if the air all around him trembled. The sensation grew stronger, more powerful.

A surge of light erupted from the dark in front of him—so bright, it almost blinded him. Wavering, beautiful, golden light like a churning cloud of energy formed and hovered before him.

Holt couldn't open his eyes, it was too bright. The whispering returned. The hissing sounds. They cut into Holt's consciousness like a razor. They were much louder now, overpowering. They were so loud, it seemed the ship (or maybe just Holt's skull) might burst.

He tried to push away from it, gritting his teeth, unnerved. His hands went to his head, trying to seal out the sounds. Max howled in pain next to him.

And then the light receded. Floated out like a bright, pulsating cloud of color into the air beyond the ship . . . and disappeared.

The whispering was gone. So was the sensation of fear and dread. Holt exhaled deeply, breathing hard, his pulse a beating drum in his ears. The light. He'd seen it before, a few times. A field of energy that lifted up and out of Assembly craft when they were destroyed, but he had never been this close to one before. Never heard . . . those sounds . . .

"Hello?" a voice came from the dark. Holt jumped, stunned. "Help . . ." The voice was human.

Holt got to his feet, pushed through the smoke toward the voice at the other end of the ship. Max followed quickly after him.

Ahead emerged a metallic chair of sorts. A figure was strapped to it, held secure like a prisoner. As Holt reached it, the smoke cleared a little and he could see more. A little girl, no more than eight or nine. Her face was covered in soot, and she coughed in the smoke, trying to breathe. But beyond that, she seemed unhurt. As he emerged from the smoke, she looked at him with wild eyes full of fear. Holt didn't blame her.

"Hold on, kid, I got you." Holt reached for the straps holding the little girl to the chair. They weren't metal; they were made of something thin but resilient. Some sort of carbon fiber maybe? They wouldn't loosen.

The girl looked at him, wide eyed and desperate to get loose. But there was something in her look that made Holt pause, too, something behind the kid's eyes. Those eyes seemed older than their owner, somehow. But wasn't that true of all kids these days? The only survivors of the invasion? Weren't they all forced to grow up fast?

"Please, we have to hurry," the girl said. "They're coming back. *Please.*"

She was right: the Assembly were definitely on their way.

Holt shouldered his shotgun and drew the red Swiss Army knife from his belt. It was faded with age now, but Holt kept it in good shape, and it had never let him down. As strong as the little girl's bonds were, the knife surprisingly cut straight through them. He made short work of all four.

Holt grabbed the kid's hand and pulled her toward the tear in the ship's hull. "Stay low, hold on to me, okay? Can you do that?" In response, Holt felt the little girl grip his hand tightly. Something in the grip implied not only her fear, but her trust in him as well. Holt wasn't sure if he liked it.

Either way, he whistled three quick notes, and Max darted back the way they had come, clearing a path through the smoke. Holt and the little girl followed and exited the crashed ship. Outside, the fires from before had extinguished, and everything was covered in shadow again. Holt and the little girl took big breaths of fresh air.

Holt drew a flashlight, knelt down before the girl, shone it all over her, looking for injuries.

"You seem all right," Holt said. It was true—if she hadn't been covered in grime and soot from the crash, no one would guess she had been through anything remotely traumatic. She stared up at Holt with huge eyes. "What's your name?" Holt asked her.

"Zoey," the little girl said, her voice still a little shaky. "My name's Zoey. We have to go. Like I said, there isn't much time."

Holt studied the kid more closely. She looked like every other little girl he had ever encountered, harmless and shy, with long blond hair that trailed down her small back, a cute button nose, and perfectly clear, deep blue eyes (still too young for the Tone to begin showing). She wasn't wearing anything unusual, just cargo pants and a small shirt. Everything about her was ordinary, and there was nothing to indicate what she was doing in that ship. The lone passenger of a strange Assembly craft shot down by its own kind. It was wrong, very wrong, but regardless, as she'd said, there wasn't much time. The Assembly would be here in force in minutes, dropships unloading walkers all throughout the forest. He had to leave now to get out before they cordoned off the whole area.

That left him with a decision to make.

Take the girl with him? Or leave her, now that she was free of the ship? His inclination was to leave her. She was a survivor, after all. If she didn't know how to take care of herself, she was doomed either way. But . . . there was something about her, something that stirred feeling in him. It was the way she looked at him, Holt decided. How her eyes held and peered into his without hesitancy, as if she were gazing *into* him. Not just at his surface, not just at who he appeared to be . . . but who he really was.

It was silly, of course, probably his imagination, but still, no one had looked at him like that in a very long time. No one since Emily.

Taking her, of course, meant a whole host of problems, and problems weren't something he was short of right now. He'd have to transport

Mira and the little girl at the same time. Concentrating on keeping the girl alive meant concentration he wasn't spending on watching Mira, who was definitely looking for an escape plan.

"Look who found a friend!" Mira shouted down from her tree, as if on cue.

He looked up at her, and she smiled back pleasantly. Holt didn't like it. She seemed smug . . . and that was the last thing the girl should be right now. She should be defeated, frightened maybe, but not smiling. Had she come up with a plan?

Holt quickly glanced around the ground near Mira, saw her pack, but it was well out of reach, so it couldn't have been that. Still . . .

A sound from the east. Far in the distance. Holt looked away from Mira toward it, but the trees were too thick to see anything. He could only hear it. A pulsing tone of sound that blared loud and rhythmic. Over and over. He had never heard anything like it, but he recognized it for what it must be. Some kind of alarm. There was one thing he was sure of, however. It was not man-made, not human. It was too . . . different. Alien.

It must be the Assembly.

But where could it be coming from? There was nothing in that direction, not until you got to—

Then it hit him. Chicago was to the east. The Presidium. The Assembly, the blue and whites as he now called them, had just raised their alarm. It could only be that. But why?

He looked back down to the girl at his feet, felt Zoey's hand grip his even tighter. She looked up at him with pleading eyes.

"We have to go," she said again, a tremor of fear in her voice. *"Please."*

"Why?" Holt asked instinctively, though he was pretty sure he already knew the answer. "What's coming?"

"Them," the girl replied. *"All* of them." The simple answer chilled him.

The alarm continued to sound from the east, frenzied and angry. Plans had been thwarted tonight. And this girl, this Zoey, was somehow at the heart of them.

"Whatever you're going to do," Mira said, listening to the echoing, distant alarm uneasily, "do it quick."

"Can you walk?" Holt asked Zoey. She nodded, holding his gaze. "If they're coming in force, we'll have to keep moving. Can you do that? Move and not stop?"

"Yes," the girl said. "Thanks, Holt."

Holt nodded, quickly started packing up the campsite. He folded up his cot and sleeping bag, put them in his pack, grabbed Mira's, too, threw it over his shoulder, then moved up the hill toward his captive.

"What do you call it?" the little girl asked in fascination behind him. She was standing over Max, staring down at him. The dog stared back, his tail thumping the ground eagerly, hopeful he had found someone to rub his head.

"That's Max," Holt said as he reached Mira and started loosening her ropes. "We have a working relationship. He helps me out, I scratch his ears."

"It's a . . . Max," Zoey said to herself. "Can I *ride* him?" she asked, her voice full of hope.

Holt laughed. "I'm not totally sure that would work out."

Zoey reached down and petted Max. Max made no attempt to stop her.

Holt started untying Mira's ropes. As they loosened around her arms, she sighed in relief.

"Don't remember tying your arms so tight," Holt said. "Should have told me, I could have loosened it."

"Don't do me any favors," she replied, watching him as he untied her bonds. He noticed her eyes again. Green, like emeralds.

Holt frowned. Emeralds or not, they weren't pretty eyes. Nothing about her was pretty, he assured himself. She was his captive, and that was that.

"Sucks to be you," Mira said. "Transporting the little girl and me at the same time, Assembly closing in. Admit it, you're losing control, you won't be able to hold it all together."

Holt untied the rest of her ropes, pulled her roughly to her feet. He spun her around, tied her hands with the same rope, then tied it to himself, so she was connected to him.

"I think I can handle it," Holt said. She stared back at him without comment.

With three clicks of Holt's tongue, Max grudgingly pulled himself away from Zoey and darted ahead into the forest to scout. Holt, Mira, and Zoey followed after him at a quick pace.

"I'm Zoey," the little girl said to Mira, stepping into line beside her.

"I heard," Mira replied.

"Why are you two tied together? Are you best friends?"

Mira chuckled at the question. "Yes. Yes, we are," she said.

Holt shook his head, trying to ignore both of them. As much as he hated to admit it, things *were* getting complicated. He had to keep it all from falling apart. Somehow he had to find a way.

In the distance, he heard the rumbling of Assembly engines headed their way. Osprey dropships, no doubt. Carrying walkers, Spiders and Mantises. In ten minutes, this area would be crawling with them. But he planned to be long gone by then, melded into the forest. He'd gotten very good at hiding from Assembly these last eight years.

It wasn't until hours later, when the sounds of engines and walker legs faded behind them, and the blaring alarm tone from the east finally silenced that he realized the little girl had used his name back at the crash site.

She used it . . . even though Holt had never said it.

11. COMPLICATIONS

THE NIGHT DRAPED AROUND MIRA as she made her way through the forest. The moon had long ago disappeared beyond the horizon, and the trees were even thicker now, which meant very little starlight got through.

They'd seen nothing of the Assembly since the crash, but they had heard them. Ships had roared by in the distance, which Mira guessed were dropships. The suspicion was confirmed when they heard the stomping of walker legs behind them. Deep, pointed thumps that shook the ground, even from far away. Only the big ones, the Spider walkers, could make those sounds from that far.

Holt wanted to be careful about attracting attention, so they weren't using lights. It was a good call, but it wasn't doing Mira's shins any good with the constant scraping and bruising from rocks and thick brush. It was just one more reason why she disliked him.

Max was several yards ahead, tail wagging delightedly as he pushed through the brush with his nose, sniffing and panting, making more noise than any of them. Mira rolled her eyes at the dog's exuberance.

Her rope stretched behind her, trailing all the way back to Holt. Every once in a while, when she got too far ahead, Holt would snap it back to keep her in place. She fumed at the situation she'd gotten herself into. *Her,* a captive. To *him.* But she still had the cylinder . . . and a plan. She clutched the Zippo lighter tightly, biding her time.

"Holt?" Zoey asked behind Mira. The little girl walked with the bounty hunter, one hand clutching the hem of his shirt. She wasn't necessarily afraid of the dark, but she didn't take to it easily either. Zoey looked at every shadow and dark spot with skepticism.

"What?" Holt said in annoyance. He snapped Mira's rope again, and her eyes thinned to angry slits. She'd show him soon enough. . . .

"We're still going the wrong way," Zoey said.

Mira heard Holt sigh in frustration. He was getting impatient with the kid, had clearly grown too used to being on his own. He didn't like having to explain himself, Mira could tell. All she needed was for him to lose his cool with Zoey, lose it enough to take his eyes off her, just for a moment. . . .

"Listen," Holt said with forced patience. "We are one hundred percent headed the right direction. And that direction is north. You can trust me on this, I'm very good at what I do."

"Not this time. We're headed right for them."

"For who?"

"The scary ones, the metal ones."

Mira heard another sigh from Holt. "The Assembly's gone, Zoey, I promise. We've left them behind, and pretty soon the sun will be up and you'll see everything is fine, okay?"

"But everything isn't fine, Holt," Zoey insisted. With every step northward they took, she seemed to get more nervous. "When the sun comes up, it will get worse. Much worse."

Like Holt, Mira didn't really buy into Zoey's concerns either. Why would the Assembly be all the way out here, when the crash site was back behind them? Still, Mira had no doubt the kid believed it. The little girl was a weird mix. Shy and scared and unassuming one moment, then certain and assertive the next. And there still remained the mystery of what exactly she was doing on that ship. But if things went according to plan, she'd be long gone and not in a position to find out.

They took a few more steps; then Zoey simply quit walking.

Mira flinched as Holt yanked her to a stop.

"Zoey, we have to keep moving. We're almost ready to stop, I promise." Holt's voice was tight with frustration.

"I don't want to stop, I want to go back the way we came."

Mira turned around to look at the pair. Zoey was staring straight ahead, past Mira, past even Max, to the shadows of the trees beyond. Her eyes were wide with fear. At the front of the line, Max stopped moving and looked back at them all with a frustrated whine.

"Look, kiddo, I'm about done being nice," Holt said, reaching for the little girl forcefully. "I got places to go and problems to solve, and you're really putting a cramp on it."

Zoey slipped away from him, stepped back a few paces. "They're right ahead of us!" she said, clear notes of fear in her voice, staring past them all.

"Zoey . . ." Holt, exasperated, moved after the little girl . . . and turned his back on Mira.

It was what she'd been waiting for. It was now or never.

She popped open the Zippo, snapped it to life. A small flame jutted from the top, but it wasn't orange like normal flame. It was purple.

Mira touched the purple flame to her bonds . . . and the entire line of rope, from her hands, to her waist, to the length stretching back to Holt, incinerated to smoke in the blink of an eye. The lighter was a major artifact from deep in the Strange Lands. The small flame it produced combusted any substance (as long as it was flammable) almost instantaneously.

Mira screamed as the incineration effect burned her wrists and waist; Holt yelled, too, as the rope on his end flared into ashes. But the pain was worth it. She was free.

Max barked in alarm and Holt ripped around. Mira hesitated long enough to see the look on his face . . . then broke into a run into the forest, quickly leaving the three behind.

She heard Max bark as she ran past, but he didn't pursue. She listened to the sound fade away behind her. Holt had probably told the stupid mutt to stay behind and watch Zoey. Good. She knew she could outrun Holt if she had enough of a headstart.

Mira darted forward. The darkness made it tough, but the hours of walking through the forest at night had accustomed her to the shapes and shadows of the trees; she could almost tell how far they extended and to where.

She leapt over roots, dodged trunks and brush. Behind her, she could hear Holt's footfalls, hot in pursuit. She kept running, breathing hard, trying to put distance between them.

She bolted left, leapt over a fallen log, hoping to lose him. If she could get far enough ahead, she might—

Mira skidded to a jarring stop, almost falling flat on her face in a desperate attempt to halt. She stared ahead at what was in front of her, felt the cold fingers of fear crawl up her spine at the sight.

Slowly, breathing hard, trembling, she started to back away . . .

. . . and Holt slammed into her from behind, drove her hard into the ground in front of another log. She groaned as the air gushed from her lungs.

Holt spun her around, opened his mouth to yell . . . then stopped when he saw her eyes. Mira knew he could see the terror in them.

Holt looked up and past her to where she had just been looking. She watched him react at the same thing she had just seen.

There was motion ahead of them. Huge shapes—visible over the top of the fallen log—moved in the dark, trailing colorful lights behind them. Strange, sinister, distorted electronic chirps echoed back and forth between them. The earth shuddered rhythmically as they moved, like giant feet pounding the ground.

Assembly walkers, half a dozen of them.

Probably the smaller Mantis type, but "smaller" was a relative term here. Holt froze with Mira under him.

"Get off me," Mira whispered as loudly as she dared, "you're on my—" Holt clamped her mouth shut with his hand. She squirmed in fury, glared knives up at him, tried to bite his—

They both went motionless as a red beam of light pulsed out toward them and split the air above their heads.

One of the Mantises was scanning near them, looking for them with its targeting laser. Had it heard them? If they were using infrared, she and Holt were done for.

12. MANTISES

HOLT KEPT MIRA pinned beneath him as the laser explored the area around them. The probe was a triangular-shaped piece of light that somehow was both solid and visible in the clear night air. It stretched back in a perfectly straight beam of red and purple to one of the huge moving shadows in the woods.

Holt ducked his head down as the beam hit and moved over the top of the log, like digital fingers caressing the surface, looking for clues. Holt had seen those beams detect heat, movement, even sounds and vibrations before.

They were in big trouble.

Mira struggled beneath him, and he clamped down on her mouth even tighter. He could tell she was boiling mad, but he really didn't care.

"Quit squirming, you're gonna get us killed," Holt whispered soft but angry into her ear. "They're all around us." Her hair smelled like mint and spice, not at all unpleasant, but Holt forced those thoughts away. *Stop it, she's your prisoner*, he told himself.

Lasers from two other shadows flared outward and found the log, moved over it curiously, examining it, seeking and looking along with the first probe.

The ground under Holt and Mira vibrated in matching drumbeats. One of the shadows appeared just on the other side of their log. Holt pushed himself as far as he could into the ground. The hulking shadow stomped closer, the vibrations filtering through the ground and into his chest. He knew if he looked up, he would see it standing over them. All it had to do was look down. . . .

The shadow emitted strange, distorted, electronic chirps. They sounded quizzical, curious, but detached and frightening, too. A few other shadows called out in response, like they were talking to one another. For all Holt knew, they were.

The dark shape kept moving, shaking the ground with its footfalls, walking on through the trees. The laser probes on their log died and the air above them went black.

The shadows thudded onward, chirping their eerie communications back and forth. The sound echoed hauntingly among the trees until they finally vanished.

When they were gone, Holt yanked Mira to her feet. They stared at each other hotly.

"Still making you work for it, aren't I?" Mira asked him, her mouth twisted in a smirk. Her arrogance infuriated Holt.

"What were you *doing*?" Holt demanded. "You struggled the whole time, those lasers can detect movement and sound, you almost got us killed!"

"You were on top of me, and I didn't particularly like it!" Mira shot back. She shoved him backwards. "Your legs were digging into my knees, and you bruised my wrist. Plus your hand smells like your stupid dog!"

"My stupid dog would have known enough to keep quiet when a patrol of Mantis walkers was just ten feet away!" Holt shoved *her* now, for good measure.

"And would he have known enough not to lead us right *into* them on our little hike through the woods? Did you even think to scout the route before we moved through it in the pitch black?"

Holt fumed, tried to find something to say . . . but couldn't. She was right. In his hurry to get them away from the crash site and all the Assembly that were certainly swarming there, he had led them right into a patrol of Mantises.

Mira smiled at his lack of comment, saw she had won. It filled him with anger. Big reward or not, emerald eyes or not, the girl was quickly starting to be more trouble than she was worth. No wonder Midnight City had a vendetta against her.

He shoved Mira forward, back the way they'd run from. "Run. That way," he said tightly. "We have to get to Zoey and Max before the walkers do."

The two darted back through the woods. As they did, Holt tried to figure out his next move. They were miles from the crash site now, and the Assembly was still searching the area. But why? For what? They had the crashed ship and whatever secrets it contained. What else could—?

Holt's thoughts trailed off as something occurred to him. *Whatever secrets it contained . . .*

There was one thing, secret or not, that spherical ship had held that was no longer there.

Zoey.

She had been in the ship. In fact, as far as he could tell from his quick jaunt inside, she was pretty much the only thing that had survived the impact in one piece. Which could mean only one thing, Holt realized grimly.

The Assembly were looking for *Zoey. . . .*

But why? She was just a little girl. A little girl who was afraid of the dark and jumped at shadows and liked dogs.

But was that *all* she was? Hadn't she warned him? Hadn't she said the Assembly were right in front of them? Somehow, impossibly . . . she had known. And Holt hadn't listened, and almost got them killed as a result. Was she connected to them somehow? If so, could they detect *her?*

Holt guessed not. If they could, they would have been overrun a long time ago. Whatever it was, it seemed to be a one-way connection, at least for now.

But did that make it any better?

The sun was rising in the east, filling the sky above the tree line with a dim glow that permeated down through the leaves. The forest would be lit up in minutes. They had to be well away from here before that.

Holt and Mira broke through the trees back onto the trail they had been following earlier. Zoey and Max were still there. The dog was engrossed in having its belly rubbed and didn't even look up when his boss reappeared. Holt frowned down at him.

"You found them," Zoey said, looking at Holt.

"They almost found *us,*" he said. "Get up, we have to move."

Holt grabbed his and Mira's pack from where he'd dropped them earlier.

Mira looked down at Zoey, smiled. "Might have to start listening to you more." Zoey gazed up at Mira with huge, blue, unreadable eyes, and smiled back.

And then two large dark shapes stomped through the underbrush behind them.

Max howled in surprise. Holt spun toward the movement and found himself staring at the same shadows from before . . . only now revealed.

Machines that stood over ten feet tall, pushed off the ground by four powerful mechanized legs, each with dozens of complicated actuators. Atop the legs was the cockpit fuselage, which held twin mounted plasma cannons, a missile battery, sensory equipment, and other ordnance. In the middle of the fuselage rested their "eyes," a triangular grouping of three polished, round sensors that glowed red, blue, and green. The machines were painted a mixture of blue and white stripes and patterns, like every other Assembly walker Holt had ever seen . . . until yesterday.

Assembly Mantis walkers. Likely two of the very walkers Holt and Mira had just escaped from. They had found them.

Earth's children, its only survivors, named them Mantises because of their four-legged bodies. But other than the legs, they didn't look anything like insects. The machine was streamlined, deadly, built for both speed and accuracy, while still possessing firepower enough to be formidable. It was an amazing mechanical construction, a marvel of engineering so advanced, it was almost art.

No one knew what the walkers were really called. *Assembly* and *Mantis* were terms coined by Earth's survivors, weak attempts to give names to something that was indifferent to what its subjugates called it.

The walkers' targeting lasers flared to life, streamed toward them. The machines called out eagerly among themselves, with frightening electronic chirps.

"Move!" Holt shouted, but it wasn't necessary.

He and everyone else, even Max, instinctively fled in panic. There was no concern for direction or path finding now. There was only the primal need to escape certain death, and any direction would work just fine.

They ran in a disorganized group through the trees, dodging rocks and roots. The dim sunlight filtering in from above made it easier than before, but it was still precarious.

Holt heard the walkers behind him, their legs pounding the ground as they chased after them.

Outrunning them simply wasn't an option. He'd seen Mantises move at upwards of forty miles an hour over open ground. Just because they had legs and not wheels didn't make them any less mobile. In fact, the way they could corner and jump and climb, in Holt's mind, it made them even more agile. Their only hope was to use their size against them.

"Hang a right!" Holt yelled as they ran.

"Why?" Mira shot back.

"Because the trees are thicker!"

Sure enough, the trunks were larger, more numerous, more tightly packed. The walkers would have to work to find paths they could squeeze through.

They rushed into the tightly packed trees, the walkers chirping sharply behind them . . . but Holt heard their footsteps slow down as they looked for ways to follow.

The four ran through the forest, actually putting distance between them and the Mantises. Holt braced himself, waiting for the high-pitched electronic whine of the plasma cannons to rip the air, the yellow bolts to shred the trees to splinters all around them . . .

. . . but nothing happened. The walkers were pursuing, but they weren't firing.

Holt was stunned. The Assembly usually fired without hesitation—what was different now?

To his left, he saw Zoey struggling to keep up with them, ducking underneath low-hanging limbs as she ran.

And the answer hit him. There was only one thing that made sense. The Mantis walkers weren't firing, for a very specific reason: They didn't want to hit Zoey.

Whoever the little girl was, *whatever* she was . . . the Assembly wanted her *alive*.

13. WATER

HOLT RAN THROUGH THE WOODS in a strange state of panicked concentration. Mira and Max were to his right, a little ahead of him, running for all they were worth. To his left was Zoey. And she wasn't doing well. She was just too young, too small, quickly being left behind.

Holt scooped her onto his back and he felt her arms tighten around his neck, holding on for her life.

"Turn left!" Zoey shouted into his ear from behind.

"But we're losing them this way!"

"Only for a little bit, then they'll be on us again. Turn *left!*"

Holt frowned, not liking the idea . . . but she'd been right once before, and it had almost cost him when he hadn't listened. With a grimace, he turned hard to the left, whistled for Max.

The dog changed course, rushing forward ahead of them. Mira did the same. Holt guessed she knew her best chance was with them, especially since Zoey's presence seemed to protect them from plasma bolts.

Behind, the thuds of the walkers were growing louder, they were gaining again, pounding after them.

The four broke from the tree line . . . and just about ran straight into a enormous river, flowing fast and full toward the east.

Holt almost cursed out loud. "It's a dead end!" he shouted, letting the little girl down off his back so he could stare at her. This was where her sixth sense had taken them?

"Swim!" she pleaded, looking up at him.

Swim? Was she serious? "You see how fast it's moving? Why would—?"

"Swim! We have to, it's the only way!"

Holt looked to Mira. Mira shrugged. "They'll be on top of us any second anyway. I don't see another choice."

Downstream, less than a hundred yards, the two Mantis walkers stormed through the tree line, turning toward them. The open sky above the river revealed the blue and white machines in even more detail. Their size, their weapons, the sharp edges of their giant legs.

Holt and company didn't wait; they ran for the river's edge.

The walkers rumbled forward in response, closing the gap fast, chirping loudly.

From behind Holt came a growl as Max stared at the walkers with an intense glint in his eyes. His hair stood up; his tail wagged furiously.

Holt knew that look, knew what was about to happen. "Max, no!"

But the dog ignored him. To Max, the walkers were bad, they were dangerous, they had chased his boss. Max charged forward, barking sharply.

The walkers stopped dead, their three-sensor eyes focusing down in confusion at the furry gray creature charging them. Holt didn't imagine Mantis walkers were used to someone charging *them*.

Mira held Zoey's hand as she ran toward the river. She stopped, turned, stared back at Holt.

Holt looked from her to Max, watched as his dog reached the four-legged walkers, futilely biting and clawing at their metallic legs, barely scampering out of the way as they stabbed down.

He wouldn't last much longer.

Holt could try to save him. But was it worth it? *Survival dictates everything,* Holt reminded himself. He would also have to let Mira out of his reach, and losing her would be a very bad thing. Plus the odds of him surviving a close encounter with two Mantis walkers were very low.

Max yelped as one of the walker's legs slammed into him, sending him rolling backwards on the ground. Holt scowled as he watched.

"Damn it," he said with a grimace. Survival was one thing, but Max was the only friend he had left. Holt didn't like it, but he made his decision.

He dropped the packs on the ground. "Get Zoey across the river!" he shouted at Mira. She considered him in a new way, a mixture of surprise, puzzlement, and . . . something else. Something softer. Holt didn't like it, whatever it was. "Go!" he yelled as he ran toward Max.

Mira didn't hesitate long. She looked to where Holt had dropped her pack . . . then rushed for it, grabbed it, and pulled Zoey toward the water. They leapt into the fast-moving current, and it ripped them downstream.

Holt drew his shotgun as he ran, pumped out the last of its cartridges, and loaded in new shells, each marked with black tape.

Max was still on the ground, dazed. He barked up at one of the four-legged Mantises as it raised its powerful leg. Max yelped and rolled out of the way as the metallic limb stabbed downwards.

The second Mantis, behind Max and out of sight, raised its own leg, about to crush the dog.

A shotgun blast hit the Mantis right in its "face," where the three-sensor eye sat. But these weren't normal shells. Normal shells wouldn't do much to a Mantis's thick armor. When these shells hit, black tar exploded all over the thing's optics and sensors. It screeched in electronic anger, wheeled back.

The first Mantis turned on Holt, targeting laser streaming out. Holt fired twice more. More shells clanged in bull's-eyes on the machine's eye, spraying black tar everywhere. The thing chirped angrily, shook, and contorted, blinded.

Holt grabbed Max and yanked him away right as the second walker's plasma cannon opened up with a scream, ripping the ground and the trees all around them to pieces. But Holt knew it was panic fire: it couldn't see.

Holt shut his eyes tight as the cannon roared behind him. He dropped Max to the ground and the two of them rushed for the water, just a dozen yards away. The ground shuddered behind Holt as the walkers moved to pursue, still covered in black goo, relying on other senses.

Max had no issue following Holt this time. A few more strides and they reached the water, leapt in, let the current rip them downstream. They were going to make it.

Or were they?

The river kept them close to the bank as it flung them forward. Holt realized they were going to pass just feet from the two walkers. All the machines had to do was step in, and he and Max were done for.

The Mantises rushed to the water. Holt shut his eyes.

But the walkers made no move to venture into the river. In fact, they stopped well short of the water.

Holt, stunned, watched the Mantises as he and Max floated right by them.

They called out furiously; their plasma cannons flashed. Yellow bolts incinerated the water all around them . . . but it was too late. The current swept Holt and Max quickly out of reach.

With what little strength he had left, Holt swam for the shore, pushing through the frothing current. The water threatened to bury him, but he finally reached the other side and painfully pulled himself onto the opposite bank, using the last of his energy to crawl onto the sandy ground. He collapsed face-first into the dirt, breathing, filling his lungs, miraculously alive.

Holt lay that way a long time, concentrating on his exhaustion and the aches in his body.

From above him came the sound of heavy breathing, in and out. A panting.

Holt knew the sound.

He pulled his face from the sand. Max sat staring down at Holt with a curious look. He was soaking wet. In his mouth was an old purple rubber ball, thoroughly chewed through and faded from repeated use. It was Max's favorite toy. But how—?

Holt looked to his right, saw where his pack lay about ten feet away, its strings opened, its contents spilled onto the sand.

The dog must have made it to shore before him. And the first thing he'd looked for . . . was his stupid purple ball from Holt's pack.

Holt glared at him. "Give me that," he said testily, grabbing the ball from the dog's mouth. Max stared at him in excitement, assuming Holt was about to throw it. Holt sighed, but smiled regardless. They had both made it.

Holt scratched Max's head . . . and threw the ball. Max barked and chased after it.

Holt scooped the spilled contents back into his pack, trying to remove as much sand as he could. He sealed it, slung it over his shoulder, checked the guns on his back, his other equipment, making sure he hadn't lost anything. Somehow, he hadn't.

Holt pulled himself to his feet as Max came running back with the ball. Holt frowned down at him, feeling the soreness in his muscles already.

"You're welcome, by the way," Holt said. Max made no comment.

Holt looked back down the river to where they had left the Mantises. There was no sign of them now. They hadn't attempted to follow.

Holt was beyond surprised. He had no idea they had an aversion to water. But somehow . . . Zoey had. She'd been right again. But where did that insight come from? And was it something to be thankful for . . . or wary of?

Holt set off down the riverbank, looking for any sign of Zoey and Mira. After fifteen minutes searching both directions, he finally found what he was looking for.

Disturbances in the sand where two people—one older, one much younger—had pulled themselves onto shore. He followed the tracks into the forest, saw where they disappeared into the overgrowth.

Mira Toombs. She'd gotten away. Again.

From nowhere, the scent of her hair, mint and soft spices, replayed in his mind. He forced the thoughts away, angry with himself.

So her hair smelled nice. So she had eyes the color of emeralds, what did it matter? She was a wanted poster to him, and that was it. She was his ticket to escaping the Menagerie once and for all. And she was absolutely, most definitely, not attractive in the slightest.

But none of that changed the fact that she'd escaped.

Max whined at his side, studying the tracks, eager to pursue.

Holt petted his head. "Don't worry, pal," he said as he pulled his pack off his shoulder, opened it, looked inside.

There, wrapped in some spare clothes, was the glass cylinder Mira had risked her life to get in Clinton Station. The strange brownish substance glittered in the center of the clear liquid.

Holt smiled when he saw it. "This time, I think she'll find *us*."

14. SHROUD

MIRA AND ZOEY MOVED through the forest as the afternoon sun pushed through the treetops, lighting everything below in a kaleidoscope of light and shadow.

The weight of the pack behind her was noticeably lighter. It felt deflated, and every step she took, it sagged against her shoulders, a constant reminder that Holt had one-upped her. When had he taken the cylinder? When she was sleeping last night?

It infuriated Mira that she'd been outsmarted. Especially by the bounty hunter. Images of Holt rushing to save that stupid dog had played in her mind all morning. The way he'd run at the Mantis walkers, shotgun drawn, like some kind of white knight.

She forced the images out of her head.

He was no white knight, she reminded herself. He was a bounty hunter intent on turning her in to Midnight City. But hadn't he let her go . . . in order to save Max? It couldn't have been an easy decision, if he needed the reward money as much as she guessed. Losing her was as big a deal for him as losing the cylinder was for her.

Then again, had he *really* let her go? He had the cylinder, he knew how important it was to her, probably even anticipated she'd come back for it. He might even expect her to just show up and turn herself in.

Well, if he did, he had another thing—

The Tone swelled in Mira's mind, blocking out all her senses in a burst of static, like from a broken television. It was so loud, it was jarring, the loudest it had ever been . . . but it went away as quickly as it had come, receding away. Was it just her, or did it seem louder now in the background, swirling and waiting in the back of her consciousness?

"Do you think we'll see the Max again?" Zoey asked in her softly casual tone. She walked and held on to Mira's shirt as they moved. The flare-up had been too quick for the little girl to notice.

"I'm fine with seeing either of them," Mira replied, forcing the last bit of the Tone away. "But I would prefer they didn't see *us*."

"Why not? Aren't you and Holt friends?"

"Most definitely not," Mira said with a frown.

Zoey smiled, looking up at Mira. "You seem like friends to me."

Mira looked down at the little girl. She stared up with her blue eyes, and there was something behind the look. A . . . pondering was the best word Mira could come up with. Every look Zoey gave her had an implied curiosity to it.

"Zoey, where are you from?" Mira asked.

"From?" the little girl asked.

"How did you get here?"

"I crashed in a ship, Holt saved me."

"Before that, I mean. Where were you before that?"

Zoey's demeanor darkened at the question. She looked away.

"Zoey?" Mira pressed.

"I don't remember," the little girl finally responded, still not looking up at Mira. Her voice was barely audible now. "I don't remember anything from before the crash."

Mira stared at Zoey as the words sank in. "Zoey, you're at least eight years old. You must remember something from before. Your parents, brothers or sisters, things you did before the Assembly, *something*."

Zoey looked up at Mira again. Her eyes were no longer calculating or calm. Now there was uneasiness in them, fear even. "I just remember waking up when the ship crashed, and Holt finding me," she said. "I know I should remember more, but I don't. I don't even know if I want to remember. What if remembering is scarier than not remembering?"

What if, indeed. Mira couldn't say she wouldn't feel the same way.

"Do you remember your parents? Do you remember who took care of you before we found you?"

Zoey shook her head.

How was that possible? Mira wondered. God, what had the Assembly *done* to her?

"Look, Mira," Zoey said, a note of brightness returning to her voice. "Now we can see the Max again!"

Mira looked ahead of them, where the woods thinned out into a small clearing. Smoke rose from a small fire there, filtering into the treetops. She could see Holt's cot lying nearby, his pack on the ground under a tree.

Mira dropped to the ground, pulling Zoey with her, silencing the little girl before she could speak.

They'd found Holt's camp. She just hoped he hadn't spotted *them* in the process.

Mira stayed on the ground, listening for any sound of alarm or pursuit. But there was none. If he had seen them, there was no indication.

Mira thought through her options.

If he wasn't expecting her, he was an idiot, would likely be easier to outwit, and deserved what he got.

But she was pretty sure it wasn't going to be that simple. Holt, as infuriating as he was, wasn't stupid. He was . . . resourceful. And clever. Mira lifted up just enough to see over the brush in front of her and look into the camp again.

The campfire burning in the open was her first clue. Holt always lit fires much more inconspicuously, so as to avoid detection. But here was one burning in the open. And his pack, conveniently away from everything else. Logically, it would be the first place she would look.

Everything in front of her was out of place. Which meant it was a trap, and Holt was lying in wait somewhere. Well, he and his smelly, furry friend had a surprise coming to them. A big one.

Mira dug through her pack, searching the artifacts inside. She pulled out two nickels, each wrapped in plastic sleeves so they couldn't touch. Strange Lands coins were highly charged artifacts, and had a bad habit of exploding if they touched one another, or anything at all if they were thrown. It came in handy in lots of situations, and she had gotten good at using them as weapons in a pinch.

Next came a small broken piece of mirror, a sealed glass vial that seemed to contain nothing at all, and a roll of duct tape. She placed the first four objects one on top of the other, forming a chain of sorts.

First, she unwrapped one of the nickels and set it so the "head" of the coin faced outward. Then the glass vial (of Strange Lands air, a very useful ingredient) to serve as the combination's Essence. Next, the mirror shard, which would be the Focuser and reflect the air Essence. At the other end, she placed the second coin, also heads facing out (which would make the polarity of the artifact combination "positive").

When she was done, she wrapped the items together with the duct tape. As the Interfusion was made, the hair on Mira's arms stood up. A slight charge sparked the air, and there was a crackling, a hum. Like something electrical was charging up. Mira opened the glass vial peeking out from under the tape. A hiss of air, a shimmer, the hum intensified for a second . . . and then everything went silent.

At the same time, Mira's hand . . . *vanished*.

She dropped the artifact. Her hand reappeared, and a small rock that the artifact landed on disappeared in its place.

Zoey stared in wonder. "How did you do that?" she whispered. "Can you do it again?"

Mira smiled, put a finger to her lips. The artifact combination created pure invisibility by reflecting air and light away from whatever it touched. Impressive . . . but not enough. Not yet. She needed to make a second combination, using the first as the new Essence.

From her pack, she pulled out more items: two dimes (also wrapped in plastic) and a large blue green marble.

Mira started with the coin (heads out). Next was the artifact combination she had just made, and then finally the marble and the second dime (again, heads out). She wrapped it all together with duct tape.

As she did, the hum came again, but this time it was louder. The air shimmered and blurred as a cocoon of invisibility enveloped her. Everything on the outside was muted and darker, like looking at the world through sunglasses.

This combination was an often-used one, called a Shroud. It incorporated the first artifact combination, increased its power, and forced the invisibility to flare outward in the form of a sphere (thanks to the marble Focuser). Now, whoever held it was surrounded by a ball of invisibility. At least until the combination's power ran out, which wouldn't be long from now.

Mira studied the artifact combination with distaste.

She prided herself on not just the ingenuity of the artifacts she created, but also their aesthetic virtues. Since leaving Midnight City, it seemed she was always making combinations in a frenzy. She didn't have the luxury to take her time anymore, to use pretty bindings like gold or silver chain, lengths of silk of varying hues, or even colored twine. Now her artifacts were hastily created lumps of duct tape or rubber bands, without form or color or artistry.

It was one more thing she had lost when she fled.

"Stay here," Mira whispered to Zoey. "I'm going into the camp."

"I can't pet the Max?" Zoey asked dejectedly.

"No, sweetheart, not right now. I need you to stay down and out of sight. Okay?"

Zoey pouted, but made no move to follow Mira as she crawled slowly forward.

Mira advanced cautiously. Though the Shroud kept her invisible, it didn't make her intangible. She would still make noise and disturb the brush, which could give her position away. She had to be patient, take her time.

Mira inched into the camp's interior, studying the layout as she did.

Holt's pack lay at the far end, resting against a collection of trees that had grown upward together and intertwined. It was isolated and apart from the rest. Mira frowned at Holt's obviousness: it was clearly where he meant her to go. It was where the trap would be sprung . . . whatever it was.

She surveyed the rest of the camp, and her eyes found Holt's cot. The sleeping bag on top looked full, the blankets pulled up tight around the supposed occupant. Mira almost laughed out loud, wondering if it had taken every piece of extra clothing Holt had to make it look like someone was inside the bag.

What kind of fool did he take her for?

There was no sign of Max either, which meant the dog was probably with his boss, waiting on her to make a grab for Holt's pack at the other end of the camp.

The question right now, though, was where the cylinder really was. If Holt could have it his way, he'd have it on him, Mira guessed. He wouldn't want to risk actually losing it by keeping it out for her to grab.

But the cylinder was big and bulky, not to mention heavy. As much as he might like to hang on to it, it would slow him down in a pursuit or fight.

No, Holt would stash it somewhere. But where? What was the least likely place for that cylinder to be?

Mira inspected the camp again, and her eyes once more found the cot. If she had fallen for his ruse and believed he was actually in that sleeping bag, the cot was the last place she would approach.

Mira smiled. The cylinder was there. It had to be.

But how was she going to snag it? The invisibility sphere generated by the Shroud moved wherever she went. If she got too close to the cot, it would absorb it, too. And Holt would definitely notice his cot and sleeping bag vanishing into thin air.

But it was possible to get close enough to reach it, without the invisibility sphere touching it. She could do it, but she'd have to be careful.

She crept toward the cot. There wasn't much brush or other obstacles between her and it. He had chosen a clear area for the camp. She stopped just short of it . . . and waited.

Mira had no way of knowing if the Shroud had absorbed the cot. To her, looking out from inside, everything was visible. It was only people looking in that couldn't see past the ball of reflected light and air.

Mira waited a few more seconds, listening for any sign she had been detected. But none came.

She examined the cot again. If she were Holt, Mira would have slid the object all the way to the rear of the sleeping bag, so that it would be the most difficult to get to.

Mira grinned and drew a knife. It would be difficult to get to only if you went in through the front.

She reached for the rear of the sleeping bag with the knife . . .

. . . and the cot in front of her flipped over as someone underneath it leapt to his feet.

As he stood, Holt whistled three times . . . and Max exploded into the campsite, charging toward them.

Mira scrambled backwards, hoping the Shroud would conceal her. It did . . . but she saw Holt turn toward her as she pushed across the ground.

He leapt forward, hands swinging wildly. He missed her completely . . .

but slid far enough that he passed through the edge of the Shroud's invisibility sphere, and inside with her.

He could see Mira now, and he looked at her with that infuriating cocky smile. "Took you long enough."

Mira kicked him hard in the face.

He yelled in pain, went reeling backwards. "Hey!" he shouted in anger, holding his nose, shocked. "What the hell?"

Mira smirked in spite of herself. That felt good. She got to her feet and ran, hoping the Shroud—

The blue gray blur that was Max ran right into her. Whether it was intentional or the dog had just gotten lucky, it was enough to trip her up.

Mira crashed to the ground. Instinctively, she put her hands out to break her fall. And one of those hands contained the Shroud. The artifact combination tumbled out of her grasp and rolled away in the dirt.

Mira was now completely visible . . . and pretty much totally screwed.

She tried to get to her feet, but Holt leapt on her from behind, pinned her hard to the ground. She struggled, trying to get loose, to get a leg free, to bite at his hands—anything—but he was too strong.

Fear swelled up in her as she felt the rope circling her hands again, felt her shoulders tighten as they were locked behind her back. It was an awful thing, the simple loss of mobility, the loss of freedom.

When she craned her neck around to glare at Holt, the smirk from before was gone. His nose was bloodied and purple, and he scowled down at her. Mira flinched as Holt pulled the ropes around her wrists extra tight. But she didn't cry out. She wouldn't give him that satisfaction.

Max continued to bark and growl at Mira, just feet away from her face. She looked at the dog . . . and barked back in her best and loudest imitation. *"Rawr, rawr, rawr!"*

Max went silent, surprised, looked from Mira to Holt, off balance.

Holt pulled Mira to her feet, turned her around to face him, wiping the blood from his nose as he stared at her.

"You knew I'd go for the cot. Knew I'd ignore your pack," she said hotly. The anger was mainly for herself, though. She hadn't even given a thought to the idea that the first trap might be a ruse.

Holt nodded. "You're smart, Mira, so I set a trap for a smart person.

It's a shame you don't give yourself more credit, you might have figured me out."

Coming from Holt, it was almost a compliment. Mira fought the instinct to blush, angered she would be flattered by a bounty hunter who wanted to turn her in for money.

Mira became conscious of a warmth on her hands. It took a moment to realize what it was. Holt was still holding on to them.

"You can let go of my hands now," she said softly.

Holt, apparently, had forgotten, too. With a start, he let them go, and stepped back.

And then Max barked excitedly, and ran for the opposite end of the camp.

"The Max!" Zoey shouted as the dog rushed to meet her, tail wagging. "The Max wants pets!"

Max rolled over as Zoey started rubbing the dog's belly. As usual, he made no move to stop her.

Mira heard Holt sigh when he saw the little girl. "Fantastic . . . ," he said in exasperation.

15. GUILT

HOLT PULLED HIS ANNOYED GAZE away from Zoey and Max and moved for the edge of the camp, where he'd left his pack.

He'd forgotten all about the little girl, hadn't factored her back in to his plans. Looked like she and Mira were a package deal, at least for the time being.

That was okay, he'd make it work. They were almost out of the forest now, nearing the river valley. The trading posts along the river would be a fine place to dump her off.

Plenty of River Rat congregations were looking for new crew, even at Zoey's age. They would take her off his hands. He'd just have to keep it to himself that the reason Assembly dropships were blanketing the area with walkers was because they were looking for the kid. That mystery would be somebody else's problem to figure out.

And then he could transport Mira back to Midnight City unhindered. Holt expected to feel the usual rush of relief at the prospect, but he didn't. The feelings were muted this time, distant and far off. They felt hollow.

But why? he wondered angrily. Mira was a criminal. At least as far as Midnight City claimed, and he had no reason to disbelieve them.

Only he did, of course.

Midnight City was a place of nonsensical politics and dangerous mind games. Its various factions weren't above falsely accusing someone of something heinous to get whatever they wanted, even if the accusation meant that person's death.

But it wasn't his problem, Holt reminded himself. He had to survive, and he couldn't very well do that with the Menagerie chasing after him.

Mira was his only shot at being rid of them once and for all, at finally escaping his troubles.

The unfinished tattoo on his hand itched under his glove, but he ignored it.

He cursed himself silently, because he knew what the problem was. Try as he might to prevent it, he had come to like Mira. She was strong and independent, a survivor like him, but also . . . not as sullen as most people he met. Somehow the cynicism of the world hadn't taken hold of her. There was an aura of optimism about her, a belief she could overcome anything. It was naïve, of course . . . but attractive nonetheless.

Attraction. Yeah, there was that, too. Her emerald eyes, the softness of her hands, the subtle scent of mint he caught when he was close to her.

Holt wasn't above such things, but anytime he had ever given in to them, it had meant trouble. And besides . . . she was his prisoner. Emerald eyes or not.

No, he had strict rules about this. He stayed detached. He didn't get involved. Regardless of how long Mira's scent might linger in his mind.

Holt moved for the edge of the camp where he'd left his pack. He reached and grabbed it, opened it, and pulled out the cylinder from Clinton Station. It still had the attached Dampener artifact, and he held it up for Mira to see.

His nose ached from her kick, and the look of anger she shot his way actually made the pain feel better.

"You had it in the *pack*?" Mira yelled at him.

"And if you'd just been as dumb as I hoped you weren't, you could have gotten it," Holt turned the water-filled cylinder over and over in his hands with curiosity, holding it up to the sun to see the light dance through the sliver of brown in its center. "What is it, anyway? What's so important you'd come back for it?"

"It's plutonium," Mira said, matter-of-fact.

The words didn't immediately register in Holt's mind.

When they did, he dropped the cylinder to the ground like it was made of hot coals and backed away.

Mira laughed out loud. "Are you always this jumpy, or just around radioactive elements?"

"It's *plutonium*?" Holt yelled back at her.

"Don't worry, killer, it's harmless as long as the Dampener's attached."

"And you're basing that theory on——?"

"Experience. I've handled it before."

"Good, then *you* can 'handle' it from now on out." He stepped around the casing, giving it a wide berth. "Why risk your life for something like that?"

"It's priceless," Mira replied.

"Yeah, you said that before," Holt said. "But why?"

"Because of the Severed Tower," Mira answered.

And then it all made sense, or at least as much as a Strange Lands myth could. Holt had heard of the Severed Tower, of course. It was a popular story, especially farther north, closer to the Strange Lands and Midnight City. But in Holt's mind, that's all it was. A story.

"You're serious?" he asked. "You're messing around with Fallout Swarms and power plants for a fairy tale?"

"You don't believe in the Tower?"

"No, I have to see something before I believe in it. I've never been to the Strange Lands, but I know it exists because I've *seen* the things that come out of there and they're anything but natural. But the Tower?" Holt shook his head. "Just sounds like a bunch of Freebooter hocus-pocus to me."

"Well, it's not," Mira replied sternly. "It's real, and people have made it there and gone inside."

"These people, you've met them?" Holt asked. "Seen them with your own eyes? Talked with them?"

Mira frowned at him, didn't answer.

"What's the Severed Tower?" Zoey asked beside them.

Holt watched Mira gather her thoughts. "It's . . . a structure," she began. "A . . . I don't know what it is exactly, but it sits in the center of the Strange Lands. A lot of people think, whatever it is, it's responsible for the Strange Lands themselves. The story says that anyone who can make it there and enter it can ask the Tower for one wish. And that somehow . . . it will make it a reality."

"Story also says you need a nice piece of garden-variety plutonium just to go inside," Holt finished for her. "I wonder how many survivors have died trying to get what you have there, throwing away the little time they had left for a pipe dream?"

Mira looked at Holt pointedly. "That just proves my point. Something people will die for is something priceless. And I need something like that to trade."

"For what?" Holt asked.

She looked at Holt differently now, and for the first time, Holt saw desperation behind her eyes. "There are things I have to . . . fix at Midnight City. Please, Holt," she continued. "You don't know how long I've looked for that, how much I had to sacrifice to get it. But you do know what it means for me to go back home in chains. I know you know what it's like."

Holt's face darkened at the words.

"You don't seem . . . completely awful," Mira pressed on. "You seem like someone who could understand. Please, taking me back to Midnight City is taking me back to die. I can pay you. I can pay you whatever—"

"It's not my problem," Holt said. He had to stop this now. He didn't like the way her words were making him feel. "I don't get involved. It's my rule. I only do what I have to do to survive, and right now that means taking you back."

"That's not true, Holt," a soft voice from across the campsite said. Holt looked past Mira at Zoey, who was still petting Max. "On the other side of the river, you went back for the Max. You did it to save him."

Holt frowned at the little girl.

"She's right," Mira said. "If you were really such a loner, you wouldn't have risked losing me to save a dog. But you did."

Holt stared at her, unsure what to say. He held her gaze, felt her green and black-laced eyes burn into him. A part of him knew she was figuring things out, knew what she was about to ask. And he dreaded it.

"Who did you lose?" Mira's words cut deep. *Lose.* Lost. Gone forever. "It must have been someone important. Someone close."

Anger swelled up inside Holt. No! He wasn't going to talk about this. Not about *her*. He'd buried that long ago, and no one was digging it back up. Especially not these two girls. His gaze turned to stone.

"We're done talking, there is no debate. The forest ends in less than a mile," he said. "Then it's a straight shot to the trading posts on the Mississippi. I'll find someone there to leave you with, Zoey. Someone to take care of you. Then Mira and I will move on to Midnight City."

"But Midnight City is where I want to go," Zoey said. "I can come with you."

Holt frowned. "*No,* Zoey, you wanna go to Midnight, you're welcome to try, you can find a boat or something else to take you north, but it won't be with us. To be honest, I'm tired of both of you, and the sooner I'm done with you, the better."

Zoey's eyes were starting to glisten. She had even stopped petting Max, and the dog was none too happy about it. He beat his tail on the ground, hoping to get her attention again.

"It's okay, Zoey," Mira said, staring at Holt sadly. "Holt's just like everyone else. He decided a long time ago to stop caring about things."

Holt turned away from them both and started packing up the camp. He shouldn't feel this way, shouldn't have to feel this guilt. He was *surviving*. He was doing what he had to do.

Wasn't he?

He had pulled Zoey out of that flaming ship and transported her to safety. He should feel good about it. He should be relieved he could escape the Menagerie soon.

But he didn't. On either count.

No one said a word as he finished breaking camp. In minutes, they were gone, moving northward through the forest once again, Max scouting ahead of them as the afternoon sun beat down through the leaves.

They walked in silence past the trees, each carrying the heavy weight of their own thoughts.

THE FOUR MOVED THROUGH THE FOREST in mutual silence. No one had uttered a word since they left the camp. It was fine by Holt. The less they talked, the better time they could make.

Within an hour, the trees began to thin. Another hour and they stopped altogether, ending in an abrupt, arbitrary line that stretched through an overgrown meadow. The field climbed gently upward beyond the tree line, to a ridge that Holt knew overlooked the river valley just on the other side.

It would be easy travel from here to the trading posts and from there, on to Midnight City. They would move faster out of the trees for sure, but the trade-off was that they were much more visible without the canopy to shield them from the prying eyes of Vultures and Raptors.

Hopefully, ditching Zoey would get the Assembly off his back. It might even make it easier, with them concentrating their forces along the river and forest instead of the plains.

Either way, the hard part was done with. The pack on his back felt lighter than it had all day; he felt energetic and optimistic. He had made it.

The four crested the top of the rise and saw the Mississippi River Valley laid out below them. A tapestry of green interlaced with patches of red and blue wildflowers stretching to the horizon. The river itself was a thick line that curved and twisted southward, flanked by trees along its entire route. The sun glittered off it from above, making it look like a band of molten silver cutting through the grasslands.

All very beautiful. And any other time, Holt might have stopped to admire it.

But when he reached the top of the ridge, the first thing he did was instantly drop to the ground, pulling Zoey and Max with him. Mira did, too, seeing the same thing he had. Holt stared in disbelief.

Assembly patrols.

Hundreds of walkers scoured the valley below, moving in groups of six or ten, completely blanketing the landscape.

And they weren't blue and white. The sun sparkled off crimson fuselages, making it look like the entire valley was ablaze in flame. These Assembly were a solid *red*.

Max whined at Holt's side as a flight of red Raptor gunships roared over them, flying escort for two huge Osprey dropships. They watched as the Ospreys unloaded four more red walkers onto the plains, saw them power up and activate, and begin patrolling. The Ospreys dusted off in a blast of engine noise and shot back into the air.

Holt shut his eyes tight.

He had never seen so many Assembly machines in one place, not even during the invasion. And these weren't the blue and whites; they were another Assembly group entirely. The same one that had shot down Zoey's ship. One or two Raptors was one thing, but this was something else; this was an *army*. And, just like the blue and whites, it must be looking for Zoey.

Holt looked down at the little girl and saw she was already looking up at him. She was frightened, uneasy. Holt understood—he felt the same way.

"See, Holt?" Zoey said. "*All* of them."

She'd used those words before. And a spark of anger blossomed in him.

"Why didn't you tell me we were walking into this?" Holt demanded. At the question, Mira looked at them, curious as to the answer herself. "You detected them before, why not this time?"

"I felt them. I just thought it would be good if you saw them for yourself."

"*Good?*" Holt asked in exasperation.

"So you would know why you had to take me with you."

On the other side of him, Mira looked away. Holt sighed, his fists clenching tightly.

What was he going to do now? He needed to get to Midnight City with Mira, but that was well on the other side of the river valley below. There was no other path, and these red Assembly knew it. They had sealed off the entire avenue. To make matters worse, he was carting around the exact thing they were all looking for.

He should just leave the girl here. Tie her up with a big bow for the aliens and leave the problem behind. He looked at Zoey again. She looked back with her clear, blue eyes, and she seemed to read his thoughts. So did Mira.

"You can't leave her," Mira said from his right. There was a note of firmness in her voice he hadn't heard before. It annoyed him.

"Oh, I can't?" he snapped, looking at her. "Last time I checked, I was the one running things, not you."

"You can't *leave* her," she reiterated, this time slower and pointed.

Holt looked away, sighed again. She didn't have to tell him that. There were some lines he wouldn't cross, even for survival's sake. And his refusal to cross those lines had gotten him into plenty of trouble in the past. It looked like it was going to do the same thing right now.

Holt looked down to Zoey. She was still gazing up at him fearfully, the idea that he might abandon her a real possibility in her mind.

"I'm not going to leave you, don't worry," he said, watching the little girl visibly relax. "We just have to find another way through to the north now."

"Thanks, Holt," Zoey said.

"Thank you," Mira said next to him. She said it so low, he wasn't sure if she meant him to hear it or not.

Another way through to the north . . .

The problem was, there wasn't one. They could turn around and try to go through St. Louis, but those ruins were overrun with Menagerie and even worse things. It wasn't an option.

Plus, turning around meant heading right back toward the blue and whites.

Something occurred to him. The truth was, the river valley wasn't the only way through to the north. There were other routes . . . but they were so dangerous, most people never factored them in as possibilities.

Holt pulled the binoculars from his belt and looked through them, scanning the valley.

"What are you looking for?" Mira asked.

"Plan B," he answered.

Holt surveyed up and down the river with his optics, examining the tributaries, the smaller branches of the river that connected to and fed the main body.

He found the specific one he was looking for, followed it to where it made a path through the ground just below the ridge and disappeared out of sight toward the west, cutting through a grouping of blufflike hills.

Interestingly, the red Assembly seemed to be avoiding it completely. Which was exactly what Holt had expected, given he now knew about their mysterious fear of water. He guessed they would give that tributary a wide berth.

"What do you see?" Mira asked again, impatient. "Tell me!"

"A different route north."

"I didn't think there was a different route north."

"By popular consensus, there's not," Holt said. "Most people, most *smart* people, avoid this way. But we are definitely not smart people—"

"True enough," Mira said.

"—and without any other choices," Holt finished.

"What are you thinking?" she asked with hesitation, sensing she wasn't going to like the answer.

Holt lowered the binoculars and looked at her. "The Drowning Plains," he said with as much confidence as he could project. It wasn't much.

He watched Mira shudder at the words. It would probably have given him a little bit of satisfaction, if he didn't feel the same way.

"What's the Drowning Plains?" Zoey asked.

"No place we want to go," Mira said.

"Used to be a floodplain downstream from a dam," Holt said, studying the tributary through the binoculars again, verifying it was devoid of the red walkers. "Dam broke during the invasion and flooded the whole thing. There were villages there, built along the river. Now the whole place is a flooded no-man's-land."

"That's the story, anyway," Mira continued. "No one who goes in ever comes out. And no one really knows why."

"Something in there isn't very hospitable. Whether it's the environment . . . or something else."

Zoey looked at each of them as they spoke, her eyes widening with fear.

"Now look what you've done," Mira said in disapproval. "You scared her."

"Me?" Holt put the binoculars down. "*You* started in with the whole 'no one who goes in ever comes out' stuff."

Max seemed to sense Zoey's discomfort, too. He put a paw on her back and licked her ear. Zoey pushed his wet nose away.

"We'll be fine, Zoey, I promise," Mira said, trying to comfort the little girl. "Holt will get us through. *Won't* you?" she asked him firmly.

"Yeah, sure, we'll make it," Holt said dismissively, concentrating on the view through his binoculars. "I've been plenty of times, it's no big deal."

"Really?" Zoey asked hopefully. "You've been before and come out?"

"Sure," Holt lied, "plenty of—"

Holt cut off as Mira gasped in pain, her hands shooting to her head. He and Zoey and even Max looked at her in surprise.

Holt reached out for her, but she shoved his hands away, curling into a ball on the ground, holding herself. "Don't . . ." She was absorbed in pain and discomfort. "Don't touch me. . . ."

Holt guessed what was happening. Mira was eighteen or thereabouts, at the point where the Tone would start to wrestle her for control. He guessed that's what was occurring. Before this, the Tone had probably reared its ugly head only temporarily, but now it was fighting her for control, maybe for the first time. The battle was always painful . . . and disturbing.

The Tone was what Earth's survivors called the telepathic signal broadcast by the Assembly only a few hours after their invasion, and it had ended any resistance against the aliens in one fell swoop.

A mind control signal, and it worked horrifically well. Anyone who heard it instantly Succumbed to Assembly control. Soldiers left their posts. Government officials walked out of their offices. Parents left their children crying in their beds. Zombielike, Earth's adult population began a unison march to the nearest Assembly Presidium, the massive ships stuck like huge daggers in the hearts of the human cities.

They marched toward them, these millions of people . . . and, one by one, they disappeared inside.

To this day, no one knew what had happened to them, or where the Tone was broadcast from, or even how it worked.

What was very quickly apparent, however, was that the Tone seemed to affect the human brain only once it matured. A chemistry that added up to something around twenty years of age. Which meant that there was an entire demographic of the population that was immune to its call. At least temporarily.

Children.

It was why Holt hadn't seen an adult in almost a decade. It was why the world was left to the devices of its youngest daughters and sons. But their time was always running out. The older they became, the more sway the ever-present Tone began to have on them.

A grim, slow, inevitable, ticking clock.

Unless they were Heedless, Holt thought bitterly. Those rare few, for whatever reason, who were immune. Like him. He would never suffer Mira's fate. He would grow old, alone in a world where everyone else had Succumbed, one of the last "lucky" few to age beyond twenty years old, alone with an entire, empty, dead planet to call his own.

"Holt . . . ," Zoey said, watching Mira in alarm.

Holt watched Mira convulse and shake, her fists clenching handfuls of grass behind her back and ripping them from the ground as she fought against the signal.

Seeing it now brought the memories flooding back. It had been the same with Emily. The convulsing, the struggle to keep her mind intact, to ward off the voices and the static hiss.

Holt watched Mira in silent horror, her eyes shut tight, trying to block out the sounds. He had prayed never to see this again. And here it was.

Prisoner or not, his way to escape the Menagerie or not, Holt instinctively reached out for Mira. She tried to push him away again, but he pulled her into his lap. "Mira," he said into her ear, listening to her sharp, painful intakes of breath. "Is this your first time to fight it?"

Mira said nothing, just shivered in his arms.

"Mira tell me, is it your first time?"

Beneath him, he noticed the briefest hint of a nod from her.

"It helps if someone talks to you, if you concentrate on their voice. It can help you push it into the background again."

Mira shuddered beneath him. Holt exhaled, thinking of what to say. With Emily, he had played games. Memory games. They always helped bring her back.

He tried to remember them, what he used to say.

"What's the thing you miss most about the World Before?" he asked Mira. "You're old enough to remember it." Mira shook silently, coping with the Tone's attack. "You can fight it, Mira. You're strong. Tell me."

"The . . ." Mira tried to speak. The words came slowly and painfully. But they came. "The . . . food . . ."

Holt smiled. "Yeah, me, too. What kind of food?"

"Junk . . . junk food . . . ," she said. The words were coming easier. It was a good sign. If she could hold on, she could push it back.

"Girl after my own heart. Pick your poison, then. What would you have right now if you could? Twinkies? Red Vines? Oreos?"

"Hostess CupCakes . . ."

Holt laughed. "Now, *that* is a stellar choice. I haven't thought about those in a while, but I remember them. The chocolate cake, the icing, right?"

"The . . . cream in the center . . ."

"Yeah," Holt said, holding her, remembering. "The cream in the center. How they came two to a pack. Do you remember that? And that little zigzag of white on the top?"

"Yes . . ."

"You know what the good news is about that choice, right, Mira?"

"What?" she said weakly but coherently. It was easing.

"Good news is, those things are virtually indestructible. Hostess Cup-Cakes, along with cockroaches, would survive a nuclear holocaust."

Mira laughed softly. "And an alien holocaust?"

"That, too," Holt said. "In fact, if you found an unexplored place, a place no one had picked over yet . . . you could probably find Hostess CupCakes, still in their packages. And they'd taste just as good now as they did back then."

"I doubt that," Mira said, opening her eyes and looking up at him. "Eight years on, they'd have to be a little stale."

Her green eyes were even more full of the black now. The Tone had spread; it was taking her over. Slowly. Day by day. She had a year left, at most, Holt realized as he studied her. The realization twisted his stomach. . . .

"A little, maybe. But you wouldn't notice," Holt said, looking back with his guiltily clear eyes. "Doing better?"

Mira nodded. "It was . . . awful. I didn't know . . . I didn't know it would be so bad. The voices . . . they were . . ."

"I know," Holt said. He did know. It was the worst part, hearing them in your head. At least that was what Emily had said. Older kids started to hear voices buried within the static. The language was incomprehensible . . . at first. But, frighteningly, the older they got, the more it seemed to make sense. The more you could understand it. Suggesting things to you, calling to you. "The next few will be easier as you get used to it. Then . . . it starts to get harder."

"How long?" Mira asked.

Holt had hoped she wouldn't ask. But he wasn't going to lie to her. "Depends on how strong you are. Average age is twenty. Some people last longer. Some less. But I'll help you. As long as I can."

"Until you turn me in?" she asked evenly. Holt stared back silently, but didn't answer. What was there to say?

They lay like that awhile longer. Holt had come to enjoy the warmness of her body beneath him, how soft she felt in his grip.

Then the roar of two more Raptors flying overhead broke the spell. Holt remembered everything. So did Mira. They separated, once again saw the enormous red army blanketing the valley below, in between them and their path north.

Zoey was studying both of them and grinning. Holt and Mira frowned at the little girl.

"What?" they both asked in unison.

Zoey just chuckled, hid her face under her arms.

Holt shook his head, got them all up. They would have to move fast. The first part of the journey would be the most dangerous. At least from an Assembly perspective. They'd be the closest to the reds then, where the tributary they intended to follow below passed near the alien patrols.

When they were ready, Holt moved to Mira. He pulled his father's

Swiss Army knife from his belt, opened the blade . . . and touched it to her bonds.

Mira looked at the knife curiously.

"You can't go back. You can't go forward," Holt told her. "You want to survive, your best chance is with me. Yes?"

Mira considered him calmly, weighing her options. "Yes," she said. "Assuming you know what you're doing."

"I said your *best* chance, not a guaranteed chance. I'm making this up as I go along."

Mira smiled at him as he cut her bonds, let the ropes fall to the ground. She rubbed her wrists appreciatively.

Holt whistled two sharp notes. Max darted westward, hugging the tree line as he scouted ahead of them. Holt, Mira, and Zoey walked after him.

"When can I ride the Max?" Zoey asked. "I'm not too big for it."

Holt and Mira shook their heads as they followed after the dog.

LONG AFTER HOLT HAD left, new shapes emerged from the tree line and climbed the same ridge that overlooked the expansive river valley. Initially, the only sign of their presence was a shimmering in the air, a slight wavering of light not unlike Mira's Shroud artifact.

If you weren't looking for it, you would never see it.

When the shapes reached the top, their invisibility shields deactivated and dropped away, revealing them for what they were.

Ten Assembly walkers, unique from any seen so far. Eight feet tall at most. Tripods, three legs, smaller, lighter, less heavily armed, built for speed and agility, not strength. But clearly deadly nonetheless. Their feet, which came to sinister sharp points, punctured the soft soil as they moved.

They were Hunters. And most strikingly, they were not blue and white . . . or even red. Their bodies were colored *green and orange*.

One of them moved forward, its body painted differently from the others. Its markings were sharper, more bold, more commanding. The other machines watched it with full attention.

The walker scanned the environment, its optics whirring as they did. Eventually, it found what it was looking for. A tangle of cut rope left on the ground. Evidence of its quarry.

Explosions flared up to the north, the sounds of plasma fire. The machine looked toward the distance and the bevy of red Assembly scouring the river valley below.

A flight of blue and white Raptors was strafing the red walkers. The reds were returning fire. One of the gunships exploded in sparks, spun out of control, and crashed to the ground in a trail of flame.

The green and orange Hunter emitted a strange, distorted trumpeting sound as it watched the fighting below. The sounds seemed . . . disdainful. The others echoed the sentiment, trumpeting electronically in response.

The walker watched the distant firefight a few moments longer.

Then it bounded off toward the west, following the path set by Holt and the others. The rest of the walkers followed without hesitation. They vanished as they moved, their cloaking shields activating and consuming them, concealing them from sight.

17. TORRENT

IT WAS A SUNKEN LANDSCAPE. What had once been a simple river was now an endlessly stretching cesspool of blackish water that stretched as far as the eye could see. The trunks of rotting, dead trees poked up from where they had been submerged and drowned years ago.

Cliff faces of sheer, sharp rock hugged the water on either side, making walking on anything dry impossible, unless you wanted to climb the cliffs and shimmy along the sides. Not the best option.

Holt, Mira, Zoey, and Max moved slowly through the Drowning Plains, sweating under the bright afternoon sun above. Of course, *moved* was only occasionally accurate. At times, the floodwater was so deep, it climbed past their waists, and walking gave way to swimming.

Right now, Holt was only up to his knees. Still, what was shallow for him was deep for Zoey. She would have been up to her neck if he wasn't carrying her on his back.

Max swam through the waters with abandon. He'd been treading water all afternoon, but didn't seem the slightest bit tired. Holt kept a watch on him nonetheless. The dog had a habit of tiring himself out with his enthusiasm, and this would be a very bad place for him to suddenly pass out.

Unsurprisingly, one person who wasn't enjoying it was Mira, at the back of the line. Since they had first plopped their feet into the water, the complaints had been almost nonstop. The water was cold. The water was dirty. The water was in her shoes. The water smelled bad.

And then there were the snakes.

Holt had anticipated them. Mira had not. The first time she saw one slither through the surface, she'd screamed and almost pulled him face-first into the water in a frantic attempt to get away.

Each snake they saw meant a delay of ten minutes or more as Holt tried to convince her to start plodding forward again, in spite of his assurances that they were harmless (which was not at all true; water moccasins were not only aggressive but venomous as well, but that wasn't something Holt felt Mira needed to know). Now when Holt saw the snakes, he kept it to himself.

For the last half hour they'd been seeing, in Holt's opinion, something much worse than snakes. Evidence of fallen civilization was becoming more and more apparent.

Sunken cars, telephone poles jutting up from the water, floating debris of all kinds . . . including backpacks, clothes, shoes, and other evidence that many people had tried to make it through this route and didn't succeed.

But there was no indication to suggest what might have stopped them. At least not yet. It would suit Holt just fine if that particular mystery remained unsolved.

They were also seeing more buildings. Or what was left of them, crumbling in the floodwater. Gas stations, motels, old diners, all partly submerged and jutting out from the glassy black surface. The buildings and the telephone poles that flanked Holt on either side suggested they were on what used to be a road. It also meant, as the buildings became more prevalent, that they were moving toward city ruins of some sort.

Holt wasn't sure if that was a good or bad thing.

He felt Zoey's grip on his neck start to loosen, could feel her forehead buried in his neck.

"Kiddo," Holt said behind him. "No falling asleep, you'll land right in the water."

"I'm tired," Zoey said with a pout.

"You're not the one carrying somebody else. Maybe you should try carrying me for a while. Or Mira."

"Yes. Please," Mira said testily behind them. "How much longer do we have to do this?"

"Until we find someplace safe," Holt replied. "Or until you don't complain for five whole minutes, whichever comes first. My money's on the former."

"I'll give *you* something to complain about," she mumbled behind him.

"Will we be at Midnight City tonight?" Zoey asked.

Holt almost laughed. Midnight City would have been days away if the reds hadn't sealed off the river valley. Now, forced to maneuver through the Drowning Plains . . . it was a much more distant goal.

Zoey was welcome to go to Midnight City; it just wasn't going to be with him. If they made it through the Drowning Plains, they'd be back along the Mississippi, and could find one of the floating trading posts. He'd get rid of Zoey there and leave this whole mess behind him.

But at the thought, Holt felt those same stirrings of guilt, and it angered him all over again. He'd be doing what he had to do by leaving Zoey. And besides, she'd be in a better position to survive with a River Rat crew. There was safety in numbers.

But Holt knew that wasn't exactly the case. He'd remained on his own for so long precisely because he believed he was safer that way. And whomever he handed Zoey off to would have no idea of the threat she brought with her. They'd likely be caught unprepared when the full force of the Assembly finally tracked her down. But . . . would she be any safer with him?

The truth was far more simple than any of that, though. He liked Mira. He liked Zoey. As much as he valued his independence and his isolation . . . their presence had shown him it came at a cost. There was an emptiness inside him he was rarely aware of, a hollow feeling he thought he had suppressed. Being with them these past few days had begun its excavation.

A part of him wanted to get the ordeal over with as fast as possible, so he could rebury it. Another part . . . wanted to dig it free and pull it back into the light.

"What the hell is that?" Mira asked behind him.

Holt refocused, looked up. Something black and otherworldly loomed out of the water ahead of them. It wasn't a building or any kind of car or truck. It was contorted and warped, frozen solid where it had fallen. As they approached it, Holt's mind found shapes within it that he recognized. But just barely.

An Assembly Spider walker, one of the big ones. It normally would have stood thirty feet tall, but this one was crumpled in the floodwaters, resting on the bottom and near unrecognizable.

It had been difficult for Holt to make out exactly what it was, mainly due to the strange substance that had completely covered it. It looked like rust, if rust could be burned, blackened, and melted. The substance, whatever it was, looked weblike, almost organic, and the Spider had been consumed underneath it, losing all its distinctive shape.

Nearby, covered in water, were two Mantis walkers. Less of their bodies poked through to the surface, they were nowhere near as large, but the black rustlike growth had consumed what was revealed of them, too. Holt had never seen anything like it.

"What did *that* to them?" Mira asked.

"I don't know," Holt said.

"The water," Zoey said into his ear. "They couldn't escape it."

"What couldn't escape it?"

"Them," she said.

Holt looked at her, her chin on his shoulder, staring at him with tired eyes. He opened his mouth to ask what she meant . . .

. . . and then stopped as he noticed something disturbing.

The water was no longer at his knees. It was up to his thighs now. And he could feel it flowing past him in the direction they were headed. Up until now, it had been stagnant and still.

Holt's eyes widened at the implication.

"What?" Mira asked, stopping next to him.

Max whined, sensing Holt's discomfort. It didn't stop him from swimming in lazy circles, though.

Holt didn't answer. He turned around, looked behind him. The floodplains stretched backwards to where they had come from, endless and long, flanked by the cliffs. And in the far distance, they were swelling and moving toward them.

Alarmed, Mira looked behind them. She saw it, too. A wall of water was barreling down on them. And fast.

"It's a flash flood," Holt said.

"You have got to be kidding me!" Mira yelled. *"More* water?"

Holt pushed forward through the murk as fast as he could.

Ahead of them, the first buildings of the ruined city loomed out of the black water like ghosts in the fading afternoon light.

They rushed for them as the flood gained on them from behind. They could hear it now, slamming against the cliffs on either side, rushing toward them.

What was left of a dry cleaners was directly in their path, its windows broken and empty, its roof teetering above the water.

They pushed desperately toward it. An old metal Dumpster sat to the side of the building, rusting but still in one piece. If they could get to it, they might be able to reach the roof. Holt moved for—

The flood caught them, tossing them forward like they weighed nothing.

They crashed hard into the side of the building. The raging waters ripped a screaming Zoey off Holt's back. Mira just managed to grab the little girl's hand as she flew by, pulled her back in.

They were pinned in place for the moment. But the water level was rising, faster and faster, threatening to rip them all away.

Holt looked up at the roof. It was their only shot, but even with the risen water level, it was still out of reach.

"Give me Zoey!" Holt shouted to Mira over the flood.

She did, handing the little girl off to him. Holt planted himself against the side of the building and lifted her toward the roof.

"Zoey, grab on!" he yelled. The little girl found a handhold on the roof's edge, pulled herself up and over.

Holt pulled Mira to him roughly, his hands encircling her waist.

"Hey!" she shouted in surprise.

"Slap me later," he said as he lifted her lithe figure upward. "Zoey! Grab her hand!"

The little girl leaned over the roof's edge, found Mira's hand, and pulled it onto the roof edge, where she could find purchase.

As Mira pulled herself up, Holt pushed from below. She scrambled onto the roof, out of the water.

The flood was getting stronger, threatening now to pull Holt off the building wall and drag him away.

He grabbed Max by the neck. The dog yelped, but Holt ignored him. He lifted the mutt up to Mira. When her hands touched him, the dog growled and barked testily.

"Cut it out! I'm trying to help!" Mira yelled, yanking Max up and over onto the roof.

Only Holt was left. He looked up at Mira. She looked down at him.

Holt read it in her eyes. She was thinking it through. And he knew what her thoughts were. It was a simple choice, to help him or not to help him. She could easily let the water take him (and all her problems) away. Just like that.

If Holt were her, it would be an easy decision. He'd let him go. He'd eliminate the bounty hunter who wanted to take him home to be killed. Why should she save him? When survival said that she should let him die?

But a part of him hoped she wouldn't. The part that had come to believe they had a connection, in spite of their differences. He realized he wanted that connection to be confirmed. And he didn't like how strong those feelings were becoming.

Time seemed to slow. What really was a second or two seemed like minutes, the two staring at each other, each reading the other's thoughts . . .

. . . and then, Mira frowned. She reached downward, offered her hand.

Holt didn't have time to be relieved. He reached up for it with his left hand, and her grip wrapped around the thick black bracelet on his wrist. Together, with her pulling and him scrambling along the wall, he climbed up and over the edge.

When he was on top, out of the water, he collapsed to the roof, breathing heavy. He heard the floodwaters still rushing by below.

Max leapt on him, started licking his face clean. Holt didn't have enough energy to stop him.

"Holt!" he heard Zoey exclaim, felt her hug him, her head sink to his chest. "You're not dead!"

"Knock on wood next chance I get," he replied, exhausted.

He looked for Mira, and saw her sitting along the edge of the roof, her back to him, hugging her knees, watching the sun set behind the cliffs to the west. The floodwaters rushed by below, dragging with them all kinds of debris—barrels, tires, car doors, a refrigerator.

She was motionless as she sat there.

"Mira's happy, too," Zoey said. "Don't worry."

Wishful thinking, Holt knew.

He, Zoey, and Max sat down next to Mira, watching the sky darken into hues of orange above them.

"Here," Holt said, pulling a piece of strawberry taffy from his pack and handing it to Zoey. "Give it to Max."

"The Max gets candy!" Zoey shouted, giving it to the dog. He sucked the whole thing into his mouth excitedly . . . and then painstakingly started trying to chew the tough piece of sugary goodness. Zoey laughed.

Holt turned back to the sunset. He didn't look at Mira. She didn't look at him. They just sat next to each other quietly, distant and close at the same time.

"Thanks," he said after a moment.

Mira nodded. "Yeah."

They sat that way a long time, listening to the sounds of the water rushing by below, until the light finally began to fade and the sky darkened.

They didn't say anything else. There was nothing else to say.

THE SKY CONTINUED TO DARKEN as the colors faded, the clouds becoming floating silhouettes of charcoal and black above them. When Holt stood up, he finally had a moment to really look at where they were. The roof of the dry cleaner's was one building in what used to be small town America from the World Before.

The ruins stretched in all directions, a hundred buildings or more poking up and out of the flooded landscape, half submerged, all crumbling and rotting where they stood. Rusted signs and decals identified them as office buildings, groceries, hardware stores, apartments, churches, a library, a courthouse.

All abandoned now. All sunken. All lifeless . . .

Holt led them to the edge of the cleaner's roof. The city had been built close together; the tops of the buildings weren't that far apart. It wouldn't be that hard to jump between them. Unless you were Zoey or Max— then it got a little more problematic.

"What we really need is a bridge," Holt said, examining the gap between the roofs.

"Maybe we can make one," Mira said. Off another edge of the dry cleaner's were the remains of a feed store. Its roof was made of rippled sheet metal, like a barn. Long rectangular holes dotted its surface where some of the pieces had collapsed and fallen through. From where they stood, the sheet metal strips seemed long enough to span the divide between most roofs in the ruins.

The top of the store looked precarious at best. Since it required someone jumping across, Mira volunteered. She was lighter, would have less of an impact when she hit the top.

The roof shook when she landed, more pieces of the sheet metal fell away into the gap. But the structure didn't collapse. Mira grabbed one of the long pieces, lifted it up, and placed it like a bridge between the feed store roof and the dry cleaner's.

It was strong enough that Zoey and Max could slide across it, if they took their time. Of course, getting Max to take his time doing anything was difficult. But Zoey kept a firm hold on him as she crossed the bridge, and the dog seemed eager to move at her pace.

"Can I ride the Max across the next bridge?" Zoey asked.

"No!" Holt and Mira said in unison.

Using the portable bridge, the four cautiously traversed building to building, Holt and Mira leaping between the gap, Zoey and Max sliding along the sheet metal.

The sun was almost down now behind the cliffs. Ahead of them was Holt's goal. A much larger building, maybe five stories tall in the center of the ruined town. A rusted sign, barely holding on to its wall, read TAVERN INN.

A hotel. Holt guessed it would be the best place to make camp for the night. Its floors were higher above the water than the other buildings, and probably drier and in better shape.

Its roof was much higher, though, and there was no way to reach it with the bridge. But they could reach the old fire escape that climbed down its side like a vine. They extended the bridge so Zoey and Max could cross; then Holt and Mira jumped to the other side.

Holt climbed several flights until he found a room with its window still intact and unlocked. He opened it and let the others inside. Before he followed, Holt looked at and appraised the city around them in the fading light.

Across from them was an old drugstore, and it didn't seem as flooded as the other buildings. Holt studied it with interest before he crawled in after the others.

The room was in tatters. Wallpaper peeled off the walls, the ceiling was a patchwork of holes and mold, and the bed and furniture were covered in dust, but it was dry and secure. The door to the hallway outside was closed, and Holt made sure it was locked and chained. A futile gesture, probably, but it didn't hurt.

Holt looked to the others. They were slumped on the floor in exhaustion, resting against the peeling wall.

"You have a look in your eye, Hawkins," Mira said as she watched him at the door. "What are you about to do?"

"There's something I want to check out, before the sun sets. Can you hold the fort?"

"Sure, it seems quiet," Mira said, turning to look out the window above her.

"Yeah," Holt said with a frown. "That's what bothers me." He slipped out the window.

As he did, Mira called after him. "Don't get lost," she said.

"You're not that lucky," he said with a slight smile, and stepped onto the fire escape.

Holt scrambled up to the roof and scanned what little of the city he could see in the fading light. He found the drugstore again, below him, but not adjacent to the wall with the fire escape.

How was he going to get down there? Holt figured he could jump, but it was a two-story drop. Even if he managed it without breaking something, the roof was most likely in just as bad a condition as all the others he'd seen. He might go crashing straight through it.

Holt looked around. There was a thick line of cable strung between the two roofs, probably a power line. It was attached by large bolts into the brick walls on both sides, then continued on to more of the submerged buildings in the distance. It was definitely thick enough to support his weight. The question was, would those bolts hold?

Worst-case scenario, they wouldn't. And he'd tumble down into the black floodwaters below. Not a good thing.

But the drugstore was worth the risk. This whole city, because of where it was, and the dangers involved in reaching it, probably hadn't been explored since the invasion.

That store most likely held things he could use, things he couldn't find anywhere else. And there would almost certainly be valuable items for trade. Medicine, writing instruments, bandages, even deodorant and toothpaste were highly valuable commodities now.

Survival dictated that he explore it, in spite of the risk.

Holt moved for the cable bolted underneath him. He could just reach it.

———

MIRA AND ZOEY SAT in the crumbling bedroom, listening to Max continue to work on the taffy Holt had given him earlier. It was tough going. He'd managed to gnaw off only about half of the thick, sticky substance.

Mira stared at the dog in annoyance. The sounds were starting to get on her nerves, a gross combination of crunching and slurping. The dog was a dirty, stinky nuisance that constantly stared at her with its dark, conniving eyes. It didn't like or trust her, which was fine for Mira, because the feeling was mutual.

Mira reached for the taffy in Max's mouth. He erupted into an enraged combination of barks and growls, advancing on her in a frenzy.

"Okay, okay! Fine!" Mira shouted, backing off. "Keep the stupid thing."

Max lay back down and picked up where he'd left off, but kept a wary gaze on Mira. She glared back at him.

"He likes candy," Zoey said beside her. When the little girl reached out to pet the dog, he didn't even bat an eye, just kept staring and chewing while Zoey rubbed his ears.

"Clearly." Mira looked out the window. It was getting dark, what was left of the daylight fading fast. The shadows grew outside, consuming more and more of the sunken, suburban landscape. The idea of spending the night in this place was starting to seem less appealing.

"The things you use," Zoey said softly. "The things that do the special stuff. What are they?"

Mira looked at Zoey. "They're things from a place called the Strange Lands. Most people call them artifacts."

"How did you learn to make them?" Zoey asked.

"I had a teacher," Mira said. "At Midnight City. But the truth is, I was just something I was good at. It came easier to me than it did to other kids."

"Have you been to the Strange Lands a lot?"

Mira smiled. "Yep. I'm a Freebooter." The words came from her easily; she was still so used to reciting them. But it wasn't totally true anymore, was it? "Or I used to be. Before . . . everything happened." She would make those words true again, she told herself. She would find a way.

"What's a Freebooter?" Zoey asked.

"Someone who travels the Strange Lands looking for artifacts to bring back and trade. Someone who knows how to survive there."

"Is it scary?"

Mira smiled at the questions. "Parts of it are, sure. Time and space don't work right there anymore."

"Why?" Zoey asked.

"I don't know—no one does. It didn't happen until the Assembly came, though, so it must have something to do with them."

It was almost a year since she had been there, but the memories were still vivid. The air in the Strange Lands had a charge to it, like static electricity, as if it were thick and tangible. The farther you went in, the more you felt it on your skin. On impulse, the hairs stood up on Mira's arms as she thought about it.

It was a dangerous place, to be sure, but also beautiful and magical in its own way. Skies full of huge antimatter storm clouds, lightning flashes of purple and blue and red. Pulsars that seemed to be all colors at once hovering over gravity wells. Geysers sprayed fountains of dark matter into the air. Floating quark spheres morphed from one incredibly complicated geometric shape to another every second like clockwork. . . .

"It's pretty," Zoey said beside her.

It took a moment for the words to sink in. When they did, Mira looked down at the little girl. "*What's* pretty, Zoey?" Mira asked.

"The Strange Lands," Zoey said. "The colors, the lights . . . even the storms are pretty."

"But you haven't been there," Mira said carefully.

"No. I saw it through you."

Mira watched Zoey turn away and look back down to Max, as if she had said nothing of importance. She saw it *through her?* She could see in Mira's mind? Mira felt a chill run up her spine at the implications. For the first time, she looked at the little girl with a touch of fear.

Who was she really?

HOLT LANDED HARD ON the roof of the drugstore, barely stopping himself from rolling forward onto his face. *Maybe sliding down the cable wasn't the best idea,* he thought as he unhooked his pack from the line. At least he wouldn't have that problem going up, though it meant he'd have to climb back to the hotel.

He canvassed the surface of the roof quickly. It was in even worse shape than the others they'd navigated before, pockmarked with cracks and crumbling plaster.

Near the corner at the rear, a large hole had formed in the roof where pooled rain water had worn its way through.

Holt moved to it with careful steps, feeling the spongy surface of the roof warp beneath his feet. It seemed inevitable that the whole thing would come crashing down, but the roof held as he reached the hole and peered down through it.

The light was fading fast around him, and everything inside the hole was dark. He pulled a flashlight from his belt and shone it downward.

The ceiling rafters were just below him, rusted and aged, but they still looked solid. Holt stuck the light in his mouth and lowered himself into the hole. His feet touched down on a metal rafter, and he heard it groan as it accepted his weight. But, like the roof, it held.

From the rafters, shining his light in the space below, he had a pretty clear view of what was left of the store.

The bottom floor was just as flooded as it looked from outside: probably four feet of the same black water. Old shelves sat half sunk, running in rows up and down the store's length. And Holt saw exactly what he'd hoped for.

The shelves above the water were still stocked with their various wares, untouched, glittering in spite of all the dust in the colorful paper and foil packages of the World Before.

No one had been here to loot this place. It was an absolute treasure trove, and Holt smiled lustfully.

"YOU'RE WORRIED," ZOEY SAID. "I can tell."

She was right: Mira *was* worried. Zoey had somehow pulled images straight out of her mind.

"I just don't know how you do the things you do, Zoey," Mira said. "I guess I'm the kind of person who needs to know how things work."

"I don't know how it works. It just does. And I can't pick when it does or doesn't."

"Do you have any new . . . memories? Since we found you? Memories of how you got this way?" asked Mira.

"Not really memories," Zoey said. "But pictures, sometimes."

"Pictures?"

"Pictures in my head, kind of. Pictures of things I've seen or places I've been. At least that's what I think they are."

"What kind of pictures, Zoey?"

"Black metal hallways that move up and down, not side to side. Glowing lights. And . . . other people. Older people. But sleeping, kind of." Zoey's voice was low, it was hard to hear her. "I don't like to think about the pictures. They scare me."

Black metal hallways? Sleeping older people? To Mira, it sounded pretty clear Zoey had been inside a Presidium, had even seen the state of Earth's adult population. But by *sleeping* did she mean just that? Or did she mean "dead"?

"Mira, how do things from the Strange Lands work?" Zoey asked, abruptly changing subjects.

"Well . . ." Mira collected her thoughts. Artifact creation wasn't the easiest thing to explain. "Things from the Strange Lands—like pencils or coins or watches—once you take them outside, they become charged with weird properties. And the farther you go in, the stronger they become. The most powerful artifacts are called 'major artifacts,' and they're found near the center.

"The really interesting thing is that with minor artifacts, you can combine them into new and stronger ones with different functions. Want to see?"

"Yes!" Zoey said with excitement. The little girl even stopped petting Max. Mira smiled and reached for her pack.

HOLT HOPPED FROM ONE ceiling rafter to the next, the toxic water ten feet or so below him. The rafters groaned with each leap, but the metal was still strong. The first thing he needed to find was another backpack, because his was almost totally full. He needed a new container for all the spoils he intended to come out of there with.

He found a whole row of backpacks on one of the aisles near the side wall, and they looked like they were mostly for children. Cartoon characters stood out on their fronts and they were dyed in bright colors, but they'd serve his purposes just fine. He grabbed a blue one.

The shelves at the rear of the store were full of medicine and pharmaceuticals, and he stuffed antiseptics, pain relievers, and bandages into the new pack. First aid supplies were some of the most in-demand items in the world now.

From there, he moved on to toiletries. Holt hung down from the beams by his knees, just barely able to reach the top shelves. He gathered toothpaste, deodorant, soap, cleaning agents, all things that would trade for a very nice price.

His new blue pack quickly bulged with the treasures, and Holt had to restrain himself from filling a second one. It was almost pitch black outside as it was, and he wanted to be back in the hotel room before night fell. The danger attributed to the Drowning Plains had seemed exaggerated so far . . . and it bothered him. He had a feeling this place hadn't shown its real teeth yet.

But Holt was interested in something at the front of the store, something specific, and he wanted to reach it before he started working his way up and out.

He hopped over two more beams and found himself sitting against the front wall of the store, looking down on the shelves behind what used to be the front counter. The old cash register sat there, probably full of money that was now useless. Crumbling signs with pictures of soft drinks and pretzels and ice cream barely held on to the blackened windows, advertising things that few even remembered anymore.

Holt looked away from the signs. More scars. More reminders of what used to be . . .

He studied the front of the store, shining the light back and forth. If he remembered right, this was where they used to keep them. He looked at the shelves, item by item . . . and found what he was looking for.

AM/FM radios, still new in their dusty boxes.

Holt smiled broadly. His radio had died on him a few months ago, and he'd been looking to replace it ever since. But working radios were becoming more and more valuable. And here he was with a shelf full of them.

He should take two or three extras for trade, Holt decided. Survival dictated it.

But before Holt reached for them, he spied something else on the smaller shelves in front of the register. Colorful packages of candy and sugary snacks of all kinds, all glittering under the beam. There was taffy for Max. Bubble gum. And there were other choices, too. One of them stood out prominently, sealed in its plastic sleeves.

Hostess CupCakes.

Holt remembered Mira's words, remembered the feeling of her head in his lap, the softness of her hair. Those feelings were still eliciting frustration from him . . . but not nearly so much as they had been.

The CupCakes were easier to reach than the radios, and Holt, almost on instinct, hung down and grabbed two packages. The new backpack was almost full now, so he placed one in the new one and another in his trusty old one.

What's the harm? he thought. It might make her more cooperative. Plus, she would certainly smile when she saw them, which wasn't a bad thing either.

Holt moved for the radios, the last thing he needed. He hung down from the rafters again, stretching for them.

As Holt's fingers brushed the tops of the radio boxes, he noticed something along the wall just in front of him, and he aimed the flashlight in his mouth toward it.

The wall contained strange, long markings, running from top to bottom. They were in groups of five. And about the same distance apart as the fingers of a human hand.

It wasn't a coincidence, Holt realized. They were scratch marks. Human scratch marks. And as Holt shone the light on the wall in all directions, he could see the entire thing was full of them, from one end to the other, dug deeply into the drywall and plaster.

Holt looked at all the scratch marks revealed in the light . . . and felt knots form in his stomach.

19. FORSAKEN

MIRA SAT ON THE FLOOR in front of Zoey and Max. The dog was almost done with his taffy, and in the resulting sugar high, was content to let Mira do what she wished.

Mira had several items from her pack laid out in front of her. Two pennies wrapped in plastic sleeves, a small magnet, a piece of copper wire tied into a circle, and the roll of duct tape.

Zoey studied each artifact in turn, curious and confused at the same time.

"It takes three types of artifacts to make the most basic combination," Mira began. "First, you need a power source, which is always two Strange Lands coins of the same denomination. The higher the denomination, the more powerful the artifact. Coins also determine the 'polarity' of the artifact combination. Placing them with the same sides facing out is a 'positive' polarity, and different sides facing out is 'negative'. Got it so far?"

Zoey looked at her with wrinkled eyebrows. She clearly didn't. Mira pushed on, making a note to try to simplify her language.

"Second, you need what's called an Essence. The Essence defines what primary effect the artifact has. And third, a Focus, which says how the effect of the Essence manifests. In this case—" Mira pointed to the artifacts from her pack. "—the pennies are the power source, which means it will be a very low-powered artifact, and we'll place them in negative polarity.

"The magnet will be the Essence. The effect of magnets with a single Focus involves gravity." Mira placed the first penny tails side out next to the magnet. Then she put the circle of copper wire next to it. "The copper wire's the Focus, and it will channel the Essence into a circle."

Mira placed the last coin on the other side of the object, heads out. "Since the coins are aligned negatively, what do you think the effect will be on the gravity generated by the Essence?"

Zoey considered the artifacts, lined up and touching, ready to be wrapped together. Mira wondered how much smarter, if at all, Zoey was than other kids her age. There was no denying she had powers, and more of them were showing every day, but was heightened intellect one of them?

"It . . . decreases the gravity?" Zoey asked, slightly unsure.

Mira smiled. "Yep. That's right. If it were positively aligned, it would *increase* the gravity." So she was smart as well. Interesting . . .

Mira taped the objects together. The air around the artifact shimmered and hummed as the Interfusion took hold, the merging of the separate artifacts into one combination. Then, the humming vanished . . .

Zoey watched the lump of duct tape on the old hotel room floor with excited expectation. Initially, nothing happened.

And then, the artifact slowly began to spin on the floor.

It spun round and round, in a slow, lazy circle. Then it spun faster. And faster. And faster. And finally . . . rose into midair and floated upward, farther and farther off the floor.

Zoey clapped her hands. Max stopped his chewing, cocking his head to look at the floating artifact. He whined at the sight of it.

It kept spinning, kept rising, until it hit the ceiling. Even there, it kept rotating, trying to push through the roof. Zoey watched it in wonder.

Mira smiled, watching the little girl stare up at the simple artifact combination she'd made incessantly spinning into the ceiling. The first time Mira had seen an artifact do something like that, she'd probably been Zoey's age. The sight had captivated her, and she immediately wanted to learn everything she could about the Strange Lands and the artifacts people brought out of it.

She had known right then that she wanted to be a Freebooter.

The artifacts were the closest thing the world had ever had to magic. For a long time, Mira had thought they were the key to everything, objects of unlimited possibility. Maybe to hold off the Tone, maybe even to repel the Assembly. Things that had happened to her, recent things, made her not so sure. But it still made her happy to see Zoey so engrossed.

"Would you like an artifact of your own, Zoey?" Mira asked.

"Yes!" Zoey exclaimed.

Mira pulled the collection of necklaces she wore out of her shirt, about half a dozen strands. One was a gold chain that held a small pair of brass dice on the end. Mira examined it somberly. She hadn't thought about that necklace, or what it represented, in a while, even though she put it on every day. She wasn't sure if that was by choice or by instinct. Quickly she stuffed it back into her shirt and looked at two of the other necklaces, each with a tiny but working compass attached to the chain as charms. Mira slipped one off her neck and handed it to Zoey. The little girl studied it oddly. It wasn't what she'd been expecting, clearly.

"These little compasses are artifacts," Mira said, "and they're linked. Instead of pointing due north . . . they always point at each other, no matter how far apart they are."

Mira watched Zoey expectantly, and the little girl slipped it over her head.

"Look at yours," Mira said, holding hers up for Zoey to see. Zoey did the same thing.

It was as Mira had said. The compass needles pointed directly at each other. Mira and Zoey smiled.

"Now we'll always be connected," Zoey said.

Mira nodded. "That's right. Always."

A sound suddenly came from one of the walls.

An odd sound, a sound that Mira didn't instantly recognize. She, Zoey, and Max turned to the wall, looked at it warily.

It came again, a long, sustained vibration that ran down its length.

It was like . . . someone scratching. On the other side of their room. As if someone had dug in their fingers and clawed slowly from top to bottom.

The sound implied movement . . . and it also implied thought and intelligence.

Max dropped the taffy and stood up. He growled low in his throat, the hair on his back rising.

"Mira . . . ," Zoey said, and she pulled the girl close.

Something was in the next room from them, in the dark. And whatever it was, it was waking up.

HOLT STARED AT THE scratch marks up and down the wall in front of him. Outside, the sunlight was completely gone. It was night, and inside the sunken drugstore everything was pitch black.

He could see only what his dim flashlight showed him, and that wasn't much. As the darkness pressed in on him, Holt realized how much of it lay between him and the hole in the roof.

The water stirred beneath him.

Holt shone his light downward. The blackish liquid below stirred in circular waves, rolling back and forth, as if something had just moved through it.

Or *in* it.

A small splash, below and to the right. His flashlight darted over, but again, there was nothing. Only shadows and black water.

Something was in the dark with him. He had a sudden, intense desire to make himself scarce.

He reached for one of the radios and quickly grabbed it. There wasn't time to get any more than that; he'd stayed too long already. In his greed, he'd ignored survival, had put himself at risk. He felt anger rising up, but pushed it back. This wasn't the time.

Holt swung up to the rafter, made ready to start jumping back . . . and then stopped, realizing he was missing something.

Batteries. For the radio.

He looked back down to the shelves behind the register. The batteries lay on the same shelf, just below him.

More splashing . . . but now from several directions. The shadows pulsed and writhed under him, and this time when he shone his light down, he caught the briefest glimpse of something tall and dark as it darted behind one of the shelves.

Holt jolted in fright.

The blue pack stuffed with the treasure fell from his hand, tumbled down, hit the register, and slid across the counter.

Holt stared down at it. It wasn't completely out of reach—he could jump down to the counter, it would probably hold him. Then he could—

More stirring of water, now all around him. He saw dark shapes rising slowly up and out of the murk, all throughout the store. If he didn't leave now, Holt had a feeling he wouldn't leave at all. The pack wasn't worth it.

"Typical . . . ," he said in frustration, staring down at the pack below him.

But it didn't have to be a total loss.

Holt rolled back over the edge of the rusty ceiling rafter, hanging by his knees. He reached for a pack of batteries and grabbed it . . .

. . . just as a human-shaped black shadow lunged at him from the dark, hissing and stammering in some crazed language.

Holt flinched, flexed his legs, and swung back onto the rafter. The shadow just missed him and slammed into the store's wall, sending the radios and batteries flying everywhere.

The flashlight fell from Holt's mouth, plummeting into the water. Everything went dark.

But Holt didn't have time to care. More of the black shapes were moving below him, rising from the water, dozens and dozens of them.

He had to leave. *Now.*

He shoved the batteries and radio into his main pack and leapt from one rafter to the next as fast as he could.

The things below him hissed and gurgled their strange sounds, moving after him.

Ahead of Holt was the rafter he'd first landed on, and above it the hole back to the roof. And two of the things, whatever they were, were crawling and scratching up onto it.

Without the flashlight, they were just dirty black shadows, but he didn't need to see them to know they wanted him dead.

Holt leapt for the last rafter, landed, and drew his pistol, a Beretta 9, to fire off three rapid shots.

The first shadow took all three, spun crazily, fell, and crashed into the shelves below.

Holt aimed at the second thing crawling toward him, but it was too late.

It leapt on him, and the scent of it washed over Holt. He gagged at the powerful combination of rotted plants and meat, oil, sweat, and whatever else made up the black water below.

But it wasn't the thing's smell, as bad as it was, that shocked Holt. Or even the sight of its leathery, blackened, crazed human face, its mouth missing half its teeth. It was its eyes, set deep back into its skull.

They were a solid *white*. The opposite of the black eyes of the Succumbed.

The figure's hand, its fingernails overgrown and curling, reached for Holt's throat.

Holt rammed his head right into the thing's face.

It hissed and wailed, stumbled off him. Holt kicked it backwards as hard as he could. The thing fell and crashed into two more of the dark, jittering shadows below.

Holt caught his breath, got to his knees. More of the shapes were climbing up the wall to get to him. The entire floor was crawling with them now. They'd been hiding in the water the whole time. The image of the white eyes was burned into his mind.

It can't be. . . .

But Holt knew it was. Holt knew now what was in the water with him, knew what had made this entire ruined city its home, knew the reason why no one who entered the Drowning Plains ever returned.

He frantically leapt upward, grabbed the edge of the roof through the hole, and pulled himself out. He had to reach the others fast, had to get them out of here. Assuming they weren't already dead . . .

MIRA STARED, WIDE EYED, at the wall. The scratching had intensified. It wasn't just louder; it seemed like it was coming from more than one place.

More scratching, this time from the opposite wall.

Mira's breath caught in her throat. It was on both sides of them now.

"Mira . . ." Zoey, terrified, tried to push even farther into her grasp.

Mira had to get them out of here fast. "Zoey, sweetheart, let go for a second," she said, pushing her off. "I'm going to open the window. When I do—"

The scratching sounds again, from a new place. The door to the room.

Zoey hugged her leg. Max barked loud and aggressive, staring at the door, ready to rush whatever came through. The sound echoed through the room, and Mira grimaced. If these things didn't know they were here before, they knew now.

Mira got to her feet, reached for the window, gripped it, and yanked upward.

It moved maybe an inch . . . then jammed.

"Oh, you gotta be kidding," Mira mumbled.

Why would it open from the outside and not now? She pulled up on the window as hard as she could. It rocked up, moved another inch, but no more. It felt even more tightly wedged than before.

The door handle at the other end of the room began to rattle. Something was trying to open it. The door was locked, but who knew what age had done to the dead bolt; it was probably ready to fall apart.

Mira looked around for anything she could break the glass with. An old armchair sat in pieces in front of a crumbling desk. She grabbed the biggest piece she could find and spun back around.

"Stay back," she warned Zoey, swinging the chair leg into the window.

It shattered and sprayed glass everywhere. She used the chair to clear out the rest of the windowpane. Broken glass covered the floor like crushed ice.

Not the most elegant solution, but—

Zoey screamed as a dark shape appeared in the window. Mira raised the chair in defense.

It was Holt.

Mira sighed in relief. "Something's—," she started desperately.

"*Forsaken,*" Holt said, cutting her off.

At the word, Mira felt icy terror grip her insides.

The Tone turned most people who heard it into the Succumbed, the mindless slaves of the Assembly. But for others it had unexpected effects. The Heedless were one: people like Holt who were immune.

Then there were the Forsaken. People who didn't Succumb to the Tone, but rather were driven completely insane by it, reduced to horribly violent, animal-like monstrosities. They were drawn to one another somehow, lived in commune-like groups in various parts of the world. At least that was what the stories said. Few who found them lived to tell about it.

"Are you . . . are you sure?" she asked, disbelieving.

The front door exploded open. Two wild-eyed humanoid shapes burst inside, their eyes completely white. Their skin was leathery and black, their bodies covered in cuts and scrapes; what was left of their clothing hung around them in soiled tatters, their hair mangled and wild. They wailed insanely, leapt for the group with curled fingernails.

Holt ripped his shotgun free, blasted the two figures out of the room and back into the hall. "Yeah. Pretty sure," he said. "Zoey, come on!"

The little girl flung herself into his arms, and he lifted her gingerly through the broken window.

"Why didn't you just *open* it?" Holt asked Mira testily.

She glared at him in anger. "I was trying to, but—"

He grabbed her and yanked her through the window, followed quickly by Max.

Behind them, more crazed blackened figures rushed past the door, hissing and jabbering.

The four didn't wait around: they rushed up the fire escape. The stairs shook and groaned as they ran and Mira could feel them ripping dangerously loose with each step.

Below them, more shadows leapt through the window, chasing after them. The stairs shook and contorted, pulling free from the brick wall.

They reached the roof. Holt ran forward, but Mira stopped short.

"Holt!" she yelled. The top of the fire escape was secured to the building by large rusted bolts, and they were barely holding on. They shook and pulled as the Forsaken rushed up the ladder below.

Mira kicked the top of the fire escape. It separated from the wall. But just a little.

She kicked it again. *"Holt!"*

He saw what she was thinking, turned and ran back. They both kicked at the fire escape in unison, tearing it loose from the wall. When the top broke away, enough supports were gone below that the whole thing pulled free from the building. Mortar and plaster sprayed everywhere as it ripped off. There was a groaning as the rusted metal contorted and warped and fell in a fury of twisted debris.

The Forsaken screeched as the entire structure crashed down, spraying black water everywhere.

They were safe. For the moment.

"This might be easier than I thought," Holt said, smiling. Mira smiled back.

They ran for the other edge of the hotel roof, where Zoey and Max stood stock-still, staring out over the breach. When they got there, Mira saw why. The hotel looked out on all of the flooded city, hundreds of buildings illuminated like ghosts in the bright moonlight.

And on every building, shapes moved. Pouring out of windows, climbing up the walls, swimming through the horrid water. Hundreds and hundreds of them, in every direction. Hissings and jabberings filled the air all around them as the Forsaken cried out in their nonsensical, insane voices.

And each one of them was rushing toward the hotel, desperate to reach them, eager to rip their curled fingernails into them.

"Then again . . . maybe not," Mira said, instinctively moving closer to Holt. He put his arm around her. All four of them stared in terror at the wave of murderous insanity flowing toward them from all sides in the darkness.

HOLT STARED DOWN AT THE DARK SHAPES of the Forsaken swarming below, hundreds (maybe thousands) of man-shaped shadows that dripped up and over the sunken buildings, surging toward them in the bright moonlight.

"What do we do?" Mira clung to him tightly, her voice strained.

The Tavern Inn was the tallest structure in the ruins, which meant the roofs of most other buildings were too far below to jump. There was only one that was close enough, an old office building. From there, they might have more choices of escape.

But escape seemed almost impossible then. The Forsaken were everywhere. No matter which direction they went, they'd run into them.

"We have to keep moving," Holt said in spite of the circumstances. "If we stop, we die—they'll overrun us."

He moved for the other edge of the roof, staring at the office building next to them. It was maybe ten feet below, and six feet away. They could make it. Maybe.

"We don't have the bridge anymore," Mira said.

"Don't have time to use it if we did." Holt looked down at Zoey, grabbed her, and flung her up onto his back. Her arms circled his neck. "I'll get Zoey, you take Max."

Below, the jittering, gurgling shadows of the Forsaken reached the hotel. They started scaling straight up the walls, from all sides. Hundreds more were right behind them.

"I'm not carrying the dog," Mira said with a scowl.

Max looked up at her, growled in response, echoing her sentiment.

"You have to take the Max!" Zoey cried.

Holt took a few steps back, stared at the edge of the roof ahead of him, and exhaled a long, slow breath.

"I'm *not* taking the *dog*," Mira said with emphasis.

"I'm sure you two can work it out," Holt said, almost smiling. "Close your eyes, kiddo."

Zoey did.

Holt ran for the edge and leapt forward as hard as he could.

He sailed into the breach, legs kicking under him in the open air. He saw the sunken ground float by below, the squirming shadows.

And then he hit the roof. His knees almost buckled, but he managed to stay up, skidding to a stop in the gravel. When he had his balance back, he quickly let Zoey down. "Still with me?" he asked.

The little girl opened her mouth to respond . . . then screamed at something behind Holt.

Holt spun, ripped his rifle loose, and fired.

Two Forsaken took slugs in the chest, shuddered, and fell to the roof. Holt spotted a third, just crawling up and over the edge, aimed, fired, missed, but the bullets sparked near it. The man-thing's hands lost their grip, and it fell gurgling off the roof into the waters waiting below.

Behind him, Mira and Max landed. Max wasn't a small dog, almost half Mira's size. He squirmed in her hands, growling and snapping.

Holt caught her before she crashed on her face.

"Get this disgusting thing off me!" Mira shouted.

Max dropped to the ground, barking furiously at her.

She glared back. "Last time I help *you!*" she yelled down at Max.

"I really think he's starting to warm to you," Holt said.

Behind them, the walls of the old hotel were covered in Forsaken: black, dirty shadows that swarmed up its side like giant spiders.

They were running out of time.

Holt ran for the edge of the new roof, scanning the buildings around them, looking for choices, looking for anything that might—

Two more Forsaken appeared in front of them, crawling up the edge, hissing, staring with their sightless, insane white eyes.

Holt fired and dropped them. But he saw the hands of more clawing at the roof, pulling themselves up.

He turned on his heel, ran toward another side of the building. Mira, Zoey, and Max followed after him. They were almost there when more hands appeared, pulling their dirty, less-than-human owners onto the roof.

Three Forsaken rushed for them madly, screeching and hissing.

Holt fired, got two shots off, dropped one of the savages . . . and then the gun clicked empty.

"Back!" Holt yelled. "Back, move back!" In one smooth motion, he shouldered the rifle, drew the shotgun, and fired.

The blast flattened one of the crazies.

The other one was on him before he could fire again, driving him to the ground. Zoey screamed; Mira grabbed her.

Max growled and slammed into the thing with all his weight. The dog knocked it off Holt, and it screeched as Max bit down on its arm, shaking it back and forth.

Holt jumped up, flipped the shotgun around, gripped it like a baseball bat, and swung.

The gun's wooden stock connected with the thing's head, hard. It slumped to the ground, out cold or dead. Either way was fine with Holt.

Max kept right on attacking the thing.

"Max! Come on!" Holt shouted, moving for—

The Forsaken swarmed over every ruined building visible around theirs. Groceries, gas stations, liquor stores, flower shops—they were everywhere, chanting and gurgling loudly in the night air. The sound was overwhelming.

Even more were climbing onto the roof of their building, an unending assault, pulling themselves up, eager to get to the four survivors on top.

There was nowhere to go. They were surrounded.

Holt looked desperately around, spotted a bank of four large, rusting air-conditioning units on the roof near them. "There!" he yelled, rushing for what was left of the machines. They were old and in disrepair, but they were still thick and big: they'd provide cover. For a little while.

As he moved, Holt blasted two more Forsaken to the ground, but more were coming.

The others ran after him. When they reached the air conditioners, they crouched down behind them.

Holt dropped his shotgun, grabbed his rifle, and started reloading it.

Mira grabbed the shotgun, and Holt tossed her shells. She started stuffing them into the barrel.

"We're, um . . ." Mira looked down at Zoey before she continued, who was staring at both of them with fear in her eyes. "We're in trouble, aren't we?" She knew they were in more than trouble.

Holt knew it, too, knew what she really meant. "Yeah," he said. "We got real problems."

They looked at each other, loading the guns, the sounds of a thousand crazed, incomprehensible yells echoing off the buildings around them. More and more Forsaken were climbing onto their roof, dozens and dozens, soon to be hundreds. They could hold them off a few minutes with the guns, but they would run out of ammo long before the Forsaken ran out of insane cannon fodder.

They were going to die. It was just that simple.

"Mira, I'm sorry, I . . . ," Holt started but trailed off. Why was it so hard? "I'm sorry . . . I got you into this," he said.

Mira smiled. "Technically, you could say I'm the one who got *you* into this."

Holt almost laughed. He liked Mira. More than he should. A part of him wanted to tell her that. Especially now. But . . . even given the finality of their situation, the words seemed pointless.

Forsaken climbed onto the roof, rushed toward them, moaning and jabbering.

Holt took the shotgun from Mira, gripped the rifle. Max growled with anticipation. Mira pulled Zoey close to her.

"Mira . . . ," Zoey moaned into her chest. "They found us."

"Ssshhh, honey," she said, never taking her eyes off Holt. "I know they did. Close your eyes."

Holt raised the rifle up and over the air conditioner, sighted down it. Dozens of Forsaken, rushing for them, more climbing up every second. God, they had maybe a minute left. Maybe two, if his aim was good. His finger tensed on the trigger. . . .

"Not the scary men, I mean," Zoey said. *"Them."*

Holt moved to fire—

—and then flinched violently as the first volley of plasma fire ripped past them, burning the air, incinerating a dozen of the Forsaken where they stood.

Holt quickly ducked back down behind the rusted machine, eyes wide.

More plasma fire flared in the night, lighting everything yellow. It slammed into the Forsaken on their building, decimating them, blowing away the ones climbing up the walls, knocking huge chunks out of the edifice.

Holt watched in shock as the Forsaken were mowed down left and right by the yellow bolts.

It took a moment for his mind to process what it meant.

Zoey was right. *They* had found them. The Assembly were here, had somehow tracked them all the way into the Drowning Plains.

Holt stood up, looked past the edge of the roof. In the dark, under the moonlight, illuminated by the flashes of their plasma cannons, Holt could see ten Assembly walkers.

They had taken up positions all around the city, on the rooftops, all along the perimeter.

And they were unlike anything Holt had ever seen.

Tripods, three legs, maybe seven feet tall, lithe, agile . . . and, most strikingly, they were *green and orange*!

If he hadn't seen it for himself, he wouldn't have believed it. How many different Assembly factions *were* there? And why the hell were they all hunting Zoey?

Holt looked at Mira. She looked back at him, stunned.

"I have a very specific policy about these things," Holt said. "Never refuse a rescue."

"That's pretty similar to my policy," Mira replied.

They all made ready to move, while the yellow bolts burned the air around them, blowing to pieces anything they touched. Holt had never been so happy to see plasma fire.

THE TOP OF THE OFFICE BUILDING was chaos. Dozens of Forsaken littered the roof, but they were being ripped apart by flying plasma bolts. Explosions flared up all around them, and Holt watched the drugstore he'd looted collapse in flames.

The Forsaken were torn between pursuing their original prey, and attacking the new, much more potent threat of the strange green and orange walkers.

Holt was glad for the confusion.

He looked over the roof, out into the sunken ruins and saw that they were at the edge of the city. Only a few more buildings lay between them and the open water, and the water appeared to be growing shallow just on the other side.

If they could make it to the waterline, they might have a chance. But jumping between buildings wasn't an option anymore. They needed something faster.

Mira screamed and covered Zoey as plasma bolts incinerated two nearby Forsaken. More of the yellow bolts slapped into the roof right next to them, barely missing them.

Between the two attacking groups, if they didn't get out of here fast, they'd be lucky to join the Succumbed in the Presidiums. More likely, they'd all be dead.

Holt saw something on the next building over. The faded letters of a radio station, KCLE, half sunk in the floodwaters. On top of it was a giant rusting radio tower.

As he considered it, a plan began to form. A crazy one. But it was all he had.

"We need to reach that tower," he announced, then promptly ducked as more plasma bolts burned past.

"We're not going to take two steps in this!" Mira yelled at him. She flinched as explosions blossomed in the distance. Holt blasted two Forsaken as they rushed toward the air conditioners.

"Got anything that can help?" he asked Mira as he reloaded the shotgun. "It's just one building over."

Mira thought about it a second. "Maybe," she finally said, digging through her pack. "Gotta buy me some time, though."

"Let me see what I can do." He lifted back up over the AC. "Zoey, stay down!" he shouted when he saw her trying to peer over the old machine with him.

His rifle flashed, dropped two Forsaken rushing them. He fired again, and a third fell.

The crazies were adjusting to the distraction of the Assembly. All around them, he saw them pouring off the buildings surrounding theirs, rushing with their insane gurgling in all directions.

They were going after the walkers.

Ten Assembly with plasma cannons versus a thousand psychopaths. Seemed like fair odds to Holt. If he was lucky, they'd all kill each other.

But the Forsaken hadn't totally forgotten them yet. Holt saw four more of the savages running for them, screeching, their tangled hair flying after them from behind.

Holt dropped two more before the rifle clicked empty.

He shouldered it, drew his Beretta. As he did, he clicked his tongue and whistled.

Max barked when he heard the command and charged forward toward the two Forsaken while Holt calmly ejected a clip from the gun, grabbed a new one, and slammed it in.

Max rammed into and drove one of the things to the ground. The other one shrieked, turned toward the dog . . .

But then Holt placed a bullet between its eyes. It fell dead to the roof.

Holt put two fingers in his mouth, whistled loudly.

Max reluctantly leapt off the Forsaken and ran back toward Holt. The crazy jumped up, shrieked and hissed, charged after the dog . . . then rocked back as another shot from Holt dropped it.

Max made it back, tail wagging, tongue lagging out of his mouth. "Good job, pal," Holt said.

"The Max is tough!" Zoey said, reaching out to pet him. The dog licked her face.

More explosions, more plasma fire, more shrieks . . .

Holt looked to Mira. "Mira, what do you got?"

"Concentrating," she replied testily.

She was combining items from her pack. Two dimes, a marble, and another combination she had already wrapped, which looked like it contained more coins, a D battery, and an old bottle cap. She placed the dimes on either end, heads facing out, then quickly wrapped the whole thing in duct tape.

There was a hum, a shimmering . . . and the air all around them flashed in a bright sphere of light. But only for a second, then it was gone.

"Gotta hurry," she said, looking at Holt. "I only had dimes left, and they won't last long."

Holt wasn't sure what that meant, but he didn't feel a pressing need for clarification right then.

"Zoey." Holt motioned the little girl onto his back. She climbed on, held on tight. He looked up at Mira. "Don't worry about Max, he'll jump on his own."

Mira fixed Holt with an icy stare. "*He'll jump on his own?* Then why did I *carry* him last time?"

"I thought it would be funny?" he said, smiling and running for the edge of the roof with Zoey. He whistled three notes and Max darted after him.

Mira glared knives after the three of them . . . then rushed to follow.

As they sprinted across the roof, a new sound overpowered even the mad ramblings of the hundreds of Forsaken. Strange, electronically distorted trumpeting sounds, coming from all directions. The walkers positioned around the sunken ruins had spotted them.

While Holt ran, he watched in awe as the strange walkers leapt toward them in pursuit, closing fast, bounding with agility and speed from roof to roof. Not even Mantises could move that fast and precisely. They'd be on them in seconds.

The nearby Forsaken hissed horribly, lunging after them, too, closing fast. Holt watched them coming closer and closer.

"Mira!" Holt shouted with concern. What was she going to do?

"Just keep going!" Mira yelled back.

The Forsaken rushed toward Holt . . . then bounced violently backwards as they ran into some kind of invisible force field. Mira's artifact, whatever it was, was working.

Holt double-timed it, leapt off the edge, and sailed across. Zoey screamed with glee behind him as they hit hard on the roof of the ruined radio station.

Max landed next to them, followed by Mira, who was still glaring at him.

But before she could say anything, something slammed into her force field and bounced off. Not one of the Forsaken, not even a plasma bolt. Something else.

A mass of some kind of metallic netting lay a few feet away.

One of the green and orange tripods was closing the gap between them quickly. Another net launched from under its body and exploded toward them.

It crashed into the shield and bounced harmlessly away just like the first. The walker trumpeted in anger, charged after them.

Holt and Mira looked at each other. They both knew the nets were for Zoey.

They dashed for the radio tower in a mad scramble. Plasma fire lit the air in bright, strobic flashes of yellow as they did. The bolts plowed into their shield, and it flared brightly, spraying sparks everywhere. Bolt after bolt hit as they moved . . . until the whole thing finally flared out. The air around them shimmered one last time as the force field died.

They all ducked behind the supports of the huge radio tower as more plasma fire burned past. The tower pressed into the night sky far above. It was rusting and aged, and leaned to the right just a little, but it was still holding on.

Holt peered out through the metal rungs of the tower.

He had a good view of the sunken city. The Forsaken were pouring over the buildings: mad, frantic, running shadows in the night, closing in from all directions. Easier to spot were the walkers, also headed for them. But they were now directly fighting the crazed humans.

Individually, the Forsaken were no match for their cannons. But more and more were coming, an unending wave of insanity that didn't care how many were decimated, only obsessively fixed on reaching the walkers and ripping them to pieces with their bare hands. Or at least trying.

They piled onto one of the machines, a dozen of them, tearing and clawing at it, ripping its cables and hoses.

The tripod trumpeted, stumbled, crashed to the roof. Even more Forsaken leapt onto it, burying it under their dirty weight.

Two or three of the walkers hadn't made the mistake of stopping to fight the Forsaken; they kept firing and moving, leaping rooftop to rooftop, making a beeline for the radio tower.

Holt guessed they'd be on them in seconds.

"We need to knock this thing over," Holt said to Mira, rapping his fist on the radio tower's thick support.

More plasma fire flashed around them, more hissing and jabbering.

Mira stared at Holt like he was crazy. "Knock it *over*?" she said, aghast. "*That's* your plan? Knock over the giant metal radio tower? Have you noticed how *big* it is?"

"I figured you had some crazy Strange Lands thing that—"

"Well, I don't! I don't carry around a storehouse of artifacts with me, Holt! There's only so much I can do with what I—"

More plasma fire ripped into the tower, spraying sparks everywhere. They all ducked. Where the yellow bolts hit, the metal flashed white hot, melted, and crumbled.

Holt stared up at the damage, thoughts swirling in his head. He looked and saw the walkers closing the distance.

With a grimace, he shouldered his rifle and shotgun, drew the Beretta. Holt aimed through the metal rungs of the support tower at the closest green and orange walker . . . and fired.

The bullet clanged harmlessly off its armor.

"What are you doing?" Mira asked, staring at him.

"Trying to piss them off." Holt knew the shot wouldn't hurt the walker; he only wanted to get its attention. And judging by the volley of plasma fire it unleashed in his direction, he guessed he had.

Holt leapt and grabbed the tower support above, pulling himself up and onto it.

"Holt!" Zoey yelled below him.

"Be right back, get ready to move!" he shouted back down.

More plasma fire sparked and flashed around him, cutting into the tower, melting and incinerating whatever it hit.

Holt barely dodged two bolts that almost took off his head. Out the corner of his eye, he caught the very visible rapid-fire flashing of the walkers' cannon again.

Maybe this hadn't been such a good idea after all.

More yellow bolts slammed into the metal around him. Holt maneuvered in a circle around the tower, drawing the fire of the walkers. More and more plasma bolts sparked and fizzled into the structure.

The tower began to groan as it weakened. The metal snapped and tore. Its ancient, rusted bolts exploded outward in sheets like gunfire, whizzing through the air.

Below, almost in slow motion, Holt saw Max barking furiously, saw Mira leap and cover Zoey, pulling her down and away.

The tower began to tip, ripping free of its supports, arcing through the air. Holt leapt clear as the whole thing thundered downward and crashed to the sunken ground below in a painful maelstrom of sound.

Holt hit the roof hard, rolled, crashed to a stop with a grunt. He coughed out lungfuls of rust and dust, and painfully pushed himself back to his feet.

The crumpled radio tower now made a bridge over the water, stretching from the radio station to the shallow waters at the other end of the sunken city.

He was glad to see Mira had figured out his intention, and wasn't wasting any time. She carried Zoey in her arms, rushed onto and down the tower toward the ground as fast as she could manage. Max rushed ahead of her, barking enthusiastically.

Behind them, one of the nets flashed by, just missing them. The walkers were on their tail, leaping from the roof of the building next door and onto the radio station.

And so were the Forsaken. The crazed shadows ran onto the tower in a swarm of dirty claws and teeth and bodies, hissing after Mira and Zoey.

"Hurry!" Holt ran after them, firing the Beretta into the mass of Forsaken until the clip emptied, dropping three or four of them.

But there were more coming. Far too many. The devastation of the tower collapse had stirred them up like a beehive: they were everywhere now.

Holt saw the top of Mira's head disappear below the roof edge, and he double-timed it.

Behind him came sounds of heavy stomping, the roof shaking with each hit. The sounds were gaining on him fast.

Holt had just enough time to look behind and see a green and orange tripod right behind him. It trumpeted and lashed out with a mechanical leg, tripping him. He went down, hit the roof, rolled.

Up close, he saw more of the walker's details. Its three pointed legs were triple jointed, the fuselage on top of them round and sleek. It was a Hunter, Holt guessed. Probably designed specifically for speed and tracking, and it had done its job well. The walker leapt for him.

He drew his shotgun, tried to twist back around to his—

The walker knocked the gun away, sent it sliding across the gravel. Holt barely dodged one of the thing's legs as it trumpeted, puncturing the roof where he'd just been standing.

He dodged again, leapt for the gun, grabbed it, rolled over, aimed.

The walker trumpeted angrily and pounced forward.

The Ithaca was fully loaded, and Holt fired every shell it had right into the thing's three-optic "eye" in the center of its body. It was the smallest Assembly walker he'd ever seen, and he just hoped he had a chance of hurting it.

Each shot rocked the thing backwards in a plume of sparks, shuddering along the roof . . . and then fire sprayed out of it in a violent arc, lighting up the night air. The walker collapsed in a whine of dying power and failing mechanics.

Holt groaned, got to his feet. This was quite a week he was—

He shut his eyes as a dazzling field of golden, wavering energy poured into the air from the wrecked green and orange machine.

Holt backed up at the light, it was so intense. His head filled with static, as it had been in Zoey's crashed ship days earlier. He held his ears, backing up, blinded and deaf.

Screeches filled the air all around him. It must be having the same effect on the Forsaken.

The energy field rose into the air, contorting and forming into a crystalline shape of near impossible geometry. As it did, the static in his head lessened, the brightness faded.

More plasma bolts slapped into the roof all around him. Two more walkers rushed for him.

Holt forgot about the golden light, made a beeline for the collapsed tower. If he could just reach it . . .

Behind him, he heard another electronic trumpeting from one of the walkers. The Forsaken swarmed it, dozens and dozens of them, pouring onto it, clawing and tearing at it. The thing trumpeted again, loud and angry.

It gave him the delay he needed. Holt reached the fallen tower and dashed down it toward the flood bank. In front of him, he saw that Mira, Zoey, and Max had already made it, were running into the night.

Behind him, the Forsaken continued to pile onto the green and orange walker. There were too many; the thing couldn't keep moving, couldn't stay up.

It fell to the side . . . right off the edge of the roof, tumbling downward with a distorted trumpet that almost sounded frightened. It crashed into the deep, black murk below, sending a giant splash of water everywhere.

As it did, a crackling explosion of energy flared out from it, fire blowing out the walker's exhaust ports. Holt stopped, stunned, and watched as a black, burned, rustlike substance formed over the walker's surface, covering it in seconds like some metallic, cancerous mass. The machine shook a few times, contorted . . . and then went still, frozen like a rusted black statue in the water.

Now it made sense. The black rust happened when the machines were destroyed *in water*, and when they did, no golden energy lifted up and out of them. It was relevant, Holt was sure . . . but he just didn't know why.

Holt looked back toward the ruined city. The Forsaken were coming, rushing after him in a mass of insanity and curled fingernails.

The remaining walkers had their hands full, their plasma bolts flashing everywhere, incinerating the crazies, knocking them back with their legs. But for every one they dispatched, five more took its place.

Holt watched the impossible chaos a moment more, then ran down the fallen tower, navigating its holes and bent metal as fast as he could. He hopped into the water and ran for the shadows of Mira, Zoey, and Max waiting up ahead. They had done it. They were going to make it— they were going to survive the Drowning Plains.

Behind them, the sunken, ruined city burned, lighting up the night in black-tinged orange shadows. Electronic cries and hissing nonsense filled the air long after they had left the flames behind.

22. NIGHTMARES

A YOUNG HOLT; his sister, Emily; and their mother pushed past the door into the dark farmhouse and ducked inside as the whine of engines outside grew to a fever pitch. Through the house's windows, Holt saw the lights of the strange ships in the sky painting the ground as they flew over. One of them lighted the house, filling the windows with brightness.

Holt's mother gasped, pulled her children back against a wall, and Holt shut his eyes tight as the engines roared above. He felt Emily shaking next to him, heard his mother's whispers that everything was going to be okay.

The searchlight flashed off; the whine of engines, mercifully, began to recede.

The three risked a glance out the window. The night sky was full of the flashing lights of the strange machines. The sight took Holt's breath away. He could never have imagined that many aircraft in the sky at once. The ground everywhere outside was being hammered by their cannon fire, yellow bolts of light flashing down and incinerating everything beneath them. From the window, Holt saw two houses in flames.

They'd made it to this abandoned farmhouse after a frantic run from Fort Connor in the family car, before it ran out of fuel and stranded them on a deserted rural road. They weren't alone long, though. In the sky, shapes moved.

Flickering lights, like airplanes, darting along the horizon at impossible speeds and angles. Yellow pinpricks flared from them, streaming toward the ground. Wherever they hit, fire blossomed up in the distance.

And they were coming closer. Hundreds of them. Thousands maybe, flying through the air, those flashes of yellow pummeling everything.

Flames shot upward where they hit, followed by the sounds of explosions, a percussive string of pops and bangs.

They had run, panicked, the roaring of strange engines growing louder behind them, until Emily spotted the farmhouse, and they dashed for it, made it inside as the machines buzzed over.

Now those things were blowing up every house in the landscape. They saw the destruction through the window as it happened. But why did they leave this one alone? They definitely saw it: the light had lit it up for a full minute. Holt didn't know the answer.

Holt, Emily, and their mother moved through the abandoned house until they found the kitchen. Holt's mother picked him up and placed him on the counter. Emily wet some rags and wiped his face, cleaning off the tearstains and the dirt. He tolerated the cleaning without complaint.

Their mother flipped on a small TV on the counter, tuned it to a cable news channel. The picture wasn't very good, it was choppy and grainy and the feed kept cutting in and out, but Holt could make out a headline running across the top of the fragmented screen.

NORTH AMERICA INVADED.

As the silent video flashed on and off, Holt tried to read the ticker tape news items scrolling across the bottom.

CONTACT LOST WITH WASHINGTON, MIAMI, HOUSTON, DENVER, BISMARCK, PHOENIX, LOS ANGELES, SAN FRANCISCO. . . .

UNCLEAR IF OTHER COUNTRIES ARE BEING ATTACKED, INTERCONTINENTAL COMMUNICATION IS DOWN . . .

NEW YORK CITY IN FLAMES . . .

UNCONFIRMED REPORTS THAT PRESIDENT GISONDI WAS EVACUATED FROM THE WHITE HOUSE TO AN UNDISCLOSED LOCATION. . . .

IDENTITY OF INVADERS STILL UNKNOWN, BUT SEEM TO POSSESS ADVANCED TECHNOLOGY AND SUPERIOR NUMBERS . . .

GROWING NUMBER OF EXPERTS BELIEVE INVASION MAY BE OF ALIEN ORIGIN. . . .

And there it was.

Alien origin. The world ground to a halt at the weight of the idea. Even though he was young, even though he had nothing to confirm the thought, Holt knew it was right. Nothing else made sense. The glowing clouds, the huge, dark shape that slammed into Denver, the aircraft that moved at impossible speeds, the yellow bolts of light . . .

Suddenly, from outside, came a low thump. Deep and powerful.

They were all instantly alert. The hair on Holt's arms stood up. What could make a sound like—?

Two more thumps, a little louder. Three more, louder, closer. Plates in the kitchen cabinets shook ominously at each impact.

The thuds were coming in threes, and they began to sound like something . . . walking. Something big. And mechanical.

A thought occurred to Holt: Maybe the airships didn't destroy the farmhouse *on purpose*. Maybe they knew it wasn't abandoned. Maybe whatever was outside . . . was coming for *them*.

The footfalls grew closer, louder, deeper. Whatever it was, it was huge.

The boy's mother grabbed her children, ran for the living room. There were stairs heading up to the bedrooms, and they climbed them quickly, peering out a window on the top floor.

Outside, the shadows moved.

Giant forms marched across the fields beyond the farmhouse. Too far off to see clearly, but they were coming.

The woman's breath quickened in fear. She saw a hatch set into the ceiling, and grabbed the string, yanked it open. The ladder to the attic descended, providing a stairway to the pitch black interior beyond.

The footfalls were growing closer.

Strange chirpings and whistles sounded from outside. Back and forth, from different directions. The sounds were electronic and distorted, and it only made them more frightening.

Downstairs, the windows exploded inward. The front door blew apart as something punched through it. Emily screamed.

Their mother didn't look; she pushed her son and daughter up into the attic as fast as she could. When they were in, she told them to hide, told them to find a place in the back, out of sight.

Emily cried louder, begged her mother not to leave them, but the woman insisted they move back, move and hide.

Holt looked from his sister to his mother, unsure. More crashing from below, something big and powerful was searching the lower floor.

Their mother told them everything would be okay. She told Emily she had to stay strong for her brother, had to take care of him, told her she was counting on it. The idea seemed to get through to the girl. She put her arms around Holt, started pulling him back and away.

Holt's mother watched them disappear into the dark for as long as she dared. Long after, Holt remembered the sight of his mother's eyes, the way they seemed to commit every detail of him to memory before she finally nodded, smiled sadly . . . and shut the attic door.

Above and outside, the sound of engines pushed into the house. One of the aircraft was hovering over it.

The stomping of machines again. Much louder, much closer.

Emily and Holt kept sliding in the dark until they hit the wall at the back. There was nowhere else to go. Holt hugged his knees and Emily wrapped her arms around him.

From outside came new sounds. The sound of someone shouting. Holt couldn't make out the words, but he recognized the voice. His mother.

The stomping of gigantic feet went silent. More yelling, more shouts.

The entire house shook as explosions rocked the ground. Emily gasped, hugged Holt tight as the roof threatened to cave in. More explosions, some kind of mechanical scream and whirring.

They heard their mother shout again, heard her strained voice start to fade into the distance as it grew more frantic.

Whatever was outside, however abhorrent it was, their mother was trying to lead it away. She was using herself as a distraction . . . and it was working.

The stomping returned. Faster, heavier . . . and trailing after their mother. The roar of the engine above them grew louder a short moment, then buzzed away also.

A minute or two later, the sounds of more explosions. But farther away now, much more distant. Whatever had been outside, it didn't return.

Holt and Emily hugged each other in the dark the rest of the night and through most the following morning before they worked up the courage to step out of the farmhouse.

When they did, the landscape was black and charred as far as they could see. Houses and barns were smoldering ruins on the hills. And most shocking, in the distance to the north, sat something foreign and awful.

An impossibly colossal black shape rose up from where downtown Denver used to be. What was left of the burning skyscrapers were completely dwarfed by the huge structure. It looked like a giant black wedge-shaped tower, and it was so tall, its top disappeared inside dark storm clouds in the sky. Even from this distance, they saw the lightning that crackled around it.

And at the bottom, where the immense black thing met the ground, dark, meandering lines stretched back from it all the way to the horizon, winding toward the tower from all directions. Holt instantly knew what they were: People. Tens of thousands of them, hundreds of thousands, all for some inexplicable reason marching toward and into that giant, vile structure in the distance.

It filled Holt with dread. It was so much like a dream, a part of him expected to wake up soon. But he knew he wouldn't, knew this was real, as impossible as it seemed.

There was no sign of their mother. Whatever had happened, she was lost. And so were they. Lost and adrift in a world that was nothing like it had been the day before.

Now they only had each other.

23. WALTZ

HOLT WOKE FROM THE DREAM WITH A START, stared at his surroundings in alarm until he realized he was no longer back there, huddled in the corner of that dark attic.

With the realization came relief. And with the relief, as always, came the guilt. Holt pushed it down and away, as he always did.

They'd made camp in the woods, several miles from the Drowning Plains. Here, the trees weren't so densely packed as they had been, and the stars twinkled through from above.

They'd run almost nonstop after their escape, the red glow of the flames reflecting off the night clouds above, chasing them until the sun finally came up.

And still, they had run. The strange green and orange walkers were seemingly being overpowered by the unfathomable mass of Forsaken in those ruins, but there was no way to know for sure. They expected the aliens to explode through the underbrush behind them at any moment.

When they could move no farther, they collapsed in the clearing. The sun was high in the sky when Holt, exhausted, finally fell asleep. Now it was night again, early evening based on the moon's position. He'd been asleep for hours.

Holt lay in his sleeping bag, thinking. The dreams hadn't been this vivid in years. He'd done a good job of stuffing those emotions away, but both Mira and Zoey's arrival into his life had clearly had an effect. Now the dreams were coming back, and with them, all the old feelings. One more reason to get rid of them both, he told himself. But those words were starting to feel very hollow.

He looked over at Mira, who lay asleep and curled up protectively around her pack. The red in her hair glistened like copper in the flickering light from the campfire.

"Did you have the same dream, Holt?" a soft voice asked from his other side. Holt rolled over.

Zoey sat cross-legged near the fire, eating jelly beans from a small jar. Max sat in front of her on his haunches, tail thumping the ground like a metronome, watching Zoey's every move. For every jelly bean stuffed into her mouth instead of his, he let out a small, sad whine.

Zoey had almost as much of a sweet tooth as Max, Holt had discovered, and he'd given her the jar before he passed out. He wondered if she and Max had been eating them this whole time. He wouldn't put it past either of them.

The little girl tossed Max a green jelly bean. He caught it in midair and swallowed it almost whole. His tail resumed its thumping.

"I give the green ones to the Max," Zoey said. "I don't like the green ones."

"Throw me a red one," Holt said quietly, trying not to wake Mira. "Or a pink one."

Zoey frowned, but tossed him one of each. He chewed them slowly, savoring the sweet yet tart flavors. Then Holt remembered Zoey's question.

"What did you ask me?" he inquired. Maybe he hadn't heard her right.

"I asked if you had the same dream," Zoey said. "You always seem to. I think it has to do with the invasion. And with a girl. Always the same girl." Zoey tossed Max another green candy.

Holt stared at her. "How do you know that?" he asked.

Zoey shrugged. "Just something I see. I see lots of things."

Holt kept studying the little girl, unsure how to respond. He had grown to believe Zoey was not a direct danger; none of the "powers" she had shown so far could harm him or Mira or Max.

But there *was* the continued threat of the Assembly.

Three separate factions (that they knew of, anyway) were hunting her. Holt understood now why the Assembly feared the water. He'd seen its effects on them with his own eyes, the inexplicable black rust that consumed them if their machines broke down while touching it. And yet, those same walkers had pursued Zoey into the Drowning Plains, a landscape flooded in water.

Her ability to sense things was important. As was this new ability to read the minds of those near her in some limited way. But were those enough to warrant such an obsessive chase by the Assembly? Was it enough to justify the massive red army they'd seen in the Mississippi River Valley just two days ago?

Holt knew it wasn't, and that was what really bothered him. It meant they hadn't seen all of what Zoey could do. It meant there were more surprises to come. And Holt wasn't a fan of surprises.

He reached for his pack, opened it, and pulled out the one radio he'd managed to take from the drugstore. The loss of that blue bag, stuffed with its priceless treasure, was still an almost tangible pain. He tried not to think about it.

"Who's the girl in your dream, Holt?" Zoey asked.

Holt tensed at the question. "Zoey, that's not something I talk about." He placed the batteries in the radio and flipped it on. There was only static, and he tuned the dials, searching for any signal out there.

"Why not?"

"It just isn't," he said more firmly, trying to make his point. And it was true. With the exception of one other person, he had never spoken of Emily to anyone. And he had no intention of breaking that trend tonight.

"Did the scary metal ones take her?"

"Zoey . . ."

"Was her name Emily?"

"*Zoey!*" Holt yelled, fixing the little girl with a stern gaze. The sound of Emily's name was like a slap in the face. The little girl's eyes bore into him.

On the other side of the camp, Mira stirred, but didn't wake.

Holt sighed, disappointed in himself. Zoey was just a little kid, after all. A little kid with a front-row look at his personal demons, but a little kid nonetheless. She didn't know any better.

When Holt looked back at her, her eyes were overwhelmed with sadness, and the raw emotion inside them struck Holt hard. He was suddenly full of shame; he hadn't meant to be so forceful.

"Zoey, I didn't mean . . . ," he began, starting to get up.

"I can feel how much you hurt, Holt," she said. The words froze him in his tracks. "You hide it, real far down, but it's there. You never let it get better."

Zoey voiced the observation with the same level of confusion as she would if she was asking why Holt wouldn't remove a knife stuck in his chest. Holt stared back at her, unsure what to say.

"Why don't you let it get better, Holt?" she asked in her soft voice.

It was a question Holt rarely allowed himself to ask. Mainly because he didn't like the answer.

"Because, Zoey," he said slowly, his voice barely louder than the crackling embers of the small fire next to them, "I'd have to feel it all over again. And I don't think I'm strong enough for that."

The sadness and pain slowly drained from Zoey's face. "Maybe that's because you've been alone too long."

When Zoey looked at him, she looked *into* him, below the surface. In a world where Holt had let very few people get close, that kind of look was rare. Perhaps the intimacy he felt with Zoey came merely by virtue of her strange powers, her inexplicable ability to automatically know what he felt . . . but did that make it any less real?

The radio in his hands suddenly came to life. The signal wasn't strong, and it was full of static, but it *was* a signal. Holt looked away from Zoey and tuned it in as best he could.

Classical music, punctuated by bits of static, filled the forest clearing.

The sounds of a hundred stringed instruments floated around them like individual pieces of air. Holt watched Zoey's eyes widen at the sounds. She'd probably never heard music, Holt realized. It was a relic now, after all, a strange, forgotten remnant of the World Before.

"What is it?" a groggy voice asked from the other side of the fire. Mira was awake, looking at him with her green eyes laced with the ever-growing black tendrils.

"A rebel station," Holt said. "Kind of far off, so it's staticky . . . but we're getting it."

A lot of survivors ran rebel radio stations throughout North America, broadcasting a variety of content that was mostly rebellion-oriented. Some of them had managed to power up the older existing radio towers that dotted the landscape's urban ruins, but most were mobile. Smaller, hastily constructed transponders made by the more industrious and electrically inclined. They had a limited range, but what they lacked in power, they made up for in the ability to move and avoid Assembly gunships from homing in on their signals. Of course, Holt figured the Assembly could pretty easily find them if they wanted to. The reality was they probably just didn't care.

"I know this." Mira climbed out of her sleeping bag and sat up, listening intently. " 'In the Fen Country,' by Vaughan Williams." The strings continued to pulse and meander around them, swelling and fluctuating in their battle with the static of the weak signal. "My dad loved Vaughan Williams, he played this one all the time."

"What was he like?" Zoey asked. Holt studied Mira along with the little girl. Max had given up on getting any more jelly beans, and was lying at Zoey's feet, letting her rub his head. Holt wondered if Zoey could feel whatever emotions Mira was feeling right now.

"I was only ten when the Assembly came. It's terrible how fast the memories fade." Even though the thoughts made her smile, her eyes didn't lose their haunted look. "I've held on to . . . glimpses of him, just images, really: making pancakes, or writing, or working in his garden. He used to set me on his lap in the car and let me pretend to drive. My mom hated that—I guess she thought it was dangerous—but I always felt safe with him. I think she did, too. When the Tone took him, took both of them, they just . . . left me. Left me and walked away."

Holt looked off into the night at that last bit. Out of the corner of his eye, he saw Zoey switch her gaze from Mira to him.

"Neither of them would ever have left me like that," Mira continued. "It was like watching who they used to be die."

Holt looked at Mira, and she at him. They held their gaze, mutual understanding passing between them. If he hadn't been connected to Mira before . . . he was now. Holt felt the frustration build. How was he going to do what he *needed* to do? Survival dictated it, but . . .

Mira looked back at him sadly, like she could sense his feelings almost as well as Zoey could.

The music built into an outpouring of emotion and sound, climaxing in the air around them. And then it receded, faded, withdrew. Holt and Mira were still staring at each other when the voice of the radio station DJ emerged from the static.

"Kid Cryptic, Cryptic Radio, broadcasting whenever and wherever he can," the rapid-fire voice of a young boy said from the other side, across who knew how many miles of wasteland. "On the road to Midnight City this week, and if you're hearing this, I'd bet you're walking the same path. May our trails cross, and our journeys intertwine, my brothers and sisters.

"That was another classic from Cryptic Radio's very limited music collection. We got more tunes coming your way, pretty much the same from last hour, but before we hit that, got some news from the rumor mill. As always, take it with a grain of salt. Further the truth travels, the more a story it becomes."

Zoey got up and moved to Mira, sat in her lap. Mira smiled and ran her fingers through the little girl's hair. Max padded over and sat next to Holt, his chin on his paws, and Holt scratched his ears.

"I keep getting reports from survivors and traders coming from the south that west of the Chicago ruins, there's a lot of *strange* Assembly activity."

Boy, was *that* the truth. Holt and Mira exchanged glances again as the voice continued.

"Kids are reporting seeing not just massive numbers of your average, everyday walkers . . . but also ones painted a solid *red*. Yeah, if I hadn't heard a multifarious quantity of reports of the same thing, I wouldn't believe it either, but this DJ keeps hearing the same damn thing over and over. To make matters worse, most reports say these red Assembly don't get along very well with our home team. Hey, if we're lucky, maybe they'll wipe each other out.

"One thing's for sure, something bad's going down out in Assembly land, and anyone hearing this would be advised to stay away from the Chicago Presidium's territory for now. I'd find an alternate route, or just sit tight until it all passes over. Whatever *it* is."

"No kidding," Mira said. Zoey looked up at her.

"In the 'good news' category," the voice continued, "Kid Cryptic has a target lock on a whole new set of CDs. I know, I know, I always say that, but this time, the trading source seems legit. And hopefully we can get something else to play besides the old school . . . not that there's anything wrong with that. I love me some strings.

"Remember, stay alert, stay alive, do what you gotta do to survive. Kid Cryptic is out."

The signal filled with static as the voice vanished. And then new music floated out from the speakers. Classical again, but older this time, with a very specific rhythm that came in sets of threes.

Holt smiled, recognizing it. "It's a waltz," he said.

"What's a waltz?" Zoey asked.

"It's an old song made for dancing," he said. "It has a certain beat, can you hear it?"

The music pulsed and moved in triplets. Zoey listened.

"One-two-three, one-two-three, one-two-three, hear it?" he asked the little girl. Zoey nodded, smiling and reclining further into Mira's arms.

"My mom was a dancer before she met my dad." Holt hugged his knees into his arms. "She taught me and my sister how to dance the waltz once. We were little, we stood on her feet while she did the steps."

"What's a dance?" Zoey asked immediately.

The question took Holt by surprise. Then he realized if Zoey didn't know music, she definitely wouldn't know what dancing was.

The music continued to churn around them. It had been a long time, maybe years, since he had heard any form of it, and it made Holt smile. The difficulties of the past few days, the pain in his muscles, the exhaustion—they seemed to recede.

Holt grabbed his pack and opened it. He dug through one of the side pockets until he found what he was looking for; then he stood up, held out a hand toward Zoey. "Come here," he said. "I'll show you."

Zoey's smile was huge as she stood up and took Holt's hand.

"Put your feet on top of my feet," he instructed.

"Won't it hurt you?" she asked.

Mira laughed behind them, leaning back on her elbows to watch.

Zoey put her right foot on top of Holt's left boot, then her left on top of his right. Holt handed her one of the things he had pulled from his pack. It was a simple black stone that had been buffed and polished until it was worn smooth and shiny. It fit neatly in Zoey's small hand. Holt held on to another stone that was exactly the same.

"The important thing is to remember which side is your right side," he continued. "Because you always move right to start, and it can get hard to remember when you're thinking about your feet. So if you hold something in your right hand and grip it really tight, you won't forget. Make sense?"

Zoey nodded, put the stone in her right palm and squeezed it.

"Okay, then." Holt took her hands. "Here we go."

He waited a few beats . . . then moved to the right.

"One-two-three, one-two-three," Holt said as he waltzed around the campsite in movements of three, carrying Zoey with him on his feet. Zoey laughed as they moved and turned, circling around the flickering campfire while the music poured from the hissing radio.

As they spun, Holt continued to catch Mira's gaze, watching him. In the dark of the dying fire, he couldn't see the black fingers of the Tone in her eyes, could see only the clear emerald green.

Maybe she was pretty, after all, he thought. This time, his rational side made no attempt to discount the notion.

Holt and Zoey danced to the music for several more rotations around the fire. Then the little girl looked up at him excitedly with her blue eyes.

"Dance with Mira now, Holt!" she exclaimed.

Mira laughed from the other side of the camp. "Holt wouldn't want *that*. I'd break his toes."

Holt looked down at Mira, still perched on her elbows, her red hair trailing gently down her shoulders. He saw the smallest question in her green eyes . . . and he knew he was asking himself the same thing: Did he really want to go there? Doing so was crossing a line, to be sure, a dangerous line for both of them. It would only complicate things. And his life was all about simplicity, keeping things in perspective.

But over the past few days, Holt had found his resolve slipping when it came to her. He was listening less and less to the voice of survival in his head. And right then, as he imagined pulling her close, having her eyes stare into his from just inches away . . . he stopped listening to it altogether.

"What's the matter?" he asked quietly, keeping his stare on her. "Can't keep up?"

The smile on Mira's face gradually sobered, like she was slowly reaching her own decision. Then she stood up and walked toward Holt.

Holt let Zoey off his feet and took the black stone from her. She moved to where Max was chewing on one of the straps of Holt's pack, grabbed the dog's ears, and twisted them gently like motorcycle controls. "Vroom, vroom . . . ," she mimicked. The dog didn't seem to mind.

Mira reached Holt. They stood before each other. He took her right hand, opened it, placed the polished black stone in her palm. Her fingers were soft and cool, like stretched silk.

"What makes you think I need that?" she asked, looking up at him.

"I've seen you run," Holt replied. "Trust me. You need it."

Mira smiled back at him.

Holt took her hands, slowly raised one up to the level of his shoulder, and placed the other one behind his back. He drew Mira close, and felt her press against his chest. She was an impossible combination of soft and firm all at the same time. They looked into each other as their bodies met.

Zoey chuckled from the fire, staring at them.

"What are *you* laughing at, kid?" Holt asked without taking his eyes off Mira. Zoey chuckled louder.

And then Holt and Mira started to move, spinning slowly with the waltz and static that floated out from the radio's tiny speakers. The music swelled around them, building toward its finale. But for Holt, the music became irrelevant. Just an audible guideline for when to move his feet and in what direction. His real focus was on the girl in front of him, her soft hands, the smell of her hair, the way the fire sparkled in her eyes.

Holt and Mira waltzed around the camp, their eyes locked on one another. Everything seemed to recede into the distance around them. The starlight, the flickering flames, the breeze that whispered in the leaves—it all faded slowly to black as they spun, faded until there was nothing but them, dancing in slow motion, the thoughts of Assembly walkers and Forsaken and bounties and death marks and plutonium and Fallout Swarms and everything else that had to do with reality vanished, faded until there was the staticky waltz and them and—

The music ended. And when it did, everything stopped.

Holt and Mira's movement slowed, then ceased altogether. When they were still, they stayed in their positions: close, staring into each other's eyes. A lock of her red hair hung loose on Mira's forehead, and Holt gently pushed it back and tucked it behind her ear. They could feel each other's hearts beating.

Then, from the distance, a sound yanked them both back to reality. Far off, the percussive booming of plasma cannon fire. The muted thumps of the after-explosions. Max, near Zoey, lifted his head up in alarm. The sounds ricocheted quietly off the thin trees, echoing eerily around them all . . . then faded.

Holt looked down at the girl in his arms and once again remembered all that she represented. A reward. His ticket to escaping the Menagerie for good. The ability to go where he wanted without always having to look over his shoulder. A chance for true freedom.

Holt could see similar thoughts playing behind Mira's green eyes.

They were back where they had been: She was his prisoner. He was her captor.

But their hands were slow to leave one another, their eyes lingering. Regardless of what the other wanted to believe, for better or worse, something had changed.

They pulled away from each other as a new orchestral piece began to play. Mira moved back to her sleeping bag while Holt reached down and turned off the radio.

"Let's rest up, we're moving at first light," he said. "We haven't had any sleep in almost a day and a half."

Zoey's face formed a disappointed frown, and she left Max and moved to Mira's sleeping bag. Mira said nothing as the little girl climbed inside, just pulled her close.

Holt climbed into his own bag, heard Max lie down next to him.

The fire was dying, the burning wood had reduced to coals now, glittering orange and red and providing only the dimmest light.

Holt, for his part, was glad for the dark. No one would see him there, his eyes open long after the fire finally died, staring sleeplessly at the stars that filtered in through the treetops above.

24. CUPCAKES

HOLT, MIRA, ZOEY, AND MAX STOOD at the top of a gently sloping hill that rolled down to the river valley below. At the bottom, where the river twisted and sparkled through the grass, something stretched from one side of the water to the other: a floating trading post made of all kinds of boats, rafts, barges, and other river craft that had been tied together into a single structure, and Mira saw a hundred or more kids swarming all over it, moving back and forth, trading supplies and necessities.

Floating trading posts like this one had the advantage of being mobile. They could set up shop in a different location every few days so as to avoid Assembly patrols. The permanent depots (like Faust or Midnight City) couldn't relocate if the aliens came calling, so their only choice was to defend themselves. Fortunately, they rarely had need to.

The four had once again left the trees behind them, and now only the occasional elm and spruce jutted up from the green hills. Holt and Mira stood in the shade of one, leaning against opposite sides of the trunk, while Zoey and Max played together in the tall grass nearby.

Mira stared down at the trading post with a tightness in her chest she hadn't expected. But why shouldn't she? After all, the place represented an end to the group dynamic that had formed ever since the strangers were forced to traverse the Drowning Plains together. A dynamic that, in spite of her better judgment, she had grown to like. It was similar to the sense of belonging she had felt in Midnight City. The coming loss of it bothered her far more than she was comfortable with.

Here, Holt would hand off Zoey to one of the congregations or boats below, and the mysteries surrounding her would be left for someone else to solve. Mira would be bound again, and led around like a trophy. Holt would trade for the supplies he needed for the inevitable march north to Midnight City, where she would be returned to her old faction and slated for execution.

In spite of the facts, her thoughts were divided between the trading post on the river . . . and the waltz from last night. What each represented were polar opposites.

Mira shook the images from her mind. She never should have let that dance happen. But watching Holt put Zoey on his feet and spin her around the fire had all been too much. The feelings that had been building inside her, feelings she had adamantly denied, were stoked to life.

Was she *insane?* There was absolutely no way she was falling for her *captor.* For the bounty hunter who planned to turn her in for a reward, who'd kept her tied up for almost a week. And then there were her . . . other responsibilities. Her other relationships. Had she forgotten them, too?

Mira sighed. Why did it have to be so complicated? Why couldn't Holt have been completely appalling like most everyone else? Why did he have to have that subtle sense of kindness, those annoying heroic impulses? Why did he have to have such strong hands, such a crooked smile?

From nowhere, the Tone swelled up from her subconscious and pushed to the forefront. The whispering, the voices, the static—they all began to press in on her. Mira groaned, gripped the tree for support, fought against the sounds, trying to push them back.

"Are you okay?" Mira barely heard Holt's voice as the incessant, swirling whispers overpowered her. "Mira?"

The static hiss in her mind slowly dissolved, and she managed to push it down to the edge of her awareness, keeping it at bay. She took a long, deep breath, steadying herself. It was over. For now.

"Mira?" Holt asked more firmly. She felt his hand on her arm. When she looked up at him, there was genuine concern in his eyes. But something else, too. Fear, it almost seemed like. An old fear. She wondered, yet again, just whom he had lost. . . .

"I'm fine," she said. "Think I'm getting better at fighting it, like you said. How often will it do that?"

"It's different for everyone," he answered. "But it's usually when you're the weakest, when you're hurt or . . . worried or frightened or

sick. Times like that are when it can get the upper hand. It's always looking for the upper hand."

He was still looking at her with worry, and she almost smiled, felt the
initial tinglings of warmth beginning to spread through her.

Then she saw the rope in his hands, and reality came flooding back.

Mira's stomach knotted. She quickly looked back down to the trading
post on the river. She couldn't believe he was really going to do it. But
here they were, back where they'd started. She felt his silent, uncomfortable gaze.

"My dad told me once how you could tell which things in life were
real," Mira said. Without looking at him, she put her hands behind her,
so that he could tie them. She felt Holt step close.

"And how's that?" Holt asked.

"When you stop believing in them . . . they don't go away. I wonder
which one last night was?"

She kept waiting for the soft rope to circle her hands. Instead, Holt
gently pried open one of her palms and set something in it. Mira couldn't
identify it at first. It was dusty, wrapped in some kind of thin plastic wrap,
and spongy.

There was a slight smile in his voice. "Don't squeeze, you'll crush it."

He didn't try to stop her as she brought the mystery slowly around
from behind her. In her hand were two black cupcakes resting inside
clear plastic packaging. Each was topped with black frosting and a zigzag of white trailed down their centers.

A smile grew on Mira's face. She couldn't believe it. It wasn't just that
he had actually found them . . . it was also that he had remembered.

Hostess CupCakes. Just as she'd described.

Mira turned slowly around and looked at Holt. He stared back. She
didn't know what this gesture meant, but all the same, there was no rope
on her hands yet.

"Where did you find them?" she asked.

"Back in the Drowning Plains, before the Forsaken tried to kill us.
I got more at first, but that was all I could save."

Mira looked at the package in her hands. It had been so long since
she'd seen one, they looked like something out of a fairy tale now. "So . . .
what is this?" Mira looked back up at Holt, searching for a sign of his
intentions. "Final meal for the accused?"

"Is that the tradition?"

"I think so, yeah."

"If it was, it would be pretty pathetic, wouldn't it?" Holt gazed at her with his clear brown eyes, made no move to use the rope. He studied Mira, weighing his thoughts, like he was trying to put words to some foreign concept he'd never expressed before.

"I think," he began, "I held on as long as I could to the way things were, you know? Telling myself the same answers to the same questions. I held on until . . . I don't know, about an hour ago, I guess, when we got here, and I knew we'd made it and things could go back to how they were."

Mira's heart beat loudly in her chest. She was sure even Holt could hear it.

"I realized I just . . . didn't want things to go back to how they were," he said, looking down, embarrassed almost. "Not now. You're . . . a friend. You saved my life, even. And you're not worth sacrificing just to solve my own stupid problems. I'll figure out some other way to deal with them."

At the words, Mira felt hope welling up inside her. "Are you saying . . . you're letting me go?"

Holt was silent a moment, then he just nodded.

When he did, a tidal wave of different emotions washed over Mira. This was more than she ever hoped. It was strange, like waking from a dream to be disappointed it wasn't real. Only in this case, it was the opposite. She was waking from a nightmare to find the reality was far better. Her throat tightened; she felt her eyes glisten. Before Holt could see her cry, she grabbed his neck and pulled him close.

Holt went stiff as she hugged him. She could feel his discomfort, his uncertainty, but she didn't care. She had no idea how much tension and worry she'd been carrying around with her until it was gone.

"Thank you, Holt," she whispered, trying to hold it together. "Thank you."

She felt his arms slowly encircle her, pull her even closer. One on her waist, the other resting on the back of her neck. His fingers stroked her red hair.

"Sorry, I . . . I haven't hugged anyone in a while," he said with a hint of nervousness.

"You're a natural," she said. And it was true. She very much liked being held by Holt; she seemed to fit perfectly in his arms. She let the moment last a little longer, and then pulled away and wiped her eyes quickly.

When she was done, she looked up at him. "I . . . don't know what to say."

"Well," he said, his voice even more nervous now. As he talked, he rushed the words, like he was trying to get all his thoughts out before the moment passed them by. "I was thinking you could come with me. You know, if you wanted, of course. It makes sense, in a way, right? I mean, people are after you, people are after me. I think I'm going southeast, toward the Low Marshes, see if I can't find someplace where no one knows who I am. Maybe that place is there for you, too."

A mass of feelings rose up in her, most of them very pleasant. "That sounds amazing . . . ," she automatically said, without thinking. And it did. But it took the time for a smile to form on Holt's face before she realized what she had almost done. "But . . . I *can't* do that, Holt."

God, she'd almost said yes! Almost threw away everything she'd worked for. Had she lost her mind? Mira watched the newly formed smile on Holt's face dissolve, and instantly hated herself for giving in to her gut reaction. Holt had just made an incredible gesture, and she'd thrown it right back at him.

"It's not that I don't want to," she continued quickly. "I'd . . . love to. It's just I have things to fix in Midnight City."

Holt looked puzzled. "But Midnight City is where you're wanted. You're going *back* there?"

"On my own terms, yes. I still have things to make right. And I left someone there, someone important, and I have to help him."

Holt shuffled on his feet. "Him?"

Mira shut her eyes a moment. Why had she said that? Did she have to divulge every little piece of information? Did she have to keep on ruining the moment? Then again . . . wasn't it the truth? Didn't Holt deserve to know, after everything he was giving up for *her*?

"His name is Ben," Mira said. "He was framed for the same thing I was, and when I had the chance to escape, it meant leaving him. They'll kill him in my place unless I go back."

"And the plutonium," Holt said. "It's for what? Trading for his life?"

Mira nodded. "More or less."

"I see," Holt said, remaining quiet. "Well, it's probably best, anyway. It's . . . harder for two people to survive than one. Besides, who knows, maybe we'll see each other again."

In that statement, Mira saw some of the walls Holt had knocked down over the last few days suddenly rebuild themselves. It hurt her. But what else could she do?

"Holt . . . ," she began gently.

Another voice cut her off before she could finish. Zoey's voice, soft and young and incapable of grasping the emotional subtleties being displayed by the two older kids in front of her.

"I want to go to Midnight City too!" the little girl said, walking up with Max following behind.

"Maybe Mira will take you with her," Holt said, "if you ask her nicely. But Max and I are headed in a different direction now."

"But . . . you and the Max have to go." Zoey's face collapsed with disappointment. "It's how it's supposed to be."

"Listen, kiddo," Holt kneeled down to her. "It's been great traveling with you, and you've become a real friend, but Max and I have things we need to do."

"But I need you to come," Zoey said.

"I promise, you don't," Holt replied. "You're gonna be okay. Had my doubts at first, but you're a survivor, I can tell."

"I *need* you to come, Holt," Zoey pressed. "Please come, you *have* to." Mira watched the little girl clutch Holt's shirt in her hands, saw her eyes begin to tear up. Mira shook her head. How did you say no to that?

Holt sighed, clearly thinking the same thing. "We'll . . . see how things shape up, okay? Maybe we can keep traveling together until you have to turn north. No promises, though, all right?"

Zoey smiled, let Holt's shirt free. "All right, Holt."

Holt looked back up at Mira. "You going to eat those or what?"

Mira realized she was still holding the CupCakes. She looked down at the dusty packages.

"Are you . . . sure they're edible?" she asked skeptically.

"Like I said, those things could outlast a nuclear winter. I'm not even sure they're technically food."

Mira laughed, and gingerly pried open the package. Then she closed her eyes as long-dormant parts of her memory recognized the scent of chocolate and moist cake that wafted up into the air. She remembered eating Hostess CupCakes in church. Her dad would slip them to her, out of sight, and she would eat them and giggle while her mom studied them both disapprovingly. But her dad always brought them, always passed them to her.

The memory wasn't something she expected: she hadn't thought of it in years. She stared down at the open package with an almost haunted look.

"Everything okay?" Holt asked.

Mira nodded. "They just . . . they just smell really good, is all. Share?"

Mira took a CupCake out of the pack, handed it to Holt. Then she broke her own CupCake in half, exposing the white creamy center, and handed a piece down to Zoey.

Mira took an experimental taste of her half. She wasn't sure how it was possible, but it tasted just as moist as she remembered, the chocolate sweet and bitter at the same time. Either her memories of the CupCakes had faded enough that she didn't notice how stale it was, or whoever had made these things put some really impressive preservatives in them. Either way, she was happy. She wasn't sure anything had ever tasted so good.

Mira stuffed the rest of it in her mouth. Below her, Zoey laughed, did the same thing, getting chocolate all over her face, smiling as she chewed.

Holt took a bite of his . . . and then stopped as Max whined next to him. The dog stared up at the CupCake in Holt's hand, his tail beating the ground.

"Fine, sure," Holt said. He tossed the rest of the cake down to Max, who caught it in his mouth and swallowed it one giant snap.

Holt looked back at Mira. For her, the look was uncomfortable . . . and frustrating. She'd gotten everything she'd hoped for. She had the plutonium, she was no longer a prisoner, she was free to go where she wanted, and she could enact the plans she'd been making for months. So, with all that accounted for . . . why did it feel so empty? Why was this look between her and Holt laced with sadness?

She knew the answer. It was the same fear she had felt a minute ago, only now it had transformed. Everything was still going back to how it was, and this brief sidestep in her life was still nearing its end.

Below them came shouts from the trading post.

Mira and Holt looked down the hill and saw a group of kids leaving the structure of boats and vessels on the river and walking through the grass toward them. They'd finally been spotted.

"Welcoming party, I guess," Holt said. He shouldered his pack and started down the hill. Max bounded after him.

Mira followed Holt with her eyes as he descended. The moment was officially over. Different paths that could have been taken had been passed by. But what else was there to do? Obligations could be a heavy thing, Mira thought.

She took Zoey's hand and followed Holt down the hill.

25. DOMINOES

HOLT AND MAX, Mira and Zoey walked down the hill. Ahead of them, the sun had begun its final descent. Even now, the light was growing softer. Warily, Holt watched the kids below moving toward them. Even though it was just a trading post, they could still be dangerous. It was a dangerous world, after all.

When they reached the bottom of the hill, they were close enough to the river to hear bubbling as it flowed peacefully past. Five kids stood protectively between them and the trading post. Holt could see four more behind them, waiting at the entrance in case they were needed.

The group in front of them was made up of four boys (between thirteen and sixteen years old, Holt guessed) and one girl, petite and short, with a pocket vest full of items and a sextant hanging from her belt. She looked younger than the boys, but in spite of her age, she radiated confidence and cunning, and Holt could tell she was sizing them all up. Even before the girl stepped forward, Holt figured she would turn out to be the Trade Master.

In Holt's experience, most River Rat boats navigated up and down a particular river, flowing with the current downstream during the fall and winter, trading for the fuel and supplies they would need to power back upstream during the spring and summer. The riverboat crews, though they were young, had become expert salvagers and traders, and often set up trading posts like this one.

Because the floating trading posts comprised many different ships all tied together, it meant that they were manned by many different crews at once. When the ships decided to set up shop, a Trade Master was selected from all the ships' Honchos (the River Rat term for "captain") to run the operations for the post.

"My name's Stephanie Freed," the tiny girl said, calmly studying them each in turn. Her eyes were beginning to show the first traces of the Tone's black tendrils. "I'm the Trade Master. How do you come?"

"With peace and profit," Holt answered in the customary way.

Zoey peeked out from behind Mira's torso, watching the kids. They didn't seem to notice her. Their attention was squarely fixed on Holt.

The boys were all armed. One had a metal pipe, two others had slingshots (nothing to laugh at—Holt had seen kids take out birds from a hundred yards with slings), and the fourth, a kid with a shaved head, held what looked like a fistful of dimes.

Holt frowned. Coins from the Strange Lands, no doubt. Or at least the bald kid wanted him to think they were. He had no intention of finding out. Artifact coins were dangerous, and he didn't need Mira to tell him so: he'd seen them used as weapons lots of times. These kids meant business. Holt smiled—he liked them already.

"Saw you from the hill. Just here to trade, that's all," Holt said.

"You're welcome to trade, no problem," Stephanie answered evenly. "But you'll have to leave the boom-sticks outside. No outside weapons are allowed on the post. Unless you mean to trade them? I know a lot of crews are looking for working guns, mine included. Getting harder to find."

Holt shook his head. "I don't trade my guns. They're too dangerous if you haven't been taught to use them, and I don't have time to teach anyone."

"Then leave them there, no one will bother them," the girl said.

With hesitation, Holt removed his rifle, shotgun, and pistol. He never liked being without his weapons; he felt naked almost, defenseless. But all the river trading posts had the same rule, even if the more dangerous depots like Faust had no problems with guns. Holt had traded many times at the river posts, left his guns, and always gotten them back.

When Stephanie saw the weapons were on the ground, she nodded. "Welcome to our decks. Trade nicely." She smiled and motioned them forward, then turned and headed back toward the giant collection of boats with the others. Holt and company followed after them.

As they did, they rounded a grove of trees, and something else was revealed behind them, tied off near the trade depot. A ship bigger than any of the watercraft on the river, only this one sat on dry land.

"Wow!" Zoey exclaimed as she got a clear look. "Look at it, it's huge!"

"It sure is, honey," Mira said with a surprised smile. "It's a Landship."

Landships were massive land craft, like boats on dry land, assembled from a variety of parts and structures and carried by huge wheels across the ground. Giant sails propelled them, and they could house two dozen kids (sometimes more). Toward the west, where the plains gave way to the deserts and flatlands of the Barren, Landships were common sights.

Holt had seen a few in his time, and he never failed to be impressed by the colossal vehicles. They were a testament to the ingenuity and imagination of Earth's survivors, misplaced though they might be.

"Must have stopped to trade at the depot," he mused as they walked.

"It's pretty far east, though," Mira replied, looking at it oddly.

She was right. Their crews generally comprised merchants and traders, and they rarely went farther east than Midnight City. It was rare seeing one this far away, and Holt wondered what it was doing out here.

Holt studied it closer. It had eight giant wheels, four on each side, two pairs of which he guessed came from either a giant construction vehicle or farm machine from the World Before. The middle wheels were custom constructions of wood and steel, meticulously fashioned and shaped. They were about ten feet tall by themselves, and held the decks of the Landship probably twenty-five to thirty feet off the ground.

Its decks had been assembled from a variety of repurposed wood and sheet metal, as well as train and boat parts. Two of its masts were formed out of polished and smoothed airplane wings, big ones, maybe even from an airliner.

The whole thing was a hodgepodge of parts, all with different origins and looks, but somehow, it all blended together into a giant, beautiful, cohesive craft that was as much a work of art as a vehicle.

"The depot's big, too!" Zoey said as she saw it.

Zoey's exclamation pulled both Mira's and Holt's attention back to the trading post on the river.

Holt nodded. "Yep. Stretches from one edge of the river to the next. It's not just a trading post, it's a crossing point for anyone who needs it. Long as you can pay the toll."

The closer they got to it, the more detail they could make out as the sun continued to sink above them. Kids of all ages and looks were traversing it, moving from boat to boat in a crowd.

It was made of more than a dozen different boats and vessels of varying sizes. River barges, fishing boats, a rusting tugboat, but most of the craft seemed to be made of pieces and sections from a whole host of other ships. The first one they stepped onto from the riverbank, for example, was made from what was once a huge, floating pier and the roof of a house, lined with floats under it. Where these kids got the roof of a house, Holt didn't know, but he guessed it was the result of some flood after the invasion. The boat crew had made a variety of ramshackle huts all around the repurposed pier, and Holt saw a bed through the attic window of the old roof, probably the Honcho's quarters.

Each vessel had set up trading areas, with all kinds of goods: clean water, nonperishable food, candy, first aid supplies, radios, knives, mechanical watches, maps, cable and rope, tools, clothing (both vintage and newly made), bags and packs, the occasional gun, and, of course, Strange Lands artifacts. Not so many as you would find in Midnight City, but still a good amount.

And the boats were swarming with kids, survivors of all ages (though none older than twenty) at various stages of the Tone's effects. They pushed through the crowd with effort, and at one point, Holt had to take Zoey onto his shoulders and hold Mira's hand, pulling her along, for fear they would get tossed overboard. Honestly, he wasn't worried about Mira, but he wasn't above taking the opportunity to feel her fingers one last time.

The center boat of a trading post was usually the most sturdy, since it anchored the entire structure. In this case, it was a large, heavy tugboat that a group of enterprising kids had gotten back up and running. The name DELIRIUM was painted on its side in crude letters.

The *Delirium* had several trading stalls along its decks, with all kinds of goods. Holt and Mira separated as they walked through them. Mira gravitated toward the Strange Lands artifacts, Holt noticed, the stalls which contained the bright δ symbols, no doubt hoping to replenish all the items she had used in the past few days. Holt was more concerned with basics. The reward he got in Midnight City would have funded his entire trip east, and given him enough of a jump start to live comfortably. Now he'd have to be frugal. If he was going to make it to the Low Marshes, he'd need water and food, not to mention swamp survival gear. He'd likely end up walking the whole way now, and he wanted to be ready.

Zoey had followed him instead of Mira for some reason, Holt noticed. He didn't like it. He was uncomfortable with the little girl's presence now, given that he had no intention of accompanying her to Midnight City. He was hoping Mira would volunteer to take her on, and he could slip away one night before she (and Mira) noticed. It would be the easiest solution. He'd grown fond of the little girl. Almost as much as he had of Mira. But he had to head east, had to get away from the Menagerie. His options had run out.

The *Delirium* had plenty of items he could use, Holt noticed as he studied the trading stalls. Nonperishables and water being the most obvious, but they also had a water purification kit and sunblock.

One of the *Delirium*'s traders stood up as he approached, a boy of fifteen, Holt guessed from the amount of black in his eyes. "Looking to trade?" he asked.

"I am," Holt replied.

"Well, we're kind of done here," the kid said dismissively. He had on a denim shirt covered in patches of all kinds of colorful fabric. "Trading post's been running three days, we're pretty much set. Unless you got something special, not sure we're gonna be interested."

"Define special," Holt said.

"Working guns, nails and screws, fuel, pharmaceuticals, radios— that's pretty much it," the kid said.

With each item, Holt kicked himself mentally. If he hadn't lost the blue bag back in the Drowning Plains, he would have all he needed to trade these kids out of their underwear. But he'd lost it. He had nothing the *Delirium* wanted.

From behind him, Zoey whispered, "Tell them you have dominoes."

Holt glanced behind him at Zoey, gave her a confused look. "How did you know I had—?" Holt began, then stopped himself. He was starting to think it was better not to know.

"Just tell them," Zoey said. The girl's eyes were locked on the boy running the trading stall, in that strangely intense way she focused on things.

Holt frowned, turned back to the boy. "We . . . have dominoes," he said without much hope.

The boy's only reaction was a slight raise of his eyebrow, but Holt noticed it nonetheless. Even if he hadn't, the four closest kids of the *Delirium*'s crew perked up like dogs being shown their favorite toy. One of them, a blond kid who wore glasses without any lenses, turned and looked at the head trader almost pleadingly.

He ignored the kid, looking from Holt, to Zoey behind his legs, then back to Holt. "We've been trying to assemble a full set for a whole year. We only need six more."

"I have a full set myself," Holt said. And he did. He'd found it buried in the ruins of what had been the St. Louis suburbs. "You're welcome to whatever pieces you need." Zoey had been right: he had them now, and they all knew it.

"I'm Russ," the boy said. "How'd you know we needed dominoes?" It wasn't a question for Holt; it was for Zoey. "I saw you tell him. It was your idea, wasn't it?"

Zoey shrugged. "I don't know how I know . . . I just know," she said.

"Sounds like a Strange Lands artifact to me," Russ guessed. "But whatever. Let's have a look at what you got."

Holt dropped his pack, started undoing the clasps. As he did, he took a closer look at the boat. There were huts and tents set up all along its rear decks. Three of them were open . . . and one was zipped shut.

In the fading light, Holt saw the glow of a flashlight inside it, moving back and forth. Someone was there. He wondered why they weren't out with the others.

"What are you looking to trade for?" Russ asked, watching him impatiently.

"Three or four nonperishables would be nice, and so would one of those water purifiers," Holt said. He saw Russ's eyebrows rise again but pushed on before the trader could object. "And the sunblock. A full canister, not a used one."

"Four nonperishables is way more than those dominoes are worth," he said. "I can't trade for the water purifier and sunblock, too."

"The way your boys got their hackles raised when I mentioned them says you can," Holt said evenly.

Russ glared at the blond kid with the empty frames. He looked away quickly.

"A couple bags of jerky," the head trader said, not pleased. "And that's it for nonperishables."

"What about bullets? Any bullets you've found here and there?"

"Get the bucket," the trader said. One of the kids disappeared around the side of the tug's rusted bridge. When he came back, he was holding a big, aging plastic bucket full of ammo. Bullets and shells of all kinds. "You can have any of that you want, getting harder to trade for, it's just dead weight."

"I bet." Holt eyed the bucket greedily. It was more ammo than he'd seen in a long time. "Getting tougher to find working guns, most people don't take care of them right."

"Or they switched to refurbished Assembly guns," Russ said.

It was true. He had shot one or two of the plasma cannon some of the more industrious kids had managed to strip off fallen Assembly walkers. They were powerful, but you lost a lot of accuracy. He'd stick with his guns until they fell apart, thank you very much.

Holt handed over the domino case . . . and the kids descended on it like happy little vultures. Holt dug through the ammo bucket, looking for calibers he could use.

Behind him, Mira was still trading for artifacts. With the ammo bucket holding his attention, Holt didn't notice Zoey move away from the group and start walking toward the one lone, sealed tent. . . .

26. BE FREE

SHE HAD CHOSEN HER MOMENT TO WALK OFF, waited until they were all absorbed in the trading.

Zoey didn't know what attracted her to the tent. Like everything that had to do with the "feelings," Zoey was simply pulled toward it. There was a certainty in her mind that there was something there for her, and ignoring it wasn't an option.

Sometimes Zoey felt like a boat in a current, being carried this way and that. She let herself be pulled and pushed, and sometimes it was scary. But she had a sense it was important to let it take her where it wanted. So she did.

Zoey reached the tent. It was zippered shut. The flashlight was still on inside, wavering back and forth. Zoey heard breathing and what she was sure was someone gently crying. She reached for the zipper near the ground and pulled it straight up, opening the tent.

Inside were two kids, both older than the others outside, approaching their twenties.

One was a girl. She was kneeling over the other figure, a boy. Her eyes were red with tears. When Zoey opened the tent, the girl's hand was resting on the boy's chest like she was feeling his breath.

The boy was on his back on the floor, unmoving, as if he were sick. But he wasn't sick, Zoey knew. She noted that his hands and feet were bound, tied with rope. And most tellingly . . . his eyes were solid black. They stared sightlessly upward, never blinking.

The Tone had taken him.

"Who are you?" the girl asked Zoey, her voice shaking with surprise. "You shouldn't be here."

The boy was blank to Zoey: she couldn't read or sense anything from him. It was the Tone, she somehow knew. Once it took someone, they were inaccessible to her.

But, the girl . . .

Zoey felt the girl's emotions wash over her, a rich mix of pain and sadness and anger and . . . fear. Of being found, Zoey sensed. She'd been hiding. Keeping the boy out of sight from Holt and Mira and herself. Obviously feeling they wouldn't understand. Her name was Elizabeth, Zoey sensed.

Elizabeth read the thoughts in Zoey's eyes. "It's . . . You don't understand," she stammered, eyes welling with tears again. "I just want to go with him. He's my best friend. I just want to wait until it takes me, too—then we can go together. So . . . we tied him. That's all . . ."

Zoey saw her eyes now, the Tone spreading through them like masses of black veins. She wouldn't have long to wait.

"Please," Elizabeth said. "Please don't tell your friends. Please don't—"

"Elizabeth," Zoey said quietly. The older girl stopped talking, staring at Zoey. "I understand. You haven't done anything wrong."

Zoey stepped into the tent and knelt down at the boy's side. Not because Zoey wanted to, but because she was compelled to. There was something here for her, she just had no idea what. Elizabeth didn't try and stop her.

Zoey's heart beat heavy in her chest, thumping in her ears. Her hands shook. Pressure built in her head, behind her eyes. Her vision blurred. Time seemed to slow. There was something *here* for her. *What am I supposed to do?*

Surrender, the answer came.

Zoey closed her eyes, let the current take her where it would.

The world receded. She felt her hands rise, one resting on the boy's chest, one covering Elizabeth's hands. But she wasn't sure it was really her moving them. From far off, as the world started to go white, and everything dissolved away, she could barely hear Elizabeth's voice say, "I'm scared. . . ."

And then it happened.

Be free. The words filled Zoey's mind . . . and everything went white.

———

THE SUN WAS SETTING on the other side of the river, and Holt was still sorting through the ammo bucket. The kids had brought him the nonperishables (mostly jerky), the sunblock, and the water purifier. He was digging out the last of the 12-gauge shotgun shells from the bucket when a scream ripped the air.

His head snapped up at the sound, eyes coming to rest on the closed tent he'd seen earlier.

Only it wasn't closed anymore. It was open. And every kid on the *Delirium* was running toward it.

Then he noticed something genuinely alarming. Zoey was nowhere to be seen.

Instinctively, he looked up at Mira at the other end of the deck, trading for artifacts. She gave him a questioning glance.

Holt cursed under his breath. He'd totally forgotten about Zoey in his excitement over the ammo. He was on his feet instantly, moving for the tent. Had the little girl done something? What *could* she do? She was eight years old at most.

Holt made it to the tent in a few strides. There was a commotion inside, the kids of the *Delirium* packed around the entrance. More were on their way, he saw, from the other boats of the trading post. An older girl pushed out of the tent excitedly, and while she was definitely upset, she wasn't angry or frightened. To Holt she seemed . . . ecstatic.

Among everyone, he saw Stephanie, the Trade Master, shoving to the head of the surging crowd.

"There was a flash and then it was gone!" the girl yelled at Stephanie and the others. "I watched it dissolve from his eyes! Look at *my* eyes!" She pointed at them, and there were gasps from the kids surrounding the tent.

"That can't be," Stephanie said, not bothering to hide her astonishment. "It just can't."

"It is!" the older girl insisted. "Look at Jim! *Look* at him!"

"What's going on?" Holt asked. He could feel Mira moving for him at the other end of the boat, but she was still far away.

The others spun around, staring at Holt. It was Stephanie who spoke up. "Jim was one of ours, the Tone took him three days ago," she began. "Elizabeth convinced us to hold him until it took her, too, so they could go to the Presidium together. They were hiding in the tent—we didn't want anyone to see."

Holt understood. Some people got real tense around the Succumbed, not seeing much of a difference between them and the Assembly. They were under alien control, after all.

"So, you're keeping him here," Holt replied. He tried to peer past the kids into the tent, but they were crammed too tightly around it. "It's not smart, but it's none of my business. Where's Zoey?"

"That's just it," Stephanie said. "Elizabeth claims your friend Zoey . . . *cured* her and Jim of the Tone."

It took a moment for that statement to fully and completely connect in Holt's mind. Then the weight of it hit him: Cured . . . *the Tone?*

"That's not possible," he managed to say. But something told Holt that it was more than possible. And that if it was, Zoey would be the one who could do it.

"That's what *I'm* saying," Stephanie replied. She nodded to Elizabeth. "But here we are. Elizabeth's eyes were almost solid black yesterday." Stephanie turned back to the tent, "Move out of the way," she ordered. "Let us inside. Move!"

The crowd parted for her, allowing a view inside the tent, and Stephanie gasped.

Zoey sat at the far end. When Holt managed to see inside, her eyes were already on him. But that wasn't what had stunned Stephanie and the others. It was the older boy, who was now sitting up on his sleeping bag, his head in his hands.

"Jim!" Stephanie exclaimed. The boy looked up at her, groggily. Looked up at her with his *perfectly clear* eyes. Holt was stunned at the sight. The world stopped as the reality hit him.

It was just as the girl had said. The Tone's effect was gone. Somehow . . . Zoey had reversed it.

"How'd you do it?" Stephanie asked, her gaze moving from Jim to Zoey.

"I don't know," was all Zoey said.

The kids stared at her. They were speechless. But only for a second. Then they started clamoring for Zoey's attention, begging her to do the same for them. To cure them.

They pushed forward almost as one, like a mad, desperate wave.

They weren't children anymore; they were something less. Something scary. They sensed survival, right in that tent, and they wanted it for themselves.

For the first time since they had met—a time that had seen Zoey crash-land in a spacecraft, on the run from various Assembly factions, and barely avoiding plasma cannon fire and death—Holt saw terror in the little girl's eyes.

"Holt!" Zoey cried as the others grabbed and pulled at her.

He lunged forward, grabbed Zoey, and hoisted her up with one fluid motion onto his shoulders. The little girl held on, arms wrapped around his neck as Holt forced his way out of the tent and moved quickly for the riverbank.

The kids followed after him desperately, dozens of them, from all different crews and origins. "Wait! *Wait!*" they shouted.

"She can save us!"

"We'll trade anything!"

"Just have her help us!"

"Please!"

They tried to stop Holt, to pull him down, to yank Zoey from his back.

"Get off!" Holt yelled. It didn't matter. They kept coming, incensed now. How was he going to get out of this? He looked around, saw Mira was already headed for the nearest exit. It was the smart thing to do; she could meet up with them back on dry land. Assuming they made it—the crowd was growing bigger and bigger, and soon everyone in the trading post would be trying to bring them down. What was he going to—?

From the near distance came an awful sound.

A powerful, distorted bellowing, like eerie, electronic whale song, but much more menacing. It was incredibly loud, echoing across the river valley, back and forth. Seconds later, another bellowing answered it, from a different direction.

Everyone stopped, even Holt, Zoey still on his back. They all looked around blindly. But there was nothing to see in the fading light or in the trees flanking the river.

Holt had heard those sounds before. He imagined many of these survivors had. And he knew what they meant: big, scary trouble.

"They're here," Zoey whispered into his ear.

The sounds came again . . . moaning on the other side of the river. The trees along the bank shook as something massive pushed through them, toppling them as if they were twigs, with huge footfalls and the violent splitting of wood.

Trees tumbled over into the river as two red Spider walkers walked powerfully into view on top of them. And the blood of everyone on the trading post went to ice.

Spiders were the larger of the Assembly's two main walkers (though the green and orange tripods they had encountered in the Drowning Plains suggested there might be other types). Spiders were thirty feet tall and wider than a city street. Agile, fast, powerful, and carrying enough firepower to decimate anything that challenged them. They got their name from the eight large, mechanized legs that held their huge fuselages far above the ground. The combination granted them superior mobility and made them the most feared sight on the planet.

And here were two. . . .

The traders and boat crews stared in stunned silence, and Holt knew that look well. He'd had it just a few days ago. These kids had never seen *red* Assembly before.

"What. In. Hell . . . ," Stephanie, the Trade Master, whispered in awe next to him. Her eyes, like everyone else's, were glued in place on the red Spiders.

When the huge walkers saw the trading post, they sounded their awful moans again, one time each . . . and opened fire.

Their plasma cannons whirred to life, screaming as they flung a thick cloud of yellow bolts toward the trading post. The plasma fire burned the air all around them, slamming into everything, spraying sparks and flame and debris.

A boat at the far end of the post exploded in a shower of fire, and Holt saw the kids on its deck thrown like rag dolls into the sky by the blast.

Screams ripped the air, and the crowd that had surrounded Holt before broke apart in panic, running every direction at once.

"Get to your boats!" Stephanie yelled as more plasma fire shredded the air around them. "Dissolve the post, man your defenses!"

Holt looked for Max, saw him a dozen feet away. He whistled two short notes, and Max barked, lunging forward through the crowd, heading back the way they had come.

Holt quickly ran after him.

Behind them, the Spider walkers bellowed as they fired, stepped into the river, and moved toward the conglomeration of boats, their footfalls rocking the ground like thunder. More concussions shook the water.

Holt pushed through the seething crowd as fast as he could. In its own way, it was even harder than before. It was chaos, with kids running everywhere, slamming into him from different directions all at once. It would have been hard enough to balance without Zoey holding on tightly to his neck.

Ahead of him, blending in and out of the crowd, he saw Mira, only a few people ahead. She was having the same problems he was.

"Mira!" he shouted, trying to yell over the plasma fire, explosions, and screams. She heard him and spun, wide eyed, finding him with her gaze.

And then the boat next to him detonated hard, spraying metallic debris and fire in a wicked arc all around him. It blew him to the deck of the barge he was trying to cross.

Holt grabbed Zoey, held her head down as more plasma fire burned past, sizzling as it slapped into three traders above them, blowing them into the water.

Holt peered over the edge of the barge. The Spider walkers were about to reach the trading post, and he could see panels sliding down on either side of their bodies, watched as missile batteries glistening with silver warheads protruded out. Apparently, these reds meant business.

"I'm a lot of trouble, aren't I?" Zoey asked under him.

Holt looked down at her. "Kid, trouble ain't the word."

THE RED WALKERS WERE ALMOST on top of the trading post, their huge cannon firing as they advanced. Another boat exploded, launching upward into the air as its fuel ignited.

Mira ran through the panicked crowd, leaping from boat to boat, trying to get to where she'd last seen Holt and Zoey before the blast. Behind her, she caught a glimpse of a gray blue blur. Max had found her and was following.

Half the traders and boat crews rushed to separate the trading post into its different vessels. The other half was readying their defenses. Some boats had guns, others prepped water cannons repurposed from firefighting ships, and a few even had primitive cannons that fired large, welded-together pieces of scrap metal. Most of it, Mira knew, wouldn't do much of anything against the massive red assault walkers. The traders were used to fighting Mantises or warding off Vultures, not engaging in open combat with Spiders.

Mira leapt onto the barge where she'd last seen Holt and Zoey . . . and barely avoided landing on them where they'd taken cover on a spool of thick rope. A few seconds later, so did Max, barking wildly.

With alarm, Mira ducked down and looked to where Zoey rested underneath Holt.

"Is she okay?" she asked with concern.

"*We're* fine," he said pointedly. She gave him an annoyed look.

Another explosion, more plasma bolts burning through the air. At the other end of the trading post, the boats had begun to detach from one another. The entire structure started to list as the current caught it.

"I think I brought them," Zoey said. Holt and Mira looked at her, heard the shakiness in her voice. "I think they found me when I . . . did what I did." She looked up at them both with genuine fear.

"Well. Okay," Holt said, peering over the edge of the barge. They watched one of the boats fire a cannonful of rusted scrap metal at the nearest walker. The projectile bounced off the red Spider's armor without making a dent. "I'd say that's an important realization, wouldn't you? Kind of a 'note to self' type thing. Right?"

"Right." Zoey nodded.

Another blast, a plume of fire shot into the sky. More bellowing from the walkers.

"We'll figure it out later," Mira said, taking Zoey's hand. "Right now, we need to make ourselves scarce."

Holt got to his feet and surveyed what was left of the trading post.

More and more boats were detaching, gunning their engines, and retreating downstream as fast as they could. Good for them, not so good for Mira and Holt. The remainder of the post was starting to spin, no longer connected to the riverbanks, and the current was carrying it away. If they didn't get off quick, they'd have to swim for it.

A rapid-fire hissing as one of the walkers launched a volley of missiles. They whizzed through the air, homing in on two of the retreating boats, and slammed home. More concussions as the vessels ignited, careened out of control, and crashed into each other.

They didn't waste any more time.

Mira pulled Zoey after them, and they all leapt from boat to boat as fast as they could, trying to make it to dry land. But they had a long way to go. More plasma fire ripped the air; trader kids ran everywhere in a panic, hurriedly undoing the ropes and clasps that kept their individual boats tethered to one another.

But it was too late.

The huge walkers reached what remained of the trading post at the same time. One of them raised its front two legs, emitted a deafening, angry sound that rent the air and stabbed downward. The powerful legs impaled straight through the old tugboat like it was made of paper. A pillar of flame shot upward; the hull of the metal ship split in half, spraying metal and bolts everywhere. Mira watched its crew leap off it as it burned, barely making it into the river before a secondary explosion consumed what was left of the ship.

The other boats were beginning to break off from the rest now, including the modified fishing boat they were on.

"Hurry!" Holt yelled, double-timing it for the edge of the last craft. He leapt off onto the solid ground, and the others followed, one at a time, hurriedly trying to—

One of the red Spiders bellowed in distorted fury. Holt and Mira spun around, looked back to where the walkers were, and saw one of them was staring with its huge three-optic eye right at them. Or, more specifically . . . *right at Zoey*.

"Oh no . . . ," Mira whispered to herself.

The giant walker moved for them, its legs spraying plumes of river water into the air as it walked. The second Spider turned, followed the gaze of its comrade, and moaned powerfully in response as its eye found Zoey, too. It marched after the first.

A hatch opened underneath the walker's body. Mira could see something spinning there, growing, moving downward. A metallic claw.

"No!" she shouted, pulling Zoey to her protectively.

And then the red Spider walker shuddered as it was hit by a stream of plasma fire.

Five blue and white Raptors roared over, cannon firing at the red walkers. The second Spider wailed angrily and unleashed a massive spray of plasma cannon fire at the Raptors.

One of them took a hit, sparked, twisted, burst in flames, and crashed into the trees on the other side of the river.

More engine sounds reverberated in the near distance. Mira looked up in time to see three blue and white Osprey dropships bank hard and slow to a hover over the river. Dangling underneath them were more walkers.

They detached from the Ospreys, dropped to the ground, and powered up immediately, flashing colors and humming as their systems came online.

Eight Mantis walkers and a Spider.

The Ospreys' engines roared loudly as they dusted off, powering straight up into the sky.

The new blue and white walkers turned their attention on the two red Spiders . . . and opened fire. Yellow plasma bolts screamed outward in a giant volley, slapping and sparking into the red walkers.

They bellowed in anger, the sound echoing up and down the valley as they turned to face the new threat.

Missiles flared from each of their batteries, roaring through the air like huge, angry bees. Blasts rocked the ground all around the blue and white walkers, already separating into smaller groups.

Plasma fire flew from both sides, screaming everywhere through the air, hissing and burning.

The flight of blue and white raptors roared by above . . . and they were now being chased by an equal number of red gunships that had appeared from nowhere, their cannons firing at the blue and whites.

Mira stared at Holt as she covered Zoey on the ground. He stared back, just as dumbstruck.

What was left of the trading post boats were speeding away downstream. Most of them were burning or damaged, but they were escaping. The red Spiders had forgotten all about them: they had bigger problems now.

Mira and Holt quickly studied the landscape. Everything was open country beyond the river; they would easily be picked off once the two sides finished blowing each other to pieces behind them. They needed another option, they needed something that—

Mira saw the huge Landship from before, still docked nearby. She saw the crew frantically scrambling over the top deck, but even so, it wasn't moving. Its sails hung limp in their masts, in spite of the breeze blowing around them.

Mira couldn't figure why they would wait so long, but she'd never been one to second-guess good luck.

"Holt!" Mira yelled as she pulled Zoey up after her and dashed forward. Holt saw where they were headed, and he didn't look too thrilled about it. The explosions that rocked the ground nearby got him and Max following regardless.

The battle raged behind them. Raptors fought in the sky, disintegrating into flames and showers of sparks. The huge Spiders fired nonstop, spraying plasma, launching missiles. And the blue and whites kept up the offensive, trying to surround the reds.

As Mira ran toward the Landship, she could make out more detail of the huge vessel. It was beautiful. In any other situation, she would have gazed up at the craft in awe. But the gunships flashing by above kind of killed the impulse.

"Hey!" Mira yelled up to the decks. *"Hey!"*

A few heads peeked over the edge and peered down at her, but then just as quickly vanished. The crew was much more concerned with es-caping than they were with listening. Mira didn't blame them. More blasts flared along the river.

"This isn't going to happen," Holt said, looking around them at the battle nervously. "Let's just go. If we get enough of a head start—"

Mira ignored him and yelled back up at the ship. "Something wrong with your Chinook? Maybe I can help!" It was a long shot, but it was possible the reason the Landship hadn't set full sail out of this place yet was because something was wrong with its main artifact.

Wind power alone just wasn't enough to move the ridiculously huge craft. Something more powerful was needed, which was why Landship crews used Strange Lands artifacts called Chinooks to enhance the power of normal wind, increasing it enough to move them. Mira had made a few Chinooks in her time—they were difficult to assemble correctly, but they always sold for a large profit.

More heads peeked over, then quickly scattered as another presence pushed to the front: a boy, probably somewhere around eighteen or nineteen, with an assuredness beyond his years and an obvious, cocky smile. Dark hair was layered back in textured waves on his head, and even from this distance, Mira could tell he was ruggedly handsome. He wore a black shirt tucked into black cargo pants, and a gun belt around his waist. As he gazed down at them, he placed a silver-tipped boot on top of the railing that circled the deck, and leaned casually on his knee.

"Say you're right," the boy said. "Say our Chinook is out. Say one of my lame-brained artifact handlers traded for a faulty component, and now we're stuck while the Assembly blows themselves to bits a couple yards away. How do *you* propose to help? Beautiful women are the world's greatest commodity, but right now, I really need someone with artifact experience."

Mira blushed in spite of the battle raging around them, and she saw Holt glare up at the Captain. "Oh, please . . . ," he said under his breath.

"I'm a Freebooter!" Mira shouted up at the captain. "I have artifacts with me, probably the right ones to fill your sails again. How's that sound?"

The captain studied her in a different way now. "Well. Beautiful *and* industrious. This could turn into a profit, after all."

More explosions, more screaming missiles. Everyone—the crew on the ship and Mira, Holt, and Zoey—instinctively turned to watch the battle rage behind them.

The trees on either side of the river were burning. Raptors roared overhead, firing at one another, crashing in flames. Glowing fields of crystal-shaped energy rose into the air over burning walkers.

What was left of the blue and whites was concentrating their fire on one of the red Spiders. It bellowed horribly, shuddering with each plasma bolt and missile hit.

Finally, it collapsed, moaning a distorted cry as it fell into the water and blew apart in flames.

But no glowing field of energy rose from it. The black rust formed on its surface, spreading impossibly fast, engulfing the giant contorting machine like a metallic cancer. And then it went still.

The remaining red walker wailed angrily and launched the last of its missiles. But it wasn't alone for long.

Behind it, two huge red Osprey drop ships suddenly burst into view, each carrying new Spider walkers.

Their engines roared as they hovered over the river, released their cargo, and quickly dusted off. When the two red Spider walkers hit the water, they came to life, whirring and flashing and rising to their full, enormous heights.

They opened fire immediately, sending plasma bolts toward the line of blue and whites, reinforcing the first Spider. The skirmish was quickly becoming a full-scale battle.

The Captain looked down at Mira, not a glint of panic in his eyes. He certainly was cool and collected. "Are we bargaining?" he asked.

Landship crews represented a subculture focused on trade and commerce. To them, everything was done as part of a bargain, and the only honorable trade was one where both sides profited. If Mira had nothing to offer the handsome Captain above, she likely wouldn't be getting on board. Fortunately for her, she did, and she had had enough dealings with Landship traders to know how the process worked.

"We're bargaining," Mira replied. "Simple trade, no conditions. I use my own artifacts to get your Chinook running. In return, you give us safe passage the hell out of here."

An errant blast of plasma bolts burned through the air right above them. The ship's crew flinched. The Captain did not; he just stared down at Mira, thinking. "It's a binding merchandise trade," he announced. "Any artifacts you use for our Chinook, you don't get them back."

"Fine!" Mira shouted, "just let us up!"

The Captain smiled. "My name's Dresden. Welcome aboard the *Wind Shear*."

Dresden disappeared and started yelling orders. On the side of the ship, a giant gangplank arched downward from the top deck and slammed onto the ground.

Mira turned to Holt, smiling with relief. But then she saw the frustrated look in his eye. "What?" she asked, even though she knew she wasn't going to like the answer.

"My guns," he said in frustration, turning around and heading back toward the chaos and the fire engulfing everything along the river. "I can't leave them."

"You have to be joking!" Mira exclaimed. "You can get more guns!"

"Not like these!" he yelled back. "Get Zoey on board. And hold that ship!"

Mira watched as Holt and Max tore back the way they'd come, toward the missiles and the flying plasma bolts. She could see his guns, lying in a heap near the line of trees that flanked the river, where he'd left them earlier. It was about a hundred yards away—he was going to have to be fast.

Mira shook her head, grabbed Zoey, and ran up the gangplank. Dresden met her, and together they rushed toward the ship's central platform, where its huge wheel sat. "Can't hold the ship for your friend, darling," he told Mira. "Either he's back on when we leave, or he gets left."

"He'll be back," Zoey said. "Holt always comes back."

Mira hoped she was right.

"Everyone to your posts!" the captain ordered as they moved. "You know what to do. Seal the ship—when our guest here gets the Chinook running, I want full sail in minimum time, hop to it."

There was a flurry of movement as the crew, more than two dozen, leapt to action, running everywhere around the deck. Ropes were untied, and giant metal plates slammed down over the Landship's windows and openings, sealing the weak spots.

The kids rushed to their stations on the deck, below deck, climbing the masts and sails toward the various crow's nests a hundred feet above the deck.

Mira and Dresden stopped in front of the wheel, where two boys were frantically sorting through a pile of all kinds of nails, screws, pins, bolts, looking for something specific. One of them was hurriedly touching the end of an artifact combination to each one, one Mira recognized: a small Recognizer, a combination that detected other artifacts. If one of these pieces on the deck were a genuinely active Strange Lands artifact, it would react to them. So far, it wasn't doing anything.

"Try the sheet metal screws!" the kid without the Recognizer shouted.

"I did already!" the other one yelled back. "They're dead, they're common. Those Rats sold us a bag of normal pieces of junk!"

"What do you need?" Mira asked them as more explosions flared up over the side of the ship.

The two boys looked up at her. "Who the hell are *you*?" the kid with the Recognizer asked.

"The one who's gonna save your asses from my foot," Dresden replied hotly. "She's a Freebooter—start listening and answer her questions."

"It's for the Chinook. It's an artifact that—"

"I know what it does, I've made them before," Mira interrupted. "What do you *need*?"

The kids looked up at her and said at the same time, "The Focuser for the fourth tier."

Mira nodded, unslung her pack. She knew what they needed, and she was pretty sure she had it. "I have a railroad tie. It's bigger than you're probably used to, but it'll work in a pinch. What are you binding it with?"

"Short-gauge chain," one of the kids answered.

"Get it!"

They rushed off toward their gear as Mira began digging through her pack.

The ship shook as more blasts rocked the ground, and she saw a second red Spider crash into the river in flames. When the Assembly were done with one another, they'd turn their attention back to finding Zoey . . . and then they were all screwed.

"And it started off such a nice day," Dresden said, leaning against the ship's wheel and watching the battle unfold.

"Tell me about it, I was having cupcakes earlier," Mira replied. Where the hell was Holt?

HOLT ALMOST FELL FACE-FIRST into the grass as he skidded to a stop in front of his guns. They were right where he'd left them, and with the explosions and fireballs just a few feet away, the sight of his old friends gave him peace of mind, if only a little.

He grabbed the weapons and quickly shoved each of them into their holsters. Now all he had to do was double-time it back to the ship and its stupid Captain. What was up with *that* guy, with his hair and his boots? "Beautiful and industrious"? He'd show *him* industri—

Holt heard a growl next to him. He turned and saw Max staring intently at the tree line ahead, his hackles raised, lips parted to show his fangs. The dog didn't like something there.

Holt looked up at the trees, but couldn't see anything. The battle was in the other direction. What could have gotten the dog so riled up?

The air shimmered as the cloaking fields dropped from more Assembly machines, small, agile ones painted green and orange. Holt's eyes widened in horrible recognition.

Only four of them had survived the Drowning Plains, and they stood in the trees like mechanical ghosts, their armor scratched and dented and soiled. Their three-optic eyes whirred as they focused on Holt.

"Son of a . . . ," Holt said as he got to his feet. "Max, let's go!"

The dog tore himself away from the tripods and they both ran as hard as they could back for the ship. Behind them, Holt heard the frightening, electronic trumpetings and the furious stomping of tripod legs.

Yellow plasma bolts flashed past and shredded the ground all around him. Max howled as they ran; he didn't seem to be enjoying himself now.

Ahead of him, the Landship stood where they'd left it. Holt could make it. All he had to do was keep running, and he could—

The ship's giant sails suddenly plumed outward like great eagle's wings.

Landship sails were beautiful, Holt had always thought, patchworks of colors and patterns, made from all kinds of fabric, and these were no exception. Orange and purple and yellow, they looked like huge pieces of art fluttering in the wind, but because Holt knew what it meant, he didn't feel the desire to stop and enjoy the view.

Mira must have fixed whatever the ship's problem was, and now it was *leaving.*

Without him.

"Hey!" Holt yelled, running even harder. *"Hey!"*

The gangplank that had been lowered to the ground arced back up to the top deck, and the ship groaned as its giant wheels began to slowly turn, crunching over the top of the rocky ground, gaining speed and momentum.

More plasma bolts burned the air. The stomping and trumpeting were almost on him. Along the river, two blue and white Raptors crashed in fireballs into their own ground forces, incinerating them where they stood. The Landship was his only ride out of this insanity.

He reached the ship just as it started rolling, running alongside it. He looked for anything he could grab on to—a window, a railing, anything—but the ship's wooden hull had been polished smooth. There was nothing to grip at all.

"Holt!" a voice cried down, and he looked up and saw Mira as she tossed over a mass of rope and wooden planks. When it extended, he saw what it really was. A rope ladder. Holt didn't waste any time—he grabbed on, found purchase with his feet, and pulled.

It wasn't a graceful process—he slid along the ground precariously, spitting rock and dirt behind him—but he finally managed to scramble onto the ladder enough to get his feet off the racing ground.

Above him, he saw the captain and some of his men grip the ladder's ropes to start pulling it up. Behind, Max barked desperately, chased by the four tripods that were closing the distance fast.

Holt whistled three short notes, and the dog hit the afterburners, galloping after Holt with all the energy he had left. The ship was gaining more speed: he had only one shot at this. Holt gripped the ladder with one hand, and then reached out for Max with the other.

The dog leapt forward with the last of his strength, the tripods closing in . . .

. . . and Holt scooped him into his arms, held him against his chest tightly.

The dog didn't seem very grateful—he squirmed and kicked, and it was all Holt could do to hold him with his one arm. "Max!" he shouted in annoyance.

Above, he heard yells as more of the ship's crew grabbed his ladder and started pulling. The ground dropped away under him . . . and just in time, too.

The tripods finally caught him, but it was too late: he was out of reach now. Holt saw one was painted differently from the others, its markings the same colors yet individual. Bolder. More striking. He stared into its eye, and to Holt, it felt like the machine was glaring up at him with a burning, electric hatred.

This was the second time Holt had beaten it. It didn't seem to sit well with the machine . . . or with whatever was controlling it.

Plasma fire erupted from the tripods, and Holt flinched as hands yanked him onto the deck right as it seared past his head.

"The Max!" he heard Zoey shout from somewhere, and the dog squirmed out of his grip and rushed to the little girl. Holt frowned. Max had a real problem with gratitude.

Holt stood up . . . and was instantly wrapped in a crushing embrace. Lithe arms hugged him, and he felt Mira press into his chest. "Holt . . . ," she said, and the emotion in her voice was plain to hear. She had been worried; he could feel it in her embrace. Slowly, hesitantly, Holt put his arms around her, too, and hugged her back.

Holt put a lot of energy into resisting caring about others. So much so that he'd forgotten what it felt like to have someone care for *him*. It was . . . not at all unpleasant.

Mira pulled away from him, blushing, looking up into his eyes. Holt looked back, and he could feel the beginnings of a smile form on his face.

"See?" Zoey said from his left. "Holt always comes back."

Holt looked down to the little girl. "That's right, kiddo," he said, smiling for real now. "I always—"

A stream of plasma bolts sliced the air, and Holt felt one rip hard into his left side. The impact sent him spinning crazily in a haze of pain and fog, and he slammed onto the deck of the Landship, then lay unmoving.

He heard Mira scream above him, felt her lunge on top of him protectively, saw the rest of the Landship crew hit the deck and take cover.

In slow motion almost, as his vision receded and darkness pressed in, he looked behind them. In the distance, explosions flared along the river as the last of the red Spiders fell in sparks and flames into the water. On the ground below, the small green and orange tripods pursued angrily, but they were being left behind as the huge ship gathered speed. Their plasma cannon fired, sending bolts streaming after the ship, and Holt stared back at the differently marked walker again. Even over the distance between them, he could feel its gaze on him, just like before, hungry and full of malice and dark intent.

And then everything went completely black, and the world flashed away.

PART TWO

MIDNIGHT CITY

28. SOMETHING

IN HIS SLOW, PAINFUL RETURN TO CONSCIOUSNESS, Holt glimpsed the world through strange vignettes of imagery that came and went and were punctuated with blackness. As unpleasant as they were, he preferred the waking moments to the unconsciousness, if only because in that confused, detached blend of sights and sounds, he wasn't dreaming. The dreams had become more vivid than ever. He knew where they were leading him . . . and he didn't want to go there.

As the blackness receded, he pushed the fog and the haze away. When he opened his eyes, he blinked at the brightness of the world. He was in a small room made completely of polished wood. The ceiling was rounded and smooth, everything blending seamlessly together, and the bed he was on seemed to have been built out from the wall. There was a wooden chest at the other end, and a small stained glass window—maybe from an old church—allowed colorful streams of light to float in the air.

And he noticed something else, too. The room rocked occasionally, shaking and jarring. It felt like the whole thing was moving. . . .

"Hey, Hawkins," said a voice he recognized. "Thanks for joining us."

Holt looked to his left and saw Mira sitting on the floor next to his bed, watching him. He wondered how long she'd been there. The idea of her protectively looking over him was both pleasing and discomforting.

"Where are we?" he asked, slowly sitting up. He regretted the movement almost instantly. His head swam and there was a burning pain along his left ribs. Now that he was moving, he could feel the sticky restraint of fresh bandages around it. Someone had treated an injury, and with the realization came the memory of the plasma bolts and the world spinning as he crashed down.

"Might want to take it slow, killer," Mira said, noticing his pain. "You took a nasty hit. I wasn't sure you were going to make it." Her voice was laced with a hint of concern. "You've been out a good twenty hours. We're on the *Wind Shear*," Mira continued. "It's taking us to Midnight City. Zoey's up with Max on the deck."

"The Landship from the trading depot?" Holt asked, remembering he had been running for it when the green and oranges had appeared. The rest of his memories were hazy at best. It explained the rocking motion of the room. "You got their . . . whatever it is fixed?"

Mira smiled. "The Chinook, yeah. They traded for a bad Focuser at the depot. I had another one, helped them rebuild it."

Holt cradled his head, letting the pain and the dizziness pass. And then something occurred to him. Something bad. "Midnight City," Holt sighed.

"Yeah," Mira replied. "I know it's the opposite direction you were hoping to go, but I figured you'd prefer that to being left behind."

He looked up at her. "Guess you'll do anything to keep me around, huh?"

Mira smiled. "It's possible you're flattering yourself right now."

Holt looked away, thinking. It meant a longer trip for him, and more chances of running into Menagerie along the way. But there was nothing he could do to change it now; he'd just have to figure it out. He closed his eyes again. It was all coming back, and with the return of his memories, he realized just how lucky they'd been.

So did Mira. "Those Hunters were almost on us," she said, "and the others were blowing each other to bits. I've never seen that much plasma fire in one place." She looked at him pointedly. "Something happened with Zoey. Didn't it?"

Holt looked at her as he thought back to the trading depot. He still wasn't sure he believed it himself, but he told her what he'd seen. The shouts from the tent, Zoey alone with the two older kids, the reaction when the others saw their clear eyes, their insistence that Zoey had "cured" them of the Tone.

Mira looked at Holt with all the shock he expected. "Do you . . . *believe* that? Did that *happen*?"

"If it did, I didn't see it," Holt answered. "But judging by the reaction of those traders, I'd say it was real. They'd have torn Zoey apart to get at her, I know that much. It's just one more reason I'm starting to wonder how safe it is keeping her around."

Mira stared at him, aghast.

"I'm not saying she'd hurt us," Holt continued, "but you saw that battle back there—it was full-scale war. And all for a *little girl*? She's dangerous. The second she . . . did whatever the hell she did, three different groups of Assembly dropped out of the sky, Mira."

She studied him. "Holt, have you thought that maybe the reason the Assembly wants Zoey . . . is because they're afraid of her?"

"She's eight years old."

"If what you're saying's true, she can *stop* the Tone, Holt."

"So what?" he said, annoyed. "What are we gonna do, line everyone up who's left alive and have her lay hands on them? A million survivors all across the world?"

"It's *something*," Mira said. "Everything starts from something."

"No, it's *nothing*," he answered. "It's ludicrous."

"I think Zoey is special," Mira said with conviction. "And I trust her."

"She's incredibly special, there's no doubt, but I don't blindly trust anything," Holt said. "I don't believe in faith, I don't believe in magic. I believe in myself and what I see with my eyes. You can't just start believing for the sake of believing. Mira, it's dangerous. It has to be about survival."

"I think that's a load of crap," Mira said, holding his gaze. "I don't think this has anything to do with survival. I think it has to do with *fear*."

Holt just stared back at her, feeling a nervous energy growing inside him.

"Who did you lose, Holt?" Mira gently asked him again.

Holt sighed and looked away. It had been a long time since he'd talked about this. In fact, he had only ever talked about it with one other person . . . and that person was very different from Mira. It surprised him when he heard his own voice. "My sister," he said. "She was leaving to join the Blacksheep. This was years ago, when I was still a kid. The Tone was almost finished with her then, but she thought she could have another year, maybe two, in Chicago, fighting with them."

No one knew why, but the Tone became weaker the closer you were to one of the base ships. In a ruin like Chicago, where the enormous Presidium towered over everything, survivors could last up to an additional year. It was no accident that the resistance groups there, like the Blacksheep Brigade, comprised primarily kids in their late teens.

As he spoke, Holt felt all the emotions coming back, feelings he'd buried and never dealt with, and to him, they still felt almost brand-new.

"I followed her even though she told me not to. When I caught her, she was furious. But I didn't care. I just didn't want to be alone, I didn't want to go on without her."

He felt Mira's gaze on him, but he didn't return it.

"We were attacked by Assembly inside an old truck stop, and the whole thing crashed down and trapped us inside. I was hurt and she had to scramble to keep me alive, and at the same time, she dug our way out of there all by herself. There was no water, no food either, and when we finally got out, we were so weak, we could barely stand. We were days away from any sort of help."

As he spoke, he felt his breathing become shallow.

"It was like, once she got us out, all the strength she'd called on to save us was just spent."

Mira sat silent, listening. "The Tone attacked her, didn't it?"

Holt nodded. "She was too sick and tired to fight it anymore. Before it took her, with the little strength she had, she told me—" Holt gazed off with a haunted stare. "—she told me . . ."

Mira remained quiet, watching him, not pressing.

"It doesn't matter," he said, forcing the memories away. "The only thing that matters is that I watched her mind drain to nothing right in front of me, watched her walk away and never look back, and it was *my fault* it happened. If I hadn't gone after her, we never would have been in that stupid building, and she would have had another year of still being her." His eyes were stinging, beginning to water, and he angrily tried to rub them dry, but that only seemed to make it worse. He didn't want Mira to see him like this.

The only sound was the shaking of the room from outside. When Mira finally spoke, her voice was gentle and delicate. "Holt, look at me," she said.

Holt kept his stare on the floor. He couldn't look at her, there was just—

"*Look* at me." He felt her fingers on his chin gently raise his eyes up to hers, and he didn't stop her. He knew they were red and full of emotion: he could feel them burning.

"What was her name?" Mira asked.

There was no sense of judgment from her, no horror or pity. There was only tenderness. In spite of everything, Mira really did care. In spite of *everything* . . .

"Emily," he replied with a cracked voice.

Mira leaned in slowly toward him, and at the closeness of her, Holt felt a wave of relaxing heat wash over him. "Listen to me," she said, looking into his eyes. "You loved Emily. And she loved you. She was lost no matter what you did—it was just a matter of time. She knew that, I promise you. I know she knew, because I live with the same thought every day. When she dug a way out of that truck stop, she wasn't saving herself . . . she was saving *you*. You were Heedless, she knew you could live a long life, and it made her happy to think that. She sacrificed the little bit of time she had left to get you out of there so you could *live*. That's as big a gesture as someone can make in this world."

He tried to look away, but she stopped him, raised his chin back up, kept his eyes on hers.

"You have nothing to feel guilty about," Mira said firmly. "And it's not just me telling you that . . . it's *her*, too. I can speak for her if anyone can."

They were just words, but they shook Holt deeply. They were words that no one had ever said to him, and it was surprising how much relief he felt at hearing them.

Holt took Mira's hand, felt her fingers wind through his. The scent of her filled him. He stared into her green eyes floating behind those black tendrils. Slowly, instinctively, magnetically almost . . . they leaned in toward each other. . . .

"Are you two finally going to kiss?" Zoey asked from the doorway to their room, and Holt and Mira stopped short inches from each other. Max was next to the little girl, tongue hanging out of his mouth.

Holt sighed, reluctantly pulled away. Mira smiled up at him and shrugged.

"Captain Dresden wanted me to tell you we're here," Zoey said.

"Already?" Mira asked. "He made good time."

"Captain Dresden says there's no Landship faster than the *Wind Shear*," Zoey replied excitedly. "He said he's outrun whole swarms of those scary metal things in the sky."

Holt frowned. "I get the impression Dresden says a lot of things."

Mira smiled and gently patted Holt's face. "Come on, killer," she said as she got to her feet. "All hands on deck." Holt watched her and Zoey exit the room and disappear down the hall on the other side of the door. Max barked excitedly and dashed in the same direction.

"Oh, sure, yeah," he called sarcastically after them. "I'll just limp my way up to the top, then. I'm sure I can make it on my own."

"You only got grazed!" he heard Mira shout from the hall. "Hurry up."

Holt could already hear the sounds of the crowd outside the ship, and try as he might, he couldn't muster the same enthusiasm as the others. Midnight City was an unpredictable place in the best of times, and dangerous in most others. At least he wouldn't be staying long.

But that was just it, wasn't it? Leaving, as necessary as it was . . . meant leaving Mira and Zoey.

How had he let it happen? Somehow he'd gotten right back in the same spot where he started. A place he'd put up walls to prevent himself from ever going again.

Survival was everything. It's what he believed, it's what he was taught, and the world had shown him it was true over and over again. How could he let this *happen*? It wasn't for lack of trying: He'd kept his distance from Mira and Zoey at first, but in spite of that, something about them refused to be ignored.

Holt shook his head. The way he saw it, he had two choices.

Leave them here at Midnight City and let Mira and Zoey face the dangers alone. It was Mira's agenda, after all, not his. Survival dictated he head east, toward the Low Marshes. The Menagerie was still looking for him, and the longer he stayed in any one place, the less safe it became. And, most important, if he left, he wouldn't have to watch it all happen again. He wouldn't have to watch someone he cared about Succumb to the Tone right in front of him.

Or . . .

He could stay. He could risk the pain and the loss, and try to find a way to make sure it *didn't* happen again. He could find a way to save Mira. And with Zoey, if what had happened in the trading post was real . . . maybe he actually *could* do it. The thought filled him with strange emotions, scary ones. Ones that felt almost like . . . hope.

Holt sat on the bed a long time, thinking, listening to the sounds of the churning masses outside float in through the small window.

All he knew was, either way, he couldn't go through all that again. . . .

MIRA EMERGED FROM THE LOWER DECKS of the *Wind Shear* into the bright morning sun with Zoey and Max.

From the ground, she could tell the ship was made of a whole host of different parts, but up close, Mira saw it all in a new light. The pieces—train, automobile, parts of buildings or boats, the airplane wings for masts—it hadn't just been haphazardly stuck together in the shape of a giant vessel. Instead, it was meticulously constructed and melded together, and the individual components gleamed in the sunlight, their rough edges polished smooth. There wasn't a hint of rust anywhere, and each piece had been shaped to flow effortlessly, one to the next, all held together by crafted wood. Pieces from old floors or boat decks or giant ceiling rafters—even a section from an old basketball court—all of it buffed and lacquered to a brilliant shine that sparkled in dozens of different colors and hues.

The *Wind Shear* wasn't just this crew's transportation; she was also their home, and you could tell by how beautifully maintained the ship was. And to think, in the Barren, there were a hundred of these ships, each one as unique as the *Wind Shear* in its own way.

Something about that made the world seem less small, Mira thought.

She watched the crew—about two dozen, Mira guessed—moving over the ship and preparing her to dock. Pulling the sails, stowing equipment, unhinging lengths of rope to tie off.

"Mira, come on!" Zoey shouted as she and Max ran past her. Mira smiled and moved to the edge of the ship's deck with them. Below was what once was a giant dam that marshaled the Missouri River, huge walls of concrete plunging over a steep drop several hundred feet below to where a diminished version of the river continued to wind southward through a huge floodplain.

It had once been called Fort Bennett Dam, but now it was the exterior of North America's largest permanent population center, a place infamously known as Midnight City.

The real "city" lay deep underground, Mira knew, in the natural cavern system behind the structure, but she stared at it with a far-off, haunted look nonetheless. It was strange, looking at a place you used to call home, a place you used to feel safe in, and knowing that it was now hostile to you, that not only did it not want you anymore, but it would also hurt you if it got the chance. Seeing the city again was both exciting and sad.

Mira felt another twinge of sadness as she realized what else the city represented. The possibility of another good-bye. Surely Holt wouldn't stay now that they had reached Midnight City, not with a price on his head. He'd said his plan was to head toward the Low Marshes, to try to outdistance his problems. That possibility, inevitable though it was, left a hollow feeling in her stomach. Mira didn't like the way it felt.

"You okay?" Holt asked beside her. He'd followed them up, had his gear slung over his back. She looked at him softly, something passing between them. And then she nodded and touched his arm.

"Wow!" Zoey exclaimed, taking Mira's hand. The little girl was staring at the port outside the ship with amazement.

Mira smiled down at her. "This is nothing—wait till we get into the city."

"What's it like?" Zoey asked.

"It's . . . beautiful, actually. Dark and bright at the same time. Full of energy, more people than you've ever seen in one place. It's not like anywhere else you'll ever go."

Zoey gazed out over the port below them.

Midnight City actually had two ports, one at the top where the *Wind Shear* was docked called Upper Berth, and one far below, where the Missouri River came out of the dam and continued south, called Lower Berth.

Lower Berth was for River Rat crews who brought their ships up from the south for trade. Mira looked over the edge of the dam, all the way down to where dozens of river boats and barges were docked far below. The crews and kids moving down there looked like ants from this far up.

Upper Berth was the land entrance to Midnight City, and traders moving on foot, as well as the occasional caravan or Landship from the Barren, docked and entered the city here. There were two other Landships tied off next to the *Wind Shear,* both a similar mix of different parts and pieces, all meticulously and artfully put together, and the crews of all three vessels had spun lines of cable between them, so that cargo or messages or even people could pass easily to and from them.

On the ground, hundreds of survivors moved between the ships and Midnight City's main entrance, a huge opening in the concrete structure at the far side of the port that probably once allowed vehicles down into the dam's interior.

"Would it be a waste of time to try to convince you to stay on?" a voice asked from behind. Mira turned and saw Dresden studying her. "It's a long road west, and your expertise would come in handy. Not to mention . . . you bring a definite beauty and charm to the ship."

Mira blushed, even as she noticed Holt's glare. The Captain was certainly cute, and he had a way with words, but he was also more kinds of trouble than she could probably name. "I'm sad to say the answer's still no. But you have a nice way of reasking the same question, Captain." Mira saw Holt roll his eyes and pretend to focus on the port below.

"I see your friend found his legs," Dresden said, looking at Holt. "That's good. When you fell, I thought you were a goner. Hell, for a second, I thought we all were. Way those things chased after us . . . you'd think they were interested in you three personally." Dresden smiled pleasantly, but it wasn't completely disarming. He had his suspicions, it was clear.

"They were probably just trying to take out the depot," Holt offered. "Tempting target."

"Three different Assembly groups?" Dresden mused doubtfully. "I've never seen red or green ones before, and they just show up and start fighting each other? No. Something was wrong there, and whatever it was, I'll be glad to put distance between it and myself. We're full sail to the west tomorrow morning. Gangplank's down, we're tied off, you can disembark whenever you want." Dresden reached out and took Mira's hand. He lifted it to his lips and kissed it gently. "I feel we are destined to meet again, you and I."

Holt had apparently had enough. "I doubt we'll be visiting the Barren anytime soon." He took Mira's hand from Dresden and started moving toward the gangplank to the port. Mira almost smiled. It surprised her how much she enjoyed seeing Holt jealous.

"You never know," Dresden said, walking next to them casually, seemingly unbothered. "The winds take us where they will, after all . . . not the other way around." He looked down at Zoey, and she looked up at him. Dresden winked at her. "Remember that, little one. Be safe."

"You, too, Captain Dresden," Zoey said.

"Winds guide you," Dresden said, giving the traditional Landship farewell as he bowed. Then he turned on his heel and disappeared back into the movements of his crew, giving orders.

The gangplank stretched before them, an ornate ramp made of sealed aspen and sparkling metal that descended to the ground of the Upper Berth below. The four walked down it and stepped onto the grass.

Throngs of people, hundreds of them, flocked everywhere, all headed to and from either the docked Landships and other vehicles or the city's main entrance. Mira looked up at Holt and found his eyes were already on her. Zoey's head turned back and forth, studying both of them.

"So . . . ," Mira said. Here it was, another crossroads.

"So . . . ," Holt said back.

They stayed like that, considering each other, both unsure what to say. Mira saw Zoey roll her eyes in frustration beneath them.

"Are you—?" Mira started.

"I was thinking—," Holt began at the same time.

They both cut off, looking at each other awkwardly.

"Go ahead," Mira said.

"No, I cut you off, you go first."

Mira sighed. Why was this so hard? She'd had plenty of good-byes in her life. It was the way the world worked, after all. Why did the possibility of this being one of them leave such a dull ache?

"Hard to believe we made it," she finally said. "After everything."

"We definitely beat the odds, I'll give us that," Holt said soberly. "We make a good team."

They stared at each other again, questions and thoughts hanging in the air. Mira heard a slight "ahem" from below, and she looked down. Zoey was giving her a firm *get it over with, already* look. Mira frowned and looked back at Holt.

She forced herself to ask, "Are you . . . heading east *now?* For the Low Marshes, I mean?"

"Is that what you think I should do?" Holt asked back.

"I think . . . you should do what you want to do," she said back, completely sidestepping what she wanted to say. What was wrong with her? "Is that . . . what you *want* to do?"

"Is that what you want me to—?"

"Mira," Zoey interrupted in agitation. They looked down at her, and she was giving them both a severe look. "Holt wants to ask if he can stay and help you do what you have to do here." Holt's eyes widened, but Zoey kept going before he could protest. "Holt, Mira wants to ask if you'll stay with us and not head east, at least not yet." She gave each of them a look in turn. "Was that so hard?"

Holt and Mira smiled and looked up at each other. "I guess not, kiddo," Holt replied.

"Are you sure? It's not going to be easy, Holt," Mira said. "In fact, it could be really dangerous."

He looked around warily at the droves of people entering the city. "Why would I expect anything else?" he said. "Besides . . . Max would miss Zoey." Holt gave her a pointed look as he said the words.

The smile on her face spread. "He would, huh?"

"Can I ride the Max just until we get to the front gate? *Please?*" Zoey pleaded.

Holt and Mira sighed, shook their heads, mouthed the word *no,* and started moving. Zoey pouted, but followed after them.

They blended in with the churning crowd headed for the main entrance, and as they moved, Mira put the hood of her top up over her face, concealing herself as best she could.

"Just . . . how recognizable are you here?" Holt asked.

"Very," Mira answered.

"What happens if I get caught with you?"

She looked at him mischievously.

"Forget I asked," Holt said.

They kept moving toward the gate amid the line of people pushing forward. As they moved, more detail of the old dam was revealed. Cannons of all kinds lined the top of the structure, makeshift ones like the boats at the trading depot had used, refurbished artillery guns from armories and old military bases, and even a few repurposed Assembly plasma guns that had been rigged to work again.

Besides the cannons, the denizens of the city had crafted gun ports all through the exterior, where they could shoot while staying behind cover. All of it was defensive, in case of an Assembly attack, but as far as Mira knew, that had never happened. They were at the edge of the Minneapolis Presidium's territory, and the aliens didn't seem to care one way or another about the city's existence. Why should they? All they had to do was wait, after all, and the Tone would deliver the rest of the survivors right to their doorstep.

The main entrance to Midnight City loomed ahead of them, two huge steel doors that had been swung open to allow entry into a concrete tunnel on the other side.

Painted above the giant doors was a symbol. A clock face, with both hands pointing straight up, and the numbers *1* through *12*, arranged in a ring around it. It was the symbol for Midnight City, and under it, a group of older kids stood guard by the entrance, checking the people as they entered.

The different factions in Midnight City alternated various responsibilities throughout the city, the entry guard being one of them. With relief, Mira saw that the kids weren't wearing shades of gray; they were wearing green.

It meant they were part of a faction called the Cavaliers. If they'd been wearing gray, it would have meant they were from the Gray Devils, Midnight City's most powerful faction, and the faction Mira herself had once belonged to.

The odds of Gray Devils members recognizing her would have been much greater.

They kept moving until they reached the city gate. The line broke into three separate paths here, each passing through a different guard purview. They were searching each person, looking for contraband or anything dangerous before allowing anyone to pass. Mira tensed at the sight. What had she been thinking? Just walk right through the main gate—had that really been her plan? Her face was well known here, and the chance of these guards recognizing her, Gray Devils or not, were pretty high.

Next to her, Holt undid his pack and dug through it, looking for something specific. He pulled out a small red cylinder with Chinese symbols written across it, and a piece of string hanging from one end.

Mira looked at him questioningly.

"When it's time," he said without looking back. "Just keep moving."

Before she could ask, Holt pulled the string on the cylinder . . . but there was no pop or bang. There was nothing. He casually slipped it into the pack of the boy in front of him. No one noticed.

The line kept moving. Holt and Max joined one line, Mira and Zoey another, but she nervously kept watching the boy in front of Holt.

Right as the kid reached the green-clad guard . . . smoke began funneling up and out from his pack, wafting into the air.

Shouts rang up from all three guards, and they automatically moved for the boy with the smoking pack. As they did, the line in front of Mira was suddenly devoid of guards.

She saw what Holt had planned, grabbed Zoey's hand, and walked quickly forward, past the distracted guards and into the tunnel ahead of her.

Behind her, Holt and Max did the same thing, moving fast for—

"Hey! *You!*" one of the guards shouted. Mira shut her eyes tight . . . and then realized the guards weren't yelling at her at all. They were moving instead toward Holt.

"You just gonna walk through the main hall carrying those guns?" the guard asked him in annoyance.

Holt looked back, unsure.

"Your guns, nimrod," the guard said. "Gotta check 'em before you go in, no firearms allowed. No slings or crossbows either. Unless they're for trade, then you need a trader's permit to carry, and they have to be empty. You trading?"

"Uh . . . no," Holt managed. "No, these are mine."

"Check them over here, then," the guard said impatiently, moving toward a group of lockers set into the wall near the entrance. Mira moved farther inside and watched as Holt hesitantly handed over his weapons to the Cavalier guard. He sealed them in a locker, handed the key to Holt, and he and Max started walking toward her and Zoey again.

Behind him, the other guards were roughly searching the kid Holt had planted the smoke bomb on, and he loudly complained that it wasn't his. The green-clad boys didn't seem to be buying it.

When Holt and Max reached Mira and Zoey, they all started down the tunnel again.

"So far, so good, I guess," Mira said, pulling her hood tighter around her head.

"Yeah," Holt replied. "But I don't like not having my guns."

They kept moving amid the mass of survivors trailing down the tunnel, which gradually descended into an ever-thickening darkness, toward whatever awaited them at the other end.

THE TUNNEL GREW GRADUALLY DARKER as they moved down it, so much so that eventually Holt had to reach out for Mira in front of him to keep from falling. In what was left of the light, Holt saw Max scamper ahead of them, darting playfully through the people.

"Max!" he yelled, trying to stop him, but he was gone, and Holt shook his head.

They passed through more of the heavy steel gates, all yawning open where they stood. They were formidable, with multiple gun ports. Further defenses, he figured. In case of an attack.

But formidable or not, if the Assembly wanted inside Midnight City, Holt had a feeling they would get in, gates or no gates.

Holt had been here only twice before, and both times he'd come in through the Lower Berth entrance, and he hadn't stayed long. Which was fine with Holt. There was just something about the city, all the people, more people than he would normally see in a whole year, crammed together in these caverns.

It was unsettling. He preferred open spaces where you could see the horizon. And he preferred a lot fewer people, too. People were untrustworthy, and the more of them you got in one place, the more fuel there was for something bad to happen.

Lights appeared ahead, dim blue and red ones along the concrete tunnel's ceiling that marked where the tunnel ended. Well, the part of it they were moving through, anyway. The man-made, concrete tunnel continued to the right, where it met a large sealed metal door. But where it forked, a hole had been punched into the wall.

Beyond it was another tunnel, but this one was natural, made of jagged rock walls, and it continued downward. The line of people moved into it, and disappeared beyond.

As Holt and the others followed after them, he finally felt the floor level out and stop its descent. There was a chill in the air, and a wetness, like fog almost, and he could taste it whenever he breathed.

And then they stepped out into somewhere amazing.

In spite of Holt's misgivings about the place, it never failed to impress him, and coming into it like this, through the darkened tunnel, only made the reveal that much more dramatic.

They stood in an enormous underground cavern system that had formed behind the dam who knew how many millions of years ago. The walls in this chamber stretched out of sight in every direction, and the ceiling soared several hundred feet above them.

All throughout the cavern, a city had been constructed. There was no other word for it. Holt twisted the bracelet on his left wrist as he took it all in. Structures made out of wood and metal and plastic, repurposed buildings from other parts of the world hammered and welded together, and refurbished components from all kinds of devices and objects climbed up the cavern walls, sometimes as high as six or seven stories off the rock floor.

Lights of all shapes and colors were strung up along the ceiling far above, in huge numbers. Because there were so many of them, and because they were so high up, they looked at first glance like stars in a night sky, bathing everything below them in flickering light. It was no mystery where the place got its name. Midnight City was a city in perpetual night.

The buildings and natural flow of the cavern created large streetlike pathways outlined with lanterns on top of poles that glowed in different colors and intensities, stretching away into the distance toward other parts of the cavern city.

The black rock made everything feel shadowy and mysterious, and the bright, colored lights seemed even more striking contrasted against it. It was as Mira had told Zoey: The city was both dark and bright at the same time.

Zoey stared in awe, her mouth hanging open. Holt watched Mira smile and kneel down to her.

"This is where you live?" Zoey asked.

Holt saw a note of sadness play on Mira's face, before she replied.

"Yes," she said. "This is the main hall—it's where everyone lives, except for the larger factions. They have their own caverns."

Mira examined the city with a melancholy look. Holt had never really felt he had a "home," as he was always on the move. Even when he'd been with the Menagerie, he didn't spend all that much time in Faust. But if he had a home, someplace he felt he belonged, and it were taken from him, he thought he could imagine how that would feel.

Hundreds of survivors moved in and out of the city's buildings, going about their business, walking in a crowd through the lantern-lit streets.

"Where do the lights come from?" Zoey asked.

Good question, now that Holt thought about it. "Electrical?" he asked. "Do they have the dam's generators working?"

Mira shook her head. "No, the dam hasn't worked in years, and no one knows how to fix it. The lights are artifact combinations, simple ones called Illuminators. Depending on the components, you never know what color you'll get. That's why they're all different."

"I like the colors," Zoey said, craning her neck to stare straight up at the cavern ceiling.

They started walking again, through the glittering city, and as they did, Max reappeared, dodging through the crowd on his way back, tongue hanging out of his mouth. "The Max!" Zoey yelled, grabbing one of the dog's ears and walking with it like it was someone's hand.

The buildings stood tall above them as they moved. There were makeshift windows all through them, but no glass. You didn't really need glass down here, Holt figured: there was no rain or wind to keep out. Inside, he could see other lanterns, people shuffling about, survivors at work in shops.

Hanging from the ceiling, far above, were twelve huge banners that draped heavily downward and hung motionless. Each had an Illuminator trained on it, lighting up the details. Each was a different set of colors, with some kind of unique symbol on it.

One was auburn red with a huge white wolf's head stitched on the front. Another was green and showed a yellow sword. A third was orange and had a red shield sewn onto its center. In the middle hung the largest banner of them all. It was deep gray and white, and embossed onto both sides was a laughing devil's face with a forked tongue snaking out of its mouth and horns on its head.

They were the banners of Midnight City's factions, Holt knew, though he didn't know which one was which. Mira certainly did, though. And he thought he saw her shiver at the sight of the imposing gray one.

As they walked, they passed underneath the arches of a large concrete and brick structure that stretched from one end of the cavern to the other, where it disappeared into smaller tunnels. Channels were built into its sides and top, and clear, sparkling water flowed through them, and Holt could hear it rippling as it drifted by. People were lined up along the channels, filling up bottles and jugs, hauling them back to their houses or workshops.

"It's an aqueduct," Mira said. "The city has almost twenty of them, and they're all run by the Gray Devils." She motioned to the same logo from the large banner above them, a horned white devil on a background of gray, which was also painted onto the walls of the archway.

"Where does the water come from?" Holt asked.

"From the Gray Devils' cavern. There's an underground river there," Mira replied. "When they discovered it, they mined it all out and built the aqueducts. A year later, they were the most powerful faction in the city. Everyone needs water . . . so everyone needs the Gray Devils."

They passed under the huge aqueduct and kept moving through the crowds and winding through the "streets" until they reached the city's business district, an area formed inside a chutelike tunnel. The walls here were spaced only about forty feet apart, and the ceiling was less than twenty high. It was still big, but nothing like the main hall they had just come from.

Dozens and dozens of trading stalls were set up along the business district's walls, selling everything from general supplies to jewelry, first aid kits to still-functional electronics, even luxury items like junk food, toys, crayons, skin moisturizer, and dusty bottles of soft drinks. Anything that there was a demand for and still existed in some quantity in the world you could find for trade here. Holt stared at it all. There was no other place he knew of where you could find so much trade merchandise and it was always surreal seeing this much product.

Holt noticed a lot of stalls bore the same δ symbol Mira wore on her pack.

It meant those stalls sold artifacts, and as Holt looked up and down the rows, he saw as many with the symbol as without. The wares at these stalls did fantastical things as they passed. Objects hovered or circled in the air, jars and bags glowed strange colors or flashed lights, things disappeared and reappeared, and cabinets lay full of minor artifacts ready for use in combinations, all of which seemed to somehow writhe and push away from one another . . . or maybe it was just a trick of the eye, Holt wasn't sure. The sight of it all sent a chill down his spine.

"Why are there so many artifacts?" Zoey asked.

"Because Midnight City is right on the border of the Strange Lands," Mira responded, staring at it all with lustful eyes. "It's the first place Freebooters come to sell what they bring back."

Holt glanced to his left and noticed a group of four kids standing at one of the artifact stalls, haggling with the Freebooter there. They looked like any other survivors, but there was something rough about them, a malicious energy that Holt recognized. He looked to the wrist of one . . . and saw a green snake etched there.

It was a tattoo. They were Menagerie.

Holt quickly turned his back to them, hiding his face. His left hand covered the glove on his right wrist. He could sense the pirates behind him, watched out of the corner of his eye carefully as they turned and left the stall. He waited until they disappeared into the crowd before he let himself relax.

His survival instincts roared like fire. He knew he shouldn't have come here. This was Midnight City, after all—he was undoubtedly going to run into Menagerie, but he'd made a choice, and he had known the risks when he did so. In spite of the danger . . . he wasn't ready to leave. He just hoped it wouldn't be his last mistake.

"What is it?" Mira asked next to him.

His alarm must have been written all over his face, and he quickly wiped it away as best he could. "Nothing," Holt replied. "Everything's good."

Mira studied him curiously, the wheels turning behind her eyes.

"I promise," Holt said, trying to assure her. Mira was smart: she would know something was up, maybe even guess what it was. But she'd also know that right now, in the middle of the crowd, wasn't the best place for the discussion. She considered him another moment . . . then took Zoey's hand. The four moved on, blending in with the surging crowd, moving toward a new room on the other side of the stalls.

When they entered it, Holt saw that it was in every way almost as big as the main hall. Which was a good thing, because it was also the busiest, and Holt pulled Max close as they moved inside.

The bulk of Midnight City's population seemed to be crammed into this huge oval-shaped cavern, throbbing and pulsing like waves trapped inside a jetty, staring and shouting at the room's one dominating feature.

The cavern's back wall was a hundred feet high and stretched to the sides for hundreds more. It had been laboriously polished to a smooth, flat, black surface, almost like a gargantuan chalkboard. Which was exactly how it was being used.

It was the Scorewall, Holt knew, and it was the single most important object in Midnight City.

Midnight City politics were a complicated and multifaceted ordeal that really made sense only to the people who lived there. Everything revolved around a complicated scoring system, where both individuals and groups were given (or penalized) Points based on who they were, whom they knew, what they had done, their position in their faction, their position in the city's hierarchies, and hundreds of other requirements and rules. These Points could also be traded like currency between individuals and factions, which made earning them even more valuable.

The number of Points you had determined your standing in the city and the amount of power you could wield over those around you. Those with the highest Points got the first choice of food, the best living locations, more voice in the forums, higher ranks in the vocations. Shopkeepers with enough Points could shut down their competitors' businesses. Freebooters with high Point totals could bring more profitable artifacts into the city, and traders could more easily corner a market on individual commodities. The gathering of Points was the central motivating force for everything that happened in Midnight City, and the Scorewall displayed a current, up-to-date representation of the totals for every faction, resident, and visitor in the city.

Faction names stood out on the right side of the wall. The farther you looked left, the more individuals you began to see, hundreds and hundreds of names, stretching out of sight in a blur of colored chalk toward the far edge of the wall, each with its own chalk-line box and number and the occasional footnote. To Holt, it looked like an impossible collection of information and data to manage, and the logistical implications made his head hurt.

Floating above the Scorewall were large, bright lights that lit up the giant surface along its entire length. The lights hovered in the air somehow, and when someone got in between them and the wall, they automatically shifted, up, down, left, right, in order to keep shining on the information. More artifacts, Holt guessed.

In front of the bright, floating lights, dozens of kids hung from ropes and pulleys attached to the cavern ceiling, allowing them not only to hover in front of the Scorewall, but also float up and down its length and height. They were called Scorekeepers, and they constantly moved around the wall, changing score totals based on the official information they received, writing in different colors of chalk, changing numbers, raising and lowering them, adding the occasional name.

The denizens of the city packed inside the giant chamber yelled up at the Scorekeepers as they did their jobs, shuffling back and forth. Everything was chaotic, energetic, ludicrous . . . and very weighted.

"Been here twice," Holt said. "But never came in this room. Always heard about it, but . . . wow . . ."

"It's hard to understand until you see it," Mira said, taking it all in like it was the first time.

Holt watched the churning crowd, watched it shout and yell and celebrate and curse, all depending on the numbers that cycled this way and that as fast as the Scorekeepers could write them. "Everyone acts like this thing is life or death."

"In Midnight City . . . it is." She looked at him, held his gaze. "Want to see something?" She moved left, pushing through the crowd, and Holt and Zoey and Max followed after her.

At the very end of the Scorewall, where the list of residents ended, past the anonymous visitors and the frozen point totals of Freebooters who had gone missing in the Strange Lands, was a section of the wall with about thirty names on it. Each of the names had one thing in common: They were written in red chalk, and the number of Points next to them was 0.

"What is it?" Holt asked, gazing up at the names.

"It's the part of the Scorewall that tracks the Unmentionables," Mira said, "people who have had all their Points removed."

She nodded to the topmost name in the section, almost in the far left corner. The box there was owned by MIRA TOOMBS. And next to the name was a single, lonely *0.*

Mira glared up at it a long time, the emotions on her face switching between anger and bitterness and sadness. Holt let her look, said nothing while she did so. He had no idea what to say, anyway. He barely understood any of this, so how could he even begin to understand what she was feeling?

Eventually, she looked back at him. "Let's get out of here," she said crisply, and then began pushing back through the churning madness of people, as if the environment had suddenly turned toxic.

31. REVELATIONS

MIRA MOVED AS QUICKLY as she could out of the Scorewall room and leaned against a cavern wall, out of breath and shaking.

Seeing her name among the Unmentionables had way more of an effect than she'd expected. She knew it would be there—where else would it be? But, still, seeing it with the rest and that zero in the box, a zero that at one time had been more than ten thousand . . .

She shuddered at the loss; it felt like she'd been physically struck.

And there was something else: The Unmentionables box was kept in order of the names added. Which meant another name should have been right above hers. But it wasn't.

Ben's.

The person she'd come all this way to save. Mira didn't know what that meant. Was he still on the main board? Or was he dead and they had moved it off completely?

Mira shook the thoughts from her head. None of them were helpful. That part of her life was over now, no matter what she did. But she had come here for something specific. She had a plan, and she would carry it out. She could still salvage some of the mess she'd made of everything.

Mira felt Holt's hand gently touch her back. She wanted to turn and hug him, to feel his arms around her . . . but that wouldn't help anything either. It would feel good, certainly, but it wouldn't help.

She wiped away the beginning traces of tears from her eyes and turned around. "I'm okay," she said, feeling Zoey's hand slip into hers.

Holt studied her. "You know, if you want me to help," he began, "it'd be good if I knew what was going on here."

Mira stared back at him. He was right, of course: he probably should know. But she still wasn't sure about having him help. This was her mess, and the idea of risking the lives of people she cared about to fix it didn't sit well with her.

Mira took in the new room they'd entered. It was in the market district, which was different from the business district in that the wares sold here were mainly for residents. The smells of all types of food filled the air, sizzling on grills and hot plates. Items in bulk gleamed on shelves, either refurbished, salvaged, or newly made. The room was lined with people, plodding in between the stalls, trading for supplies.

Mira moved for a hut made out of an old, green Volkswagen van someone had found a way to get inside, with tables and a counter attached to it. A lone girl wearing the orange color of the Lost Knights stood behind the counter, and she smiled as Mira ordered three cups of tea. The shop had a good stockpile of tea bags on a shelf behind her, still in their dusty packaging.

When it was brewed, Mira offered the girl a small sewing and repair kit she'd picked up somewhere as trade. It was enough. Normally she would have traded Points, but as she'd just personally witnessed, she didn't have those anymore. She, Holt, and Zoey sat down at a makeshift table attached to the doorframe of the old van, while Max curled up at Holt's feet, gently chewing on his boot heel.

"I don't like this," Zoey said as she sipped her tea and crinkled her nose. "It's not sweet."

"It's tea, sweetheart. Try some of this in it." Mira pushed a tube of honey on the table toward the little girl.

Mira watched the crowd as it seethed past them, churning among the stalls and booths. They were completely surrounded by people who might recognize Mira, but she knew that wasn't likely. If there was one thing certain about Midnight City, it was that it had a short attention span.

"Making artifact combinations always came easy to me," Mira finally said. "The more complicated it was, the more I liked it. Portals. Chinooks. Magnatrons. But the best was when someone asked for something new, something that had never been made before. A new artifact, with new properties and powers." She smiled as she remembered the feelings. "Making an established artifact can still be challenging, but there's no sense of danger. It's like putting a puzzle together you've done

a dozen times before. But . . . a *new* combination? Starting from nothing, trying to figure out the right mix of components, the right Focusers,
the right Essences? There's nothing like it."

Next to her, Zoey was still pouring the honey into her tea from the
plastic squeeze bottle, and Mira took it from her with a frown. "That's
enough, Zoey, you'll make yourself sick."

The little girl sipped her tea, then looked up at Mira and smiled.

"So, you were making something new," Holt guessed.

Mira nodded. "Something I'd experimented with for years, and as I got
closer to finding the right pairings, I started passing over paid commissions
to work on it. My Points started declining, the rest of the faction wondered
what I was doing, why I kept making trips into the Strange Lands."

Zoey looked up from her tea curiously. "What were you making,
Mira?"

Mira ran a hand through the girl's hair, straightening it. "An artifact
that would slow down the Tone." She felt Holt's stare refocus on her.
"And after a few dozen tries, I thought I had it, too. But I was wrong."

"It didn't work?" Holt asked.

"No, it worked," she answered. "Just not the way I intended. I did
something wrong—I still don't know what, I never got to analyze it. But
the artifact didn't slow down the Tone. It did the *opposite*. It accelerated
it, made it spread *faster*."

Holt shifted in his seat uncomfortably. "How much faster?" he asked.

"Less than a minute of exposure, and you'd Succumb, no matter how
young you were," Mira said, looking back up at him. "Even if you were
Heedless."

"Wait a second . . ." Holt was trying to put the pieces together, and it
wasn't easy. "How could you know that's what this thing would do?"

"Because I tested it," Mira replied. "I tested it on myself."

"Mira . . ." Holt's voice dropped low.

"It was my creation, it was my responsibility, who else would I test it
on?" she said before he could finish. "I probably lost six months to the
Tone in the few seconds I used it. It was . . . awful. Like how the Tone is
now, only worse, much worse. It felt like . . . things crawling around in
my head . . ." Mira trailed off, not wanting to remember.

She could see the horror in Holt's eyes. "God, anyone who had that
could . . ." He paused as he processed the realization.

"Quietly get rid of anyone they wanted, for starters," Mira said. "And if you were good enough, you could use that combination as the essence in a new one, extend and focus the ability, make it into a weapon you could project at dozens of people at the same time."

"That has to be destroyed," Holt said. Mira could hear the tightness in his voice, and it was a tightness reserved for people who had experienced the true horror of the Tone, who had watched the minds of people they knew be replaced with . . . nothing at all. Mira knew about his sister now, and she didn't blame him.

"I tried to destroy it," Mira said. "But the Interfusion had already sealed it. Which meant it could only be destroyed in the Strange Lands. Ben and I were going to take it back, make sure it was dismantled, but Lenore somehow found out about it."

"Who's Lenore?" Holt asked, but Mira could tell Lenore wasn't the one he wanted to ask about.

"The leader of the Gray Devils," Mira said. "Which means she has the most Points of any single individual in Midnight City. She is a very, very powerful person here, and she's Heedless, like you. I still don't know how she found out about it, but when she did, she came with all her guards to stop us from leaving. I did the only thing I could think of. I hid the artifact so Lenore couldn't have it. For a Heedless, the power to wield the Tone like a weapon would be a horrible thing. She hasn't faced the realities like you have, and she doesn't care to."

"This is the leader of the faction you belonged to?" Holt asked in surprise.

"Lenore and I had a . . . complicated relationship," Mira said. "In lots of ways, she was like a sister. A mentor, even. But the pressure to hold on to the Prime Movership is intense. It would probably change anyone for the worse. Eventually, when you start to run out of conventional ways to stay on top, you start looking for other alternatives. *Any* alternatives."

"But she never found the artifact? You're sure?" Holt asked.

"They never found it and they never will, not without me," she said. "It's the only reason I'm not dead. But before I escaped, Lenore came up with a new way to pressure me."

"Ben," Holt guessed, and Mira nodded. "Who is he?"

Mira felt a twinge of nervousness. Ben was the one thing she didn't want to discuss with Holt, but the way she saw it, he deserved the basics at least. "Ben was . . . *is* a friend. A close one, a Freebooter in the Gray Devils. Lenore had him accused and found guilty of Point Fabrication, just like me. It's the most severe crime you can commit here, and it carries a death sentence. She said if I told her where the artifact was, she would let us go. We wouldn't have our Points anymore, we were Unmentionable, but we could live. As long as she got the artifact."

"And you said no," Holt said.

"I said no . . . and then I escaped," Mira answered, feeling the sting of the decision all over again. "There was no way to get Ben. I . . . I left him here. With Lenore. I gambled she would keep him alive for leverage, but for all I know, he's already dead. And if he is, it's my fault." The anguish in her voice was palpable, and Mira felt Zoey's hand on hers.

"You know that's not true," Holt said softly. "You couldn't let Lenore have that thing. If you did, you'd be responsible for a lot more than just Ben's death. You did the only thing you could—you did the brave thing."

"Yeah?" Mira asked. "Well, it sure doesn't feel that way."

Holt was silent, thinking, and she felt his eyes on her. "You've come all the way back here," he said. "Risked everything to do it. But why, Mira? What do you want to do?"

Mira looked back at Holt. There was something about him that was different from everyone else in her life. She knew what it was. He'd sacrificed his own interests for hers. He was here for her when it would be much better for him to be somewhere else. Those were unheard of gestures in the world as it was now, and from what she knew of Holt, they were just as unheard of for him. Yet, here he was. . . .

Mira smiled at him, gently stroked his face with her hand. Then her stare hardened as she contemplated what they had to do, and she knew it wasn't going to be easy.

"There's someone we have to go see," Mira said.

Holt looked back at her with more than a little trepidation. To be honest, Mira felt the same way, but she laid out her plans all the same, talking as they finished the rest of their tea.

32. THE CESAR

WHEN HOLT AND THE OTHERS REACHED the main gate, they were instantly stopped by Los Lobos compound guards: two big, older kids wearing auburn red, the color of their faction, the black of the Tone creeping through their eyes.

"No visitors today, we don't want Pledges," one of the guards said. "You can turn around and head back."

"We're definitely not here to Pledge," Mira said as she lowered the hood from her head. "Tell Cesar that Mira Toombs wants to see him."

The guards stared at Mira like she was a ghost. Zoey chuckled at the looks on their faces.

"Wait here," one of them mumbled before running into the compound on the other side of the gate. A few minutes later, he reemerged with four other Lobos, two more boys and two girls. "The Cesar will see you. But the dog stays outside—there's no animals in the compound."

"I'll stay with the Max," Zoey said, kneeling down and wrapping her hands around the dog protectively. Holt looked up to Mira questioningly.

"She'll be fine," Mira said. "We're guests under the faction's protection. For the moment, anyway."

Holt didn't see that they had much choice, and he looked back at Zoey. "We'll be back in a minute, kiddo," Holt said, and Zoey smiled up at him. She didn't seem worried at all.

Holt envied her.

He was in as uncharted a territory as he'd ever been, and he was following someone else's lead on top of it. He didn't like not being the one making the decisions. He just hoped Mira knew what she was doing.

They walked through the main gate into the compound, flanked on all sides by guards, and while they were definitely being "protected," it didn't do much to put Holt's mind at ease.

Major factions in Midnight City were given caverns of their own in which to build compounds, and Los Lobos had one made of concrete and strong wood. It looked more like a fort than a clubhouse, somehow blended and bolted into the chaotic shapes of the cavern walls, which only reinforced it further. It was blocky, but it wasn't all utilitarian. The concrete had been spray-painted graffiti style in shades of red, with swirling images and letters all centering around a huge stylistic rendering of a wolf's head that covered the main wall.

"Los Lobos' specialty is construction," Mira told Holt quietly. "It's the source of their Points. With the exception of the Gray Devils' aqueducts, they built pretty much every structure in Midnight City, including the other faction compounds."

Ahead of them was the main entryway, and it was an amazing sight: a giant refurbished bank vault door that had been bolted into a steel frame in the compound's main wall. It still had the hand levers and combination lock, but they were backwards, facing toward the interior of the compound.

So it could be locked from the inside, Holt realized. He studied it appreciatively. It had been no small feat, repurposing something that big.

"How'd they get that all the way down here?" Holt asked. The door must have weighed several tons, at least.

"No one but Los Lobos knows that," Mira said as they passed through the door. "But it involved artifacts, probably a Portal combined with half a dozen Aleves. Whatever they did, it took them only one night. Pretty impressive, and it got them a lot of Points."

On the Scorewall, Midnight City reserved twelve spots for what were simply called "factions," organized groups of resident survivors who lived and made their way together, not unlike the thousands of congregations that existed on the surface. The difference was, the factions were interested in Points.

A faction's Points were determined by a complicated equation that took into account the point totals of its members, of its enemies, and of the achievements and failings of the faction as a whole. The faction that had the most Points was called the Prime Movers, a position that granted it a dominant voting percentage on the city's supreme council. Which essentially meant, in no uncertain terms, that the Prime Movers ran Midnight City.

The current Prime Movers were the Gray Devils, Mira's old faction, and they had held the title for more than three years.

After the main door, the concrete of the exterior gave way to yet more cavern walls. The outside was a fortified façade, Holt saw, which protected the more diverse cavern system of the compound beyond.

But it wasn't just a cavern, either. A small "hall" opened up into an enormous room, several hundred feet in diameter. There were natural formed ledges on some of the walls, and ladders led up to them. On the ledges, Holt saw dozens of doors of all shapes and colors and origins built into nooks and crannies, leading to different parts of the compound.

But it was the huge room itself that was most impressive.

Dozens of cone-shaped stalactites dripped downward from far above, each circled with strings of Illuminators, hanging like petrified Christmas trees from the ceiling and bathing the room in a warm glow of pale white. The ceiling itself had been polished smooth, like rough wood sanded down.

And on the smooth surface, in between the stalactite formations, was an incredible collection of graffiti art. Images and symbols and shapes and writing, and not just in auburn red like the ones outside, but a myriad of colors that filled the ceiling, sparkling brightly underneath the stalactites.

Scaffolding and rope climbed up to the center of the ceiling, where a boy hung on his back, wearing goggles and a mask, and holding cans of paint in both hands. He was spraying the ceiling above him, adding to the giant canvas's already brilliant colors, bringing to life a flowing script of writing.

The letters weaved in and out of a series of stalactites, a mix of purple and red and blue. Whatever it said, it was written in Spanish.

"Cesar!" one of the guards yelled up at the boy. He kept painting; if he'd heard the call, he showed no sign. "*Cesar!* There's a Gray Devil in the hall."

The spray paint in the boy's hand shut off, but he didn't look down. "You're wrong," the boy said, and he slapped a set of clamps on his chest. The ropes that held him to the ceiling dropped him toward the floor, and he rode them down easily, slapping the clamps back into place right before he hit, stopping his fall. "She's not a Gray Devil anymore. Are you, Mira?"

The boy who stood before them was all of fifteen, Hispanic with curly black hair, wearing a red T-shirt over black cargo pants, and easily the shortest person in the room. But short or tall, the way the other kids in the hall eyed him warily suggested he had a way of commanding respect. He stepped out of the harness, keeping his gaze on Mira.

"No, Cesar," Mira said. "Not anymore."

Cesar handed the two cans of spray paint to one of the other boys without looking at him and removed his mask and goggles. "My Sistine Chapel," he said, motioning to the multicolored ceiling above them and smiling proudly. "What do you think?"

"I think it took a lot of paint," Mira said without much enthusiasm. At the dismissive comment, the other faction members tensed.

But Cesar only laughed out loud, long and hard—though, to Holt's ears, the sound contained a hint of menace. "You always were difficult to impress, Mira," the little kid said, smiling wickedly. "But I always liked that about you."

"The writing up there," Holt said. "What does it say?"

At the sound of Holt's voice, the smile vanished from Cesar's face. His eyes moved from Mira to Holt, and Holt felt the weight of the little kid's stare. There was something dangerous about the way the boy held himself, an unpredictability in his eyes that Holt had seen before with youths who got too much power too quickly. When you thought no one would stand up to you, there was very little you wouldn't do if the urge struck you.

"It says '*Al mal paso, darle prisa,*'" Cesar said.

"Which means—?"

Cesar studied Holt a moment more, then looked back to Mira. "This one wears no colors—he's an Outsider. Why bring him into my compound?"

"He's my friend, Outsider or not," Mira said. "You'd be surprised, there's lots of people worth knowing on the surface."

Cesar spit, moved away, gazing up at the ceiling again. "The surface is past tense. Pathetic, ragtag groups scrounging in what's left of a dead world, just trying to survive. Here, we do more than survive: We *build* things. We *thrive*."

"Thriving, perhaps," Mira replied. "But still in second place."

Cesar stiffened. He kept his back to them as he slowly looked down from the ceiling. "Did I ever tell you, Mira, that your name is a word in Spanish? It means 'look.'" What little warmth was in his voice before, it vanished now. "It's fitting, I think. You're always looking for something, aren't you? It's what got you into trouble in the first place. And it's what's about to get you into trouble now." He turned around, fixing her with a cold gaze. Any pretense of cordiality was gone, and the other Lobos instinctively took a step back. "What did you come here *looking* for, Mira Toombs? You're either very brave or very stupid. My Points are on stupid, especially if you think I won't hand you straight over to the council. You have any idea how much you're worth now?"

"Turning me over would get you Points, that's for sure," Mira replied. "But handing me to the council is handing me to the Gray Devils."

Cesar considered her as she spoke, his face unreadable.

"I was at the Scorewall earlier," Mira continued. "I saw the totals, saw how much further ahead they are than you. Even further than when I left. And what have you been doing about it, Cesar?" She looked up at the graffiti winding through the brightly lit stalactites, unimpressed. "Painting on a ceiling."

Cesar took a slow, dangerous step toward her. Holt moved forward as well, but Mira held up a hand. As much as he didn't like it, he stopped and watched Cesar slowly inch toward her like a wolf.

"Nowhere in any of that did I hear an answer to my question," he said.

"I wanna break into the Gray Devils compound," Mira replied. "And I want your help to do it."

The laughter from the faction members echoed all around them in the large room. Cesar, however, did not laugh.

"You know the caverns better than any faction," she continued, "especially the unmapped areas. It's a source of a lot of Points for you. I'm betting you know secret ways into pretty much every main cavern or compound in the system."

Cesar studied her evenly, weighing things. "Maybe. Maybe not. Even if I did, why would I risk helping a treacherous, double-dealing little Freebooter like you?"

"Aw, Cesar," Mira said with a slight smile. "Name calling? Really?"

"When you're caught," Cesar said, ignoring her, "and word comes down how you got inside, someone's gonna lose Points for that. And you don't got any more Points, which means it'll be Los Lobos who loses 'em."

"You're right," Mira said. "But *only* if I get caught. If I pull it off, the Gray Devils are the ones who are going to lose Points. A lot of them. Probably enough to reestablish you as the Prime Movers."

Murmurings from Los Lobos filled the air, ideas and calculations passing through the hall. Mira had their attention now.

"The Gray Devils say you're a Point Fabricator," Cesar said.

"The Gray Devils say a lot of things. You're not stupid—you know that's not true," Mira replied. "They lied to make a problem go away."

"Wouldn't surprise me. Lenore's the best liar I've ever seen, and she's lied about far less," Cesar said, musing. "But it's the 'problem' you mention that I wonder about. They have something of yours, don't they? What is it? An artifact, something you built? Whatever it is, it must be incredibly valuable or incredibly dangerous for them to go to these lengths to get rid of you."

"That's my business and no one else's," Mira said sharply.

Cesar shrugged and stepped away from her, pacing in the huge cavern, thinking. "So maybe you do pull it off, maybe you steal back whatever it is they took, maybe you reveal them for the lying, pathetic losers they are—that would definitely drop their total a lot. But that's a lot of maybes, and you're just one Freebooter and one Outsider."

"We have a dog and a little girl, too," Holt said.

Cesar ignored him. "I still don't see why it's worth all the risk for me to help you. Help me understand."

"Happy to," Mira said, reaching into her pack. The guards around her all tensed, but Cesar waved them down in annoyance. She pulled free the glass cylinder with the brownish sliver of plutonium still floating within the clear liquid inside. The Dampener was still attached by its watchband.

When Cesar saw it, his eyes widened. It was the first time since the conversation began that Holt had seen the Lobos leader surprised or off balance.

"Is that . . . what I think it is?" Cesar asked.

"How long have you been trying to mount a Severed Tower expedition, Cesar? Two years? Three? I wonder how many Points entering the Tower is worth these days." Mira said with a smile, "You get me into the Gray Devils compound . . . you can find out."

Cesar gazed at the plutonium lustfully a moment more, then tore his eyes away and looked at one of his boys standing nearby, a giant of a kid who towered over the others, with a black ponytail and a wicked-looking hunting knife on his belt. "Marcus, answer this Freebooter's question. You need to check the maps?"

"Nah," the big kid responded. "There's two ways into the Devils' caverns, both side chutes that connect through the Crawlway. They're tight, no fun pushing through 'em, but they'll get her there."

"Where do they come out?" Mira asked.

"One near the lab, the other in a hallway deeper in, near the residences, I think, by the falls."

"I want the one near the residences," Mira said.

Cesar studied her. "Guess it would be useless of me to ask for the plutonium in advance?"

"Useless isn't the right word." Mira smiled.

"Then two of my boys go with you, Marcus and someone else," Cesar announced. "Just to make sure you feel like paying up once all's said and done."

Mira shrugged. "If that's how it needs to be, then fine."

Cesar's eyes raked over her. "Either way, Mira Toombs, things go to plan, or things go to hell, you and I won't be seeing each other again. You're through in Midnight City. But you knew that coming in. There ain't no coming back from Unmentionable."

"This place has always cramped my style anyway," Mira replied. Holt was impressed by her composure, how she didn't give off even a slight hint at the pain he knew she felt at the words.

33. CRAWLWAY

HOLT PUSHED MAX FORWARD through the unbelievably tight cavern tunnel, but the dog was less than cooperative. He struggled every few feet, whining and sometimes growling. "Max, just move!" Holt whispered roughly as he shoved on the dog's rear. He was afraid to make too much noise. Marcus had sent word down the line that they were getting close to the Gray Devils now, and they needed to be quiet.

The Lobo was easily one of the biggest kids Holt had ever seen, all muscle and built like an oak tree. He looked like he was carved out of granite, and for the life of him, Holt couldn't figure out how the kid managed to fit through the horror they were traversing right now, much less remain calm.

The "Crawlway" was a densely packed collection of cavern tunnels that wound through most of the system's larger rooms, and the name was definitely deserved. For Holt, it was a claustrophobic nightmare, a tunnel so tight, he had to keep his hands stretched out in front of him, because it wasn't wide enough to fit with them at his sides.

The first hundred feet or so hadn't been too bad, but now the novelty had definitely worn off. He felt buried alive, like the walls were pushing in on him and the tunnel was shrinking the farther they moved through it.

Max was enjoying the experience even less, it seemed.

"Max, you can do it, wiggle like a worm!" he heard Zoey say encouragingly from the other side of the dog. There was no trace of discomfort or uneasiness in her voice, but then again, she was the smallest one out of all of them. Hell, she was probably having fun.

Max whined and moved forward, following Zoey's voice, and Holt sighed in relief. He crawled forward through the crushing tunnel, foot after foot, until he looked up and noticed Max was no longer in front of him.

In fact, nothing was, just a wall of darkness. Holt shone his light ahead, but it didn't help much. The rock was so black, you couldn't tell if you'd lit up a wall or were looking at shadow.

Holt eyed the darkness ahead warily. "Max? Zoey?" No answer, no sound at all. How could they have disappeared so fast?

He pulled himself cautiously forward, conscious of the rock pressing down on him. There was still no sign of—

The floor fell away from under him as the tunnel made a sudden, sharp descent downward.

Holt yelled in surprise as he slid face-first down the slick, rocky slope, picking up speed, faster and faster toward . . . whatever lay below.

He shut his eyes, waited for the moment when his face would slam into some rock wall, but instead he tumbled out of the tunnel into a larger one, rolling right into Max and almost bowling the dog over. Everyone else was picking themselves up off the floor, and Holt glared at the Lobos. "Would a heads-up have killed you?" he asked testily.

They just smirked at him. "You're still in one piece, Outsider," Marcus said. "Now shut up from here on out—sound carries bad and this passage connects to the compound."

Marcus and his fellow set off, and Holt made to follow . . . when he caught Mira's eye ahead of him. She had a strange look, hesitant and contemplative, with a touch of guilt. Was she having second thoughts about the plan? If she was, it was a little late for that now.

He watched her move on, crawling after the Lobos. Zoey went next, waving Max to follow, which he did. The dog was walking on all fours now, and by the incessant wagging of his tail, it was clear Max was feeling better. And when Holt examined the new tunnel, so did he. The ceiling was low enough that he had trouble sitting in a crouch, and he couldn't extend his arms straight out to the sides, but after that last tunnel, it felt like the inside of Grand Central Station.

Ahead of him, he saw the flashlights switch off, and he followed suit. They must almost be there.

Ahead, the others were crouched around a hole in the floor. Through the hole, light filtered up, and Holt took a spot around it and looked.

Another cavern ran below them, wide compared to theirs, and Holt saw glimpses of painted doors inset into its wall spaced several feet apart.

He leaned forward for a better view, but Marcus's hand clamped onto his shoulder, held him in place. When Holt looked up at the big kid, he held a finger to his lips.

Beneath them came the sound of voices. Seconds later, two figures walked by, a girl and a boy, each dressed in something gray. They didn't even glance up as they moved, but if they had, they would have seen five faces and a dog snout staring down at them.

When the sounds of their voices finally faded away, Marcus glared at each of them. "This is the tunnel to the main residence hall," he whispered.

"What side of the compound are we on?" Mira asked, just as quietly.

"The northern side, near the falls. Best you're gonna get," he responded, and his stare hardened. "We'll take that plutonium now."

"I'm going to assume that's a joke," Mira replied.

"What was that?" Marcus asked dangerously.

"The Crawlway's a maze," Mira replied. "I don't wanna spend a month lost back there."

"We'll wait," Marcus said with a grin.

"I know you will, because you're not getting paid until I'm back." A very displeased look formed on Marcus's face, but Mira just smiled sweetly at him. "It's not like I'm not coming back, is it? How else am I gonna get out—walk out the front gate?"

Marcus and his compatriot looked at each other, considering.

"I need something else from you, or there's no deal," Mira pressed on before they could say no. She turned and looked at Holt, and something passed between them. "I'm going by myself, and I don't want anyone else following."

"Wait, *what?*" Holt exclaimed.

"Mira . . . ," Zoey started, staring up at Mira.

"We have to keep your friends on ice, too?" Marcus asked.

"Just think of them as collateral," Mira said. "Something you know I'll come back for."

Marcus and the other Lobo shared a look; then they both shrugged. Marcus reached out and grabbed Holt with a concretelike grip, sealing him in place. Holt struggled, but the giant hand was clamped down on him like a vise.

The other kid reached out for Zoey. She tried to scamper away, but the kid pulled her back, muzzling her with a palm over her mouth.

"Don't hurt her," Mira whispered, genuine anger in her glare.

"No guarantee there. No guarantee at all," Marcus said, slowly drawing the hunting knife from his belt and holding it up for Mira to see. It was a big knife. "You wanna play games, fine, we can play games. But if an hour comes and goes and you're still not back, I might take it upon myself to start cutting off little pieces of your friends here. We got an understanding, you and I?"

Mira stared back at the giant of a boy, her fists clenching at her sides. "Pretty clear, yeah." Mira looked at Zoey. "Zoey, it's gonna be all right, I promise. Okay?"

Zoey continued to struggle in spite of the assurances.

"Mira, don't do this . . . ," Holt said, then groaned as Marcus's hand dug into his shoulder.

"I'm sorry, Holt," Mira said. When he looked up, her eyes were on him again. They were filled with a steady resolution; she had her plan, and she was sticking with it. But there was guilt there, too. "This is my problem . . . and my mistake. And no one else is getting hurt trying to fix it." She reached out and gently touched his hand. "But thank you for coming this far with me."

Holt felt her hand on his a moment more, then watched as she leapt through the opening in the floor down to the Gray Devils cavern below and disappeared.

34. PHOTOGRAPH

MIRA FELL FROM THE HOLE and hit the floor running, leaving it quickly behind. It was funny. When she had lived here, she walked past that opening every day, but never really gave it much thought. Just another cramped, impassable chute that wound off into the unmapped areas of the caverns, or so she'd believed. She wondered how many times a Lobo spy had watched her walk right under it.

Mira saw she was in the tunnel to the Gray Devils residence hall, just like Marcus had said. Illuminators floated near the ceiling, providing light, and a few smaller rooms branched off it. They were all sealed with doors brought in from the outside and framed into the openings. They were also all locked, Mira knew.

She dug through her pack and pulled out a key chain loaded with about a dozen small keys of different colors and shapes, each marked with the δ symbol. They were Skeleton Keys, major artifacts from the Strange Lands' deeper parts, and they would open any lock that took a key. Not every key from the Strange Lands was a Skeleton Key—only certain ones developed the right properties, and Mira usually found only one for every eight she brought out. They were rare, very valuable, and this key ring, which held about half a dozen, represented her entire collection.

She plucked two of them from the ring as she moved. Ahead of her was one of the doors, inset into the wall. When she reached it, she shoved one of the Skeleton Keys into the lock. There was a spark and a hum, and Mira could feel the door handle vibrate slightly in her hand.

She twisted the key and, with a flash, the door clicked as it unlocked. Mira quickly opened the door, stepping into the small, rocky room beyond. When she removed the key, there was another flash . . . and the entire thing crumbled into a palmful of metallic shavings and dust in her fingers. Mira brushed off the residue as she stepped inside the room and shut the door behind her. Skeleton Keys could be used only once.

It was a supply closet, as she'd expected, lined with cabinets full of all kinds of things: paint cans, scrap metal, boxes of nails, tools, car batteries, thick chain, rope and pulleys, pieces of plywood. Mira set her pack down amid it all, and quickly dug through it, removing two dimes, a small piece of a mirror, and a glass vial.

Mira assembled the components and hurriedly wrapped them with her ever-dwindling supply of duct tape. As she did, a crackling charged the air, and a light humming sound built and faded away.

Mira examined at the artifact, another Shroud, but this one wasn't for her. She just hoped he remembered what she'd told him. She set the newly Interfused Shroud on her pack and tossed the ring of Skeleton Keys on top of them as well.

She left the closet, leaving the door unlocked. From a pocket, she pulled out a line of red string and quickly wrapped it around the door handle. It didn't stand out completely. If you weren't looking for it, you probably wouldn't notice it.

The hallway was still empty and quiet, and she moved down it again, heading for where the tunnel ended and widened into a new room. As she approached it, a deep sound, like constantly rumbling thunder, grew louder the farther she went.

The Gray Devils residence hall was a massive, cylindrical cavern that rose hundreds of feet straight up. There were ledges and indentations all through the rough, black rock walls, and built out from them were dozens of platforms made of wood and sheet metal, bolted and hung with rope and chains into the sides of the cavern.

Each platform was the personal space of a Gray Devils member, and each person made the space their own, customizing it with different furnishings and possessions. They were painted shades of gray and white, but most had additional drawings or writing underneath them, so they were visible from the ground. Seen from below, it made a kaleidoscope of color and personality that ascended far above to the cavern ceiling.

Ladders climbed up the walls, and precarious bridges stretched between them all the way to the top.

Large Illuminators floated in the air at the top of the ceiling, bathing everything in dim light, while even smaller ones had been strung between the ceiling's stalactites. Hanging down from that same ceiling were two huge banners, each emblazoned with the smiling devil logo. And between them, at the very top of the cavern, was something like a balcony, where light from candles and lanterns gleamed in the dark. It was Lenore's residence, and Mira stared up at it warily before turning to examine the room's most prominent feature.

A large underground waterfall burst out of the cavern wall far above and tumbled downward, crashing into a pool at the far end of the room, draining away through some hidden underwater tunnel system. A grid of latticework and sheet metal hung next to it, attached to mechanical arms, but there was no indication what they were used for.

Large blue Illuminators were installed behind the tumbling water, and the light that shone through made the falls glow like sapphire in the dark. It was an impressive sight, and Mira paused to admire it. She had built and installed those blue Illuminators herself, a project that won her enough Points to finally become the top Freebooter in Midnight City, and she smiled as she looked at it.

Mira had forgotten how loud the falls were, and marveled that she had ever been able to sleep in here. But she'd gotten used to it. Eventually, you stopped hearing it altogether.

The good news was, because the waterfall was so loud, she didn't have to worry about being quiet. She did, however, have to worry about being seen.

Mira ducked into the shadows of the closest wall and looked upward at the multitude of colorful platforms above her. Her eye moved to two of them, on the fifth level, close to each other, and both of them were dark and lifeless.

Her platform, and a few down to the left, Ben's. Two places where, in another life, she'd made a lot of memories. Seeing them again, dark and without any indication of life, caused a hollow ache in her stomach. Going back to how things were wasn't why she'd come here, Mira reminded herself. There was *no* going back.

Mira looked away, found the nearest ladder, and started scaling it. It was a wooden one, and pretty sturdy, but she could see it went only as far as the third level. From there, she'd have to take one of the bridges to a new ladder.

She kept climbing, and passed by one of the lower-level platforms. She knew this one: it belonged to a boy named Daniel who led salvage runs into the ruins on the surface and always came back with nice items, a few of which she had traded for. His cavern wall was still decorated with dozens of faded postcards from the old world, some of them with writing on them. They were all from city ruins he had explored, Mira knew. Daniel always had a rule that he first found a postcard as a memento before doing any treasure hunting. It was bad luck otherwise.

She had liked Daniel; he was always nice to her. Now if he saw her, he would most surely raise an alarm and help run her down. Funny how quickly things could change here.

Mira continued upward and reached the end of the ladder, where it connected to one of the cavern's many rope bridges. The thing swayed precariously when she climbed onto it. It was the same for all the bridges here, and Mira had never gotten comfortable crossing them. They always seemed on the verge of falling apart or tipping you off, but as far as she could recall, none of them had ever collapsed, a testament to just how solid they really were, in spite of their appearance.

She moved over the bridge as quickly as she dared, holding on to the rope railings that ran along the sides. She kept an eye on the dark platforms as she went, looking for any sign of movement. From a few came the flickering light of candles or lanterns, but they were all mostly dark, which is what she'd counted on. From a distance, anyone looking would assume she was just another faction member heading to bed. That was the plan, at least.

Ahead of her, the bridge connected with two other ladders that moved diagonally to a far wall. Mira took the one she needed and started climbing, moving past the fourth level and stopping at the fifth.

Her quarters were dark and empty, as she'd expected, and Mira jumped silently off the ladder onto her platform and ducked out of sight.

Everything was, for the most part, exactly as she'd left it, though somewhat dusty now. Her hammock and blankets still hung between the cavern wall and a pole she'd attached to the floor in the middle of the platform. A row of blue metal shelves were at the far end, about half empty, which wasn't surprising. It was where Mira had kept her favorite major artifacts, which would all have definitely been stolen by now.

There were still a few things left, though. Candles, a tea jar, old books, a binder of Strange Lands maps, a jewelry box. A Polaroid picture was glued to the wall behind the shelf, and a small lump of jagged, purple crystals sat in the middle. On the bottom shelf was a small, ornate wooden chest made of a flowing combination of cherrywood and gold and silver.

The crystal was a remnant of a lightning strike from one of the numerous antimatter storms that hovered over the Strange Lands' fourth ring. In spite of how dangerous it could be, Mira had always thought the antimatter lightning was beautiful. It ripped the air in a whole range of colors, and wherever it hit, its flash incinerated the ground into crystal of the same color. As a result, navigating through the fourth ring was like traversing a neon-colored crystalline maze. The first time she'd explored it, she brought back this chunk as a keepsake.

The Polaroid was even more meaningful: a picture she'd snapped at the edge of the fourth ring, the farthest she had ever gone in. The picture showed huge wavering bands of color filling the sky over a horizon of city ruins, like a borealis. Silhouetted against them were two massive blurry wedges of darkness, spinning powerfully in the distance. They were tornadoes, but not like any in the normal world—six times as big and made entirely of swirling dark energy. They were isolated to the core, the deepest, most deadly part of the Strange Lands, and whatever they touched, they absorbed into themselves, ripping it from existence. She had taken this picture the morning before she and Ben returned home, and she remembered having to pull him away. Exploring the core was his obsession, and it hadn't been easy to make him leave.

She studied the entire platform with a mixture of emotions. It felt so comfortable here, and part of her expected Ben to swing down onto her dais as he always used to. But the rest of her knew things had changed beyond repair, and that those times were gone forever.

Mira focused on each individual object in her old space, wondering which one Lenore had chosen. It would be something meaningful, something Mira would absolutely take, but there were several choices that fit that criteria.

Mira hesitated. She was about to move past the point of no return, and by doing so, she would put others at risk—people she cared about, maybe even loved. She could always leave now, go back to the secret tunnel, forfeit the plutonium she had worked so hard to get. But this was what she'd come here for. And she had to go forward. She had to make things right . . . as much as she could.

Mira exhaled and moved for the small chest at the bottom of the shelf. She pulled out the second Skeleton Key and shoved it into the lock. The lock was made for a much smaller key, but that made no difference. When the artifact hit the keyhole, there was a spark and a hum, and it somehow reorganized its shape to fit inside the smaller lock.

She turned the key, and it flashed as it unlocked the chest, then dissolved away into a small pile of metallic dust that fell through her fingers onto the floor when she removed it.

Mira lifted the top half of the chest with trepidation . . . but nothing unexpected happened; it simply opened. Inside rested a tarnished but well taken care of brass stopwatch, a circular mirror with a frame of silver, and a magnet about the size of a silver dollar attached to a very long length of gold chain.

Mira smiled at the sight of her tools. With just these three items, she could survive 80 percent of Strange Lands anomalies, and these specific ones had gotten her all the way to the fourth ring. When she had escaped Midnight City, there wasn't enough time to grab these on her way out, and she had always regretted it.

Mira reached into the chest and pulled the items out one at a time. Each time, she expected the worst . . . but still, nothing alarming happened.

Mira contemplated the tools in her hand, thinking. If it wasn't them, then what was it?

She stuffed the three items in a pocket. It was good to feel their familiar weight and shape again. Their absence had felt like she was missing an arm or a hand.

Mira reached up and touched the purple crystal remnant on the shelf. Nothing. She touched the Polaroid. Nothing. She ran her hands over the books, picked up her old tea jar, touched the candles one at a time.

Nothing.

Mira was becoming worried. Had she been wrong about everything? If so, then her plan wasn't going to work . . . and she was in a lot of trouble.

Quickly, she looked around the rest of her space. There wasn't much else; she had always kept it fairly minimal. There was just the hammock, and . . .

Mira stopped, staring at something on the cavern wall behind the hammock. A small, faded, black-and-white photograph. Slowly, Mira stood up and moved to the item, staring down at it with a haunted look. It was a picture of a man leaning against an old station wagon, holding a small girl on his shoulders. Behind them, the ocean stretched to the horizon.

The girl was Mira, years ago, and the man was her father. It was the only picture she had of him, taken by her mother during one of their summer visits to Portland.

It was a long time since she had seen his face, and the sight of it here filled her with sudden sadness. Another part of her life that was over and would never come again, and one that had even less chance of being set right.

It was the one thing still left from that time, the thing she'd had the longest of any of her possessions, and anyone who knew her knew how much that photograph meant.

Mira scrutinized it a moment more, then slowly, carefully, she reached toward it . . .

. . . and everything around her flashed, bright and forceful.

The world spun crazily as Mira's feet were ripped off the floor of the platform and she was flung through the air toward the center of the giant room. When she reached it, she hung there, immobile, spinning around in a cocoon of light and inertia a hundred feet above the cavern floor, the result of some sort of artifact trap.

Of *course* it had been the picture, Mira thought. Her first instinct was to feel a small bit of relief. But as the Illuminators on the cavern ceiling far above lit up and filled the room with brightness, and the kids on the platforms began to stir from their sleep, the feeling quickly vanished.

All around her, the members of the Gray Devils looked up at the person trapped and spinning helplessly in the Gravity Void in the center of their residence hall. As they did, they all came to realize who she was. The trap that had been sprung was designed to catch one specific person, and it had done its job well.

Throughout the giant cylindrical cavern, a cheer sprang up, repeated over and over, echoing back and forth in the air around Mira.

"*Gray! . . . Gray! . . . Gray! . . . Gray! . . . Gray! . . .*" The more people who joined the shout, the more hostile it seemed. Mira felt a surge of heat in her face as she spun and stared at her former fellow faction members. She recognized most of them. The faction's top Information Peddlers, Johnny Ringo and Sam Smythe. Another salvage expert, like Daniel, named Oscar. Two young Freebooters named Summer and Meadow, girls who had always looked up to her, girls she had mentored. The Devils' main enforcers, big, scary kids named Hawke and Waylan. And many more. Some had been friends, others acquaintances, and a few had been competitors, but now they were all her enemies, and they glared up at her maliciously.

"*Gray! . . . Gray! . . . Gray! . . . Gray! . . .*" The hostile shouts continued, bouncing everywhere around her.

There was definitely no going back now.

THEY HAD LEFT MIRA'S LEGS UNBOUND, but her hands were tied behind her back. She stood alone in a cavern that rose to a smooth roof where blue and white Illuminators floated. It had been a long time since she'd been here, but it didn't look like Lenore had changed it all that much.

At the back of the room was the "balcony," a cliff ledge that looked out over the rest of the compound's residence hall below. The sounds of the thundering waterfall filtered up and into the room from outside.

A large four-poster bed sat in the back draped with gray curtains, and a big Victorian armoire stood next to it. One wall was lined with shelves full of books, and there was a reading area nearby with chairs and a sofa. In a corner, a few workbenches held photographic equipment. It was all old, but it was clear that it had been meticulously taken care of.

The room was clean and neat and feminine, and the older furniture blended well with the dark walls of the cavern, but it was not at all lavish, which wasn't surprising. Like any powerful faction leader in Midnight City, Lenore was obsessed with Points, and she spent much more time at the Scorewall than she did in her own room.

One indulgence, however, was apparent: All along the walls hung large framed black-and-white photographs from the World Before, famous ones. Prints by Adams, Strand, and Cartier-Bresson, all mounted throughout the room. It would have been a priceless collection in another time, but now it had only sentimental value.

Still, Lenore had spent a lot of resources to get these prints, Mira knew. To her, photographs were memories made physical, almost like freezing time. Mira didn't disagree, and the thoughts made her remember the photograph of her father.

There was a click as the room's large double doors were unlocked. Ornate and worn, they were still beautiful, and had been taken from an old Spanish mission somewhere down south and installed into the cavern room's opening. As they parted, Mira caught a glimpse of two burly Gray Devil guards outside as another figure passed by them and entered.

It was hard to say how old Lenore Rowe was. Mira so rarely saw anyone older than twenty, her frame of reference was skewed, and Lenore never disclosed her age. But if she had to guess, Mira would say somewhere close to thirty. Her eyes were clear and radiant green, and whenever Mira had looked at them, she couldn't help but bitterly think that they were how her own might appear, if not for the slowly spreading presence of the Tone.

Lenore was tall and thin, with long, shimmering black hair that fell down her back in a wide, loose braid. She wore a gray dress lined with a colorful floral print, which clung to all the right spots. Lenore was very aware she was a woman in a world of girls, and she used it to her advantage, both within and without the Gray Devils. She was beautiful and feminine, there was no doubt, but the beauty was tempered with a cold hardness that always kept you at arm's length, no matter how close you thought you might be.

Lenore's gaze found Mira and slowly scanned her up and down. Her expression was unreadable, as usual, and she said nothing as she slowly walked closer. Lenore always moved meticulously, almost in slow motion, and there was something mesmerizing in it. Mira swallowed as the woman approached. This was a moment she had, in some ways, looked forward to since she'd left. A confrontation, a reckoning of sorts, but now that it was here, all she felt was dread.

Lenore had no weapons that Mira could see, there was nothing in her hands, but with Mira's wrists tied behind her back, she had no real way of defending herself regardless. She was completely at Lenore's mercy, and that was never a good place to be.

When Lenore was close enough, Mira flinched as the woman took the last few steps quickly . . . and unexpectedly threw her arms around Mira, pulling her close into an embrace.

It took a moment for the shock to wear off and for Mira to realize what was happening. Amazingly, Lenore was *hugging* her.

"Mira," Lenore said softly, stroking the back of her red hair. "I am . . . so sorry. For everything."

It was surreal. Lenore held her another moment, then slowly pulled away, and Mira saw that Lenore's eyes had the beginnings of tears in them.

"I never said to tie her," Lenore said, looking at Mira's hands with agitation. "Take the ropes off." The guards jumped forward and quickly cut the ropes free. When she was untied, Mira rubbed her wrists. Ever since the first part of her journey with Holt, she'd come to really hate having her hands bound. "Now leave us," Lenore commanded.

The two boys, dressed in gray, closed the doors behind them as they left, and Mira and Lenore considered each other in the quiet room.

"Let me see you," Lenore said, moving closer. "I know it's only been months, but it feels like years. You look good, darling. A little tired, perhaps, but still good. And your hair is longer. I always told you to try it like that, do you remember? I like it."

Lenore's clear green eyes held Mira in their gaze a few more seconds; then she moved casually toward a cabinet along one of the walls. On it sat glasses and a carafe of clear water with strips of limes and lemons floating inside. She poured some of the drink into a glass.

"Water?" Lenore handed it to Mira, but Mira studied it hesitantly. Who knew what may have been put in it.

Lenore read the source of Mira's hesitation sadly. "How far we've come from where we were." She took the water from Mira's hand and drank a sip before handing it back. The look Lenore gave her almost made Mira feel ashamed. Almost. She took a deep drink, and it was good, the citrus flavors sparkling in her mouth, and she realized just how thirsty she was. She drank more.

Lenore held something up to show her. It was the photograph of Mira's father. "I had them link the artifacts to the picture. Of all that you left, it was the only thing that was irreplaceable, and the one I was sure you would take if you ever came back. I know how much it meant to you."

Lenore handed it to Mira, and she pondered the little girl frozen inside it, on the man's shoulders. She would be there forever, and there was something comforting about that.

"It's a nice composition," Lenore said. "Your mother had a good eye—I wish I could have known her."

Mira remained silent. She still wasn't sure what to make of all this, of Lenore's sympathy and tenderness, two traits she didn't often exhibit.

"How did you get inside?" Lenore asked. "The front gate has been sealed for hours, and the Rectifiers you built are still there, so you didn't use a Shroud."

Mira knew she would have to talk eventually, no matter what. It might as well be now. "Cesar was very eager to help," Mira said.

Lenore thought the comment through, putting the pieces together. "So. Los Lobos know tunnels that connect to our cavern. I shouldn't be surprised—they know the Crawlway better than anyone." Lenore smiled at the thought. "Still, once word reaches the city that you've returned home, I'm not sure Cesar will be as enthusiastic."

"Returned home?" Mira asked.

Lenore contemplated Mira carefully, weighing her thoughts. "Before you left, I handled things . . . poorly," she said. "Beyond poorly, and it's something I regret. You were more than a faction member to me, Mira, you were . . . family. And family doesn't do to each other the things I did to you."

Mira stared back at Lenore, unsure what to think. They were words she never expected to hear, and the skepticism, she was sure, showed in her eyes.

"You don't trust me," Lenore continued. "I probably wouldn't either. I did some very unpleasant things, after all."

"*Unpleasant?*" Mira's reaction was incredulous. "You accused me of Point Fabrication, Lenore. You stripped my Points and had me declared Unmentionable. You threatened to *torture and kill* my best friend."

"I know," Lenore replied evenly. "I'm not going to pretend what I did wasn't wrong. I want to make amends, as best I can."

"And what? I'm just supposed to believe that?" Mira asked.

Lenore sighed, looked away. "I knew you'd return, Mira. You've never been able to leave things unfinished. My hope was that when you did, Ben would be here. If you could hear it from him, it would make it so much easier to convince you."

Hearing Ben's name sent tremors of dread down her spine. "Where is he?" Mira asked.

"Set free." Lenore smiled. "He still has his Points."

"I don't believe you."

"You must have gone to the Scorewall, to see your own name if nothing else. Did you see Ben's there with yours? Did you?" Mira remembered the absence of his name in the Unmentionables box, and she felt the first stirrings of hope in her mind. "All you have to do is check the wall and you'll see his name, and his Points. He's alive, Mira . . . and still a Gray Devil."

"You didn't answer the question," Mira said. "*Where* is he? Why isn't he here?"

"He's leading an expedition."

"Into the Strange Lands? For what?"

"For Points," Lenore replied.

"For *Points?* That doesn't make any sense. Not unless he's going . . ." She faded off as the answer occurred to her.

"The *Severed Tower*, Mira. He'll be the first Gray Devil ever to enter it and return. You, if anyone, know how many Points that would be worth."

Indeed, Mira did. A massive amount. No Gray Devil Freebooter had ever been to the Severed Tower and survived. If it could be done, the faction would gain enough Points to solidify its hold as the Prime Mover for years to come. But it was a big *if*. Less than half a dozen people had ever even made it inside the Tower, let alone returned. Navigating the core was essentially suicide.

"He'll be killed," Mira said. "No one has made it into the Tower in years."

"It's what he wanted, Mira. He asked me and I gave my approval as a gesture of reconciliation." Lenore's gaze softened. "He wished you could have gone with him. There was no one he trusted more."

It was true: They had worked well together, had even set records for the fastest crossings of the second and third rings. Since she had known Ben, they never went into the Strange Lands without the other, and the thought of him navigating it alone made an unpleasant emptiness in her chest.

"His chances would be much better if you were there," Lenore said, and the words resonated with Mira. "You can still go with him, Mira. You can help him, enter the Tower together, the way he always wanted.

The expedition left only a few days ago. You could catch them. If not before the crossroads, then at Polestar."

"And you would just . . . let me leave, Lenore?" Mira asked dubiously. "Just like that? After everything that's happened?"

"No, Mira," Lenore said, taking a step closer. "I am willing to do much more than that. I would give you your life back, the one I so callously took."

Mira looked at Lenore like she had lost her mind. "You made me Unmentionable. There's no coming back from that."

"Your Points, I'm afraid, are lost," Lenore said. "But the Unmentionable status can be removed."

"But the Codex—"

"Allows for the removal of an Unmentionable brand," Lenore said, "if the denizen belongs to a faction willing to sacrifice one-fifth of its Points as a penalty."

Mira was speechless. The Codex was Midnight City's constitution, its founding principles, and it was a very dense, very complicated document. It explained in exacting detail the impossibly complex Points system, as well as the city's political structure. Mira had read it only a few times, and the one thing she had learned was that there were no absolutes in the Codex. Everything in it seemed to have a loophole. Even the loopholes had loopholes. But still, it was a steep price to pay.

"One-*fifth*?" Mira asked. "That would put you below Los Lobos—it would knock you out as the Prime Mover. You don't seriously expect me to believe that *you* would give up all that power, just to bring me home?"

"I'd consider it a trade," Lenore replied. "We would get back the Points we lost and more when your artifact was no longer a rumor, when the rest of the factions knew we had it."

And finally, there it was, the point of this whole song and dance. Mira felt her anger begin to rise. "We've already had this conversation."

"No, this is different. I don't want to *use* it, Mira," Lenore responded. "You're right: It's too awful to even think about."

Mira hesitated. Again, it wasn't what she'd expected. "Then you would . . . let me destroy it?"

"It's far too valuable to simply destroy. Don't you see?"

"No, I don't see. I must be missing something," Mira retorted. "You don't want to use it, but you won't destroy it either. You can't have everything—it's either one or the other."

"Think for a moment, Mira. It doesn't have to be *used* to be valuable. It can be a *deterrent*," Lenore said pointedly, moving closer to her as she spoke. "I would establish that we had it, I would make sure all the factions knew the power the Gray Devils wielded . . . and then I would let that power simply sit, untouched and protected in the Vault, forever. Isn't that a fair trade, a good compromise? I get what I want; you get your life back. You'll be welcomed with open arms, watch your name be put back on the Scorewall, and that monstrosity you made will never see the light of day."

Mira opened her mouth to speak before she realized she had no idea what to say. She had always thought the only option was to destroy her artifact. But what if Lenore meant what she said? What if she really could get her life back, a life she had come to believe was lost forever . . . and still have the threat of the artifact gone?

But . . . did she really *want* that life back? So much had changed for her since then.

"Your hesitation makes me hopeful," Lenore finally said. "I'm glad you're considering it."

"This . . . isn't something I ever thought about. It's . . . I don't know what to think," Mira admitted. "But there's something I don't get. You said you would establish that the Gray Devils had it. But how could you do that without using it?"

Lenore looked away, and her mood seemed to darken. "You always think a problem through to the end, Mira. It was one of the reasons I trusted you. And why I miss you, too." When Lenore looked back up at Mira, there was an unpleasant glint in her eyes. "You're right, of course. We couldn't expect the other factions to just take our word that we had the power. We would have to demonstrate it."

Mira's gaze turned dangerous.

"There are those who would volunteer to have your artifact used on them," Lenore said.

"Volunteer?" Mira demanded.

"Those whose loyalty to the Gray Devils is so great, they would make the sacrifice."

"No, Lenore," Mira said, shaking her head in disgust.

"Just consider it, for a moment—it isn't as insidious as it sounds. We have members who are close to Succumbing and have no desire to join a resistance group and live near a Presidium. They know they're lost, no matter what, so why not do *something* in the end that matters?"

"How can that possibly *matter*?" Mira asked heatedly.

"Because it's an end with a *purpose*. One that profits their faction and strengthens its position! Isn't that more meaningful than just ambiguously disappearing into the wilderness to lose their minds?"

Mira sighed, closed her eyes, turned away.

"Just once, Mira," Lenore assured her. "Only once. Isn't it worth the one time, for all the good that will come from it?"

Mira was silent a long moment, and Lenore said nothing further. She had made her argument, and it was Mira's decision now. She would be lying if she said the proposal didn't make sense on some levels, or that a part of her didn't want her old life back. She and Ben could navigate the core together, and as hazardous as it was, she knew that if they worked together, they could beat it. They could see the Severed Tower.

But everything in Lenore's scenario was at the mercy of one thing, and it was that one thing that Mira knew would be the failing of anyone with access to the artifact she had created: human nature.

"You say 'just once,' Lenore," Mira finally replied. "Just once. And I think you really do believe it. But you and I both know Midnight City has a short memory. The factions will be intimidated for a while, your Points will go up. But it won't last. The others will forget, eventually. The fear will fade—it always does. And the Points you earned from the artifact will start to drop." Mira slowly turned back around to look at Lenore, held her gaze without trepidation now. "I know you, Lenore— you won't let that stand. Not when the Points start to circle the drain, not you. You'll use it a second time. And it'll be the same justification: *just one more*. But when you've done something twice, three times doesn't seem so awful anymore. Four seems even less. Five. Six. Another enemy who could just disappear. Another rival it would be nice to no longer have to worry about. I'm sorry, Lenore, but I don't think you have the strength *not* to use it. I'm not sure anyone does."

As Mira spoke, Lenore's glare slowly turned darker, but she remained quiet throughout.

"The answer is the same as before," Mira said. "The answer is no. It has to be destroyed. And if you let me destroy it, if you can give it up, like you should . . . then I *will* come home. I'll be proud to."

Mira stood silently after she finished, watching Lenore, but the woman just remained quiet and motionless, like a statue, perfectly still. "Is that your final answer, then?" Lenore asked.

"Yes. It's the only answer I can give."

Lenore's calm demeanor evaporated in front of Mira, her expression changing subtly into a muted form of disgust. "You would come home?" she asked mockingly. "You would *come home*? You *have* no home. I offered you salvation. Forgiveness. A genuine compromise, and you throw it back in my face for the same selfish, misguided reasons as before."

The words stung, but Mira kept her composure. "Only *you* would call what I'm doing selfish," Mira retorted calmly. "And if everyone else here feels the same way, then you're right, this isn't my home. It never was."

"Ben said you would never come around," Lenore remarked. "I believed you would see reason. But he was right about you, of course. He knows you better than anyone."

Something about what Lenore had just said was off, and it took a moment for Mira to figure out what it was. "Ben knows you want to use the artifact?"

Lenore gave Mira a pitying look. "Oh, Mira, how sad. You really don't know? Didn't you even at least suspect? Or did your feelings for him cloud everything?"

Mira didn't like where this was going.

"How do you think I learned about the artifact?" Lenore asked. "How was it I knew with time enough to stop you from taking it out of the city? Did you never wonder that?"

In truth, Mira never really had wondered. Everything had happened so fast after she was caught, and then there was her escape, and she had been on the run ever since. She didn't have time to think the details through. But Lenore was right: It didn't add up.

"It was *Ben*, Mira," Lenore said venomously. "Ben came to me. Told me what you had made in the lab. And that, like a fool, you wanted to destroy it."

Mira felt her heart thudding in her chest, felt her knees begin to weaken. "You're . . . lying," she said, her voice cracking. Suddenly, her throat felt very dry. "I . . . don't believe that."

Lenore smiled. "Think, Mira. Who else knew? Was there anyone else who could have told me? Anyone?"

The truth was, of course . . . there wasn't. And Mira knew it. But, still, she refused to believe. "Why would—?" she trailed off, uncertain. The world seemed dreamlike now.

"Why would he *do* it?" Lenore asked sarcastically for her. "Why would he betray his best friend, the person he loved? Ben's best friend has always been himself, Mira. What was the one thing he always wanted? More than anything else. The thing he asked me for repeatedly."

"An expedition," Mira managed, but her voice was nothing but a whisper now. "A fully supplied expedition into the core, so he could try for the Severed Tower."

"And now you see," Lenore replied. "He traded what he knew about your artifact for your position as the top Freebooter in Midnight City, for your Points, and for the opportunity to lead a Gray Devil expedition into the core. And I was only too happy to oblige him, if it stopped you from destroying what you made."

Mira felt sick to her stomach. It all added up, and she was ashamed at never having put the pieces together herself. But still, she didn't want to believe it, *couldn't* believe it. . . .

Lenore moved away from her. "The ironic thing is, you'll give it to me, regardless. After I'm done, you'll tell me everything I want to know, you'll hand it to me yourself. It will take months, most likely. Months and months of pain in the dark. You'll be an example to the others, that even the highest of us can fall. And when it's time to demonstrate to the city the power of what you've created . . . it will be *you* who your artifact destroys. In that way, you can make amends for all you've done . . . and for how much you've hurt me."

Lenore looked back at Mira, and her eyes held both malice and triumph.

"Guards!" Lenore shouted, and waited on the doors to open behind her, for the two burly Gray Devils to enter and bind her prisoner again and take her away to the cavern dungeon.

But the doors didn't open.

Lenore looked to it, annoyed. "Guards!" she shouted again. When the door remained shut, she strode angrily toward the entryway, grabbed the handles, and swung the doors wide open.

The guards were there, but not as before. Now they were in heaps on the floor, unconscious.

Mira saw Lenore's eyes widen, then look down the cavern tunnel for any sign of—

There was a hissing sound, a whine of energy, and then the air in the shape of a large sphere flashed once, twice, and shimmered away, revealing two people and a dog standing in the doorway.

Holt was holding a copper pipe he had picked up somewhere. Lenore was stunned, and Holt smiled back.

"You must be Lenore," Holt said. "Heard a lot about you." He swung the pipe hard into Lenore's head. She spun crazily and dropped to the floor, out cold like the guards.

Holt looked up at Mira proudly.

Mira didn't react. "Took you long enough," she said, and Holt frowned.

HOLT FROWNED BACK AT MIRA, held up the small compass pendant of Zoey's. "Hey, I'm sure this thing's way easy to use *outside*," he said, "but in *this* place, it's a little harder."

Zoey reached up and grabbed the pendant from Holt. "You said I could have it back," she complained. Holt sighed and let her have it, then held up the Shroud artifact Mira had made earlier, wrapped in duct tape.

"This thing's toast, right?" he asked.

"Toss it," Mira replied, and he threw it to the floor. "Did you ditch Los Lobos?"

"Yeah." Holt grinned and held up Marcus's big hunting knife, admiring it. "And look what I got."

Mira patted him on the face. "That's so cute. Where's my pack?"

Holt handed over her backpack and watched as she started digging through it. "Was it like you thought?" Holt asked. "Your old room?"

"They trapped it, yeah," Mira said as she pulled out an artifact of some kind. "Too bad they didn't know getting caught was part of the plan."

"What now, we find your thing? How far away is it?"

Mira stood up, looking around the room. "Not far at all," Mira said, stepping over Lenore and moving to the corner of the room where the photographic equipment sat.

"What's that one, Mira?" Zoey asked, looking at the artifact Mira was holding. It looked like several different combinations woven into one, with coins, batteries, two magnets, a big yellow marble, and strips of copper wire, all wrapped in tape.

"A Rectifier, sweetheart. It cancels out artifact effects, shuts them off." Mira passed the Rectifier through the air in the corner, and as it moved, blurred trails of light followed after it, like lens flares in a photo-graph. It was a disorienting thing to watch; it made Holt wince. Every-thing seemed to waver and shimmer in the air where Mira passed the thing, growing brighter and brighter. Then something materialized and fell toward the ground.

Mira caught it before it landed—a small black bag. Holt looked at it. "You hid the artifact *here?*" he asked in surprise. "In the Ice Queen's lair?"

"Last place she'd look, right?" Now Mira gave him a devilish look.

Holt was impressed. Mira was smart and clever, self-sufficient, and yet still vulnerable. She didn't need anyone to take care of her—that much was clear—but that didn't mean she didn't want someone to try. Her red hair hung loosely around her neck, and even though only a few flecks of green peeked through the black in her eyes now, she was still beautiful, he thought. Had there been a time when he really didn't think so?

"You sure are something," he said.

Mira smiled and untied the bag. She pulled out a very large, very strange-looking artifact combination. It wasn't a simple one like the oth-ers Holt had seen; this one was made up of over a dozen different objects (that he could make out), all tied together with linked silver chain and purple leather twine. The main aspect of the combination seemed to be an antique gold pocket watch on the exterior of the artifact. A silver δ was ornately etched into the watch's metallic cover.

Mira held it in her hand, staring down at the thing that had cost her so much. Holt could sense her trepidation. "Want me to carry it?" he asked. Considering how much he disliked artifacts, it wasn't a small gesture.

"No," Mira said. "I made it, I should be the one to deal with it." She stuck it in her pack and looked up at Holt.

Holt nodded, then glared at the unconscious form of Lenore. "What about her?"

Mira forced her gaze back onto Lenore's still body. When she did, Holt couldn't tell if she was frightened, remorseful, or angry. It might have been all three. "Leave her," Mira finally said in a low voice.

"She won't stop coming after you, you know, not after this. She'll send the entire faction to find you."

Mira looked down at Lenore, her face the same combination of emotions. "I'm not going to kill her," Mira said firmly. "I'm not her, and I never will be. Let's get out of here."

"How are we going to do that without the invisibility thing?" Holt asked.

Mira smiled up at him. "It's called a Shroud. And I said not to worry—we have a plan." She took Zoey's hand and quickly started moving.

"Okay." Holt frowned after them. "Is it possible I could know the details of this plan at some point?"

"Trust me, you'd rather not." Mira and Zoey ran through Lenore's cavern toward the balcony at the opposite end. He and Max followed.

The view from the balcony was amazing. It looked out over the residence hall from above, the dozens of platforms circling down the steep walls of the cavern to the floor far below, and all the bridges and ladders that connected them. The waterfall was directly underneath, roaring up at them, and the cavern's highest walkway passed just seven feet below.

From here, they were almost close enough to touch the two big Gray Devils banners that hung from the ceiling, and the static hum of the big Illuminators that were lighting them and hovering in the air a few feet away floated around them.

Mira slipped on her pack and looked at Zoey. "Get on my back, honey." The little girl jumped up and wrapped her arms around Mira's neck.

Holt stared apprehensively at the cavern floor far, far below. "Are we jumping?" he asked uneasily. "Tell me we're not jumping."

"The tunnel up here is tight and one-way," Mira said. "It takes too long, and we need to get out now. Plus, if anyone's coming up to check on us, we're screwed. We jump to the banners, ride them down, jump off. They're bolted into the ceiling—they'll hold us." Mira moved to the ledge, seemingly unbothered by the sheer drop below her. "In theory."

"That's comforting." Holt groaned, looking down at the giant drop with trepidation. "And how's Max supposed to get down?"

"I'm sure the mutt will figure it out," Mira said, looking at the dog unpleasantly. He growled low back up at her.

"I bet he beats you down to the floor," Holt replied.

"You're on," Mira said as she leapt from the edge, sailed through the air, and grabbed hold of the huge gray banner. The giant piece of fabric sailed backwards, propelled by her momentum.

Holt picked Max up, leaned over the edge, and carefully dropped him. The dog yelped slightly as he fell, then landed on the walkway underneath them. When his legs stopped wobbling, he looked back up at Holt.

"Go!" Holt said, pointing to the floor far below. The dog took off in a dash, circling down and around the walkway toward the bottom of the cavern in a blur of motion.

Mira was still hanging from the banner, gathering it all up into her chest. She wrapped her arms around it . . . and started sliding down it like a pole.

Holt frowned as he watched her, envying how easy she made it look. He studied the second banner, the same distance away. He exhaled his tension, long and slow, trying to work up the courage for the leap. "In theory," he skeptically said to himself. Then he ran and leapt off the edge.

He flew through the air, felt it rush around him, saw the gray of the banner coming toward him.

Holt slammed into it, tried to grab it . . . and missed badly, kept falling.

In a panic, he felt the angle of his flight shift to a downward trajectory toward the ground. The gray fabric flared all around him, and he tried to get his hands around it, but it was going too fast now.

Any moment, he would run out of banner to grab, and slam right into the floor.

He did the only thing he could think of. Marcus's hunting knife was still in his hand. Holt drove it down into the banner as he fell.

The sharp blade punctured it easily, catching the fabric. It jarred violently when Holt's weight slammed onto it, and he almost lost it. But he held on, grabbing it with both hands.

The knife ripped through the banner as he fell, slowing his fall. And the sharp sound of tearing fabric echoed throughout the cavern.

The big knife sliced through the remainder of the banner; then Holt was free-falling again toward—

He slammed into a rope bridge just below him, and the whole thing shook loudly. Above him, the huge banner swayed and rocked, split in two . . . and tore loose from the ceiling, falling downward in a flurry of gray fabric.

Holt, wide eyed, tried to roll out of the way, but it was too late. The giant mass of falling cloth buried him as it crashed down, pinning him under its increasing weight.

He struggled underneath it, trying to breathe and get it off him any way he—

Someone yanked the remains of the banner away, and he stared up into angry green and black eyes. He braced himself as Mira opened her mouth to yell at him . . .

. . . and a dog barked under them. They all looked down to the floor below, saw Max there, staring up at them impatiently, his tail wagging.

"The Max beat you!" Zoey exclaimed.

Mira rolled her eyes, looked back to Holt. "Real nice work," she said.

All around them, people were stirring. Lights were flashing on in the platforms that circled the giant cavern, and Holt realized he'd just woken the entire Gray Devils faction.

Mira was up and moving, pulling Zoey along with her toward the edge of the bridge. "Jump after me when I get down," she told the little girl.

Holt pulled himself loose from the heavy banner as Mira crawled off the edge of the bridge and dropped to the floor about ten feet below. All around, he could hear shouts starting to ring out as the faction members slowly realized what was happening. Their prized captive was escaping, aided by a little girl, a dog, and a clumsy moron.

Zoey dropped from the bridge into Mira's arms, and Holt ducked under its railing, falling as well, landing on the ground, and moving after them.

But Mira wasn't running back the way they had come. Instead, she was running toward the waterfall.

The torrent of water thundered down in front of them, and Mira reached for a length of thick chain that ran up the side of the wall next to it.

When she yanked it, more chains above them began sliding through pulleys as counterweights fell downward. A large latticework of sheet metal that Holt hadn't noticed before began slowly tilting down on the other side of the waterfall. He wasn't sure what was happening, but whatever it was, it needed to happen fast.

Above, dozens of figures were leaping from the platforms, scaling ladders, and running over bridges. Max barked up at them.

The large wing of sheet metal continued to lower . . . and finally passed into and under the water that was crashing down from above. The sheet metal wing shuddered under the impact, but it held together as it deflected the waterfall outward, shifting the flow a few dozen feet to the left.

With the falls diverted, a new tunnel that had been hidden behind the water was revealed. Mira raced into it, pulling Zoey along.

The Gray Devils reached the floor, and Holt raced after Mira and Zoey, signaling Max to follow.

Behind him, Holt heard a new sound that overpowered even the roaring waterfall: bells, all kinds and tones, ringing incessantly. The Gray Devils had raised the alarm; the entire faction would be waking now to hunt them down.

HOLT SPLASHED THROUGH THE NEW TUNNEL, noting that he was ankle deep in flowing water. "Where does this thing go?" he shouted at Mira up ahead.

"Nowhere, if we don't outrun all the trouble you just stirred up!" she yelled back.

"It wasn't my idea to leap off a ledge twenty stories off the floor!"

Behind him, Holt heard the cries of kids splashing after them. Ahead, the tunnel widened into a new room, and Holt raced after Mira into it.

It was huge and it wasn't what he'd expected. Several other tunnels converged in this same spot, and they all contained flowing water. Where it collected sat a big crystal-clear pool that stretched from one end to the other, and branching out from it were more of the aqueducts Holt had seen in the main hall. They traveled in different directions, disappearing into tunnels that looked like they'd been cut through the rock by human hands.

Each aqueduct was labeled with large letters, which read things like, MAIN HALL, LOST KNIGHTS, CROSSMEN, LOS LOBOS, and MARKET HALL. Each went to a different part of Midnight City, Holt realized, and each had a large iron gate hovering above it, which could seal off the flow.

No wonder the Gray Devils had amassed so many Points: they could shut off the water supply to any part of the city with the turn of a handle.

Mira and Zoey didn't stop to admire the view in the same way as Holt; they just rushed forward and jumped into the flowing water of a specific aqueduct, which flowed fast toward the other end of the room. They were quickly whipped under and out of sight.

"Hey!" Holt yelled angrily as he leapt in after them. The water ripped him forward. It was deep, probably up to his chest, and it was flowing fast. He tumbled and rolled a few times before he finally righted himself.

Ahead of him, he spotted Mira and Zoey again, right before they disappeared into a tunnel. Seconds later, everything went dark as he did, too. He felt himself sucked under and tossed back and forth against the rocky walls. Try as he might, he couldn't reach the surface in the current, and he was starting to worry he—

He felt a hand grab him by the hair and yank him to the surface.

"Grab on!" Mira's voice shouted above him. "Pull yourself out!"

Holt saw Mira and Zoey standing on the edge of another aqueduct, trying to keep him from sailing past. He grabbed the edge, started to pull himself up . . . when Max tumbled past.

Holt grabbed him by the scruff of his neck, and the dog coughed out water and inhaled. "Zoey!" Holt yelled. "Get Max out!"

The little girl reached for the dog, helping him scramble over the side of the structure. Holt did the same thing, and when he was out, collapsed on top of the aqueduct. His heart beat heavy in his chest as he breathed deeply.

"Come on, you can pass out later," Mira said, leaping quickly down from the aqueduct.

Holt opened his eyes and took in the new cavern underneath the aqueduct. It wasn't as big as the aqueduct hub or the residence hall, but it was still large. Half a dozen workbenches were dotted around the room, cramped with tools and supplies. The walls were lined with metal cabinets and cases, each of them filled with objects that glowed or sparked or hovered or flashed colors. On the room's largest, flattest wall, a giant gray δ was painted, with the Gray Devils logo resting inside the round circle on its bottom.

Holt realized he was in the faction's artifacts lab. He was surrounded by objects from the Strange Lands.

Next to him, Zoey and Max both climbed down from the aqueduct.

"Holt! Get down here!" Mira yelled under him, and he rolled off the aqueduct and landed on the floor.

Mira was near one of the cabinets, building something from the components there. As she did, Holt studied the room more closely. There was only one exit, and it seemed to head right back where they had come from. Other than that, he saw no other way out.

"This is a dead end," Holt said in exasperation.

"Not according to Marcus," Mira answered, hurriedly building her artifact combination.

Marcus? What did the Lobos member have to do with—?

And then it hit him. "The other secret tunnel," Holt said, looking around.

"Yeah, and I need you to find it," Mira answered, concentrating on her work.

Holt scanned the room again, trying to find any sign of another tunnel, but he couldn't find anything. The walls were solid, there was nothing behind any of the workbenches that—

"Is that it, Holt?" Zoey asked from beside him. The little girl was pointing with a finger straight up.

Holt stared upward. Above them, a hundred feet or more, was a small black opening in the ceiling. It was also, of course, completely out of reach.

"Son of a . . . ," he started.

Mira looked over, following his gaze upward. When she saw it, her face dropped.

"Real nice work," Holt said, echoing her tone from before.

And then, from the tunnel came the sounds of running feet and angry yells. The faction was almost on them again.

Mira sprinted for the tunnel entrance, holding her new combination. Holt saw it was made of a pencil, a D battery, and two dimes wrapped together with red string.

She reached the tunnel entrance, took the artifact, and drew a long line with the head of the pencil, starting at the floor, then up one side, along the top, down the other side, and back to where she'd started.

When the two lines connected, there was a bright flash of light in the air contained by the square. Everything hummed powerfully for a moment, and then the tunnel entrance was darkened by some kind of fluctuating, black energy.

Mira stepped back and away from it . . . as two Gray Devils rounded the corner at full speed and slammed into the field of black energy. They were tossed back as though they had just run into a wall, crashing to the ground and staring up at the field of energy in surprise.

Then the boys glared at Mira, realizing what she'd done.

More and more kids were appearing in the cramped tunnel. A few others slammed into the energy field before they all figured it out. They piled up next to it, kicking and punching, trying to break through. But for the moment, the shield was holding.

"How long will that thing last?" Holt asked.

"I used dimes, so not long," Mira said, looking up at the hole in the ceiling. "We have to find a way up there."

"Can't you just . . . make another one of those gravity things?"

"I need magnet shavings for that, and there's none here."

"There has to be *something*, we're surrounded by Strange Lands stuff!" he yelled.

"It's not that simple!" she yelled back. "The combinations do very specific things—you can't just make them do whatever you want!"

The kids continued pounding on the black force field, trying to weaken it. Holt shook his head in frustration, looking for anything that might help. "Well, what *can* you make?"

Mira quickly canvassed the contents of the shelves that circled them, mentally taking inventory. "Um . . . I can do a Vortex, a Gravitron, another Grid—"

"I don't know what any of that is!"

"I can make something freeze in time," Mira started over in frustration. "I can make something that increases gravity in a certain area, I can do another of those force fields—"

"None of that helps us, what else?" Holt asked, looking back to the black force field. The kids kept pounding on it, and some of them were using bats and crowbars and other things against it. It was starting to flicker.

Mira's voice was nervous. "I can . . . I don't know! I can do a . . . an Accelerator. . . ."

"What's that?" Holt asked.

"If you throw something, it accelerates whatever it is to a much higher speed."

At the description, Holt looked at her. "How fast?"

"It depends on the coins you use, but if I can find quarters, it'll be pretty damn fast," she replied. "The speed of sound."

Holt eyes widened. "The speed of *sound*?" That was incredibly fast . . . but was it enough? They were talking about solid rock here. It was a long shot, but at the moment, he didn't see any other option. "Make it," he said, ripping the pack off his back.

"Why, what are you—"

"Just hurry!" he shouted, taking off the thick black bracelet he always wore, then pulling out a small harness from his pack. Holt looked up at Zoey as Mira bolted for one of the workbenches. "Zoey, I need your help."

The little girl ran to him and he handed her the harness. It was too small for a person, but it would fit a dog perfectly, and it had a metallic clip on top of it, woven into the fabric. "I need you to put this on Max for me, okay?" Zoey took it from him and nodded. "He hates wearing it, so you'll have to convince him, and we don't have a lot of time."

"I can do it, Holt," Zoey said with confidence.

"I know you can, kiddo—get to it." Holt reached for his corded black bracelet. When he started unwinding it, it became apparent what it actually was: about fifty feet of 550 mil spec paracord that had been tightly coiled into the shape of a bracelet. They were called Survival Straps, and Holt always wore one. You never knew when you might need a length of really strong rope.

When it was unwound, Holt grabbed Marcus's knife. He quickly slipped one end of the rope through the hole at the bottom of the handle, pulled a length of it through, then tied a knot called a buntline hitch. It was a strong knot, though it had a tendency to jam. But since Holt didn't plan on ever untying it, it didn't really matter.

"Girls, how's it coming?" he asked as he finished the knot.

Mira was hurriedly piecing things together at the workbench, while Zoey was wrestling with Max on the ground, trying to force his head through the harness's main loop. The dog was having none of it. Holt looked back to the lab's entrance. There were so many Gray Devils in the tunnel beyond the shield now that they completely filled it, and most were yelling threats as they beat against the shield. Others just glared at him, eager to rush inside when the barrier finally collapsed.

They were running out of time.

"Got it!" Mira exclaimed, and ran back to him. In her hand was another combination, made of two quarters, a piece of copper tubing, and a round gear that looked like it used to power a bicycle. It was all wrapped with rubber bands, and Holt stared at it skeptically.

"It's Interfused, it'll hold together, and it works fine," she said impatiently. "What do you want to do with it?"

"Can you tie it on the knife handle?" he asked back. "I need the blade to be free."

It was Mira's turn to look skeptical as she figured out what he intended. "*This* is your idea?" she asked as she wrapped the artifact combination to the knife's handle with her duct tape. When it was done, it looked like a gray tumor sticking off the side of the blade, and Holt examined it without much enthusiasm.

"Okay, then," he said, holding the knife by the rope it was attached to. "How does it work?"

"The copper pipe is the Focuser," Mira explained quickly. "It's straight, which means the artifact will accelerate motion *only* in a straight line."

"So I can spin it around before I throw it?"

"Right," Mira answered. "But once it gets moving straight . . . *look out.*"

Behind them, Max whined, struggling against Zoey's attempts to get the harness around the dog's head. "Go see if you can help her," Holt said, looking up at the ceiling and the dark tunnel inset into it. He'd get only one shot at this.

Mira ran to Zoey and Max, tried to shove the dog into the harness, but he growled and snapped at her. "You're working on getting left behind, you stupid mutt!" Mira shouted, struggling with the dog.

Holt surveyed the ceiling a moment more . . . then began spinning the artifact and the thick knife it was attached to in a circle next to him, like he was priming a sling. There was nothing to indicate that the artifact was even working, but he didn't have a choice now. When he thought he had the aim right, he slung it all straight upwards . . .

. . . and there was a flash and a loud, deep explosion of sound so thunderous, it almost knocked him to the ground.

The Gray Devils pounding on the energy field fell back, stunned. Mira held her ears, and Max scampered backwards, frightened. As he did, Zoey pulled the dog's head all the way through the harness and secured it to his waist. "Got you!" she yelled at the distracted canine.

Holt's ears were ringing, his equilibrium was all wrong, but he looked up anyway . . . and saw the knife impaled straight into the thick rock of the cavern wall right above. The speed at which the blade had flashed through the air was enough to puncture the rock, but it wasn't a bull's-eye. The rope dangled downward to the floor a foot or so away from the opening in the ceiling. It would have to do.

"That's a big climb," Zoey said as she brought Max to him.

"Don't worry, I'll carry you just like in the Drowning Plains, remember?"

Zoey nodded. "But who's gonna carry the Max?"

"We're gonna pull him up last," Holt said, passing the end of the rope through the clip in Max's harness and tying the same knot he'd made before. "Get on my back, kiddo."

Zoey climbed onto Holt, and he stood up, feeling the little girl's weight. She was getting heavier every day. His gaze moved up the rope to the ceiling above. It was going to be one hell of a climb.

"You sure you can do this?" Mira asked with her hand on his arm.

Holt looked back at her. "Don't have much of a choice." He smiled and felt his tension melt away. It would work or it wouldn't; either way, it would be over soon. "Wait till I make it inside before you start climbing, I don't know how much weight this will hold." Holt grabbed the rope and started hauling himself up.

From the tunnel, where the kids were still blocked, came cries of anger as they saw their prey now had a chance to escape. With renewed effort, they went back to pounding on the field of energy. It was wavering badly.

Holt felt his arms start to burn as they pulled both he and Zoey toward the ceiling.

He kept climbing, pulling himself up, groaning with each effort. His hands ached, but he felt a sense of relief knowing he would at least make it to the ceiling, and also a sense of dread as he realized he still had to find the strength to crawl into the tunnel once he did.

Holt reached the top and looked to the tunnel entrance a foot away from him. It was dark inside, but mercifully he could tell it leveled out quickly, making a ledge they could scamper onto. Barely.

"Zoey," Holt said. "Can you reach that ledge? If I swing you over?" It was dangerous, for both of them, but they were running out of options fast. The shield below was almost down—he didn't need to be a Freebooter to see that—and Mira hadn't even started to climb yet.

"I think so," Zoey said with nervousness in her voice. "But we're so high, if I—"

"Just don't look down. We have to do this fast, and I know you can do it, okay?"

"Holt, no!" Mira exclaimed under them. "She'll fall, she's not strong enough!"

"She can do it!" he yelled back. *She has to,* he thought. "Can't you?"

Zoey nodded.

"Okay, get ready." Holt used his weight to swing them both toward the hole in the ceiling. "Now!" As he did, Zoey reached up, grabbed the ledge, and let go of him.

Her feet dangled precariously in open air for a moment.

"Zoey!" Mira called out in terror below.

Then the little girl pulled herself up into the dark tunnel, twisting and wiggling until she disappeared inside.

Holt smiled in relief. This just might work.

He grabbed the rope below him in his hand. "Zoey, take this!" He handed it up to the little girl. When she had it, he swung back over, and reached up with one hand to grab the ledge.

Holt let loose of the rope and forced himself to grab the ledge with his other hand. His weight pulled him downward, and he almost fell, but Zoey grabbed his hand, pressing it into place on the rough rock. Desperately, Holt started pulling himself up onto the ledge, groaning with the effort. With the last bit of his strength, he climbed into the tunnel with Zoey.

"Holt!" the little girl cried, wrapping her arms around him.

"Hi, kiddo," he said, breathing hard. "Back up for me—we have to get the others up."

He took the rope from Zoey, held it in his hand, and pressed his back into the wall of the tunnel, bracing himself with his feet.

"Mira, go!" he shouted down.

The rope pulled tight in his hands as her weight hit it and she began to climb. She was lighter and wasn't carrying anyone else, so she made much better time than he had. Max stared up at them all, whining softly.

When Mira reached the tunnel, Zoey helped pull her inside and over Holt. Then they all started pulling the rope upward, end over end.

There was a yelp as Max's feet left the floor, and he dangled helplessly as he rose in fits and starts.

And then came a flash as the black energy field finally collapsed below. Dozens of kids poured inside, looking furiously up at them. They had slings, and rocks quickly flew through the air, sparking all around the tunnel entrance.

But it was too late. Holt and Mira pulled Max up and into the tunnel, free and clear.

"Mira!" an intense, feminine voice yelled from underneath them. Holt watched Mira lean out over the tunnel and peer down to the floor far below.

Lenore stood there, glaring up at them, a purple bruise on the side of her head.

Mira gazed down at her. "It was good seeing you, Lenore. But I think this'll be the last time."

"If you do this, Mira, if you steal what's mine"—Lenore replied—"I *guarantee* it won't."

"The artifact isn't yours. It never was."

"What belongs to one Gray Devil belongs to them all," Lenore stated.

"Yeah, it's like you said, though," Mira answered. "I'm not a Gray Devil anymore." And then she pulled away from the hole in the ceiling, and they all quickly crawled into the dark.

Even with all the thick rock between them, Holt could still hear Lenore scream Mira's name.

38. DIFFICULT QUESTIONS

TO ZOEY, the unmapped parts of the cavern seemed beyond massive. They were frightening, twisting pathways of darkness that opened and closed, widened and shrunk, and the only details she could make out were what was revealed by Holt and Mira's flashlights.

Max walked next to her, which made her feel better. He didn't seem bothered by all the jagged rock and the strange, eerie shadows the lights projected onto the walls. If he could be brave, then so could she.

Holt made sure they wound through as much of the cavern as possible before stopping, so that even if the Grey Devils did manage to follow them, the odds of them finding the four would be slim. That was the plan anyway, and Zoey hoped it would work. Mira's old faction hadn't seemed very friendly at all.

The cavern they finally stopped in was oval shaped, and a hole in one of its walls provided an overlook to one of the city's main areas: the Scorewall—the strange, massive collection of names and numbers Zoey had seen before. They were situated far above it, staring down into the room from a corner of its ceiling.

Zoey wondered just how many little caverns and entrances there were that blended unnoticed into the walls all throughout Midnight City.

They all laid on their bellies at the edge of the cavern, studying the Scorewall room underneath them, trying to stay out of sight. Even though it was early morning, people were already gathering below.

"Why do they get here so early?" Zoey asked.

"For the best spots," Mira answered. "It fills up quick. Give me your binoculars." The last part was meant for Holt, and he handed them to Mira.

The calls of large horns of some kind, dozens and dozens of them, suddenly blared all throughout the city, echoing against the thick, black rock. The sounds seemed angry to Zoey, angry and urgent. She saw the people below stop as the sounds bounced everywhere, continuing for a few more moments before shutting off. Even then, it took a long time for the noise to dissipate, ricocheting back and forth between the thick cavern walls until it was finally drowned out by angry murmurings and yells from the kids below. Zoey watched them turn away from the Scorewall in disgust and head away.

"What was that?" Zoey asked.

"The Gray Devils just sealed the city," Mira said. "No one comes in, no one goes out."

Holt looked up at Mira, surprised. "They can do that?"

"They're the Prime Movers, so yes, but the other factions won't be happy. Closing the city means no trade comes in, and it also means faction members on the surface can't get in either. It all effects the Scorewall, and the Gray Devils' Points will start to drop the longer they keep the city shut down."

"You don't seem all that surprised," Holt said.

"It was the only thing Lenore could do. Trap us inside, try to find us before they lose too many Points."

"That's all well and good, but how the hell are we supposed to get out of here now? Los Lobos are after us too, now that they didn't get their plutonium."

"We needed it to barter our way out of here," Mira said. "And Cesar can't help with that."

"But you said no one comes in, no ones goes out," Zoey said, confused.

Mira smiled, stroked Zoey's hair. "There's always a way." She lifted Holt's binoculars up to her eyes and trained them on the Scorewall below. Zoey could sense she was looking for something specific, and when she found it, she felt a wave of emotion from Mira. Shock mostly, but also pain tinged with anger.

Holt couldn't feel it the same way Zoey could, but he sensed it nonetheless.

"What?" he asked.

Mira lowered the binoculars, but kept staring at the Scorewall.

"Mira?" Holt asked again.

She blinked, looked up at him. "It's Ben," she said. "He *is* on the Scorewall, Lenore was telling the truth. And he has his Points. Twice as many as he ever had. There's no way he could have got that many without . . ."

"Taking *your* Points," Holt finished for her after her voice faded away. She was visibly shaken.

Back in the dark passages, Mira had told them everything Lenore had said about Ben. That he had tricked her and taken her Points, that he was in the Strange Lands now, trying to reach "the core." Zoey didn't know what that was, but it sounded scary. When Mira recounted Lenore's story, Zoey had felt only a little bit of doubt from her. Now, it was much stronger. A large part of her was starting to think Lenore had told the truth, and the more she came to think that way, the more it hurt.

"Maybe she staged the Points to incriminate him, in case you ever came back," Holt suggested.

Mira shook her head. "That's Point Fabrication. It's the worst crime you can commit here, it's what Lenore accused me of, and it means death, even for the faction leader of the Prime Movers. She wouldn't risk it." Mira looked back up at the Scorewall in the distance with a dark stare. "No, those Points are real. Ben is alive and he's free."

Holt looked away from Mira, staring at the Scorewall along with her. "Do you love him?" he asked after a long moment of silence.

It took awhile for the words to register, but when they did, Zoey felt new emotions from Mira. Doubt, guilt, confusion . . . and something warmer, something Zoey had felt growing in Mira for a while.

Mira stared at Holt, hesitant and conflicted. "Ben and I were . . . close," she said. "There was no one better than him in the Strange Lands. He had an almost sixth sense when it came to it. He could tell you just from how the air felt on his skin whether a Pulsar Chain was nearby or an Ion Storm was coming, and the farther we went in, the harder it was to get him to come out. We made it all the way to the end of the fourth ring once, even though I never wanted to go that far. That was how Ben was. He always had a way of convincing me to do things I shouldn't. Sometimes I didn't feel safe with him at all."

Holt listened, but it wasn't until she finished that he finally looked at her. "That wasn't what I asked," he said. "It's not a hard question, Mira," he said. "Either you do or you don't."

They stared at each other in uncomfortable silence . . .

. . . and then Zoey felt the Tone flare powerfully inside Mira's mind.

Mira instantly curled into a ball, moaning in pain. Zoey could almost hear the voices erupting within the static and hissing inside Mira's head.

Holt wrapped his hands around her, pulled her to him, and Zoey felt the desperation overtake him. He looked up at her, and she didn't need her powers to read what was written in his eyes. "Zoey, I need you to do your thing here," he said. "For Mira."

Zoey looked up at Holt in fear. Zoey had no idea how to re-create what had happened in the tent. The feelings had risen inside her and she'd had nothing to do with that. She searched for them regardless, trying to find them in the recesses of her mind . . . but there was nothing. And Mira continued to groan and shake on the floor.

"I need you to stop the Tone," Holt clarified. "Like you did back at the river. I need you to do it for Mira."

"That wasn't me," Zoey said simply.

Holt stared at her, and she could feel his frustration. "What?" he asked.

"I mean . . . it was me, but it wasn't me either. It was—"

"Zoey, I don't have time for riddles right now," Holt said, grabbing her and pulling her close. "I need to you to save Mira. You've done it before, I need you do it again. Right now."

"I don't know how," Zoey pleaded. She could feel her eyes starting to tear.

"But you did it *before*," Holt said, his voice cracking. Mira continued to shake in his arms. "Please, Zoey, just try? Just try once . . ." He tried to pull her down farther, to put her tiny hands on Mira, but Zoey yanked free.

"Zoey!" His voice was full of panic and rage, and Zoey stared at him with wide, startled eyes. She knew he wouldn't hurt her, but she flinched nonetheless at the pain that swelled inside him. She felt it too, just as intense.

"I don't know how!" she screamed, tears starting to flow. "Something did it on its own, and it wasn't me! *I don't know how!*"

"Holt." Mira's weak voice stopped everything. Holt looked down at her. Her eyes were open, she was staring up at him. "It's not . . . her fault."

At the words, Holt looked from Mira to Zoey, trembling in his hands. Tears ran down her face, and she felt an outpouring of guilt and shame from him, with an intensity she'd never felt from anyone.

Instantly, he let her go, and Zoey pushed back away from him.

"I'm . . . sorry, Zoey," Holt said. "I didn't mean—"

Mira spasmed again underneath him and Holt wrapped his arms around her, held her as tight as he could, whispering into her ear, trying to keep her attention on the real world. It took her almost ten minutes to fight it off and shove it back down into her subconscious, where it whispered just out of reach, but she finally did, and Zoey felt the tension in her body mercifully release.

"Zoey . . ." Mira said weakly from beneath them. Her contortions had stopped, her eyes were open. It had passed, the Tone was beaten back, and she was fine . . . for now. "It's okay, Zoey."

When Zoey looked into Mira's eyes, the Tone seemed even more prominent, lacing and crawling through her irises. Mira reached up and pulled the little girl down to her, holding her gently. "It's all okay," Mira said. "It's not your fault."

But to Zoey it felt like it *was* her fault nonetheless. Above her, she saw Holt look away, his face torn with anger and pain.

Zoey felt the tension drain out of Mira, could sense her exhaustion. It didn't take long for her to drift off to sleep.

Behind her, Holt moved moved to the edge of the cavern, to where it overlooked the city, and sat there, staring down quietly at all the activity near the Scorewall. Max whined a little, padded over and sat with his head in Holt's lap. He scratched the dog's ears absently.

The intensity of Holt's emotions had calmed, but they hadn't changed. Zoey could still feel the worry and the fear projecting from him, but there was something else, too. Resolution. Commitment. Holt had chosen to stay with them instead of heading east, and it had been a difficult decision, she knew. He was risking a great deal for the possibility of saving Mira.

Zoey suddenly realized where all his plans hinged. On *her*. Holt had stayed in a desperate attempt to help Zoey remember the one power that was lost to her. The one she had just shown she couldn't use. And the realization filled her with dread. What if she couldn't remember? What if she failed both of them? What if she lost them both?

Quietly, Zoey pulled free from Mira's arms and sat next to Holt. Below them, the Scorekeepers had arrived, darting over the huge wall on their ropes, moving up and down, left and right, changing the bevy of numbers that were listed there. Zoey and Holt watched it all dispassionately.

"I still don't know what I need to do here," Zoey said. "I don't know how I can know and feel so many other things . . . and not that."

Holt just kept staring down at the people filing into the huge cavern below. "Do you have any clues? Anything at all to help?"

Zoey shook her head. "No. I just know there's something here for me."

Holt stayed quiet, thinking. She could feel him bury his doubts and fear, push them back down, the same way he always did. It was what he had to do to keep moving forward, and he'd had lots of practice at it.

"Well . . . it's something," he finally said. "Everything starts from something. Right?"

"Right, Holt."

They both kept staring down at the Scorewall and the kids hovering over it. Zoey slowly reached over and took Holt's hand. Holt squeezed it back.

"Don't worry," he said. "We'll figure it out. You and me. Okay?"

Zoey nodded and tried to take solace in his words, but it was hard. Behind them, Mira stirred, lost in some dream, and the crowd continued to grow below, churning and cramming forward, completely oblivious to the three figures staring somberly at them from above.

HOLT AND EMILY LAY exhausted underneath the bright afternoon sky, outside the collapsed truck stop. It was a long moment before Holt heard his sister weakly say his name.

He turned and looked. The color was gone from her eyes; there were only little specks of white peeking out through all the black now. It was the worst he had ever seen it.

No words came to him, and even if they had, he wasn't sure he could have found his voice. Emily took his hand and stared into him. He felt her fingers trembling.

When she spoke, her voice was ragged, just weak, fragmented whispers. She was fading, Holt could tell. But there were no spasms this time, no moans, no curling into a ball as she fought against the Tone's waves of voices and static in her mind.

She was calm now, motionless . . . peaceful almost. The sight filled him with anguish.

Holt felt tears in his eyes; he knew this was all his fault. If he hadn't gone after her, if he had just done what she'd told him . . .

Emily was trying to marshal her strength, trying to speak. She could manage only one or two slow, painful words at a time, but she held on long enough to deliver them.

She told him to be strong and brave.

She told him to be smart, like their father.

He needed to understand how happy it made her knowing he would carry all their memories forward.

And he had to absolutely, above all else . . . *survive*.

Tears fell down Holt's face as he listened.

Emily asked him to promise. Promise he would do everything she asked. Holt forced himself to nod, but it wasn't enough. She made Holt say the words, made him tell her that he promised. Promised to survive. Survival had to be everything for him now, or what she had done here might all be for nothing.

Holt found his voice, promised her, said it with as much conviction as he could.

At his words, Emily nodded and finally relaxed.

Holt watched her body tense and shake one last time, and then her muscles all released. Emily deflated into the grass underneath her, went so completely still, she could have been sleeping.

Holt said her name. She didn't respond.

He said it again, touched her arm, tried to wake her. But she didn't stir.

Holt pulled himself up, looked at her eyes. They stared blankly up at the sky.

They were solid black now, and Holt knew what that meant.

He heard a sudden wail of anguish release from some far-off place, and it took a moment for him to realize it had come from him. Everything was like a dream now, blurry and slow motion, and he looked at the world through a haze.

In it, he watched his sister rise from the grass to stand above him. Saw her turn and look to the north with that same mindless, black stare.

Instinctively more than anything else, he reached for his sister's hand. But it hung limp there, the fingers did not close around his.

A moment more, and she began to walk toward something just visible in the far distance. Something that towered into the sky, black and vile and ominous. The Assembly Presidium.

Holt held on to Emily's hand, willing her to stop and turn around and be herself again, but she didn't. Her arm trailed limply behind her as she moved . . . and then fell loose when her hand tore away from his.

She kept walking, one slow step after another, moving farther and farther away.

The world shifted and rocked, and Holt realized he must have fallen to his knees. He couldn't feel the tears running down his face. He didn't feel anything anymore.

He stared after Emily for almost an hour, watching her gradually become smaller and smaller in the distance, until she finally disappeared somewhere between the horizon and the sky.

Not once, in all that time, did she look back.

HOLT PUSHED THROUGH THE TIGHTLY crammed mass of people in the Scorewall room, who were all staring up at the gigantic wall of polished black rock filled with its insane, arbitrary, mathematical nonsense. The survivors here stood shoulder to shoulder, and it took a lot of effort to move through them.

He looked to where he was headed: a platform built against the far wall, maybe fifteen feet off the floor, which stretched the length of the giant room. It was divided into sections by walls of polished wood or gleaming metal, or hanging sheets of colored glass, and hanging over each section were the giant, colorful banners of the Midnight City factions. Some he'd come to recognize. The horned, laughing face of the Gray Devils, the red wolf's head of Los Lobos. Neither of those platforms were populated right now, which was a good thing, seeing as how they were both looking for him.

There were other banners, too, of course: a yellow sword, a black scorpion, a white Celtic cross, and others, twelve in all. Most were filled with a dozen or more people, watching the action unfold on the Scorewall. Dedicated runners for the factions dashed back and forth between the platform and the Scorekeepers, exchanging and bartering information, watching the Point totals rise and fall.

Holt studied each banner until he found the one Mira had described. Orange with a red shield sewn brilliantly into it. He saw people there, each wearing some piece of clothing that was orange, watching the action in the room below them.

It took a few more minutes to push through and reach the platform, and when he did, two large orange-clad youths moved to block him.

"Your business?" one of them asked coldly.

Holt reminded himself what Mira had told him about the Lost Knights. It was a faction without an official leader. No one had any doubt there actually was a leader, but whoever it was didn't make his or her identity known. On the Scorewall, the leader's Points were listed under the name Rebus, and that was all anyone knew. Direct audiences with Rebus were generally refused, so as to preserve the figure's anonymity. But that didn't mean there weren't ways to communicate with him or her.

"I'm here to speak with the platform's emissary," Holt said, exactly as Mira had told him. The response he got was the expected one.

"The emissary's too busy to waste time speaking with an Outsider who has no Points," the other guard said with contempt. "Turn around and start walking."

"I have information the emissary will want to hear."

One of the guards raised an eyebrow. "And what information is that?"

"The location of Mira Toombs," Holt said, holding the boy's gaze.

The two guards looked at each other, then turned back to Holt. "Wait here a second." One of them moved to the platform, where a small wooden tray hung from a rope tied to the very top. Next to it was a notepad and a pencil. He wrote something, tore a page loose, set it in the tray, and then nodded to a girl at the very top. She reeled it up and disappeared out of sight on the platform above.

The response took a few minutes to come, but when it did, it wasn't verbal. A large drawbridge-like ramp that was stained in various shades of orange began to lower from the top of the platform. When it did, the guards motioned Holt past, and he climbed the ramp. As he did, he noticed the factions up and down the platform all watching him with curious looks, trying to determine who he was and how he might be valuable.

Holt crested the ramp and stepped onto the Lost Knights' platform. It was more extravagantly appointed than it looked from the floor. Telescopes of different types were installed along the railing, probably for examining specific parts of the Scorewall, which loomed above them. An orange rug filled the space, and the platform contained two sitting areas, a work area, and a large, cushioned, elevated chair that looked almost like a throne. Behind it all was an orange curtain, covering something he couldn't see.

Holt counted nine kids, all younger than him, watching him suspiciously as he stepped onto the platform.

A boy, older than the rest, maybe sixteen, sat in the large chair in the center of the platform, the Tone beginning its slow creep through his brown eyes. The kid watched in a bored fashion as Holt approached and stopped in front of him, but he said nothing. Holt studied the boy impatiently, waiting for some sign of communication.

"Are you the emissary? I'm here to—"

The emissary, if that's what he was, raised a disinterested hand and shook his head.

From the curtain emerged a little girl, no bigger or older than Zoey, adorned in orange. She kept her eyes low as she moved quickly to sit next to the boy in the chair.

She carried a small black velvet bag in one hand, and when she opened it, an array of brightly colored crystal stones fell onto a small table next to the boy's chair. Holt watched the girl swirl the crystals around on the table.

"My name is Digby, an emissary of Rebus," the boy said. "And I'm a superstitious sort of person."

Holt looked at Digby and the crystals. "What are they? Strange Lands pieces?"

"Not in the slightest," Digby replied. "What are you here for?"

Holt considered the boy. He was nondescript, didn't look particularly shrewd or capable. In fact, there was little, if anything, to distinguish him from the other kids dotted around the platform. But if there was one thing Holt had learned, it was that first impressions could be misleading. "I'm here to barter," Holt said.

"Yes, I figured that," the boy said, agitated. "You're offering the location of Mira Toombs, which isn't a small thing these days. But what are you looking to trade it *for*?"

Holt exhaled, remembering what Mira had told him. "The Lost Knights have something I need, and you're mistaken. I don't want to trade Mira for it."

The boy's look turned dangerous . . . and then the small girl next to him shuffled the crystals, pulled one from the bunch, and set it on the table. It was a red stone. At the sight of it, the boy's annoyance turned to genuine anger. He looked back up at Holt. "The stones don't favor you,

Outsider." Digby nodded to two of the guards nearby, and they moved for Holt, ready to toss him off the platform. "I don't like having my time wasted."

"I have something more valuable than Mira Toombs," Holt said quickly, while he still had the chance. The guards didn't stop moving for him, however, and Digby said nothing.

But the girl next to him swirled the stones around again, pulled another loose, set it on the table. A green stone.

At the sight of it, Digby's anger softened, and he motioned the guards to stop. They hovered a few feet away from Holt. "The stones encourage patience," Digby said. "But I've got only so much. You lied to get yourself up here, why should I bother listening to anything you have to say?"

Holt removed his pack and pulled free the glass cylinder of plutonium. When he did, the disinterested looks from the Lost Knights around him vanished, and their eyebrows all rose as they stared at the brownish-tinged sliver inside the casing.

Even Digby's eyes widened, and when he looked back up at Holt, it was in a new way. The little girl whirled the crystals on the table once more and pushed an orange one toward Digby.

"Plutonium's as rare a commodity as they come, and very valuable," the boy said, looking up from the crystal to stare at Holt. "What do you want to trade it for?"

Holt didn't immediately answer. Things were wrong here, somehow. Something had been bugging him about the colored crystals ever since the little girl brought them out. The way Digby consulted them, the way he waited to begin their discussion until they appeared. Something occurred to Holt.

"We want safe passage out of the city," Holt said. "Today."

The tiny girl swirled the crystals again, and as she did, Holt watched the boy gaze down at them expectantly.

"Why don't we quit this little puppet show?" Holt said sternly, looking not at Digby, but at the small, unassuming girl next to him. "So you and I can talk directly."

"I don't know what you think you—," Digby began.

"I'm not talking to you anymore," Holt cut him off without looking up. "I'm talking to her. The one pulling your strings."

Digby stared down at the little girl in alarm. She stopped swirling the stones, and for the first time, looked up at Holt. The unassuming, innocent gleam in her eyes vanished, suddenly replaced with a shrewdness and self-awareness far beyond her age. She hid them very well, Holt thought: he'd almost overlooked her completely. She examined him with a mix of annoyance and respect.

"Who do you think you—?" Digby started hotly, but was cut off again.

"Be quiet," the little girl said. Her voice was soft and low, but it contained a notable measure of harshness as well. The boy silenced immediately. "The dance is over." The girl stood, scooped the stones into the black bag, and moved for the orange curtain at the back of the platform. "Follow me," she said without looking back.

Holt sighed. Why wasn't anything in this place ever straightforward?

He followed the girl through the curtain. Inside was a bizarrely appointed room. Mismatched pieces of furniture, a Crystal Castles arcade machine, shelves full of vinyl record sleeves, and the walls were covered with what looked like large, framed crayon drawings, in all kinds of colors and shapes. Each bore the same signature, but Holt couldn't make it out.

The little girl sauntered to a black sofa and sat down, slowly raising her eyes up to Holt.

"You're not what I expected," Holt said.

"Expected of what?" she asked.

"Of Rebus," he said with a smile. "You're a little shorter than I pictured."

The little girl didn't return the smile. "Well, that's the whole point, isn't it? And call me Amelia—it's my name, after all. You're the Outsider working with Mira Toombs. I hope she's . . . healthy."

It was strange, listening to her. It didn't fit, the maturity and the confidence, the subtle hints of maliciousness, all exuding from the tiny person on the couch. But while it was certainly unsettling, it wasn't surprising. In a world where the Tone made every second count, people grew up incredibly quick.

"Mira's fine," Holt responded. "She can take care of herself."

"Yes, I know. She had a lot of Points once. No one believes the charges against her, but Lenore is meticulous. Her false evidence was very convincing."

"If no one believes the charges, then why is everyone so willing to kill her for them?"

"Because in Midnight City, the truth always takes a backseat to principle. Point Fabrication is our most serious crime, and if someone is found guilty of it, innocent or not . . . examples must be made."

"Well, I don't think a whole lot of your city," Holt said. "It's a self-absorbed, dangerous melting pot of craziness, focused on a meaningless game I don't have any interest in playing."

"Really?" For the first time, Amelia smiled. "That's interesting. Given how many Points you've managed to collect. Did you even know you were on the Wall?"

The words jarred Holt. Being on the Scorewall was a concept he'd never considered, and he stared at Amelia hesitantly.

She kept smiling, stood up, and walked to a separate curtain at the other end of the room. Opening it revealed a private view of the Scorewall, with a conveniently placed brass telescope on the floor. Amelia sighted through the scope, adjusted it until she found what she was looking for. Then she stepped back and motioned Holt over. "See for yourself," she said.

Holt stepped to the telescope and peered through. It was pointed at a specific block on the Scorewall's left side, which was full of titles, most beginning with OS. The one dead center in view was OS107 and there was a number written next to it.

872.

"OS one-oh-seven?" Holt asked skeptically.

"*OS* stands for 'Outsider,' " Amelia replied evenly as she reached up for a thin red rope hanging from the ceiling. When she pulled it, a small bell rang loudly on the platform outside the curtain. "And one-oh-seven is the number of the Outsider helping Mira Toombs."

A boy, clad in orange, entered through the curtain and nodded to Amelia expectantly, but the little girl's eyes remained on Holt.

"There's a rumor that my faction has, in its compound, a secret exit out of Midnight City." Amelia picked up a small notepad and pencil next to the telescope and began writing on it. "You want to trade the plutonium to use that exit."

"Yes," Holt said.

"The good news is the exit's real. The bad is that it's going to cost you three things. The first of which is your full name."

Holt studied her uneasily, saying nothing.

Amelia smiled again. "It's a small price to pay. Tiny, really. Especially for someone who isn't at all interested in our games."

Holt frowned. He didn't see that he had much choice, but he wasn't sure he was going to like where this went. "Holt Hawkins," he said.

Amelia wrote something else on the notepad, then ripped a sheet loose, handed it to the boy waiting by the curtain. He analyzed it quietly, then disappeared back through the orange fabric. Holt didn't know what to make of it, but Amelia's next words quickly made him forget.

"There are two more prices for the use of our exit, and neither of them is your plutonium," she said, and Holt's eyes widened in surprise. "It is valuable, but only if you have the drive to use it, and I'm afraid I don't. Entering the Severed Tower isn't something that interests me. Points, however, do."

Holt tried to contain his shock. Mira had never even mentioned the possibility of the Lost Knights not wanting the plutonium. To her, it was the most priceless substance on the planet, and the reaction of every person he had ever seen had been nothing less than lustful.

"You . . . don't want the plutonium?" Holt asked.

"No," she said. "I first want the sum total of all Points you earn here, an amount I have a feeling will be very large. In one day, you've acquired almost a thousand. It's impressive."

"Fine," Holt said with distaste. "You're welcome to them. What else?"

"It's called the Chance Generator," she said, and her voice was wistful as she said the words. "A major artifact from the Strange Lands that belongs to the Crossmen. They keep it in the Artifact Vault."

"Which is what?"

"You really are an Outsider, aren't you? The Artifact Vault is a storage cavern for powerful artifacts that their owners want to keep secure, or which are too dangerous to remain in the city. Only Freebooters can get past its main gate, and once inside, the Librarian protects everything else."

"And the Librarian would be who?" Holt asked with thinly veiled annoyance. He was starting to lose his patience with this whole thing.

"The fool keeper of the Vault," Amelia replied. "A moron who took it upon himself to stand watch over all that power below the city. He rarely ventures outside of his lab and his school, but don't let his appearance fool you. He's cunning . . . and dangerous. Even the faction leaders won't cross him willingly."

This was sounding less and less like a good trade. "Well, that's just great. Enlighten me—what makes you think we can pull all this off?"

"Because you have no other choice, Holt Hawkins," Amelia said. The little girl looked away from him and peered through the telescope again. When she pulled away, she was smiling. "Look."

Holt frowned but did as she said, bending over and peering through the lens.

He saw the same section as before, but now one of the Scorekeepers filled the frame, hovering over the black wall. Holt saw that the title OS107 had been erased, replaced with something else. He felt a chill run down his back.

It now read HOLT HAWKINS. And the number next to it had grown to *945.*

Holt looked up at Amelia, more than a little disturbed.

"You see, Holt?" she asked with amusement and malevolence. "Everyone in Midnight City plays our games. Whether they want to or not."

Holt just stared at the little girl silently.

"Bring me the Chance Generator," she continued. "Mira will know where to find it. Do that . . . and you escape Lenore's grasp."

Holt frowned at her, but knew there was no real choice. Maybe it would have been better to head east when he had the chance after all.

40. SHRINE

HOLT FOLLOWED MIRA through an ever-tightening tunnel that stretched and wound out of sight ahead. While the ceiling mercifully stayed the same height, the walls had pushed in to the point where they had to sidle through the cavern.

"Glad I skipped breakfast," Holt remarked, wiggling through a particularly tight section. Behind him, Max and Zoey followed, annoyed at the slow progress. They were a lot smaller, after all.

"You're sure she said the Chance Generator?" Mira asked. She'd been only slightly surprised that the Lost Knights hadn't wanted the plutonium; they marched to a different beat, apparently. But their desire for the Chance Generator was something she just couldn't seem to understand.

"Yeah," Holt answered. "What is it, anyway?"

"It's a major artifact, a scary one, probably fourth ring, maybe even the core. A Crossmen Freebooter brought it out, I don't know who." Mira said, "Basically, it makes a sphere of 'good luck' around the user."

"Good luck?" Holt asked.

"Mmm-hmm. Once you're inside the influence sphere, you become . . . incredibly lucky—I don't how else to put it. Things that normally might go bad for you, go right instead. And they go right over and over again."

"That doesn't sound so bad," Zoey piped up from the end of the line.

"Yeah, I gotta agree," Holt replied, pushing past another tight intersection. "It not only doesn't sound bad, it sounds valuable."

"It isn't," Mira said. "It's horribly dangerous. In order to increase your luck, it reduces someone else's to the same degree. Say it lets you win at dice. Someone else nearby loses. Maybe it saves you from a falling rock? Someone else has an accident."

"And what if someone tries to kill you?" Holt asked, but he had a pretty good idea what the answer was.

"You live . . . someone else dies," she answered. "The more you use it, the more negative effects it has to generate to keep your own luck going. And the more dependent on it you grow, the more it becomes like a paranoid addiction. You don't feel comfortable doing anything without the artifact. The only good thing about it is that it can be used only so many times a day before it runs out of power and has to recharge. It's been kept in the Vault for years by the Crossmen. They're terrified of it, never use it, only hold on to it for Points. If it were me, I wouldn't even do that much. I'd send it back to the Strange Lands to be destroyed."

"Seems like a lot of things that come out of that place need to be destroyed," Holt said pointedly. Mira opened her mouth to retort . . . then shut it. What was there to say? Most artifacts *were* scary, and they did scary things. Including the one that had gotten her banished from Midnight City, the one she'd made herself. . . .

The four stepped out of the cramped tunnel and into a small round room lit with two Illuminators that hummed on the ceiling just ten feet above their heads.

The walls all around them were brimming with objects, glued or somehow else attached permanently in place, and they filled the room with all kinds of colors and shapes. Postcards, Polaroid pictures, drawings, notes, from what Holt could see. Some were worn and wrinkled and faded; others looked like they'd been placed in the room just recently.

"Where are we?" Zoey asked, standing in the center of the room, spinning to look at all of it at once. Max watched her spin and cocked his head to the side as he studied her.

"The Shrine," Mira said. "These are mementos for Freebooters who've died or gone missing in the Strange Lands." Mira gazed at the walls silently, and Holt could tell the chaotic conglomeration of things and images had deep meaning for her.

"Did you know a lot of them?" Holt asked.

"Yeah," Mira answered. "I did."

Holt moved around the room, looking at everything that was revealed under the dim lights of the Illuminators. Hundreds of photographs of kids, some in Midnight City, but most were standing in a strange, almost alien landscape, where the backgrounds were blurred or flashing colors or contorted like the air had somehow been bent. There were drawings, too, of Strange Lands landmarks, some better than others, labeled things like POLESTAR, KALEIDOSCOPE, AXIS, TORNADO ALLEY, or COMPRESSOR. Next to the drawings were notes, sometimes several pages thick, that seemed to describe the adventures of the lost ones, their journeys, the obstacles they overcame, the artifacts they brought back.

The name was well earned. It really was a shrine, Holt thought.

Mira looked away from all the history and moved toward something set into the far wall. A heavy steel door that looked like something from an old castle. It had been permanently affixed in front of the next tunnel, blocking the path past the room, and next to a large handle near one of its edges was an ornate keyhole. The words FREEBOOTERS AND ACOLYTES ONLY were stenciled across the door in faded red paint.

Holt eyed the wall and the writing hesitantly. "Is this—?" he started to ask.

"An artifact," Mira finished for him. "A really dangerous one." From a pocket she pulled out a large key inscribed with the δ symbol, and Holt saw a length of chain attached to it that ran back to her belt. "I'd move back if I were you—it can malfunction," she said as she stepped toward the metallic gate.

She didn't need to tell him twice. Max whined as Holt pulled Zoey a few steps away, watching Mira hold the key in front of the keyhole.

She stayed like that, hesitantly studying the door. "You may want to move back more. It's not pretty when it backfires," Mira said.

Holt stepped backwards again without hesitation, keeping his eyes on the door. What the hell did this thing *do?*

"A little farther," Mira said again. Holt backed up, eyeing her. "A little more," she said again, and Holt took another step back. "Seriously, you want to be *really* far back for this."

Holt frowned and dragged Zoey and Max with him. He was starting to wonder just what—

He flinched as he hit his head on a low-hanging part of the ceiling. "Ouch," he said painfully, rubbing the back of his skull. Below him, Zoey looked up and stared at him in exasperation, shaking her head.

Mira laughed out loud. "Sometimes it's just too easy," she said as she shoved the big key into the gate and turned it. Holt watched as the door groaned and slowly cranked open, revealing more dark tunnel beyond . . . and nothing else. No flash of light, no killer emission of energy, nothing remotely dangerous. "It's just a big metal gate with a lock," Mira said. "All Freebooters get a key. Come on, tough guy."

Holt glared after her, felt his ears start to redden. "Oh, that was supposed to be funny, I guess?"

"It *was* funny," Mira clarified, pushing past the gate and stuffing the key back in her pocket. "Lock it behind you."

Holt watched her disappear on the other side of the door, then felt Zoey take his hand and pull him forward. "Holt, try not to be so gullible, okay?" the little girl encouraged as he followed after her.

"Well, isn't your vocabulary growing?" he said as he shut the gate behind Max. The dog barked and ran after the little girl, just as excited. Holt rolled his eyes and followed after them, without the same enthusiasm.

WHEN THEY ENTERED THE CAVERN that made up the Vault, they emerged into its topmost level, the stalactites that spanned its ceilings right in everyone's eye-line, and the vastness of it was staggering. It was by far the largest cavern in the whole system, and it stretched downward out of sight into a massive pit. The walls below them were lined with row after row of shelves and cabinets, sitting on ledges that had been carved into the rock face. Even from the top of the Vault, it was apparent what they held: Thousands of artifacts flashed, glowed, pulsed, wavered, hummed, floated, disintegrated and reappeared on those shelves, filling the pit with a kaleidoscopic sea of flickering, colorful lights that spiraled down brightly into the darkness.

In all the times that Mira had come here, the Artifact Vault had never failed to take her breath away. Long ago, when she was young, it was here she'd first learned about the Strange Lands and the artifacts that came from them, and the magnificence of the Vault had played a sizable role in putting her on the path she'd eventually taken, for better or worse.

At first, there was no discernible way to get to the artifacts in the huge pit. There were no stairs or ladders, no poles to slide, or handholds in the rock to climb. The answer was on the ceiling.

A large grid-work of metal had been bolted into the rock there, circling the entire cavern. Hanging from the grid by thick ropes and chains were two large boxes made of ornately polished wood, each bearing a δ symbol inlaid in brilliant gold and resting on a platform at the edge of the pit. The boxes were large enough to hold two people, and it was fairly clear what they were. Elevators.

The ropes and chains passed through pulleys in the grid-work, and traveled to a bank of switches and cranks on the landing platform. There were other things there as well—more cabinets and shelves, work spaces—and flickering candles and lanterns illuminated it all. But if there was anyone there, Mira saw no sign.

She stared at all of it, enraptured once again, and didn't even notice that the others had stepped up beside her. Even Max was still as he gazed at the Vault.

"Wow . . . ," Zoey said, her voice an awed whisper. "It's so big."

Mira smiled and looked at Holt, curious to see his reaction. He looked down at the expansive view with a gaze that held only amazement. In a room crammed to the gills with thousands of powerful Strange Lands artifacts, he wasn't slowly backing toward the exit, and that spoke volumes.

When she slipped her hand into his, he turned and looked at her. There was something about the fact that her touch was enough to tear him away from the sight of the Vault that Mira liked. "What do you think?" she asked.

"Beautiful," he answered, and there was a tone in his voice that implied he was talking about more than just the Vault. Mira smiled.

"Are we going down to the bottom?" Zoey asked.

Mira pulled her gaze from Holt's. "I don't know yet, honey," Mira answered. "We have to find the thing we're looking for first."

"Can I ride the Max down to the bottom if we do?" Zoey asked hopefully.

Holt sighed next to her. "What is it with you? Just because he has four legs doesn't mean he's a horse."

"The Max can carry me, he's strong!"

"I don't think it's the best idea right now, Zoey," Mira replied. "Besides, there aren't any stairs. We use the lifts."

Zoey pouted, but didn't complain further as they all started moving for the opposite end of the cavern, where the platform sat, as well as the work and study area. There was still no sign of movement there, no indication anyone was nearby; there was only the light from a few dozen glimmering candles and lanterns. Still, someone had to have lit them.

"Old man?" Mira yelled as they approached, her voice echoing back and forth amid the stalactites that hung over their heads. There was no response.

"Is that the best idea?" Holt asked.

"The Librarian knew we were here the moment we passed the Shrine," Mira said. She looked ahead of them and yelled again, *"Old man?"* They all listened to her voice as it echoed between the walls, unsettlingly loud. But after it died away there was nothing, only silence.

"Amelia said the Librarian protects the Vault," Holt said, taking in the big, empty cavern with trepidation.

"He's a teacher, too—he taught me everything I know," she answered darkly. It was true; she had learned a great deal from him, but there had been a price to pay for that knowledge.

Mira kept moving, growing more uncertain with each step. Did he not recognize her? Or had her reputation in Midnight City tarnished even this relationship, her oldest one in the city? She wasn't sure, but—

Mira stopped when she heard something. A crackling in the air around her. It was distinctive, metallic and thin, like someone was crinkling giant wads of tinfoil next to them. And because of its distinctiveness, she knew what it was almost immediately. "Get back!" Mira shouted in alarm, trying to drag them back, but it was too late.

The air flashed around them as the Restrictor took effect. Mira felt her limbs, her muscles, her extremities, even her hair, all exponentially increase in weight, and as they did so, her movement gradually slowed down. She struggled against the force building around her, but it was no use. She watched as Holt, Zoey, and even Max froze solid in place, bit by bit, unable to move—even their eyes wouldn't blink.

Mira had been caught in a Restrictor only one other time, and that had felt like her body was transforming into dense, unyielding stone, until she finally froze completely. It was the same now, but the reality was altogether different. A Restrictor was an artifact combination that continually reversed the force of inertia. The longer it stayed on, the more difficult it became to move, until you just couldn't move at all. With a strong enough Restrictor, you could probably freeze a Spider walker in place.

They were all trapped now, unable to move, their eyes glued to where they had last been looking before the artifact was activated.

In front of Mira, the air shimmered suddenly and parted like a curtain. A silhouette stepped through and revealed itself, and in a world where youth reigned supreme by virtue of complicated circumstances, the sight of the figure before them was shocking, even for Mira, who had seen him countless times growing up.

She'd never had the gall to ask the Librarian how old he really was, but she was positive it was more than seventy years. His appearance was beyond disheveled. His clothes were a patchwork of pieces from all manner of garments, some of them having been sewn into places that were the opposite of what they came from. Pieces of jeans for shirtsleeves, and coat arms pieced together to make leggings. A pair of eyeglasses hung from his neck by red twine, half from one pair, the other half from another, and taped together to form a complete set. Despite his chaotic appearance, the man had neatly and meticulously trimmed his beard, and it hung down half the length of his wrinkled neck. And, of course, there were his eyes: clear of the Tone. The hazel of his irises sparkled in the candlelight that filled this part of the cavern.

Leather straps like belts crisscrossed his body, and attached to them were a dozen amazingly intricate and beautiful artifact combinations of his own creation. The lights of one of them, near his left shoulder, glowed and flashed in different colors, and Mira guessed it was probably the Restrictor that was holding all of them.

The old man examined each of the four trespassers one at a time without emotion, and then his eyes finally settled on Mira. When they did, his brow furrowed deeply and he fixed her with an irritable gaze.

"If anyone should not be here in this place, Mira Toombs, it is you," he said in an annoyed voice that sounded like he had swallowed a mouthful of gravel and cut glass. "Explain why I shouldn't hand you over to your old faction right now. It would be a fitting punishment, the way I see it."

The Librarian tapped the glowing artifact on his shoulder, and some of the lights on the combination—a mixture of magnets, vials of black metallic shavings, a circuit board, and a strand of interlocking paper clips, all held together by spun silver and gold chain—wavered and died away.

With a groan, Mira collapsed to the ground in a heap, and her entire body ached. It was a normal side effect from being restrained in a Restrictor's field, and she painfully looked up . . . and was shocked to see the others—Holt, Zoey, and Max—still frozen in place.

A typical Restrictor simply emitted a single field that slowed down everything it touched. The Librarian, however, had managed to construct a combination that could selectively apply a Restrictor's effect to multiple and separate targets. It was an amazing achievement, a testament to the Librarian's reputation as the greatest crafter of artifacts in the world, and her head spun as she tried to figure out the complicated combination of Essences and Focuses necessary to—

"You were asked a question, Mira Toombs," the Librarian stated with unveiled displeasure. He was not used to being ignored, and it made her face redden the way he spoke to her as if she were still a little girl. "By coming here, you have violated the sanctity of something I long ago taught you to revere."

"I do revere this place, old man," Mira said. "Just not the city that holds it."

The Librarian gazed down at her curiously. "Not a completely uninspired response, to be sure, and one that echoes sentiments I also hold, but it fails to answer the question, doesn't it? Why are you *here?*"

Mira swallowed, thinking through her words carefully. "I need something from the Vault," she said. "Something that doesn't belong to me."

The Librarian frowned. "You aren't making a very good argument, little one. Why would I allow you to steal from my Vault? Why would I break the oaths I have taken?"

Mira made herself look up at the Librarian forcefully. "You've broken them before—don't pretend you haven't. It's me you're talking to, old man, not some silly acolyte." She spoke with as much strength as she could muster, and hoped it was enough.

The Librarian stared back evenly . . . and then smiled. Or at least as much as he could. The only indication Mira had ever attributed to a smile from him was a slight wrinkling of the beard around his cheeks, and that was what he gave her now. "I didn't say I had never broken them, only that I wanted to know the reasons why I might do so again. Is this about that wretched little creation of yours? The one I warned you against?"

"Yes," Mira said with shame. "I'm trying to undo that mistake."

"If you had listened to me in the first place, you wouldn't have anything to undo, would you?" he said with contempt. "You're all the same, once you leave here. Arrogant and sure of yourselves. It's a wonder any of you survive that place."

"I'm trying to fix things, old man," Mira said through clenched teeth, feeling her face burn at his scolding, just as it always had. Why did she still feel so tiny around him? Hadn't any of her achievements impressed him? Hadn't she earned the right to make a few mistakes?

"You want to take it back to the Strange Lands and destroy it," he surmised. "A wise course, but it still doesn't explain why you're here. You must need something else," the old man said contemplatively, and Mira could see him putting the pieces together in his head, tugging on his beard absently as he did so. "The Gray Devils have sealed the city; I heard the horns. Looking for you, no doubt. There must be something here someone else wants in order to grant you passage out of the city. The only other way out is through the Lost Knights' infamous secret exit . . . and they have always lusted after the Chance Generator." His mood, if it were possible, darkened even more as he figured it out. "Is that why you're here?"

Mira just nodded. She could sense Holt and Zoey frozen in place above her, but was powerless to do anything for them. The old man had all the cards now, and he stood over her stoically a long time, still tugging on his beard, thinking things through. "The price for my aid is this, Mira Toombs," he finally said. "You may take the artifact . . . but in return, you must carry it back into the Strange Lands and destroy it along with your own. It's another hideous aberration that doesn't deserve to exist, as far as I'm concerned, but my tenure as the Vault's Librarian prevents me from taking matters into my own hands. You are already Unmentionable here. One further insult will have little effect."

"Gee, thanks," Mira said tartly, glaring up at him. She could feel her patience starting to run out. "How exactly am I supposed to arrange all *that*? We need the artifact to bargain our way *out* of here."

"You've always been industrious," he said, his beard wrinkling in a quasi-smile once more. "I trust you to find a way. But if I should hear that the Lost Knights have the Chance Generator and are actively using it to increase their Points, I will be . . . most disappointed." The stare he fixed Mira with almost instantly made her cringe, and it was infuriating.

The old man tapped the same artifact again, and this time all the lights on it went out. When they did, both Zoey and Holt exhaled deeply as they fell to the floor. Max whined as the same thing happened to him. He just squirmed on the ground with the others, feeling the painful sensations of motor control returning.

"What . . . the . . . *hell*," Holt managed to say in between gasps of air, and the anger in his voice was apparent. He looked up at the Librarian with red eyes. "I am going . . . to *stomp* this guy."

Before Mira could warn him, Holt pushed himself shakily to his feet. The old man, however, simply rotated a ring of dimes around a different artifact, one near his waist, until a specific coin clicked in place. When it did, the combination hummed loudly and glowed in muted red light. "That decision would be . . . ill advised," he said calmly.

Holt eyed the glowing artifact, and didn't make another move. He wasn't a fool, Mira knew; he'd survived this long on his own by being able to read a situation in spite of his emotions, and his instincts were probably telling him the old man was a lot more capable than his feeble, disheveled exterior implied. If he wasn't, the Librarian wouldn't be so unintimidated. And for good reason, she knew. The Librarian was the one person in all Midnight City that even Lenore feared.

"Now that that's resolved . . . ," the old man said as he moved toward the nearby work area. It was filled with rows of tables and seats in front of shelves that contained all manner of minor artifacts for combinations. It had been a school for Mira, a hallmark of what little "youth" she'd had, and the place always stirred emotions in her when she saw it. Here, sitting at these desks, she and dozens of others had been taught the cursory skills they needed to become Freebooters.

The basics of artifact creation: coins, Focusers, Essences. How to combine them into more powerful entities. The properties of hundreds of minor artifacts for creating their own. And the Strange Lands and its obstacles and its different rings. They learned about antimatter storms and dark energy tornadoes, discovered the mysteries of the core and the Severed Tower, and dreamed of seeing Polestar, the famous Freebooter outpost that stood in the middle of the third ring in defiance of the chaos that surrounded it.

Mira's head, like those of all the other students, had been filled with the Librarian's teachings, but he'd warned it was only theoretical knowledge. The only true way to learn to survive in that place was through experience. The Strange Lands were a harsh teacher . . . but so was the old man. Mira could still feel the shocks on her wrists and back when she got the polarity of a coin set wrong or chose the wrong Essence for a combination. The Librarian's methods had seemed unnecessarily severe at the time, but the truth was, he was preparing them for the reality to come, Mira knew. The Strange Lands were unforgiving, and the punishment for failure there was far worse than the sting of an electrical charge.

Though his demeanor was cold, there was more to the Librarian than his harsh teaching style. He had spent his life since the invasion preparing countless children to become Freebooters, and had watched his teachings consistently not be enough to keep them alive. Mira knew he drove his students hard out of an interest to protect them—because, deep down, he really did care.

The Librarian stepped to a large, ornate pedestal holding a huge, hardcover bound book. He grabbed the mismatched pair of eyeglasses that hung from his neck and slipped them onto his nose. The book was as wide as he was, and he flipped the tome open and scanned its pages one at a time with a discerning eye, running his finger down the length of each, looking for something specific. Eventually, he found it.

"The Chance Generator," he said in disdain, peering up at them over the rim of his glasses. "Are you ready for the key?"

Mira nodded. "Yes, old man."

"Six of clubs," he began, spouting out the list of settings that would program the lift. "Purple eight, and three-twenty-five. You and the Outsider can go—the little one and the dog can remain with me. I always have plenty of chores to be done, as you well know."

Zoey looked up at Mira and Holt curiously, neither frightened nor eager.

"I'm not a fan of leaving her with Merlin here," Holt said, fixing his gaze on the Librarian. The old man just stared back silently.

"He can be . . . difficult, I know, but he won't hurt her," Mira said, pulling Holt's attention away from the Librarian. "I promise, it's the last thing he would do."

Mira could tell Holt didn't like it, but her word seemed to be enough for him. He nodded, and Mira kneeled down to Zoey, ran her fingers gently through the little girl's hair. "We'll be right back, okay. Zoey?" Mira said. "Do what the old man says. There's no reason to be scared."

"I'm not scared, Mira," Zoey said, matter-of-fact.

"Of course you're not," Mira replied. Then she stood up and moved for the large, heavy wooden platform that extended out over the breach of the pit, and the two wooden lifts that sat there. "Come on," she said to Holt, and he followed after.

"Mira," the old man called out gently behind her, and she stopped and looked at him. There was a different feel to his eyes now. "It is not . . . unpleasant to see you alive."

Mira smiled. It was as close as you got to tenderness from the Librarian. "You too, old man." She turned and kept walking with Holt toward the lifts.

Along each side of the platform were small, open shacks full of chains, ropes, pulleys, cranks, and wheels, and Mira stopped in front of one.

She reached for a long, antique brass crank attached to huge spoked metal gears. Interestingly, each gear was marked at certain points with old, faded playing cards—clubs, hearts, spades, diamonds—and the gear threaded through a series of giant rusted chains. Mira turned the crank handle, and the gear spun with it, pulling up lengths of chain and winding them through pulleys and slots up above the shed. Outside on the platform, one of the lifts shook slightly as the tension of the chains rippled down to it.

As Mira turned the crank, the cards began to rotate on the surface of the gears. She kept cranking, loading more and more chain, until she finally saw the card she wanted: the six of clubs. She kept cranking until it was pointed straight up, above all the others, and then locked the wheel in place.

The first axis was set, but there were two more to go. And using the formula the Librarian had given her, she set the remaining ones. She pulled a long stretch of thick rope downward, lined with numbers in different colored paint, until a purple 8 appeared. More tension shook the lift outside. For the last axis, she moved over to where additional chain hung, and an assortment of metallic weights hung with it.

"Help me," she said to Holt. "We need three hundred and twenty-five pounds." Holt was clearly confused at what they were doing, but he helped anyway. They added weights in different increments—ten pounds, twenty pounds, fifty—linking them into hooks on the chains' surface, until it was the right amount. The chains didn't move; they were locked over the breach with all the added weight, waiting to descend.

Mira and Holt stepped out of the shed and moved to the closest lift. It was not a quickly cobbled-together box of scrap wood; its pieces had been chosen from strong sources, blended together and rounded into soft curves, and polished and lacquered to a brilliant sheen. Mira opened the door to the closest one and stepped inside, feeling it tilt as her and Holt's combined weight shifted it.

Inside was a small wooden panel with two large metallic handles. One was marked LOWER and the other RAISE. Mira looked at Holt as he shut the door behind them. "This can be a pretty wild ride," she said.

Holt studied her soberly. "Yeah, that was my guess."

Mira smiled and yanked the lever labeled LOWER down and back.

Outside the lift, the huge chains and weights they had just configured in the shed raced through their pulleys as the tension released. The lift lurched and they were flung off the platform and up into the air.

Mira felt gravity catch them as they moved not just upward, but also sideways. Looking up through the small window shaped into the ceiling of the lift, she and Holt saw the ropes and chains that suspended them from the grid-work on the ceiling shift through various metallic rails and tracks as the tension pulled them to a specific spot.

When they reached it, the lift swung to a halt, swaying precariously over the hundreds of feet of empty air between them and the rock floor below.

Holt pushed back against the wall, probably in an attempt to feel something solid and not think about the sheer drop underneath them. Mira held his gaze, finding his discomfort pretty cute, if she were to be honest about it.

"Going down," she said with another smile . . .

. . . and then the lift plummeted at breakneck speed toward the dark of the Vault below them.

42. VAULT

MAX WATCHED, chin on his paws, as Zoey rummaged through a collection of items on a desk and placed them one at a time back on the study area's cabinets. They were all things she assumed were from the Strange Lands—pens, circuit boards, coins in plastic sleeves, springs, candles, spoons, doorknobs—and she watched as they all seemed to writhe and push away from one another, ever so slightly. Or was it a trick of the eye? Zoey couldn't tell.

"You were supposed to organize them by color," a stern, gravelly voice said behind her. Zoey turned and saw the Librarian watching her inquisitively, standing near the bottom of the teaching area, where the steps began.

She couldn't read the old man as easily as she could other people. His emotions were weaker than everyone else's, but not because he was without feeling. There were feelings there, but she guessed he was so in control of them, they never stood out. There had been only two times when she felt something from him, and both had been mixtures of sadness and apprehension, but so brief, she barely felt them at all. Zoey wasn't sure if the mastery came from the old man's age or from some facet of his personality. Either way, that restraint wasn't something she experienced often.

"I was lining them up by how strong they felt," Zoey replied, holding the old man's gaze. She watched as his eyes thinned, and there, right then, she felt something from him: a stir of emotion, surprise mainly, but it fell away almost as quickly as it came.

"And how do you know which are 'stronger,' little one?" he asked.

"I don't know. I just . . . feel it, sort of."

The Librarian studied her even more closely now, and she felt the weight of his scrutiny on her. It wasn't pleasant—she felt like one of his artifacts, like something to be analyzed and cataloged.

"Your name, girl," the Librarian said bluntly after a moment. "Tell it to me."

"Zoey," she answered simply.

"Zoey," he said in a slow, musing tone, as if deciding whether it truly fit her. "There is an air about you. A vibration almost, like a static charge. It's something I encounter frequently, but never in people."

Zoey had no idea what he was talking about, but it was interesting. "Where *do* you notice it, sir?"

He held her gaze pointedly. "Only in artifacts from the Strange Lands." There seemed to be some implication in the statement, some musing, but she had no idea what it was. But before she could ask, he spoke again. "Where are you from?"

"I don't know," she said.

"Where did you grow up, I mean," he pressed.

"I don't know," she said again in a lower voice, reaching for more of the artifacts. This subject wasn't something she liked talking about. "I don't have many memories."

The Librarian contemplated her even more intently. There was a long pause before he finally spoke again. "You sensed the artifacts' power as you touched them. I'd bet you can sense other things, too, can't you, Zoey?" he asked.

Zoey went still at the question, hands holding the artifacts she was about to stack, and Max's ears perked up curiously. No one had ever guessed her ability, not from simple observation, and she was suddenly uneasy about the old man. If he was that perceptive, who knew what else he might be able to deduce.

"Emotions, thoughts, memories?" the Librarian kept on. "Which is it?"

Zoey said nothing, just stared at the old man at the bottom of the steps.

"You can tell me, girl. There's no danger in it," he told her. "You can tell me if anyone, I assure you."

Zoey wasn't convinced. Should she tell him? He already seemed to know the truth, but was it smart to confirm it? What would Mira or Holt say? Mira trusted the old man—Zoey could sense that much—and there was even some affection there, but she was also cautious around him.

Suddenly, she felt a stirring in the back of her mind. The feelings blossoming and coming to life, the ones that had guided her before. When she noticed them this time, the first thing she felt was anger. Why now? Why hadn't they appeared earlier, when she could have saved Mira from the Tone?

The feelings washed over her, and she absorbed them, discerning their meaning, and it was almost instantly clear: She should trust the old man. There was no hint as to why; she sensed only that it was important she do so. They wanted her to tell him everything.

The feelings were unpredictable, it was true, but they had never steered her wrong, as far as Zoey could tell. In fact, in spite of the frustrations she sometimes had, she'd come to trust them, almost as much as she trusted Holt and Mira. So she followed their lead yet again. . . .

"Feelings," she said. "Other people's feelings."

The Librarian nodded, as if he'd expected that answer. "You can sense them," he said.

"It's more than that. It's like I'm the one feeling them," she answered. "Sometimes it's scary."

"I can imagine, Zoey," the old man said with sincerity. "But there's more, isn't there? A lot more."

Zoey told him the rest. Told him about the feelings, how they came and went, how they guided her. She told him how they had helped her cure two survivors of the Tone, how she had wiped it away by just touching them and willing it to happen. And how she couldn't make it happen when she tried to heal Mira, how it never seemed to be *her* doing it at all.

Through it all, the Librarian remained quiet, listening and absorbing her words. When Zoey was done, he stood in silence, thinking. "Keep stocking the shelves," he said absently. "It's work that needs doing."

Zoey started stacking the artifacts again, moving them around so that they were grouped in matching colors, as the old man wanted. As she did so, she noticed the Librarian was no longer watching her. He was too deep in thought.

"Why are you here, Zoey?" he finally asked. "In Midnight City. You came here for a reason, not just to help Mira. Am I right?"

"The feelings pushed me to come," she said. "But I don't know why. I just know there's something here for me."

The Librarian was silent a moment more; then he looked at Zoey. "It's possible that your inability to use your powers is tied to your memory loss. Memories are what make us who we are. It's also possible the memories were taken from you. Maybe to repress your abilities. If that's the case, these . . . feelings of yours may have brought you here for the Oracle."

The name itself meant nothing to Zoey, and it was so vague, she wasn't sure how she was supposed to feel about it.

"It makes sense," the old man continued, thinking out loud, "that they would send you here for that, but how did they know? Could they be more prescient than I thought? Or . . ." His eyes refocused, locking back on to Zoey. He seemed to be considering things, important things, but she couldn't sense any of it, and that frustrated her.

"Do you see the curtain hanging over the wall at the back of the study area?" he asked.

Zoey looked past the desks and chairs, past the cabinets lined with glowing artifacts, to the wall in the far back. Hanging there was a curtain, red and blue, with a diamond pattern. It was probably an old rug the Librarian had repurposed, but it added a splash of color to the black walls that dominated everything. "I see it," Zoey said.

"On the other side lies what you seek," he declared.

"The 'orkle'?" Zoey asked.

The Librarian's beard crinkled around his cheeks, signaling a smile, but it lasted only a second. "Yes, Zoey," he told her. "The Oracle. All my students visit it once. Mira herself did so, but she was much older than you. In fact, when you speak to it, you will be the youngest ever to have done so."

"What does it do?" Zoey asked, looking at the curtain on the wall, wondering what was on the other side.

"It's a powerful artifact," he said, "maybe the most powerful ever to be brought out. I found it many years ago, when I still had the strength for such things." He paused a moment, considering his next words. "The Oracle reveals to you your three greatest truths, Zoey. Who you were, who you are . . . who you will be. The revelations are not always . . . pleasant. Nor are they always clear. Some of them you will have to deci-

pher for yourself, but they should be enough to tell us what you are meant
to do."

"You think I'm here for something important," Zoey said, and it
wasn't a question.

The old man considered her. "If you are what I think you are . . .
then yes. I would believe that. I'd believe it's no coincidence that you're
here, Zoey. In this place, at this time. In fact, where you're concerned . . .
I'd wager that coincidences cease to exist altogether."

Zoey looked away from the curtain and back at the Librarian, confused.

"It doesn't make sense, I know. But it will, Zoey. And sooner than
you might think." They held each other's gaze a long time before he finally spoke again. "Set the artifacts down—you can finish it later," he
told her, and Zoey set the last of the artifacts on the shelves. "To the side
of the curtain is a small chest on a shelf, made of golden wood. Open it
and take one of the coins inside. They are Strange Lands coins, so use
caution—don't remove it from the plastic sleeve until it's time."

"How will I know when?" Zoey asked.

"You will know, little one," the old man answered. "I have no doubt
of that. Go now."

Zoey hesitated; then she motioned Max to follow her. He jumped to
his feet and padded ahead of her up the steps that led past the rows of
desks and chairs of the study area, toward the red and blue curtain.
When they reached it, Zoey looked at a row of shelves to the left side and
saw a small antique chest, which had been brushed a long time ago with
a dry, gold substance that flaked off it like old leaves.

Zoey opened the chest, and inside lay dozens of quarters, tarnished
and faded, each in separate plastic sleeves. She grabbed one of them in
her hand. It was the first time she'd ever held a Strange Lands coin, and
she felt it subtly vibrate and pulse, moving around in her palm. She
gripped it tighter to stop it from squirming out.

Zoey looked at the thick curtain in front of her.

She couldn't see past it; there was no indication of what was on the
other side. Whatever was there apparently was the reason she'd come all
this way, why she had traversed such a dangerous path. Now that she
was faced with the truth of it all, an ending of sorts, it was suddenly not
the easiest thing to draw open that curtain.

She did as she always did now when faced with difficult moments like this. She asked herself what Holt and Mira would do, and the answer was always the same: They would be brave, she told herself. They would do what they had to do.

Zoey reached for the curtain and pulled it open.

Nothing but darkness waited for her beyond. The entrance to another tunnel stretched out of sight and into the shadows far ahead. Max whined apprehensively next to her. She knew how the dog felt. Zoey exhaled a long, slow breath, and together, they stepped past the curtain.

THE LIFT JARRED AS IT lurched to a halt directly in front of one of the Vault's many ledges. The initial plummet had been so steep, Holt had thought he was going to fly up into the ceiling, and when it stopped, his stomach felt like it had dropped into his shoes. He'd been sure the entire contraption was going to come apart in midair and send them hurtling to the cavern floor below.

But the lift had held, and it had stopped. He looked at Mira, and she was smiling back at him, seemingly unfazed by the experience. "What?" he asked, frowning.

"I don't know why," she said with an amused look, "but it's very cute seeing you scared."

"I'm not *scared,*" Holt insisted, even though his heart was still pounding.

Mira took his hand as she moved past him. "Come on," she said, and her arm brushed against his. The quick, soft feel of her and the scent of her hair helped to slow his pulse.

Holt let her pull him out of the lift, and as she did, he took in the sight of the Vault up close. At the top, it had been deceiving to look at—the rows of hung shelves and cabinets that spiraled down the walls looked like they had somehow been bolted or attached to the rock—but from here, it was clear that the architecture was much more complicated.

Just outside the lift was a rocky outcrop that had been cut into the cavern's walls, one of many Holt could see: a man-made ledge that stretched probably a hundred feet in either direction, and another twenty feet or so into the cavern wall. It was on this ledge that the cabinets sat, two rows deep. The pattern continued all around him, up and down the circular cavern's walls, stretching out of sight in every direction. Ledges, cut into the rock, containing hundreds of cabinets and shelves, and within them, thousands of artifacts.

Holt stepped out of the lift onto the ledge and made the mistake of looking down. In spite of how far the lift had unceremoniously dropped them, they were still very, very far from the bottom of the chasm. He quickly moved forward, out of sight of the drop below. As he did so, he noticed the cabinets were all labeled, and the labels placed inside etchings of the δ symbol.

Mira walked to a specific cabinet, pulling Holt gently along, and turned down its row. "What does that symbol mean, anyway?" Holt asked, watching the way her red hair brushed the turn of her neck.

"Which one?" Mira asked back.

"The one you guys put everywhere, the one that means 'artifact.' The one on these shelves, the upside-down Q thing."

"It's called the Feigenbaum constant," she said absently, scanning the artifacts on the shelf. "In the World Before, it was a number that appeared everywhere in nature, in things that were supposed to be random but really weren't. Dripping faucets, falling leaves, blooming flowers. It was one of the main numbers in chaos theory."

"But why choose it to mean artifacts?"

"Ask the Librarian—he's the one who picked it," she answered. "But I'd guess it's because the artifacts themselves are pretty much pure natural chaos."

Holt followed her progress through the shelves. "Who was the old man before the invasion?"

"A scientist, a famous one, but that's all I know," she said. "He doesn't talk much about the past. But he was the first one to travel the Strange Lands, the first to see the core. No one knows more about that place than him. Hell, no one probably knows more about *anything* than him now."

Mira kept examining the shelves, and it was then that Holt finally looked at them himself. His stomach tightened as he realized he was surrounded by not just artifacts, but major ones as well. Potent artifacts from deep inside the Strange Lands, things that didn't need to be combined with other pieces in order to do frightening things. These were powerful enough on their own.

Next to him, a bright, prismatic, laserlike beam shot out from the lens of an old microscope. What Holt would see if he looked through it, he had no desire to know. On the other side of him, the two pieces of an old, faded slide rule floated and rotated around each other, like a planet and a moon, inside a large cork-sealed glass jar. On the right, a small clock stood ticking away time, but its hands were moving backwards, not forward, and they glowed with a dim yellow light. And there were more, many more, all around him, stretching to the end of the row, lining the shelves and filling the ledge with colors and flickering light and strange sounds.

Ahead of him, Mira came to a stop, looking at something specific on the second shelf of a cabinet. "Here," she said, and Holt didn't need to be Zoey to read the apprehension in her expression. He looked to see what all the fuss was about.

Admittedly, it didn't seem all that threatening. It was an abacus, Holt knew, an ancient counting device, with little red beads that slid across tiny wires in a wooden frame. It wasn't glowing or moving; it didn't pulse or float or make strange sounds. It just sat there, silent and unassuming.

It made Holt all the more wary.

"You'll have to carry it," Mira said, looking away from the artifact to stare at him now. "I can't hold it with my artifact. They might not affect one each other, but then again, they might, and as dangerous as they both are, I don't want to risk it."

Holt looked at the simple abacus, sitting serene on its shelf. He wanted to argue the issue, but what was the point? It was their only way out of here, wasn't it? He forced himself to reach out and take the thing.

Nothing happened. It sat cold in his hand, feeling no different from any other item. He studied it cautiously nonetheless. "How does it work?" Holt asked, keeping his eyes on the thing. "You know, so I know how *not* to activate it."

Mira held him in a skeptical look. "I think it's safer not answering that," she said.

ZOEY AND MAX MOVED DOWN the dark tunnel that lay behind the curtain. The little girl was scared, but she pushed forward regardless, holding the slightly vibrating quarter in her hand, reminding herself to be like Holt and Mira. Max padded along silently behind her, and whenever she stopped, he bumped his fuzzy head into the backs of her knees.

She didn't get the sense that the tunnel was all that long, but it was moving in a curve, and since she had started down it, a glowing red light had been building ahead of her, becoming brighter and brighter. The light didn't flicker or waver: it was constant, providing the only real illumination inside the dark tunnel. Whatever it was, it was just around the end of the curve.

A few more steps, and Zoey came face-to-face with it . . . and it was nothing like she expected.

In front of her sat a machine about as big as a refrigerator, with a base of wood and the top half encircled in a square of glass. It was once painted in colorful colors, but now it was faded and old. Along the top, the words DORINA THE DIVINER were written in an elaborate script whose paint had mostly worn away from years of weathering.

She stepped closer, finally able to see what sat inside the glass box at the top of the machine. When she did, Zoey jumped back in fright, almost tripping over Max.

Inside the glass, the slumped, lifeless body of an old lady stared back at her through the glowing red light. Around her head was a sparkling, jewel-encrusted cloth. Dozens of chipped and broken gold necklaces draped down her neck. Zoey tensed, staring at the figure inside, expecting her to leap straight through the glass . . . but the old woman just lay there completely still, her eyes open and staring sightlessly, blankly ahead. Max growled low behind Zoey, apparently not liking the figure much either.

It took a moment for the truth to connect in Zoey's mind. The woman was not—nor ever had been—real. Looking closer, Zoey saw that the woman was actually made of *wood*. There was only half of her, the top half. One of her wooden arms had fallen off, and Zoey could see the mechanical parts and gears that had once probably made her move and gesture and maybe even speak. The machine looked like something you would find in an old carnival, and it had definitely seen better days.

Zoey moved closer, staring into the blank eyes of the gypsy. Red light bled out from the machine in spite of the fact that there was no way it could be plugged in and working here. A slight rumbling emanated from the box, which Zoey could hear when she was close enough, deep and low but muted, like the crashing of a waterfall from someplace far away. Still, those things were the only indications the machine was anything other than what it appeared to be.

Zoey's eyes traveled down the front of it . . . then stopped as she noticed the slot on the bottom half, inside the ring of the faded question mark. A rusted, metallic one, just the right size for a quarter.

She knew she had come to her moment. A decision point. There were no feelings to guide her here, nothing to tell her what to do. But she knew anyway.

Zoey carefully unwrapped the coin in her hand and held it over the slot. The far-off rumbling seemed to grow louder now. Behind her, Max whined uneasily, watching Zoey, reading her intentions.

"It'll be okay," she said, trying to assure herself as much as the dog. "I don't know what's gonna happen, but it'll all be okay." Max looked at her, unconvinced.

Zoey looked back to the coin that hovered over the slot, and sighed. As always, going back wasn't a real choice. Pushing forward was her only option.

With forced courage, Zoey shoved the coin into the slot.

IT WAS LIKE ZOEY had been sucked into space. Light receded and swirled away until everything around her was an impossibly dense field of pitch black, completely absent of anything resembling light, and Zoey floated through it all in a delirium of senses, none of which worked the way she was used to. Touch, sound, sight, smell—they all morphed and bled into one another, and she couldn't tell where one ended and the next began.

As Zoey floated, she felt the rumbling again, growing and building and rushing toward her like the footfalls of a thousand horses, but she couldn't see it coming, whatever it was. She tried to duck or spin, to twist out of the way, but in that solid haze of blackness, there was no way to tell if she was even moving at all.

The sound grew louder and stronger until it roared over her, filling her fractured, disjointed senses with an intense surge of noise and heat. Zoey tried to scream, but nothing came. In this place, she had no mouth, no lungs, nothing physical to her at all . . . and the realization was frightening.

The rumbling went on, roaring around her, sweeping her down and away toward a place that felt both solid and intangible, a nowhere place. But a place nonetheless. When she reached it, her consciousness, such as it was, filled with imagery. . . .

ZOEY SAW A GIRL.

This girl was younger. Much younger. So young, she hadn't yet learned to speak.

The little girl was in a crowd, with her mother. It was dark, and stars filled a clear black sky.

The girl had never been allowed to stay up this late, but tonight was special. Tonight was the meteor shower her mother had told her about.

They were gathered with dozens of other people on top of an overlook, where the lights of a city flashed in the distance.

The girl's mother hoisted the giggling child up onto her shoulders. It was one of her favorite things, Zoey somehow knew, seeing the world from her mother's vantage, being so high up.

Zoey didn't wonder where the girl's father was. She simply knew he had never been there. For as long as the little girl had been aware, there had only been her mother. And that had always been enough.

Zoey heard the mother's voice tell the girl to look up, and saw her finger pointing to the stars.

The little girl followed the gesture excitedly, and gasped. Above them, the stars were moving. They were *falling*. Streaking through the sky in pinpricks of light.

But something seemed wrong. They weren't as far away as she would have thought.

In fact, they seemed very close. Too close. And they were coming closer still.

As Zoey and the little girl watched, the falling stars transformed before her eyes into trails of fire, raining through the sky all around them, stretching from horizon to horizon, hundreds of them. Maybe thousands . . .

It became clear one of the "stars" was directly above them, falling toward the city in the distance. It was huge, they could tell, even from this far. The little girl never would have guessed stars could be so big.

Screams erupted in the crowd. Zoey and the little girl watched as the people around them began to run. They slammed into the mother, and the woman struggled to keep a grip on the girl.

The woman turned to run herself . . . and then stopped, as above them, the sky suddenly ripped itself apart in a maelstrom of sound and color.

Zoey and the little girl looked up in time to see the air all around the falling "star" waver in a strange way . . . and then, impossibly, watched the huge shape begin to slow as it fell, as if it were somehow freezing in place in the air.

A wave of clear, rippling energy erupted from the huge thing, flaring powerfully outward.

The mother screamed, pulled the little girl from her shoulders, held her tight . . .

. . . and then the wave hit and everything went white.

Zoey was there when the little girl awoke, watched her groggily come to. She was alone, they both realized at the same time. The mother was gone. So was the crowd of people. She was the only one left, and there was no explanation why. . . .

It was early morning now. Dim, yellowish light was everywhere, but the sun was hidden. Where was it? The sky above her was a strange, sickly shade of orange, like nothing she had ever seen.

The little girl looked around in fear. Where had everyone gone? Why was she alone? Where was her mother?

Zoey watched the girl slowly pull herself forward, toward the edge of the high point they had been standing on earlier. When she saw where she was, her eyes widened.

The city was burning ruins now. But that was the least of what she and Zoey saw.

What was in front of them was almost beyond description.

Amid the fractured landscape, they saw huge tornadoes of swirling black energy. Lightning that flashed in bright streaks of purple and red. They saw rolling waves of energy, glittering spheres of light and dark . . . and something like a tower in the distance, split in half, frozen in the air, spanning high above what remained of the city.

And then something roared above the little girl.

They looked up, and the sky was filled with machines painted blue and white, listing and turning in the crazy currents of wind and energy that swept through everything.

One of them hovered over her, descending down, closer and closer, the sound of its engines whining loudly.

There was a flash as a metallic claw attached to a long length of cable shot down toward her.

The moment it fired, Zoey realized she wasn't watching the little girl anymore; she was no longer an outside observer.

Zoey *was* the little girl, looking through her eyes as the Vulture claw raced toward her.

The girl was *her*, Zoey now knew. This was who she used to be.

And then the claw slammed into her, and everything went black.

THE DARKNESS ENVELOPED ZOEY again, a solid, unmoving pitch black of nothingness.

The rumbling swarmed around her still, furious and loud and unknowable. To Zoey, it felt like she was swept upward now, through the dark, but there was no real way to know. Here, there was no up or down, no true direction at all.

The sounds intensified, drowning out everything, even her thoughts. And her mind was flooded with imagery again. . . .

ZOEY WAS SOMEWHERE COLD. Cold and dark.

Not so dark as the place from before: nothing was as dark as that. But dark, still.

Zoey knew it had been years since *they* had found her in that broken, chaotic landscape, all alone. And she knew this room, too. The same room they always brought her. And she knew she was strapped to the same table made of black, rippled steel, held in place by the same strange, fibrous strands.

Dread filled her, because she knew what was coming. Any moment, it would begin. Any moment . . .

Lights flashed on above her.

They were harsh and bright, instantly blinding.

It *was* the same room, its walls made of metallic, black plates that moved in organic wavelike shapes, up and down, circling her and stretching upward out of sight. In her position, Zoey was forced to look straight up, and far above her, impossibly far, she saw odd glimmering golden lights moving back and forth.

The same ones she always saw.

Whatever the lights really were, it was always mesmerizing watching them, pulsing around each other far above. In a way, it was almost comforting. Almost.

She heard a strange sound then. Like a whistle, but electronic and distorted. And she knew *they* were there. Zoey shook as she looked down her immobile body to the rest of the room.

Two machines stood on either side of her. Strange machines, each about as tall as a human being, with four powerful, articulated legs and a rounded torso that held a variety of mechanical arms, the appendages containing all kinds of instruments and tools. Each had a three-optic eye, and they made whirring sounds as they rotated and focused on Zoey.

As always, the machines were painted in the same blue and white color pattern.

Now it would begin again, Zoey knew. Now they would move to her and raise their arms. Now the cutting and the prodding and the pain would start. Zoey felt tears forming, felt the fear building inside her. Why did they have to hurt her? Why did it never end?

But, strangely, this time, as she watched and waited, the machines didn't move.

They just watched her with their electronic eyes, whistling disturbing, electronic notes back and forth.

She wasn't sure if that was a good thing or not. Did it mean they were through hurting her? Or was there some new way they planned to—?

She noticed a glow wavering on the skin of her hands, and it wasn't the same harsh illumination of the room.

Curiously, she looked up . . . and saw one of those wavering lights high above, the ones that had always been there, now descending toward her.

It had gotten close enough that Zoey could see what it really was.

A field of intense, wavering energy compressed and formed into an incredibly complex crystalline shape. She had seen them before in this frightening black place, but none like this one. Usually, the light that poured from them was a brilliant shade of gold. This one, however, was a mix of two colors.

Blue and white. Like the colors of the machines on either side of her.

The colors mixed together throughout its shape so perfectly, it was impossible to tell where one began and the other ended. At the same time, both colors were distinct and prominent, and as it floated down toward her, it lit the interior in hues of sapphire and fallen snow.

It was beautiful, Zoey thought, watching it. Like a snowflake of pure, swirling color falling gently toward her.

It wasn't until she heard the first whispers in her mind that the sense of awe vanished.

The sounds were like no language she had ever heard, and they repeated over and over in her head. There was a hissing, too, like static, and it all built and grew louder the closer the energy field came to her.

It was just a few feet away now, and the colorful light was so bright, it filled her vision with blue and white stars.

Zoey blinked and looked away, but there was no looking away from the sounds in her mind, the growing static, the agitated whispers. They grew louder and louder, overpowering her other thoughts, until her head threatened to explode. It was terrifying, and there was nowhere to run, nowhere to hide.

Zoey struggled against her bonds, trying to tear them loose, but they were too strong.

Even though her eyes were shut, bright blue and white color filtered through her lids, and she knew the thing was right above her now.

The sounds in her mind, the whispers, the static—all of it combined into a single, powerful, frightening tone that filled her head and smothered her thoughts. She snapped her eyes open . . .

. . . and watched as the giant, hovering, blue and white energy field sank itself into her small body.

A surge of heat and pain flashed through her, and Zoey screamed as the thing burned slowly into her skin.

The whispers and the static vanished.

In their place were images. A flood of them.

Hundreds. Thousands. Millions. Flashing through her mind's eye one after the other. But horribly, somehow, Zoey's brain registered each one, making sense of it, cataloging it, absorbing it, over and over and over again.

Strange planets circled strange suns. Machines painted in different colors marched across thousands of worlds. Stars imploded into black holes. Golden energy fields floated through space, surrounded by fleets of black ships.

The intense blue and white light vanished as it completely buried itself inside Zoey, and the room became visible again.

The images kept coming, streaking past one after the other, and pain built in her head as her mind tried to absorb all of it. It was like seeing the collective memories of a million different people all at once.

She heard the electronic whistling again, could barely make it out over all the sensations, but she heard it nonetheless.

Zoey saw the two machines advance on her, their arms rising . . . and she was suddenly filled with an intense anger that overrode her fear. She felt . . . something else, too. A feeling. A feeling that she could stop this if she wanted to. That she knew *how* to stop it. The feelings, wherever they came from, spurred her, gave her direction . . . and she let herself be carried along.

Automatically, without thinking, Zoey mentally reached out toward the two machines in front of her, projecting herself *into* them. There was no other way to describe the experience, and it was as if she had done it countless times before, even though she knew she never had.

She could feel them now, the machines. More than that, she *was* them. Both machines at once. She felt the power of them, the energy coursing through their bodies, the strength of their gears and mechanics. She saw through their electronic eyes, heard through their digital ears.

Something inside each one fought her for control . . . but she could tell they were no match for her.

Zoey had no idea how she did it. She just watched as the machines stuttered and sparked, trying to resist her will. She felt a surge of satisfaction as she forced them to lash out with their arms, to cut and scrape and pummel each other in the same ways they had done to her so many times before.

Flame spurted from the machines as they crumpled and died.

A pulsing, electronic sound, ripped through the room like some kind of alarm.

Above her, lights began to flash on, hundreds of them, lighting up the insides of what Zoey now saw was a massive black shaft of the same organic, wavelike walls made of rippled metal, stretching upward out of sight.

Things moved within that space, hurtling down toward her. Things of both light and shadow.

The pain in Zoey's head peaked. Her vision blurred. Something was wrong. Something was—

Everything went black.

When Zoey woke, she was inside another dark room . . . and her lungs were filling with smoke. She coughed painfully, trying to breathe. Flames punctuated the shadows, but she couldn't make out any details.

It occurred to her suddenly that she had no idea how she had gotten here, wherever here was.

In fact . . . she didn't know anything at all.

She didn't remember the other room; there were no memories of the machines crushing each other, or of the lights and the alarm. There was nothing now. Her mind was a blank. She knew only her name, and even that seemed foreign to her. Like the name of a stranger.

To her right, something moved.

She called out for help. She called out again, until a figure appeared, standing over her.

A boy, older than her, with disheveled hair and a skeptical, impatient look in his eye.

His name was Holt, Zoey somehow could tell, though she had no idea how. And the feelings told her to trust him.

———

THE BLACKNESS AGAIN. SOLID and complete nothingness.

The rumbling was still around her, angry and insistent, and it shoved Zoey forward through the dark, overpowering everything.

As it did, her mind was overflowed with imagery one more time. . . .

SOMETHING HUGE AND MASSIVE stretched high into the sky. Particles of energy and darkness swirled around it in a powerful maelstrom that obscured her view, but Zoey could still recognize its silhouette: the same towerlike structure she had seen in her first vision, split in half and frozen in the air, surrounded by the same insane, chaotic landscape.

Zoey saw no sign of herself, but she knew she was here somewhere. In fact, what it really felt like was that she was *everywhere*.

She realized that by looking at the tower, she was looking at herself. Zoey *was* the tower, impossible as that seemed. She was the black, broken, monolithic structure rising above everything.

With this realization came others, things she sensed and felt: Pasts. Futures. Presents. Every possible combination of every potential possibility converged within her at that exact moment. And every other moment.

Right then, she knew who she was, knew the truth, as scary as it was. And she also knew that once the vision was over, the knowledge would be gone. But it didn't matter. This would all happen again. She would be here once more.

She saw other things in the swirl of times and places.

Saw how the ends connected, how every event since she had been found on that hilltop had led her back to this place.

If only the Librarian could see this. Would he believe it? Or did the old man already suspect?

She saw more.

Mira's eyes filling in with solid black, Holt crying in grief.

Figures holding strange spear-like weapons that glowed on either end, spinning and darting through the air.

Holt and another girl, not Mira, a girl with raven black hair, kissing each other, surrounded by the shouts and jeers of people in some kind of huge arena.

More Assembly walkers, all the kinds she had ever seen, but these had no colors; they had been stripped to their silver, bare metal without explanation.

Landships like the *Wind Shear,* dozens of them, storming forward toward a wall of Assembly walkers, cannons along their decks flashing as they fired.

And then the images all burst apart as one, in a powerful flash of color and light. . . .

BLACKNESS. NOTHINGNESS.

The rumbling roared around Zoey as the images and places and possibilities vanished. But in their place came realization. Memories re-formed in her disjointed mind, all that she had witnessed fusing together in patterns that slowly began to make sense. And she could sense the feelings, the ones that had sporadically guided her in the past. It was as if they had been hidden behind a curtain, and that curtain had been lifted away. They welcomed her. Even in this dark place, they gave her warmth.

But Zoey could sense other things now as well. Other presences. Similar to the feelings . . . but not. She felt their eyes turn to her, felt them notice and sense her as she did them. There were hundreds of thousands of them. Millions, maybe. Some close, some far. And Zoey knew what they were: the ones who were hunting her, the ones she was running from. With her memories restored, now she could tap into parts of herself that had been denied. Parts that they had sealed away from her in hopes of curbing her power.

Now they knew where she was. Now . . . they would be coming. *All of them.*

The rumbling peaked one last time, filling Zoey's senses with pain. Then it receded, leaving only peace and quiet, and Zoey felt herself waking, returning to her body with a host of new feelings and memories that felt frighteningly foreign.

44. APEX

HOLT HELD ON TO THE RAILS inside the lift as its chains and ropes screamed through their pulleys, and slammed it roughly back down onto the platform.

When it was done, he breathed a sigh of relief. Going up had seemed even worse than going down, and he gratefully stepped out of the lift and onto the cavern floor.

"Hey, was that fun or what?" Mira asked behind him.

"'Or what,'" he answered dryly. Holt thought he could feel the specific weight of the Chance Generator inside his pack. He expected it to start vibrating or giving off heat or explode any moment, but it just sat in there, harmless and inactive. Its silence only made him more apprehensive.

"Where's Zoey?" he heard Mira ask, and alarmed, Holt looked up to where they had left her and Max. There was no sign of them. Only the Librarian, standing at the back of the study area.

Holt's gaze fixed on the old man. He knew he shouldn't have trusted him, but he had let Mira talk him into it. Mira tried to grab him, but he broke loose and stormed toward the Librarian. "Holt!" she yelled, but he ignored her.

"Where the hell's Zoey?" Holt demanded as he moved. The old man said nothing. *"Where?"*

The Librarian looked down at Holt calmly as he reached the bottom of the study area. "With the Oracle," he said, and Holt heard a sharp intake of breath from Mira.

"You sent her . . . to the *Oracle?*" Mira asked aghast, staring at the Librarian in horror.

"It's what she came here to find," the old man answered.

"But she's too young, it could kill her!"

"If Zoey is what I think, then she is more special than either of you realize," he replied evenly. "The Oracle won't kill her; it will unlock her potential. As it did with you, you might remember."

Mira glanced away with a haunted look. Whatever the Oracle was, it hadn't left a good impression on her, Holt could tell. "What if you're wrong?" she asked in a whisper.

"Then the weak have been rooted out, as is our way," he said, matter-of-fact. "But the simple truth is . . . I am seldom wrong."

Holt had heard enough of the old man's riddles. They made less sense than Zoey's. He looked back at Mira. "Where's this Oracle thing? I'll go get her."

Mira opened her mouth to respond, but the Librarian cut her off. "I think you have more pressing concerns," he said, looking past them.

Holt spun around and saw something on the ceiling above him. Amid the collection of stalactites was a small hole. And from the hole, three or four thick ropes suddenly tumbled down to the lift platform.

Seconds later, boys swung down them—more than two dozen, it looked like, spilling toward the platform, one after the other. Holt noticed they were all dressed in auburn red.

"Los Lobos!" Mira said in alarm. Apparently, the faction knew secret ways even into the Artifact Vault. If Holt didn't get them out of here fast, they were all most likely dead.

The Librarian's gaze hardened, and his hand touched a silver and black artifact strapped to his left arm. It glowed and hummed briefly, and then a curtain of light parted behind him. The Librarian stepped into it without a second glance and disappeared as the curtain closed.

Holt frowned. "Great, thanks for the help." He spun back around to Mira. "Where's this Oracle thing?"

"Behind the curtain," she said, backing up and watching the Lobos warriors landing on the platform behind them, their eyes all coming to rest on them.

Holt grabbed Mira and ran for the curtain at the back of the teaching area. He guessed there was a tunnel on the other side of it, and he just hoped it would take them out of—

The jarring report of a gunshot ripped the air inside the cavern.

The sound meant it was over, and both Holt and Mira stopped short.

"Always running somewhere, aren't you, Mira?" a familiar, dispassionate voice asked. "Even when there's nowhere left to go."

When Holt turned around, amid the dozen or so Lobos, he saw exactly whom he expected to see, glaring straight at Mira.

"Cesar," Mira began, and it was obvious she was trying to keep the note of fear out of her voice. "I can explain all of this."

"I'm sure you can, *roja*," Cesar said. He looked even shorter than Holt remembered, and even more inflamed. "And I'm gonna give you that chance. Bring 'em here. Drag 'em by the hair if you have to."

"I'd rather you didn't!" another voice, a new one, yelled from the opposite end of the cavern, and everyone turned toward it.

Another group of kids stood in the main entrance to the Vault, glaring at both Los Lobos and Mira, each dressed in varying pieces of gray and white.

Gray Devils, about a dozen of them, blocking the exit out.

Holt sized up the situation quickly, noted with a sinking feeling that both groups were armed with guns. Supposedly, firearms were illegal in Midnight City, but Holt would have been surprised if the various factions didn't hide some away for special occasions. And this situation, apparently, was *extremely* special.

All three groups tensed at the sight of one another, and it was clear from the menace in their looks that there was no love lost between Los Lobos and the Gray Devils. Slowly, their hands began to creep toward the triggers of their guns or the knives on their belts.

How could both Los Lobos and the Gray Devils know they were here? Holt wondered. They had covered their tracks well. Something didn't add up, but Holt didn't have time to worry about that now. He and Mira were trapped in the middle of both groups, the Librarian was gone, and there was nowhere left to run.

"Los Lobos," one of the Gray Devils said with disdain. "You're outgunned, so slink back the way you came before you get hurt. Mira Toombs is Gray Devils business."

The Lobos members stared back defiantly, and made no move to leave. "Outgunned, maybe," Cesar replied with an equal amount of scorn. "But never outmatched, especially by gray and white. Toombs owes us more than she can repay. Try to take her, if you wanna bleed for it."

Holt started pulling Mira back and away to where Zoey must be. If there wasn't an exit through that curtain, they were all in a lot of trouble.

"Fine," the Gray Devil leader said casually. "You wanna die and give us your Points, that works for me. But let's stop standing around talking about it."

The tension lasted a few seconds more . . . and then the Gray Devils charged forward with yells of fury. So did Los Lobos.

Gunfire erupted everywhere, and bullets sparked along the walls and floor. The two sides slammed full-speed into each other, knives and clubs swinging, the groups clawing and kicking, trying to kill and maim.

Holt grabbed Mira and ran toward the curtain. But before they reached it, Mira screamed as more gunfire flashed behind them. They flinched as bullets streaked past.

Holt pulled Mira behind a table for protection as more bullets flew.

Six or so Lobos were running for them, Holt saw. Frustration washed over him as he realized there was nothing he could do. When they reached him, he fought anyway. He took out two of them before the others jumped him, and even landed a few punches in on a third.

From somewhere far away, he heard Mira scream as they pummeled him.

Just as the black began to push in around Holt's vision, they started dragging him. He felt Mira struggling above him, being carried as well, away from the teaching area, back toward the lift platform. Holt tried to struggle, but there wasn't much left in him now.

He heard the faint sounds of gunfire and screams. Through blurred vision, Holt saw four Gray Devils racing toward them, guns and knives ready. He heard Mira scream again. . . .

"Stop!" a small voice yelled from somewhere close by. Even though it was small, it carried through the large, empty space loud enough to draw everyone's attention.

Holt craned his neck and saw Zoey standing in the study area. Max was next to her, growling low.

Zoey's face was unreadable, neither alarmed nor frightened.

And then a voice echoed all around them, from nowhere in particular, filling the giant cavern. "Tell me what you saw, girl. Did you see the Tower?" It was the Librarian's voice, and it halted the chaotic battle in place.

Zoey looked at the blank air around her and nodded.

"You were there when it happened, then? When the Strange Lands formed?" the voice asked eagerly, echoing off the walls of the Vault.

"Yes," Zoey replied. "And I think I'll be there again soon."

There was a bright flash as the curtain of energy parted once more, and the Librarian stepped through. He looked at Zoey and nodded, and his shoulders seemed to sag in relief, as if a great tension had released. "Then you understand. Good."

From his belt, he pulled a large, red encased artifact wrapped in silver chain, and then pushed a set of quarters down like buttons. When they clicked into place, the artifact began to glow and hum.

"Hey!" Cesar shouted. "Get that thing away from him!"

But the kids didn't move. None of them were eager to rush the old man.

"I won't let you harm the girl or her friends," the Librarian said, and his voice was amplified again, filling the chamber, bouncing powerfully off the walls. The Lobos took a step back. "They all have much to do, more than any of them know." His gaze focused on Mira, and she stared back at him. "Zoey is the Apex, Mira. The one I *knew* existed."

Holt had no idea what that meant, but Mira's eyes widened in absolute shock at the words.

"I know it's hard to believe." The red and silver artifact in his hands continued to glow and hum, as if it were building power. "But she will convince you on her own, I think. Protect and trust her, both of you. There is nothing more important in this world. And Mira . . ." He trailed off as his look turned poignant and deep. "You were always my favorite. Do not lament, girl. There's no time for it."

The Librarian tossed his artifact forward, and it sailed like a ball of flashing lights and colors through the air and disappeared into the depths of the pit.

He and Mira held their gaze a few moments more . . . and then, from below, came an angry, furious howl that ripped the air like thunder. Everyone in the cavern was blown off their feet as torrents of wind suddenly ripped past them, sucking them into the bottom of the pit like it was a whirlpool.

The two factions screamed as they flew backwards, dragged across the ground, disappearing over the edge and into the dark below.

The Librarian, however, stood still, letting the winds rip him from the cavern floor and fling him into the pit, where he plummeted out of sight.

"No!" Mira screamed in anguish, watching the old man fall and disappear, gone forever.

Zoey grabbed a howling Max with one hand and held on to the solid leg of a workbench with the other, struggling to keep them both from being yanked away.

"Holt! The lifts!" Mira shouted as the maelstrom of air yanked everyone on the platform backwards.

Mira managed to grab on to the door of one as she flew past, dragging herself inside. Holt did the same, Lobos yelling in terror as they flew past him in the air.

Holt groaned as he started pulling himself inside the lift . . .

. . . and then another figure flew through its door and slammed into the back wall.

Cesar.

He and Holt glared at each other, and then the Lobos leader sneered and lunged toward him as the wind howled everywhere outside. It was so powerful, the lifts began to slide back on the platform toward the sheer drop on the other side of the ledge.

Cesar clamped on to Holt's fingers, started prying them loose from the edge.

As Holt struggled with him, he looked the boy in the eyes. *"Al mal paso, darle prisa,"* Holt said. "Take bad steps quickly." Cesar hesitated. Holt smiled. "It's good advice." He grabbed Cesar by the hair and yanked as hard as he could. The wind blowing through the cavern filled the lift enough to make the kid buoyant, and he flew through the door and fell screaming into the long drop below.

Holt pulled himself into the lift as it bucked and spun in the tumultuous winds. And then, finally, it all died down. The lifts slid back to their original position. The angry howl silenced. Everything was eerily quiet.

Holt and Mira crawled weakly out. There were six or seven Lobos and Gray Devils warriors left, but they were too exhausted for the moment to do anything.

Holt instinctively looked up to find—

Max rammed into him, licking and rubbing against him, and Holt sighed in relief. Zoey was running up behind the dog. "Holt!" she yelled.

Holt and Mira pushed to their feet, grabbed Zoey, and ran, heading for the tunnel back to the Shrine. Holt stared at it with intensity. They could make it if they hurried. They could *make* it. . . .

But behind them, what was left of the factions began to stir.

HOLT AND THE OTHERS DASHED into Midnight City's main hall, the haphazard buildings climbing up the black rock above them on either side of the underground street. They moved fast toward the Lost Knights compound, which lay on the northern end, on the other side of the Scorewall. The secret exit was their only hope of escape, and time was running out.

People all around Holt gasped as they recognized Mira. Holt kept moving, but the crowd thickened and pushed in on them, everyone trying to get a look or stopping to point, hundreds of them. It was getting tough to shove through it all.

"Move it, come on!" Holt yelled as he pushed to the front, trying to clear a path, taking Mira and Zoey's hands. He was frantic, could feel their window of opportunity closing, in spite of all they had achieved. Getting Mira's artifact. Escaping the Vault. Most important, Zoey had apparently found what she had come here for. Maybe she could heal Mira now, Holt thought with hope. Maybe everything was finally in his grasp. But the only way to find out was to get out of this cursed place.

His stomach twisted into knots as it always did when a goal was in sight. The last few steps were always the most precarious, the most dangerous, the point at which everything could be lost. And the feeling of Mira's hand in his reminded him that he, for better or worse, once again had a lot to lose. The thought spurred him onward, and he pushed through all the people, dragging Mira and Zoey with him.

They were almost through. They were almost—

Shouts rang out from behind them. "Stop them! Stop Mira Toombs!"

Holt and Mira looked behind them . . . and saw dozens of kids dressed in gray and white pushing after them. At the front ran Lenore, a purplish red bruise on the side of her head where Holt had knocked her out. She glared at Mira with burning eyes. The rage that radiated from Lenore was enough to easily part the crowd before her. He felt Mira's grip on his hand tighten.

"Out of the way!" Holt yelled in despair, turning back to the crowd in front of him. They were almost *through.* . . .

But the crowd reached for them. Max barked viciously, lunging and driving them back, but it wasn't enough.

"Holt!" Zoey yelled in fear behind him. But there was nothing he could do.

Holt felt dozens of hands on him, grabbing and tearing and punching. He felt searing pain in his head and ribs, and most horribly, he felt Mira and Zoey's hands ripped out of his, heard their screams over the yells of the Midnight City mob, heard Max growl as two kids kicked him out of sight.

Holt struggled, but there were just too many hands on him, too many people to fight off.

The crowd calmed and suddenly parted, and the Gray Devils pushed into view, led by Lenore. Holt saw Zoey and Mira, both struggling, held in place by groups of kids, hands clamped over their mouths.

Lenore moved forward with a slow, predatory walk, her eyes holding Mira's. Mira, for her part, glared right back, refusing to look away. When Lenore reached her, she smiled thinly, gently ran her hand down Mira's cheek.

"My Mira," Lenore said softly. Mira tried to squirm away, but the kids all around her held her in place. "I don't think I can ever hurt you like you've hurt me." The gentle, almost tender caress of Lenore's hand shifted as she slapped Mira hard across the face. "But I'm going to try all the same."

Fury roared to life inside Holt. "Touch her again, bitch, and I'll *kill* you!" he shouted at Lenore maliciously, pulling and struggling against his captors. His anger was so intense, he didn't even notice the first in a series of punches that finally got him in line.

Lenore never looked at him. "I'll touch her, Outsider," the woman replied drawing a knife from her belt in a smooth, patient gesture. The blade gleamed, as it moved toward Mira's face. "Touch her, and much more. Make him keep his eyes on this. I want him to watch."

Mira screamed a muffled cry, pulled against the hands holding her. Holt struggled violently, but it was no use. The hands on him were too strong. The knife approached . . .

. . . and then the entire cavern shook.

Debris and rock fell from the ceiling and the buildings, crashing to the ground and spraying splinters of sediment. From outside came a strange rumbling.

Everyone in the hall, even Lenore, looked up in alarm.

The room shook again, more intense this time, and sounds filtered in from the surface. Deep, percussive booms that could be only one thing: explosions.

Alarm horns began sounding throughout the city, echoing loudly against the thick cavern walls.

The crowd went stock-still, their eyes wide. Whatever those horns meant, very few had ever heard them, and judging by the looks on their faces, they had never expected to.

But Holt didn't need to know what the horns meant. He'd heard enough plasma explosions in his life to recognize an Assembly attack when one was happening.

The kids all around him panicked as the horns continued to sound. Holt felt the hands holding him disappear. As everyone fled one way or another.

In the chaos that consumed the huge room, Holt saw Lenore knocked backwards and away, disappearing into a crowd of stampeding people.

Holt hit the floor as Mira and Zoey dropped, too.

He moved for them, but now the crowd was a completely different obstacle. It wasn't fixed in place anymore. Instead, it was spilling in a panic in every conceivable direction, and Holt yelled out as feet stepped on his arms and legs and chest.

He had to claw his way to his feet and push with all his strength against being swept away in the frothing, manic crowd.

"Holt!" he heard Zoey shout from somewhere up ahead, but everything had blended into a sea of desperate, running kids.

"Zoey!" he yelled back, trying to find her, trying to push toward her.

"Holt, here!" he heard her shout to his right, and he moved, punching and kicking his way through until he saw the little girl huddled on the floor, covering her head with her arms. He yanked her up onto his shoulders.

"It's all my fault," Zoey said into his ear. "When I was with the Oracle, they sensed me. I felt them. I think they felt me, too."

Holt gripped her leg encouragingly. "Don't worry about it, kiddo," he said, pushing through the crowd. "Probably the only time I've ever been happy to see the Assembly."

Holt heard barking to his left and saw Max dodging and weaving his way toward them through the crowd. The dog seemed no worse for the wear, and Holt nodded in relief. There was only one person left to find, and he looked out over the tops of all the bobbing heads around him, a hurricane of panicking people stretching in every direction.

But there was no sign of Mira. She was gone, buried in the crowd somewhere.

"She's that way," Zoey said, pointing ahead and to the left. Holt instantly started moving and yelled for Max. The dog followed after them as they all pushed through the desperate, pulsing crowd of people.

DOZENS OF BLUE AND white walkers, Spiders and Mantises, swarmed toward the dam, marching through the floodplain at its base, plasma cannons flashing and hammering the giant structure as they moved. Fire burst out from its side, spraying plumes of concrete everywhere. Flights of Raptors roared by above, circling the action, providing cover for Osprey dropships to touch down and unload even more walkers onto the field.

It was a terrifying show of force. Clearly, the Assembly planned to overpower Midnight City quickly.

But the city wasn't without its defenses. Kids wearing the colors of many different factions, differences forgotten now, ran to and from the cannon emplacements on the walls—old artillery and other human weapons, new guns that fired large, compacted balls of scrap metal, and one or two repurposed Assembly cannon. The weapons exploded to life, returning fire, flinging shrapnel and plasma bolts down toward the invading army.

Explosions flared up and rocked the ground of the floodplain, and the river valley was quickly a battle zone.

But the Assembly pushed through it easily. For every one walker Midnight City managed to drop, four more were unloaded from Ospreys behind it. The walkers' cannons and missile batteries opened up, flinging death upward through the sky.

More explosions rocked the dam, kids went flying everywhere, cannons burst apart and crumpled.

The Raptor gunships opened fire as well, hammering the defenses from above. Metallic claws from Vultures shot down from the sky, grabbed and yanked the defenders from their positions, screaming as they were ripped up and away.

The Mantises swarmed ahead of the Spiders, headed for the main entrances to the city. They were small enough to fit in and through the tunnels that connected to the main hall. If they got inside . . . it would all be over. And quick.

Orders and commands were yelled into the air, and some of the defenders began abandoning their posts, running for the entrances, readying to man the tunnel defenses to slow down the Assembly attack.

MIRA AND LENORE CLAWED at each other as they rolled on the floor. The crowd was all around them, a chaotic tempest of stomping feet and legs. Mira's pack tore loose and fell away from her just as Lenore pinned her down. She tried to squirm free, to find a defense, but Lenore had locked her in place.

The woman's hands slipped around Mira's throat and began to squeeze. "All of this," Lenore sneered, squeezing tight, "*all* of it is *your* fault."

Mira looked around for anything that might save her, anything that could—

Next to her, just within arm's reach, was her pack, torn and ripped open.

For a moment, she forgot about Lenore's hands choking her life away, forgot the pain. All she knew was that there was a way out of this, and it lay within reach. She knew it was something she had sworn never to use. But she had things to live for. Things to make right and people to see again, people she cared about. She would do what she had to do, even if it sickened her. Even if it damned her.

Her hand stretched out for the pack, she frantically dug around inside it with her fingers.

Lenore didn't notice; she was too focused on Mira's face. "Do you know what hurts the most, Mira?"

Mira was seeing stars, her vision was blackening, her lungs burned. Her hands found what she was looking for inside the pack, struggled to hold on to it, lost it . . . then found it again.

"What you've done wipes away our past," she said, her fingers digging in. "All the memories of us, all our times together, how much you meant to me—it's all ruined now. You killed it. Like you've killed this place."

Mira's hand pulled free of her pack, holding something tightly.

"Like I'm going to kill *you,*" Lenore spat, gripping harder.

And with the last of her strength, Mira shoved her artifact—the one that both repulsed and frightened her—in front of Lenore and snapped open the casing of the brass stopwatch.

Black light flared out from the watch's interior in a cone of pulsing, bright shadows that seemed to squirm and contort like it was made of millions of dark, putrid worms.

Lenore shrieked as the light hit her, and her grip loosened automatically. She tried to pull back, but the beam of darkness held her in place, leaving her to scream and shake.

And Mira screamed with her. While the full force of the artifact had hit Lenore, the bleed effect from it sprayed outward and struck her as well.

Her mind filled with the static and whispers and hisses of the Tone, but in a way she had only felt one other time. It was almost tangible, like some kind of slimy, oily, pestilent energy working through her mind. And it hurt. A lot. More than she remembered.

Above her, Lenore continued to shriek. With horror, Mira watched as Lenore's previously clear green eyes—eyes that had looked so much like her own—filled in with spidering, black, veinlike fingers. She watched until the black solidified, until the woman's eyes were completely black, watched until what was left of her grip on Mira's throat released, and the person who used to be Lenore rolled off her.

Mira forced every bit of concentration she could muster on closing the watch. And slowly, painfully, she somehow did it.

When it shut, the vile, black, squirming energy vanished away, and Mira slumped on her side, barely conscious.

The Tone continued to sound in her mind, raging and whispering and filling her, and she knew, even though she had been only partially hit by the beam, in her advanced state, it was enough to finish the job.

She wasn't scared. She felt calm, in fact, could hear the whispers more clearly now, could tell what they meant, could make out their insistent rambling for the first time.

Come, they seemed to say. *Walk. Follow. Belong. Surrender.* The words repeated. Over and over, gaining power and momentum. And slowly, she could feel herself starting to give in to them. . . .

She noticed a familiar presence above her suddenly, a presence she loved, and it almost pushed through the crushing darkness. Almost.

The presence held her; she felt his arms circle her. Her mind was slowly shutting down, but she knew he must be sad, knew he must be tortured.

But it was too late now. She had gotten what she deserved.

HOLT HELD MIRA IN his arms, staring into her nearly black eyes, watching her on the verge of fading away, just like Emily.

Lenore lay comatose and Succumbed next to them, staring sightlessly up at the ceiling of the main hall. Mira wasn't in much better shape, but she was still herself, still conscious. Barely. He saw Mira's artifact lying on the floor next to her hand. She must have used it to save herself from Lenore, but it had affected her as well.

"Zoey!" Holt shouted. "Grab Mira's stuff quick!"

The little girl grabbed the awful thing with its tarnished pocket watch face and stuffed it into Mira's pack as the mad crowd churned and frothed around them. Explosions continued to push into the city, louder, closer. Holt knew it was only a matter of time before the Assembly burst in.

"Mira!" he yelled, shaking her hard, trying to break through the fog in her mind. He was *not* going to lose her, not now—"Mira! Wake up. You can do it, focus on my voice!"

"Holt . . . ," she whispered, staring up at him. Her eyes were so black, he couldn't tell if she was even looking at him. "I used it . . . I used it. . . ."

"I know," Holt said, looking around, trying to find an avenue of escape. "I know. It's okay."

"It's not . . . ," she replied weakly. "Said . . . I never would . . ." The strain in her voice, the obvious effort it took her even to speak now, ripped Holt's heart in half. He *had* to get them out of here.

"Leave me . . . ," she managed to say, and Holt felt his blood run cold. "Out of time . . . what I deserve . . . leave me . . . get Zoey to—"

Holt shook her as he spoke, this time with ferocity. "Don't you *ever* tell me that!" he yelled. "I will *never* leave you! Do you understand, Mira? And you aren't going to leave me! You will *not!*"

Mira slumped in his arms, but he kept shaking her regardless. Shook her until she finally responded. "Okay . . . Holt . . . ," she said weakly. "Won't . . . leave . . ."

"Damn right you won't," he said, pulling her up. He hefted her over his shoulder, fighting off the panicking, seething crowd as he stood.

He saw the Scorewall room ahead of them, but there were hundreds of panicked people in between. It was going to take a lot of energy to—

Screams filled the interior of the main hall. Holt looked behind them and saw the gates of the city burst open, and dozens of Mantis walkers erupt inside, plasma cannons firing and decimating everything. People were being cut down, falling or blown backwards.

The Assembly had penetrated the interior of the city. It was all but over now. And they would be looking for Zoey, Holt knew.

46. CHANCE GENERATOR

PLASMA BOLTS SEARED THROUGH THE AIR as more and more Mantises pushed inside the city. Holt watched as panels opened up on the sides of the walkers and small, deadly, buzzing objects sparked and hovered to life, rising up into the air, dozens and dozens of them.

They were about the size of soccer balls, with small turbine engines underneath that held them aloft. Survivors called them Seekers, small machines that could squeeze into tight spaces where the larger walkers couldn't go. Their plasma cannons were small, but no less lethal, and they had the nasty ability to blow themselves apart at will.

Holt had seen one of them take out a dozen kids that way, inside the drainage pit of some city ruin. It wasn't something he liked to think about much.

Max barked as the Seekers rose up and buzzed forward, raining down heated death from above. The Mantises pushed into the crowd, stomping through the people, sending them flying.

What was left of the Midnight City defenders were fighting valiantly against the aliens, but the effort wasn't enough. Their guns and slings sparked harmlessly off the walkers, and the Seekers were too agile to be easily hit.

Still they kept at it, refusing to let their home be taken without a fight. Some had clubs and bats and swung them at the buzzing drones in the air, knocking them down. Others piled on top of the walkers in large groups, trying to drag them down, pulling at their cables and electronics, trying to rip them apart on the spot.

It was chaos. Holt had to get everyone out of here. And he had to do it now.

He looked to the Scorewall room, a hundred feet away, but the crowd in front of him was still thick and panicked, dashing wildly everywhere. Mantis walkers and Seekers were all over, shooting and buzzing and exploding.

His heart sank. He would have to carry Mira, and see to Zoey and Max as well. It would be nearly impossible for them to make it.

He heard Mira's words in his mind once more: *Leave me,* she'd said. *Leave me and go.*

Holt shoved the thoughts away angrily. He wouldn't leave her. He would never do that. There must be a way. There was always an answer.

Holt paused as something occurred to him. A solution. A dark and drastic one. But a solution nonetheless.

Quickly, he pulled out the aging abacus from his pack, held it in his hand. The Chance Generator did nothing, just sat in his palm, waiting, and Holt stared down at it with apprehension.

"No . . . ," Mira said next to him, barely brushing his hand with her fingers. "Not . . . worth it . . ."

Holt flinched as more explosions rocked the main hall. The Mantises were almost on them, the plasma fire intensifying. Mira looked up at him weakly, fading, slipping away from him, just like Emily. And when it happened, it would be his fault all over again. . . .

Holt scowled, looked down at Zoey and Max. "Stay close to me, okay?" he said as he studied the abacus with uncertainty, deciding how it worked. Experimentally, he did the only thing he could think of. He slid one row of beads up to the top.

There was a flash of yellow energy in the shape of a perfect sphere all around them, just big enough to cover all four of them.

"No . . . ," Holt heard Mira mumble. But it was too late. It was done. Even though he couldn't say he felt any "luckier" than before.

More plasma fire, more explosions. One of the larger buildings along the street came tumbling down in a mass of debris. They had to move.

"Go!" he shouted, and they all moved forward as one. The crowd was still in front of him; so were the Assembly, their cannons flashing and spraying lethal energy everywhere, their legs pinning and stomping people as they ran.

Holt expected the crowd to push and pull against him, to stop them from moving, to force them back.

But the panicked masses cleared out as they approached, giving them a way through. Holt smiled. It was working. He could almost run full-speed through the churning crowd.

As he moved, Holt noticed others nearby who were trying to push through at the same time, watched them get blocked and sucked down, trampled underfoot. But that had to be a coincidence, didn't it? Surely there wasn't a connection between—

A pair of Mantis walkers stomped in front of them, blocking their path, guns rising.

Holt shoved another row of beads to the top of the abacus, and an orange sphere of energy flashed around them.

Flame exploded from the base of another building as missiles buried themselves into it.

The structure collapsed in a shower of concrete and wood and metal, falling right on top of the two Mantises, burying them before they had the chance to fire.

Nearby, another group of people were blocked by a similar pair of Mantises . . . and he watched plasma bolts burn into them and send them flying.

Holt shut his eyes momentarily but forced himself to keep moving. He had to save her. It was all worth it to save her.

His luck parted the sea of people in front of them, and they pushed inside the Scorewall room. He stared at the cavern, the giant wall of numbers and names and lists stretching high above them. It was eerie somehow. This place was the hub of the city, and seeing it so empty drove home just how desperate the situation was.

"Everyone's gone," Zoey said quietly below him, and she slipped her hand into his.

"Yeah," he murmured, studying the layout of the cavern. Screams and explosions echoed behind them. There were three offshoot tunnels to the Scorewall, and only one of them led to the Lost Knights. "Mira," Holt said, looking over his shoulder at her. "Mira, which way? I don't know which cavern to take."

Mira mumbled something he couldn't hear. She was almost lost, slowly slipping away. Holt had to hurry. He looked at his options: the three different openings in the black walls. He picked one . . . and just hoped the Chance Generator's effects extended to picking tunnels as much as it did to avoiding plasma bolts.

There were more explosions behind them. He saw a troop of Mantis walkers rushing toward them.

He ran, pulling Zoey along, and Max darted out in front of them. Plasma bolts shredded the air and the floor all around them, and Holt prayed the abacus could keep them alive long enough to reach the compound. Mira had told him it worked for only so long, and he had no way of knowing when it was about to run out of power.

"Hold on, Mira," he said as he ran. "Hold on." Mira made no sound, didn't even move on his shoulders, except to bounce up and down. *Please let her still be there. Please . . .*

THEY PASSED THROUGH THE TUNNEL, and then through an opening that spit them out into a room that wasn't anything like what Holt had expected. It wasn't a cavern like the others. Walls of concrete and steel stretched high up to a flat, smooth ceiling several hundred feet above. Metal pipes snaked all along the walls, and rusted, old ladders and walkways stretched among them. At the very top, skylights had long ago been built into the ceiling, allowing sunlight to filter in from the surface.

The Lost Knights had found and inhabited a part of the old dam itself.

The room was full of Lost Knights warriors, gearing up to fight the aliens that had invaded the city and were about to beat on their own gate. As Holt entered, they all aimed their weapons squarely at him. Max growled, and Zoey instinctively moved behind Holt's legs.

Just outside, he could hear screams and yells, gunfire and explosions, and the buzzing of Seekers. Everyone in the room nervously looked at the tunnel that led outside.

"No pulling triggers!" a voice shouted from the center of the room. A small feminine voice, not unlike Zoey's, only this one was laced with venom and guile. "At least not yet." Holt watched as the kids, all dressed in red and orange, parted so that a little girl could push past them.

It was Amelia.

Her eyes moved between each of them intently, studying Holt, Zoey, Max, then finally settling on Mira, slumped across Holt's shoulders. She smiled mockingly. "If you brought her here to sell, I don't think she's worth much anymore."

Holt's eyes thinned. "What's that supposed to mean?"

"I mean her bounty was payable by the Gray Devils," Amelia said, walking slowly toward them, holding Holt's eyes. "And from what I hear, the Gray Devils aren't the faction they used to be. Their leader's gone. Their numbers are dwindled. In fact . . . I hear pretty much the same thing about Los Lobos, too. It all sounds very tragic."

The explosions and sounds of battle outside were suddenly forgotten as Holt put the pieces together. "*You* told them," he said, glaring at the little girl in front of him. "You told them both we were in the Vault. That's how they knew." Holt watched as Amelia's smile broadened, and he felt his anger building. "You gambled they'd kill each other off in their frenzy to get Mira, and then the Lost Knights would be on top of that stupid wall of numbers back there."

Amelia's smile vanished. "That wall of numbers is *everything*," she fumed. "You just don't see it. The Scorewall is order and structure. It's *meaning*. Where you come from, there are no systems, no designs, no formulas to tell you what to do, nothing to spell out what's right or wrong. Here . . . there are rules. And the rules make sense. We live or die by them. Midnight City is the world, Holt, like it used to be, only more honest. We rebuilt the world inside this cave, only we made it better. And if I could, I'd thank the Assembly for giving us the chance to create it."

Holt stared at her, at all of them, like they were insane. "You wanna thank the Assembly?" he asked. "I think you're about to get your chance." He held up the Chance Generator for Amelia to see, and her gaze turned dangerous. "You want this thing or not?"

"Oh, yes, Holt. I do. And while we're at it . . . why don't you hand over Mira's artifact, too? Lenore was Heedless, and if the rumors about her Succumbing are true, then I have a pretty good idea what it does . . . which makes it even more valuable than the Chance Generator."

"That's not gonna happen," Holt said firmly.

Amelia laughed, and so did the others. "Well, aren't we confident?" she asked with a malicious glint. "Kill them quick. We have other visitors to deal with."

The Lost Knights all raised their weapons. Max growled viciously.

"Holt . . . ," Zoey whispered behind him, fear in her voice.

Holt did the only thing he could think of. There were two more rows of beads left on the abacus in his hand. He shoved them both to the top.

The air around them briefly flashed into a crimson sphere . . .

. . . right as the Lost Knights pulled their triggers.

Holt flinched as every gun in the room simultaneously misfired and exploded, sending their owners crashing backwards, dead or badly hurt. Everyone who was left jumped back in shock, staring around wildly.

"He's using the generator!" Amelia shouted, figuring it out. "Rush him!"

The Lost Knights stared at Holt, but none of them made a move.

"*Now!*" Amelia yelled.

The kids tensed, their fear of Amelia stronger than their fear of Holt's luck. They moved forward . . . and plasma fire filled the air, punching holes in the concrete wall above them, raining debris down everywhere.

The kids in front of him panicked and scrambled.

Holt grabbed Zoey and ran forward through the chaos as the buzzing of Seekers filled the room. He knew that the Mantis walkers would be close behind now.

Two Lost Knights moved to block his path . . . but were quickly cut down by plasma bolts from above.

He kept moving, picking a door at random in the side of the wall across the room.

"Stop him!" he heard Amelia yell behind him. "*Stop him bef—*" The sound of her voice was lost in the roar of an explosion. Holt felt the heat of it on his neck as he ran.

More Lost Knights moved to block him . . . and were just as quickly crushed by a downpour of falling concrete and glass as one of the skylights crumpled above them. His luck was holding, awful as it was.

Gunfire erupted everywhere, but none of it was aimed at him. What was left of the Lost Knights defenders were firing at the walkers and buzzing Seekers. He heard screams and cries of pain and the sounds of bodies hitting the concrete. But Holt didn't look back. He had to get Mira out of here. Had to save her. He *had* to . . .

Holt reached the door set into the corner of the room. A faded stenciling of letters on it read, CONTROL ROOM ACCESS—AUTHORIZED PERSONNEL ONLY.

He yanked it open, shoved Zoey and Max inside . . . and risked a look behind him.

The room was chaos now. Half a dozen Mantis walkers had pushed inside, and were firing and bowling over Lost Knights defenders. And then he saw something even worse. Every one of the walkers were headed right for Zoey, chirping loudly. They had seen her, Holt guessed. And it meant every walker in the city would be headed this way soon.

Holt lunged through the door and slammed it behind him. There was a dead bolt on it, and he rammed it home. It wouldn't keep the Assembly out long, but it would buy them time.

Just on the other side was a flight of stairs leading up into darkness. They rushed up, taking the steps as fast as they could. Mira's weight was becoming a major burden, and his legs were starting to weaken. But he kept going, forcing himself to climb.

Below, he heard sparks and a high-pitched whine as something began cutting through the door. When it blew open again, a storm of Seekers would explode inside after them.

But it didn't matter now. Above them was a door set into the concrete wall at the end of the stairs. And beyond that . . . was freedom. They were going to make it, Holt told himself. They were going to *make* it.

Holt reached the door and burst through.

On the other side was another concrete room. It was small, only about forty square feet. One wall was full of windows, and underneath them was a long bank of aging, rusted, useless buttons and knobs and screens, which he guessed used to control the dam's functions. Sunlight filtered in from outside.

Holt stopped dead as he stared through the windows. The breadth of the entire floodplain stretched out before him, and he watched the battle raging below.

Dozens of blue and white Spider walkers marched toward the dam. Massive volleys of plasma bolts and missiles burned through the air, slamming into the structure, spraying fire and rock everywhere. He felt the floor under him shake with each hit.

Flights of Raptors filled the sky, roaring over the control center, hammering it with their own cannons. Vultures and Ospreys circled high above, watching the action, ready to pick off anything that moved.

"No . . . ," Holt said to himself in dread. It couldn't be as bad as it looked. There had to be a way.

A ladder in the center of the room led up to the ceiling only half a dozen feet above their heads, where there was another door, square and metallic with a big handle that kept it shut.

Holt set Mira on the floor and scaled the ladder. He cranked the small handle and shoved the metal door open . . .

. . . and then leapt off as blasts of plasma bolts seared past, inches from his face.

He hit the floor hard, rolled, stared up into the sky beyond the ceiling, watching the yellow bolts of heated death flashing past, shredding the air right outside. Anyone who stepped out would be nearly instantly cut down.

Holt grabbed the Chance Generator. It had helped them this far; it could get them a little further. The only problem was, there were no more beads to push up. He had used all of them. He pulled a row down, pushed it back. Nothing happened. No flash of light, no colors in the air. It sat in his hand, lifeless. He tried again. Still nothing.

With a sinking feeling, Holt knew the truth: It was used up. His luck was gone.

Explosions rocked the room, plasma burned the air just outside, missiles screamed and blew apart against the dam. This was it. This was as far as they could go.

It was over.

A buzzing echoed inside from the stairwell, and the sound ripped Holt from his depression. The Seekers were coming up the stairs.

"Get back!" Holt yelled at Zoey as he lunged for the door and slammed it shut, twisting the dead bolt into place.

The door rocked hard as something crashed into it. Again. And again. The sound of buzzing grew louder.

Holt looked at the door, backing up. There must be *dozens* of them in the stairwell. God, when they broke in . . .

"Holt . . ." Mira's weak voice reached him from behind.

He spun around instantly, dropped to the ground at her side. She was trembling, staring upward with her almost black eyes, oblivious of the explosions and the coming death that surrounded them. She was trembling, fading . . . and there was nothing he could do about it. Not anymore.

"Holt . . . ," Mira repeated.

"Right here," he forced himself to reply, and he heard the tones of defeat in his voice. He took her hand.

"Zoey . . . ," Mira said next, and the little girl moved closer. Zoey wasn't crying. She looked down at Mira with gentle tenderness.

Explosions flared outside again, shaking the room. The glass along one wall shattered and crumbled to the floor.

Mira's free hand rose and took Zoey's, then delicately placed it on Holt's. Holt and the little girl looked at each other.

"Trust . . ." Mira tried to speak, but it was getting hard. Holt's stomach dropped as it occurred to him that this was the last time he would hear her voice. "Trust . . . Zoey . . . ," she finally managed to say. The words barely registered for Holt. He felt himself going numb, felt any semblance of feeling or emotion dying where he sat. Fading away with Mira. "And . . . thank you . . . ," she continued, her words barely audible now, just broken whispers that floated out on her final, conscious breath. ". . . for . . . the dance. . . ."

While Holt was forced to watch, the Tone finally took Mira Toombs.

Her eyes swirled and went completely black. Her body relaxed and slumped in Holt's arms. He looked down at her with a dead gaze. It was over. She was gone. And just as before . . . he was to blame.

The anguish he felt now wasn't intense. It was more like a numbing cold. An icy grip on his heart he knew without doubt would never end.

The explosions outside were inconsequential. Escape was meaningless now. Everything was over. Everything he had fought for, everything he had come to this place for.

He'd gambled, and he'd lost.

To his left, he heard a sizzling sound. The fine, red sliver of a laser beam burned through the door and began to cut into the room. It would all be over soon; that was one consolation. And Holt would sit here, with her in his arms, until it happened.

48. BELIEF

HOLT SAT LIKE A STATUE with Mira in his arms. She just lay there, unmoving and mindless. She would rise up soon, Holt knew, try to start her walk toward the nearest Presidium, but with the battle raging outside and the air full of searing plasma, there wasn't much chance she would make it. Next to them, the laser continued to cut through the room's door. It wouldn't be long now. . . .

"Holt," a small voice said beside him, and the sound dragged him out of his stupor.

He glanced to his right . . . and saw Zoey.

In his grief he'd forgotten about her. Max sat next to them both, watching him with sorrowful eyes.

Explosions flared outside; the room shook. Holt's hand was still in Zoey's, and he looked at the little girl. The mere sight of her, someone so small and fragile amid all this chaos, drove home that it was more than just Mira he had failed.

"Zoey . . . ," Holt began with a cracked voice. A flight of Raptors roared by outside, their cannon screaming, shaking the room as they flew past. "Zoey, I'm sorry. This . . . this is all my . . ." The words rang in his mind as he spoke them, because he knew they were true. "We shouldn't have come here. I shouldn't have brought you."

"Why *did* you come, Holt?" Zoey asked, studying him curiously. Almost like she was seeing him for the first time.

"I wanted to save Mira and you, but I failed. Just like before." Holt stroked Mira's hair absently. "I should have known better."

Zoey was silent next to him. She didn't seem to be weighing her own words, so much as Holt's. "There's a reason all this is happening, Holt," she continued. "Not like how you think . . . but there's reasons."

Holt looked away from Zoey. He suddenly felt tired, more tired than he'd ever felt. He just wanted it all to be over. "If there are reasons, kiddo, I sure as hell don't see them. I don't see any purpose at all, to be honest."

Zoey's hand remained in Holt's a second longer . . . then she pulled free, stood up, and moved for the ladder that led to the open air beyond, where shrapnel and fire filled the sky.

"Zoey!" Holt grabbed the little girl and pulled her back. *"What are you doing?"*

Zoey looked at him evenly. "I need to go outside, Holt."

He was so stunned that all he could do was stare. Explosions erupted against the dam, and he heard the haunting, electronic bellow of dozens of giant Spider walkers outside. "Zoey you'll be cut to pieces out there!"

"I know it looks like I'll be hurt, Holt," she said, "but I promise . . . I won't. I can see how things work now. I don't have all the answers, but I have a sense of things. I kind of know who I am. And what I have to do. But to do those things, I need your help. I need you to *believe*, Holt. It's the only way we're ever going to make it."

Holt kept his grip on her arm. He had no idea what to say. "Zoey—"

"I can help you, Holt," she said before he could finish. "I can find your hope again. I can show you that great things can happen. Even *right now.*" Holt looked at the little girl, listening to the calm, assured words that came from her. She had never spoken this way before, and something about it was . . . comforting somehow. "But I need you to let me go. I need you to trust me, Holt. You've trusted me before." Her eyes held Holt's intently. "Trust me again."

Holt watched her with a contorted mix of emotions. *Trust Zoey,* Mira had said. So had the Librarian. A part of him, what was left of who he used to be, wanted to do just that. But could he? Could he gamble again, after everything he'd already lost?

The laser continued to cut the door. It was almost through now. The dam shook outside, screams of pain mixed with triumphant, electronic bellowing echoed in. Another pane of glass shattered right next to them.

"Let me go, Holt," Zoey said gently. "Let me go, and everything will be all right."

Holt felt his hands shake as they slowly began to loosen their grip on

Zoey. It wasn't a completely conscious decision. It was more like some other part was driving him, a subconscious part that had maybe put the pieces together on its own. Either way . . . he couldn't believe he was doing it.

It felt wrong. Incredibly wrong. The grief and guilt he felt a second ago were gone, replaced with a muted horror as he watched his hands let go of Zoey.

When she was free, the little girl reached out and touched his face gently . . . then scaled the ladder, climbing up through the ceiling. Max whined fearfully as he watched her go.

"Zoey . . . ," Holt called after her, his voice barely audible. She didn't look back. He watched her climb through and disappear outside, amid the flurry of plasma bolts streaking by everywhere.

To his left, the laser had almost cut a complete line through the door's hinges, but Holt didn't notice. Explosions flared outside again, and he shut his eyes, sank his head into his hands. God, what had he just done? What had he done? . . .

ZOEY WALKED SLOWLY ALONG the roof of the old control center, feeling the hard concrete beneath her feet. She saw the missiles and the yellow bolts and the debris flying through the air all around her, but she didn't really hear any of it.

To her, it seemed like she was moving in slow motion toward the edge of the roof, and everything was calm and tranquil, and there was no sound. Just the feelings, deep in the background of her mind, but she could sense them easily now. They weren't closed to her anymore.

The Oracle, in showing Zoey her past, had removed a block of some kind. It was as the Librarian had said. The feelings were tied to her memories, because memories were what made people who they are. She didn't have all the answers yet, but she knew which questions to ask . . . and she knew where she needed to ask them.

But that was for later. Right now, people she cared about were in danger. Their time was almost up.

The roof came to an end at her feet in a sheer drop down the massive height of the dam's main wall. Plasma fire streaked all around her, but none of it hit her. None of it even came close. And Zoey knew it wouldn't.

Below her, she could see the entire battlefield, filled with Assembly

Spider walkers obliterating what was left of the Midnight City defenders. Raptors roared through the sky, their cannons flashing, blanketing everything in fire.

Zoey stared at all of it calmly, without fear. She called for the feelings buried somewhere inside herself, and this time she knew they would answer. When they came, they flooded her with strength and peace. And then they waited.

Waited for *her*.

It would always be her decision, Zoey knew. Always her choice. And in that as well, the Librarian had been right. She wasn't sure what the feelings really were yet, but it didn't matter. All that mattered was they were there.

Zoey took a long, deep breath. She closed her eyes and let herself go.

She sank into the flowing river that was the feelings, let it take her where it wished. She felt her hands rise at her sides. The feelings guided her, showed her where to look, and she reached out with her senses. When she did . . . she felt what the feelings intended. She felt the dam's pieces and parts, the old mechanics that used to drive it, the generators that once controlled its enormous power.

And she knew what to do with all of it.

HOLT SAT WITH HIS head sunk in his hands. Mira lay silent and motionless in his lap, staring blankly up at the ceiling with black eyes.

The laser was sizzling in the door, almost through. The Seekers would pour inside soon, and when they did, that would be that. Holt was fine with it; he just wanted it done now. Wanted it over.

Beyond the windows, there were more explosions, more bellows, more roaring Raptors. Zoey was surely dead: there was no way she could survive outside in all of that. No one could.

And then, in front of him, at the other end of the concrete room . . . one of the control banks sparked.

Holt looked up from his hands at it, confused. Why would—?

Another spark. More. Lights flashed on the terminals; buttons began to illuminate. One of the monitors burst apart but the others flickered as they started to come back to life. Somehow, the dam's controls were *powering up*.

Holt stared at all of it in awe. It was impossible. The machines had died long ago; their circuits must all be rusted and broken. There was no way they could work.

From beneath him, he heard a rumbling. Deep and powerful, and it vibrated the concrete floor as it began to build.

It couldn't be. Could it? Could Zoey—?

The cutting laser flashed off, and the door shook in its frame.

Max barked wildly, and Holt lunged to his feet and slammed into the door, driving it back right before it fell open.

He heard a furious buzzing on the other side, felt the door shake as the Seekers tried to ram it open. It was just a piece of wood without hinges now, and the only thing keeping them out was Holt.

He looked back to the controls, watched them continue to light up and glow through all the dust and grime that had collected on them over the years. Beneath him, the rumbling continued to build.

Holt pushed back against the door with all the strength he had left, trying to hold on. Before, he would have let the machines pour inside and tear them to pieces, but now . . . now he felt a spark of something almost forgotten: hope. And he held on to it for all he was worth.

DEEP INSIDE THE BOWELS of the dam, its old, broken pieces and parts began to reanimate, like the organs of some long-dead metallic creature that was being resuscitated. And it wasn't a smooth process.

Turbines lining a huge dust-caked room sprayed sparks in torrents as their components turned and spun. Gears that had long ago been rusted into singular pieces groaned angrily as they were forced to rip apart. Electricity popped and fizzled through frayed wires. Fire exploded from vents and grates along the walls. Metal whined as it tore and bent itself in an effort to function once again.

And all through the dam, the sound of a rumbling grew, louder and louder, as more and more of the old machinery inexplicably began to reactivate.

THE DOOR BUCKED AND kicked behind Holt, and he desperately tried to keep it shut.

The lights on the control panel were flashing with urgency now, faster and faster. Information scrolled down the monitors that still worked. The rumbling underneath him continued to build.

The windows of the control center overlooked the dam's main wall as it stretched in both directions. The structure's huge metal gates lay along its length, keeping an unmeasurable amount of water behind them at bay.

Even though Holt had an idea what was coming, when it happened, he still couldn't believe it. He felt his knees shake and buckle.

"Oh my God . . . ," Holt managed to whisper. And then the unthinkable occurred.

ZOEY LOOKED AT HER hands and arms and saw they were covered in golden, wavering energy.

Her real body was forgotten. She was the dam now. She was its turbines and generators and controls; she was the energy that coursed through its cables, and the pressure that was building in its pipes and lines.

She traveled through the structure, feeling it as individual pieces and as one giant whole. She found the parts she was looking for, the dam's main function, and she forced herself into them, filling them with her energy and willing them to obey.

Beneath her, and in every direction, came a sound like rolling thunder.

The giant gates set into the concrete wall began to slide open, groaning and rumbling and spraying sparks and rust.

But they opened nonetheless.

Zoey watched as huge cascades of water exploded out the side of the dam, roaring downward like giant liquid obelisks that slammed and burst apart on the floodplain below.

Bellows erupted from the Spider walkers on the field, no longer tones of triumph or confidence. Instead they were sounds of shock and fear, and Zoey watched as dozens upon dozens of the huge machines, which had been on the verge of victory, turned and ran away from the dam, as fast as their powerful legs would propel them, toward the edges of the floodplain.

But it was too late.

The massive wall of water roared toward them, burying everything as it surged forward.

The flood plowed into the Assembly. Zoey watched them almost instantaneously be hammered forward and disappear under the giant swell.

The Spiders' panicked, fearful electronic calls were suddenly drowned out as the water pounded them to the ground and enveloped them completely. Zoey watched the giant machines disappear in the torrent as it roared forward, saw them tossed and flipped as if they weighed nothing. And she felt them, too. Sensed their fear and terror as their shells broke open and the water gushed inside. And then, a moment later, the sensations were gone, wiped away. . . .

The main force of blue and white walkers had been completely washed out of existence.

WHAT REMAINED OF THE dam's defenders stared in awe as the gates of the dam slowly closed, sealing off the powerful flow. As the main surge of water began to recede, they saw dozens of motionless blue and white Spider walkers spread out before them, all crushed and destroyed and lying crumpled in the water like mechanical corpses.

The color on their armor didn't stand out for long. A thick, black, rust-like substance formed on their surfaces, spreading and consuming the machines where they lay, like a metallic cancer. No golden fields of energy rose from their bodies, no crystalline shapes of light. There was only the rust.

Above, the Raptors ceased their firing, circled a few more times, and then their engines roared as they banked hard and flew toward the east, followed by the Vultures and Ospreys. Watching them recede was like watching a giant black cloud move toward the horizon, shrinking and diminishing in the sky until it vanished.

When they were gone, the river valley was filled with a strange, surreal silence that felt very out of place. The crackling of fires on the walls and the lapping of water against the new shoreline were the only sounds.

Eventually, a shocked, disbelieving cheer went up on one side of the dam. It was quickly echoed all along the walls by a hundred young, ecstatic voices.

As they roared in victory, some looked upward toward the very top of the structure. There, a silhouette against the bright sky, stood what looked like a tiny figure, a young girl, her arms extended, her hands and eyes glowing with an unearthly golden light.

The figure stood a moment longer . . . and then she vanished.

Rumors blossomed from that brief sighting, stories that would be told over the months to come. Tales of a young girl who had stood at the head of the dam while plasma bolts filled the air all around her, and somehow willed the old structure back to life. Willed it back to life . . . and saved them all.

They were only rumors, of course. But they would spread nonetheless. . . .

HOLT STARED, JUST AS astonished as those outside, watching the water cease its flow and everything return to normal.

It took him a moment to realize that the door was no longer shaking at his back, and the buzzing of the Seekers was gone. He stepped to the side and let the ruined door fall to the floor. Beyond it, there was nothing but a dark, empty staircase descending downward.

They were gone. Holt guessed that the pattern had repeated itself all throughout Midnight City. Without the support of the larger force outside, what remained of the smaller Mantis group had withdrawn, taking their Seekers with them.

The city was saved. And Zoey had done it all. Somehow.

He watched as the little girl stepped back through the hole in the ceiling, descending the ladder to the floor. When she finally stood before him, Holt stared at her in a whole new way. His heart beat heavy and fast in his chest. He was stunned.

"Zoey . . . ," he managed to say. But there were no more words.

Max barked and rushed to Zoey, brushing up against her, and the little girl petted his head and scratched his ears.

Then she kneeled down before Mira and her empty, black eyes. Zoey placed her hands on Mira's chest.

"Holt," she said. Something strong in her voice made him look down at her, down at them both. "I need to know," she continued. "Do you *believe?*"

Holt looked back at her. Ten minutes ago, he would have answered no without hesitation. But not now. Regardless of what had happened to him, or what might happen to all of them . . . there was finally, ultimately, a reason to hope. He only wished Mira were able to hear the answer herself. "Yes," Holt said firmly. "I believe."

Zoey was silent, reading him or weighing his answer, he wasn't sure which. Then she nodded and looked back down to Mira. "Hold her hand," Zoey said.

Holt felt his heart begin to pound again. He kneeled down before Mira, on the other side from Zoey, and took her small, still hand in his own.

Zoey closed her eyes. Holt watched expectantly, waiting. . . .

"Be free," Zoey said, and a flash of rippling golden light blossomed around all three of them.

When it faded, Mira inhaled a gasping breath. Her whole body shook, and Holt held her down until the spasm ended.

When it did, she opened her eyes. And the world seemed to stop.

They were perfectly clear. Clear and conscious and alive. The vein-like black tendrils of the Tone were gone, leaving only twin seas of intense emerald green.

Her eyes blinked and focused as her awareness returned, and when she saw Holt, she smiled. "Hi," she said softly, staring back at him.

"Hi," Holt replied. He brushed the strands of hair off her face, ran his fingers across her cheek and chin, feeling all of her. He couldn't believe it.

"Still making you work for it," she whispered. "Aren't I?"

Holt stared back a moment, feeling life and warmth return to him. When he had held off as long as he could . . . Holt pulled Mira to him.

The world faded away as they kissed, absorbed and lost in each other, their closeness overriding every other sensation.

Max whined next to them, and Zoey reached out and covered the dog's eyes. She smiled broadly, and watched as the moment went on and on. . . .

MIRA SAT WITH HER BACK against the wall of the old barn they'd made camp in the previous night. After they escaped Midnight City, Holt had doubled back with Max to get his guns and other things from the security lockers at the main gate where he'd left them.

There had been little resistance, everything was still disorganized after the attack, and when he got back, the four set off toward the east. They didn't stop moving until the sun began to set on the horizon, and they saw the old, abandoned farm surrounded by thick reeds of overgrown wheat.

It was odd, Mira thought. The silence and clarity of life without the Tone. She hadn't realized how she'd become used to the constant, insistent whisperings and hisses in the back of her subconscious, and she had lain awake in wonder, listening to the sounds of crickets and night birds in the dark outside the barn's old wooden doors for hours.

Before, she never would have noticed. The sounds of the Tone would have blocked them all out. It was going to take some getting used to.

Mira looked up and saw Max, sleeping near what was left of the embers of their campfire. Next to him, Holt was collecting his things, discarding supplies he no longer needed, sorting and organizing the others. He did everything so meticulously, so exactly, repeating over and over again actions he had drilled into himself in order to survive. Mira smiled, knowing that part of him would never change, even though others might. She was happy about it, actually. It was a part of him she liked.

She watched him pause suddenly, considering something in his hand. She recognized it immediately, the old abacus that was the Chance Generator. He looked at it in a slow, haunted way, and something about it bothered Mira. He hadn't said what he'd done to get them out of Midnight City alive, but she knew the artifact had played a role. But whether he was disturbed by the results or by something else was unclear. She watched him gently place the artifact beside his pack.

Zoey sat next to her, looking up at beams of sunlight that trailed through the dust-heavy air.

The little girl was different now, too. But wasn't that to be expected? Hadn't Mira been affected in her own way by the Oracle? That thing changed you, no matter who you were. Sometimes a little . . . sometimes a lot.

"You're thinking about the Oracle," Zoey said, and Mira felt no sense of surprise at the observation. After everything they'd been through, it was difficult to be surprised by Zoey's abilities anymore. "I didn't like it," the little girl confided.

"What did it show you?" Mira asked.

"Lots of things," Zoey replied, looking away from the sunlight and back at Mira. "Things I understood and . . . things I didn't. It made me remember. Not everything, but some things. Things I shouldn't know, things it scares me to think about."

"We don't have to keep going," Holt said from behind them, and they both turned to him. "We can stop right here. You don't have to do anything you don't want to. Mira and I will still protect you, no matter what."

Zoey was silent. "I don't think I could if I wanted," she said. "And I don't think it's right, either. If there's one thing I have to do . . . it's keep going. But thanks, Holt." She smiled at him.

Mira watched Holt's gaze harden. "Then I'll help you," he said. "However you need. You asked me to believe, and I do, and before you and Mira . . . that wasn't anything I ever thought I'd be able to do again."

Mira felt a strange emotion at his words. They were closer than they had ever been, but ever since she had kissed him, kissed him in a way she had wanted to for a long time, something had been bothering her. She knew why, too. He had asked her, after all. She owed him the truth. But how could she tell him? Especially now, after everything that had passed between them? Was it even the best thing to do?

"Did it tell you what you need to do next?" Holt asked Zoey.

Zoey looked thoughtful, and Mira guessed she was reliving what she'd experienced in the Oracle. It had taken years before Mira slept through a night without dreaming those images.

"It showed me the beginning," Zoey said.

"The beginning?" Mira was puzzled. "You mean you need to go where something started?"

Zoey nodded.

"Is it a place?" Mira pushed. "What does it look like?"

Zoey described part of what the Oracle had shown her, and as she did, Mira recognized the images. A destroyed, insane landscape filled with impossibilities. Something like a tower in the distance, split in half, frozen in midair. Mira knew what it was even though she had never seen it herself. There was only one thing it could be, and somehow, it seemed to make sense.

"The Severed Tower," Mira said, her voice almost a whisper.

Both Holt and Zoey looked at her. Even Max looked up at the tone in her voice.

"That's what she just described," Mira said. "I haven't seen it, but I know Freebooters who have."

Holt was at a loss for words, but he always recovered quickly from moments like that, and usually with a sour look on his face. This time was no exception. "The Severed Tower," he said sarcastically. "Well, that's a relief. I was worried it was going to be something difficult."

Zoey looked at Mira questioningly. "It's 'diff-cult'?"

Mira smiled at the little girl.

"It's in the middle of the *Strange Lands*, Zoey," Holt said before Mira could answer. "Where the artifacts come from. It's *full* of the damn things, and now we have to go marching right through the center of it."

"You said we needed something before." Zoey looked at Mira. "To go inside the tower."

"That's right." Mira reached inside her pack. "A radioactive substance." She pulled out the glass cylinder and the Dampener. The plutonium she'd intended to trade for Ben's life. She showed it to Zoey. "Something we just happen to have."

Zoey smiled. "See Holt? It'll be easy."

Holt looked up again, eyeing the glass cylinder. "Yeah . . ."

"Why don't you take Max outside to play?" Mira suggested.

"Keep away fetch with the Max!" Zoey exclaimed, and Holt tossed her the dog's chewed-up purple ball. Max watched Zoey with excited, perked-up ears. He ran after the little girl, barking enthusiastically, and they both disappeared into the bright sunlight on the other side of the doors.

Holt and Mira, alone now, looked at each other.

"Can we really make it to the Tower?" Holt asked, simply and pointedly.

"I've never been," she answered back. "Ben was the only person I've ever known who'd seen it. Well, Ben and the *Librarian*, of course. But others have done it. A few have even gone inside."

"How many?" Holt asked.

"Five," she said, and Holt sighed in exasperation. The small number was a testament to how difficult the quest would be. "At least according to the records in the Vault, but there could have been others, I suppose. Freebooters not registered with Midnight City . . . but it's unlikely. It's inside the core, the deepest part of the Strange Lands . . . and the most dangerous. The Anomalies there are more deadly than anything in the other rings. Only the best Freebooters can stay alive in the core."

Holt rubbed his eyes tiredly. "Well," he replied, thinking it through. "It's lucky we *have* the best, then." He looked at her and Mira looked back.

"What did the Librarian mean when he called Zoey the Apex?" Holt asked.

Mira had forgotten about that; it had been in the middle of a tense situation. Had he really meant that? If so, how could he have known? Surely he was wrong. . . .

"Mira?"

"You know that when the Strange Lands formed, during the invasion, no one who lived in that part of the world ever came out, right? They just vanished?"

Holt nodded with a dark expression.

"The Librarian believed that one person *did* come out," she continued. "He thought that the life forces of everyone inside the zone were split and merged . . . except for one. He called that person the Apex."

Holt looked dubious. "How did he come up with *that* theory?"

Mira shook her head. "Who knows? He was part genius, part crazy. It was some complicated equation he was always working on. The thing was too technical for me, it took up six blackboards inside the Vault, but he believed it, I know that much, and he felt that whoever it was, was very important. But he never told me why."

"Do you believe him?" Holt asked, holding her gaze.

"I don't know," Mira said. "Do *you* believe Zoey really controlled the dam?"

"It's the only thing I can figure," Holt said with a perturbed look.

"But there's been nothing to show she has that kind of power," Mira said. "And why *would* she have it? It's so specific."

"And there's the fact that that entire thing was run-down and rusting where it sat. It shouldn't have been able to work at all." Holt winced suddenly and sat down on an old hay bale next to him.

He lifted up his shirt and studied a wicked-looking gash over the back of his left ribs. Mira winced along with him at the sight of it. It must have been something that happened yesterday during their escape.

"God, Holt, did you *sleep* with that?" she asked in annoyance. "You need to dress it."

"I was too tired last night," he said, still looking at the wound. It had stopped bleeding, but it was caked with dried blood and dirt. "I didn't think it was this bad."

"Well, you thought wrong," Mira said as she stood up. "I'll get your med-kit."

"Actually," Holt said. "I was . . . kind of hoping you might help me do it."

Mira went still with her back to Holt as the weight of what he was saying occurred to her. "I thought Holt Hawkins did everything himself," she said, reaching for the med-kit near the campfire. When she turned around, they stared at each other as implications passed between them.

"Well, I can't totally reach it," he replied slowly. "At least . . . not without you."

Mira felt a gentle warmth flow through her as she held his look. She moved toward and around him, kneeling down behind his back. "I look after you . . . you look after me? Is that the idea?" Mira asked softly. She felt Holt breathe as her hands found the wound and started cleaning it. He relaxed at her touch.

"That's the idea," he said.

"I have to tell you something, Holt," she said, and her mouth suddenly felt dry. "You asked me a question," Mira said. "About Ben. And . . . I think I owe you an answer. I think you deserve to—"

"Hey." Holt's voice was almost a whisper, but it was enough to stop her. Mira looked up and saw he was looking gently down at her. "Do you think you could maybe tell me this tomorrow?" he asked. "Instead of today?"

Mira held his gaze as long as she could . . . and then looked away, back to his injury. She nodded. It was funny the way life threw things at you. It could be unfair. It hit you with things you wanted, things that made you happy, things you knew you needed . . . but it never seemed to do it at the right time, did it?

When she was done dressing the injury, they packed in silence, and were gone an hour later.

MOVING NORTHWARD THROUGH THE plains turned out to be a painstaking journey. Holt wanted to avoid the more direct routes and not push through the tall grass or the wheat fields, since it would leave an obvious trail behind them. The decision made her remember the price on Holt's head, and she wondered again exactly who was looking for him. And why. It was something he had yet to tell her, but she was patient. He would tell her when it was time.

As they moved, Mira looked up into the air. They had spent so much time in forests or under Midnight City's cavernous ceilings that the open sky felt impossibly tall and deep. There were kids who lived most of their lives in Midnight City, never feeling the warmth of the daylight, and most who ventured outside the cavern were terrified of the sky.

It was disorienting, dizzying to look at when the ceiling had always been a few hundred feet above you. They said it felt like they were going to fall up and *into* it, and whenever Mira left Midnight City, she always got a sense of what they meant.

Ahead of them, the ground sloped upward, and the crest of a grassy hill blocked the view of the horizon.

"The Max!" Zoey shouted, and dashed forward. Max barked excitedly and chased after her.

"Zoey, don't get too far ahead, please," Mira called after her.

"We won't!" the little girl yelled back as she and the dog raced up the hill to see what lay on the other side. It left Mira and Holt to walk together, and she noticed something else, something in Holt's hand. The sight of it caused a pang of concern.

"Holt," she said. "Why isn't the Chance Generator in your pack?"

"I don't like it in there," he said without looking back. "I like it out where I can see it."

Mira studied it closer. She wasn't sure, but it looked like a few of the beads had been slid upward. It looked like it was *active*. Surely, Holt of all people wouldn't be using the abacus. "Holt, why don't you put the abacus in your pack?"

"It's okay, I can hold it," he said. "I don't mind."

"Holt, I'd really like it if you put it in your pack. It's not something you should be touching."

Holt glanced back at her, and when he did, there was an odd look in his eyes. Thoughts and calculations seemed to swirl behind them, dark ones, and it was something she had never seen from him before. But it lasted only a second.

"Yeah, okay," he said. "Thing makes me cringe anyway." He undid a pocket on his pack and stuffed the abacus inside. Mira couldn't tell if it had been turned on or not, but at least he wasn't holding it anymore. He'd used it only once, and she was doubtful that short an exposure could lead to compulsion . . . but who knew? It was a powerful artifact, and he had been tight-lipped about his experience with it. She had assumed it was just a hesitancy to discuss the negative effects it had caused in order to save them all. But what if it was more than that? What if he had used it at full power?

"Guys!" Zoey's shouts from on top of the hill tore Mira from her thoughts. "Come see! Hurry!"

They both looked up and saw Zoey staring down at them impatiently. Holt smiled at Mira, and shrugged. "After you," he said, motioning her forward.

Mira smiled back. He seemed himself again—it probably wasn't anything to worry about. She kept walking and felt the ground start to incline under her feet.

They climbed to the top of the hill and crested the rise to where Zoey and Max sat, looking at the horizon that was now revealed before them.

When Holt saw what was there, Mira saw his body sag as his brain tried to make sense of it. "Holy God . . . ," he exclaimed, though it was barely a whisper. He had never seen it before, she guessed.

Mira instinctively slipped her hand into Holt's, felt him squeeze it back tightly. She looked to the north, and saw the beginnings of a landscape that was beyond description. She had seen vistas like this over and over again, but the first sighting of it, from a distance like this, always brought goose bumps to her skin. It carried with it a tangible excitement and wonder, and she had never not felt a thrill looking at it.

The horizon in front of them was covered in impossibly black, rolling storm clouds as far as the eye could see, towering powerfully over everything. Lightning flashed from those clouds, but not like any normal lightning. This was purple and green and red, and when it struck the ground, flashes of white energy sparked upward. The sky, where it peeked through, seemed to waver and distort somehow, like a borealis, only in daylight. Near the ground, strange colors faded in and out of view, disappearing in one place and reappearing in another. And the sound of deep thunder reached and rolled around them, rumbling in the air longer than it should.

Mira looked down at Zoey. The little girl was looking to the north, but unlike Holt, she looked more thoughtful than astonished. "It's the Strange Lands, sweetheart," Mira told her, petting the girl's hair. "It's where we're going."

"I know," Zoey replied. "It's where I was born."

The comment was enough to pull Holt's stare away, and he and Mira shared a look. "What's that supposed to mean?" he asked.

In the back of her mind, Mira couldn't help but hear the final words of the Librarian again. His words . . . and his warning . . .

"Can I ride the Max to the Strange Lands?" Zoey begged, ignoring Holt's question and looking up at them. Holt frowned.

"She's just going to keep asking until you give in," Mira said.

"I'm not sure that's a great reason to let her do it," he answered back.

"Please, Holt?" Zoey asked. "Please?" Zoey looked at him with her clear eyes, waiting hopefully. Holt considered his options . . . and finally sighed.

"All right," he said, "but just for a little ways. You're gonna be too big for Max soon. He's not a Saint Bernard."

Zoey's eyes widened with excitement. "I'll never be too big for the Max," she said as she moved to him and crawled onto his back. Max, for his part, wasn't as shocked as Mira would have expected. He sniffed Zoey a few times when she lay down on top of him, but otherwise seemed unconcerned.

"Wrap your arms around his neck, hold on tight," Holt instructed.

Zoey did, her arms encircling the dog, and she laid her head down across the back of his neck.

Holt studied them both a few more seconds . . . and then he whistled three sharp notes.

Max responded instantly, darting across the open ground like a rocket. He moved so fast, it didn't even seem like he felt Zoey's weight at all.

The little girl screamed in delight as they raced down the hill, Max's legs darting them forward at breakneck speed, until they reached the bottom and rushed over the grass, heading north.

Holt and Mira silently looked after the disappearing pair, their hands still intertwined. After a moment, Holt looked at Mira. "Ready?" he asked.

Mira hesitated, enjoying the soft warmth of his hand. There was so much she wanted to say. Why was it so hard?

"Sure," she said, but the word rang hollow in the afternoon air.

Holt held her gaze a moment more; then he started down the hill, slowly following after Zoey and Max. Mira held on to his hand until it slid away and out of her grasp. When it was gone, her hand felt cold, even in the sunlight.

Mira followed after Holt, and as she moved, she withdrew one of the necklaces from her shirt: a gold chain with two small, worn, golden dice cubes attached at the end. It was a necklace Ben had given her years ago, one she still wore.

As she contemplated it, she reached in a pocket and pulled something else out. When she opened her hand, a polished black stone lay in her palm.

Mira's gaze moved between the necklace and the stone as she walked.

Ahead, in the far distance, purple and red lightning flashed from storm clouds amid a prismatic, wavering sky. Strange thunder rolled ominously in the air, and it seemed to follow them as they walked north, toward whatever fate awaited them within that strange, surreal horizon.

EPILOGUE

NORTH OF MIDNIGHT CITY, amid a grove of trees that looked out over a rippling ocean of grass and wheat, something stirred.

Fields of energy shimmered as they bled away, revealing the machines that were hidden underneath them. Three legs, small and agile, painted green and orange. There were only four of them now—they had lost many since landing on the continent, and the ones that remained had deep gashes, dangling wires ripped free by crazed human hands, and gaping holes from shotgun blasts.

But they were still functional. They would hunt and track without question, until they finally fell apart.

The one in the middle had bold, differently colored armor, and it stood out next to the others, which gave it a cautious berth. It scanned the sky impatiently.

In a few moments, it found what it was expecting.

There was a roar above them. Larger cloaking fields wavered and fell away, revealing three huge ships hovering in the air directly above the tripods.

They were green and orange as well, and of a different design than either the reds or the blue and whites. Dangling underneath each one were four other walkers.

A mechanical whine echoed as clamps and grips released. The walkers dropped to the ground, and as they did, lights flashed and engines hummed to life. They were of a similar design to the others . . . yet different.

Still tripods, still lithe and agile, but these had missile batteries next to their plasma cannon, the small warheads gleaming in the sunlight. They looked more heavily armored as well, with thicker, mesh plates, all painted in brilliant green and orange. What looked like an array of optics and sensors sat atop them, and square, armored storage cases of some kind were affixed to their backs.

The new walkers stood tall as they activated, trumpeting affirmatively. But not all of them. Eight rose and activated, but four sat where they were on the ground, lifeless and unpowered.

From the old walkers came a rumbling as bright, wavering fields of energy lifted out of each one. Three crystalline shapes of golden light . . . and one of something entirely unexpected. The energy field that rose out of the boldly marked walker wasn't gold . . . it was a perfect, flickering blend of *green and orange,* like emerald sunlight.

Each floated to one of the new dormant walkers. They hovered above them for a moment, and then sank downward and absorbed into them. As they did, the machines powered up just like the others, coming to life.

The dropships collected the old, damaged walkers, sucking them up into hydraulic racks. When they were finished, their engines roared as they lifted up and away into the sky. Seconds later, their cloaking fields flashed back to life, concealing them from sight as they flew toward the west.

The walkers stared at their leader with anticipation, its new armor marked in the same unique, bold color pattern. Before it could sound its orders, however, a rumbling echoed from the distance.

The Hunters turned in unison, staring to the West, where something moved amid the plains, miles away.

The machines' optics whirred silently as they zoomed in on the movement and revealed it for what it was.

More Assembly walkers, dozens of them, all moving northward. Familiar kinds—Spiders, Mantises—and others less familiar. Some with five legs, some with six.

But one thing was common among all of them. They had no colors painted on their armor. There was only bare metal. And each of them gleamed in flashes of blindingly bright silver in the afternoon sun.

The boldly marked walker trumpeted with electronic disdain at the sight. More Assembly had arrived to join in the hunt.

The walker trumpeted once more, this time with urgency . . . and then it and the rest of its Hunters bounded off toward the north, searching for the trail that would lead them to their priceless quarry.

Don't miss the second book in the
THE CONQUERED EARTH SERIES

THE
SEVERED
TOWER

AVAILABLE FALL 2013